HEARTLAND

THE SECOND BOOK OF THE CODEX OF SOULS

The Codex of Souls by Mark Teppo:

Lightbreaker
Heartland
Angel Tongue (Forthcoming)

HEARTLAND

THE SECOND BOOK OF THE CODEX OF SOULS

MARK TEPPO

NIGHT SHADE BOOKS
SAN FRANCISCO

Heartland: The Second Book of the Codex of Souls
© 2010 by Mark Teppo
This edition of
Heartland: The Second Book of the Codex of Souls
© 2010 by Night Shade Books

Art © 2010 by Chris McGrath
Design by Michael Gin
Interior layout and design by Ross E. Lockhart
Edited by Marty Halpern

Printed in Canada

First Edition
ISBN   978-1-59780-155-3

Night Shade Books
Please visit us on the web at
http://www.nightshadebooks.com

This one is for Mom and Dad.

Lost in the winter
Ghosts of today

– Fields of the Nephilim

THE FIRST WORK

"Yet, poor old heart, he helped the heavens to rain.
If wolves had at thy gate howl'd that stern time,
Thou shouldst have said 'Good porter, turn the key,'
All cruels else subscribed: but I shall see
The winged vengeance overtake such children."

William Shakespeare, *King Lear*

I

"Is the nature of your trip business or pleasure?"

"Business," I said. I showed the customs agent one of my generic business cards. "Meetings, actually."

He gave the card a cursory glance, as there wasn't much on it. Minimalist design aesthetic, that leave-much-to-the-imagination attitude that made it easier when I had to use a different passport. "Antiques," he said. The corners of his mouth moved up. "In Los Angeles."

"Hollywood," I explained. "Scouting for movie props, and for some private clients. That's why I'm here, actually. I figure if I can open an office in Paris, then—" A well-timed shrug. "—you know, they're all about façades out there."

As compared to *here*—at Charles de Gaulle Airport—not far from Paris, that glittering cultural center of the universe. But the rule still applied: tell someone what they want to hear, and without meaning to, they let you become invisible.

The agent's stoic expression eased, his lips edging toward a real smile, and he thumbed through several pages of my passport. "Yes," he said, nodding. "They are fascinated with how things look."

Like a well-used passport. He had been doing this job for some time as he had unconsciously started looking to match port of entry stamps with whatever his computer screen was telling him. But the old method of stamping passports was

3

another victim of computerization. A lot of countries didn't even bother stamping the pages anymore, but that didn't wipe away the old rituals, the old way of thinking. Banishing the cultural and muscle memory took longer.

Piotr's contact had liked my suggestion of modeling the travel history on my own. Easier to keep the lies straight that way. The really clever bit had been to reuse a majority of the pages of my old passport so as to include those few places that still did the stamps. Authenticity is a matter of matching enough details to fool the experts, and more often than not, they presuppose what they should see anyway.

"Your French…" he said as he turned back to the front, "…it is very good." An inflection in his voice, just a hint there at the end of the word, suggesting a question.

"Thank you." I swallowed, pushing down the knot forming in my throat. In the past, my French had been serviceable; now, it was much better, but then I wasn't relying on my experiences alone. The Chorus twisted in my chest, a memory of old snakes, and from their coils, I heard the rising echo of their voice—the susurrating echo of many pretending to be one. I had always absorbed language quickly from the Chorus, but this time the connection was different, and my fluency was nearly perfect.

The customs agent nodded, his attention on my passport picture, and I realized he was waiting for me to elaborate. We had used the picture from my old passport as well, instead of playing games with image manipulation. My hair was shorter now, and lighter. Looking at the picture, I could see how haunted I had been: the stain of the *Qliphoth* in the flesh below my eyes, the distant stare, the slack skin of my face, the shadows at the base of my throat. I looked like a man worn out before his time, and the only distinguishing feature—the one detail that made the rest irrelevant—was the white band of hair. A narrow braid of fine hair ran around my throat. A gift from Reija, my Finnish witch. A reminder of what I had both lost and gained with the Chorus.

Piotr had vouched for the forger. A Five of Disks man. Reliable. Very competent. There was nothing to worry about. *This is one man's curiosity. Nothing more. Keep the lie simple. Make it* true.

"My mother's uncle lived along the Aude," I explained. The lie came easily—much like my new fluency with the language—as if it was *true.* As if *I* believed it. "We used to visit every year when I was younger." The Chorus coalesced into a stream of images: the farm house, its brick chimney leaning toward the east; the wooden railing of the horse pasture fence; the trees along the slow water. It wasn't my past, but the memory was mine now, part of the mental travelogue of my life.

There, in my head, the image of a dark-haired girl, chasing white geese across the pale field. Yellow flowers, early to bloom. Spring at the farm.

"But not recently," the customs agent said. His gaze flickered toward his computer screen.

"No," I said carefully. "I've been… *traveling* elsewhere."

He gave no indication he had heard my emphasis, and for a moment, I felt like a fool for trying such a trick. *They weren't watching. Not this way.*

A few months ago, when I had been interrogated in Seattle by the local Watcher, Lt. Pender of the Metropolitan Division of the SPD, he had pulled an extensive list of countries I had visited from TSA. It hadn't even occurred to me until a few days later that if Pender could pull that data so quickly, who was to say that other members of *La Société Lumineuse* weren't equally able to query this data? I had been careful to stay hidden on a magickal level, but I had been trusting to security through obscurity—stay off the watch lists, give the security agencies no reason to notice me, and trust that the avalanche of data could never be properly mined to track me.

Even with the reassurance in my head from the Chorus that they weren't Watching this way, even with the added obscuration of the fake passport, I couldn't help that momentary spasm of panic that I was being a fool for coming back to Paris. That I was doing exactly what someone wanted me to do.

You are, a spirit in the Chorus whispered, and the rest of them turned the hiss of these two words into echoing laughter.

"Just the one bag?" the agent asked, oblivious to the tension knotting up my spine.

I nodded.

The agent's gaze flickered toward the line of waiting passengers behind me. "Most don't travel lightly," he said. "Lots of baggage."

I forced my heart to slow down. I exhaled slowly through my nose, pulling a Kundalini warmth up from my belly, up through the tension in my spine, up to my throat and face where it could lift the corners of my mouth. "I travel a lot," I said, the words falling through the warmth in my throat. "I learned the lesson some time ago: travel light; you never need as much baggage as you think you do." Each word came easier, drawing the tension out of my body. Growing lighter with each letter, shedding the weight of old paranoia. It was still so easy to be bound by that old way of thinking, that bleak fury that had driven me for so long, that restless need for revenge. In the dim chambers of my heart, it was easy to welcome back that old animal instinct. "Besides, the airlines charge now for extra weight. I tell you, they're getting cheaper all the time. Soon they'll be weighing us when we board…"

The customs agent nodded, no longer listening to me, as he tapped a few keys. "Welcome to Paris, M. Dupont," he said as he slid my passport across the counter. "Have a nice visit."

I took the folio. "Thank you," I said, making a small show of being annoyed that he had cut me off. Something to give him the satisfaction of having controlled the conversation. Something to make me seem smaller. As I walked past him, he had already waved the next person forward. With each step, I was vanishing from his mind.

They aren't Watching.

I walked toward the arch that separated the security area from the main terminal. De Gaulle was a series of pods, built years before modern security theater, and even after every attempt to turn it into a series of dehumanizing little boxes, it still evoked the interior of a gothic cathedral. The new arch was a faux wall, built from pressed wood products and molded plastic, and it certainly didn't have the grandeur of any of the arches of Notre-Dame. But it had its own magic: by virtue of its shape and design, it was a threshold; a portal between here and there, one magickal space and another. Arches, doors, entryways, thresholds: they were all symbols of change. Once I crossed it, I would be in a different world.

I would be back in France.

I had caught an earlier flight than the one that had been provided for me. The direct flight was too obvious, and I couldn't believe that someone wouldn't have been Watching there. Especially when my real name had been on the ticket. I had gone out to Sea-Tac much earlier in the day and had talked my way on to standby for the less direct flight. At the last minute, the gate attendant released a first class seat. I had feigned surprise and eagerly paid full price for the ticket. The airline had been happy to gouge me.

The flight went through Heathrow, where I had sat for several hours in the British Airways lounge and tried not to think about my final destination. Or the phone call I wasn't making. Excuses were plentiful: it was an international call; I didn't have a cell phone; she might not be home; what was the point of leaving a message. After all this time? *Hi, it's Michael; I'm not as dead as you thought.*

Baggage. Lots of baggage. Physically, I had grown accustomed to traveling light, but, in my head, I was standing at the curb, waiting for a Sky Cap and a cart. The *rapture* in Portland had graced me with a new burden—a different sort of baggage—and not all of my old mistakes had been forgiven. Sins may be absolved, but the stains left behind were another matter entirely.

The Chorus flushed through the braid of white hair around my throat, leaving—in their wake—a tingling sensation that flowed down into my chest like a film of water racing across glass. An involuntary shiver followed, a purely physical reaction to the mystic flow. I still wasn't accustomed to this new freedom they enjoyed, this new independence from my Will. Certainly less of the malignant taint that had been eating at my spirit for the last decade, and there was a constant hum to them now, as if they were some sort of autonomous holistic system, keyed to maintaining my shell.

Too much like a guardian angel for my liking.

Then there was the issue with the Old Man. Maybe he was too strong of a spark to be subsumed quickly. Maybe the process of mapping history to mine was slower with the new Chorus. They weren't as ravenous as the last bunch, and it had only been twenty-four hours since Philippe and I had met in Seattle. In Harvey Alleningham's library, where we had talked. Father to son. Teacher to student. Magus to magus.

Less than a day had passed since we had had our talk, and I had taken his soul.

Staring at the arch that separated Customs from the main airport, I was reminded of Aleister Crowley's commentary on the Moon, the nineteenth card of the Major Arcana of the tarot. Well, the Moon was never far from my mind these days. Not since Portland. Not since Devorah nearly cut my throat with it.

On the Moon card, there is a void between the pillars, a threshold between the two paths represented by the pillars. A bloodied moon hangs low in the sky. The card represented the cusp of possibility. The Moon was the edge of midnight. On *this side* of its pillars, you were still in the real world, on *the other side* was both dream and nightmare. Unrealized until you stepped across. Until you actualized the future.

You See it, Michael, it becomes so; that is the key to the ego of the Moon.

While in the lounge at Heathrow, I had looked at the deck I had brought with me, and the Moon had been warm, the ink seemingly still wet on the card. Unlike Crowley's symbolic explosion, the Marseille Moon was like a surrealist landscape painting, a flat illustration of disparate objects: the pillars, the dogs, the rays thrusting forth from the lunar disk, the crab in the river, the moon itself. But it was a syncretic whole, all the objects to be treated equally, and not read solely as a representation of the swollen eye of midnight. The meaning of the pillars and the space between them was but a piece of the puzzle, as were the tears falling from the gibbous eye and the crab reaching up for them.

You could hold yourself on this threshold, balanced on this moment of possibility. You could live your life here, never crossing over, but it was a life in abeyance. A life never fully realized. You had to cross the threshold. You had to move forward and pass between the pillars. You had to decipher the mysteries offered by your existence, otherwise the river would—eventually—wash you away.

I had to unlock the puzzle in my head. I had to know why the Chorus came back. I had to know what Philippe gave me when I took him. There were too many pieces still unknown. Too many strands of the mystic knot in my head that I couldn't follow.

I had to cross the threshold into the future.

A fellow passenger, clearly under no apprehension about arches, strode past, clipping my foot with the edge of her suitcase. *Don't be a rock in the stream,* the Chorus whispered, and I knew they were right. Time to move on. I took a deep breath, held it, and walked through the arch.

I don't know what I expected: lights and sirens; a bolt of lightning from Heaven; a demonic army bursting through the floor. Like most transitions we go through in life, there was no sign the Universe carried or noticed. Nothing happened. The lights didn't even flicker. I took a step to the side, hauling my suitcase out of the way, and watched as other passengers moved past me. Souls, moving from one realm to another. Thousands did it every day. It was just another portal. Part of the endless cycle of our lives. We pass through portals and don't realize—or don't care—that nothing—or everything—has changed. We pass through, and go on.

"Paranoia," I whispered to myself. "Looking too hard to find connections." In the last six months, I had started talking to myself. It was the only way I could be sure the voice was mine and not theirs. The first few times I had been furtive about it, as if I were hiding something, but from who? The voices in my head? I could imagine Detective Nicols making a note in his little black book: *Schizophrenia. How many symptoms is he exhibiting now?*

The Chorus read the terminal, overlaying my vision with the glittering silver of etheric energy. A sea of dancing lights, filled with currents and eddies, this magickal overlay was a visual filter that transformed the terminal into a fluid map. Allowing the Chorus to enhance my vision was becoming an unconscious reflex; prior to Portland, this had been an act of Will, and now it was merely an aspect of evaluating the environment. I could read the leys more easily now; I could see the patterns of force that affected the world and those caught in its rhythms. I could see the lights without having to worry about my own; the Chorus was no longer a constant threat, waiting for me to weaken, waiting for their chance to take over my body.

The souls in the terminal were like a profusion of stars in the night sky: some were bigger, some brighter, some twinkled. One appeared to be strong enough to exert a subtle influence on the souls around it. The Chorus reached for this light, but I held them back, flushing them from my vision. I wanted to see who this was without the benefit of mystic sight, as there was something about its resonance that was achingly familiar. Something about its pulse that seemed so close to my own.

At the farm house, along the Aude. The memory of the little dark-haired girl, chasing the geese. One of Philippe's memories. I hadn't known her then. But as the Chorus left my eyes, and I saw her standing by the wall, the memory of the little girl became fused with my history of the child as a grown woman.

She was standing near a wall of burnished steel, out of the flow of traffic. Her hair was shorter and straighter, a sculpted salon cut that seemed like a frozen arc of water. Highlights too, honey and gold. A black overcoat, tailored tightly to the curve of her body. Underneath she wore a burgundy silk top, scoop neck to highlight the cluster of stones held at the base of her throat by a silver cord. The sight of her, as always, made me feel like a scruffy vagrant caught dumpster diving behind the sleaziest bar in town. A tongue-tied, clumsy, lovesick vagrant who wanted nothing more than to find a bouquet of roses in the trash.

Marielle.

She was waiting for someone, her gaze moving from face to face as more passengers streamed through the gate. She had seen me when I had first come out, but she hadn't recognized me. But I was standing still now, staring at her; feeling my gaze, she gave me another look.

Her pulse jumped and the Chorus sparked in syncopation, and recovering, noted another spike elsewhere.

She wasn't the only one waiting.

On my left, further back in the terminal, the Chorus targeted a magus trying to be invisible. He was wearing sunglasses and a black coat with a gray sweatshirt underneath. Hardly inconspicuous in this day and age, but he was using magick to bend light. Most of the people in the terminal wouldn't register him as being there, but to those of us with extra-sensory perceptions, he wasn't that clever.

Before I could examine him more closely, the Chorus tagged another cluster of lights—a more active threat. Three magi, coming from my left, walking through the terminal, checking all the gates. The Chorus touched the trio before I could prevent them, and having licked their lights, the spirits knew who the three men were.

What I know, I pass to you. What you know, passes to me. Father. Son. Holy Spirit. Let these secrets be revealed.

Jerome Theirault, third-degree Traveler. Tall and lanky, he looked awkward in his winter coat as if he were nothing but sticks and birds' nests underneath. Charles Lentier, sixth-degree Traveler. Florid, trending toward round; face shaped like a pug dog's. He knew he would never make another grade, and his bitterness and resignation was imprinted deeply on his face. And Henri Vaschax. First-degree Viator. One of a pair. He limped.

I knew why Henri limped. The Chorus twisted around the memory of that night in Béchenaux.

Henri wouldn't have forgotten either.

I maneuvered through the flow of bodies in the terminal, heading for Marielle. "They're on the prowl," I said as I reached her. "They shouldn't be here." So much for the cordial opening. *Hi. How've you been? I've missed—*

"No," she said. Her gaze was magnetic and I couldn't look away for a second. "Neither should you." Nothing accusatory in her tone, but I could read it all in her eyes.

"I'll explain later. We need to go."

I touched her arm and the Chorus whined at the contact. She was a gravity well. *Gravitas.* It was as if she were standing on a nexus of ley energies, and they were grounding her. It would take more power than I had at my ready call to move her. "No," she said. "Not after all this time. Don't brush me off."

I glanced back at the trio of Watchers, and the Chorus could taste the etheric disturbance forming around Henri's head. *Viator*, I thought. One who has returned from Traveling; a walker between worlds. Seven steps removed from Protector. Enough of a magus to flatten me, given the chance.

Since I had left Paris, I'd been scatter-shot in my education, learning what I could, when I could. I hadn't been keeping up with the ritualized procession of the degrees within the society. If pressed, I could probably pass the Traveler trial without much preparation. But Viator? Not a chance. Which put Henri way outside my comfort zone. I didn't want to have to face him. Not here. Not now.

"Your father isn't on this flight," I said to Marielle, rushing past the truth and into the lie. "He's on a later flight. He gave up his seat to me." And before she could ask, I pushed on, compounding the falsehood with some more truth. "He came to see me. In Seattle. Asked me to come back to Paris. But there are some—" My tongue caught on the word. "—circumstances that forced him to stay behind."

"Why?" she asked. Her eyebrows pulled together as she looked past my shoulder, at the three magi approaching.

Not here. Not now.

And then I knew how to unroot her. "They've exposed themselves," I said. "That's why he sent me first. To draw them out. Now we know who they are."

"But—" she started.

"Markham," Henri Whispered. That line-of-sight magick trick whereby magi spoke directly to one another.

Too late.

"Henri Vaschax," I said, turning to greet the three men. The fabric of Marielle's coat brushed my hand; my suitcase rocked on its wheels, but remained upright. "It's been a while." The Chorus twisted in my throat, some of their old humor lacing my words. "How's the knee?"

Nunc, the Chorus breathed, echoing a ritual moment two

months ago. A whisper of a dry wind, twisting through old bones. Waking old ghosts, beginning the cycle anew.

This is how it begins.

II

I had been part of the family once, one of the many brothers sworn to serve the Hierarch. *La Société Lumineuse* had its roots in the early days of Templar history, though its design and intent didn't really crystallize until after de Molay and the others were burned at the stake in 1314. Then, fleeing the greedy hand of Philip the Fair and every other king and bishop who thought they could follow the French king's lead, the organization became invisible. Over the next seven hundred years, they became much better at manipulating events and people from the shadows. The Watchers, as they've become known in occult circles, are True Seeing Witnesses to history. Their charter—somewhat self-appointed—was to keep the mystery mysterious, to protect the rest of humanity from its darker secrets. *They need us to be in the shadows.*

Critics of the organization—and there were a few, discreet and careful to whom they spoke of such things—saw them as yet another group of elitists who wanted to keep all the toys to themselves. Their mission of obscuring the occult mysteries was simply another means of control, an act that ran counter to much of the mystical philosophy they protected. How could mankind learn its true place in the universe if all the keys were hidden?

I hadn't had such quibbles. I wanted access to the secrets; they were granted to initiates. I signed up. Simple as that.

The Old Man, the Hierarch of the order, was based in Paris, and if you wanted to learn, that's where you went. After the disaster in Tibet, I realized I needed a better education. I needed something organized. Flailing about in the dark was getting people killed, some of them at my hand, and that was becoming problematic. I needed to be smarter.

They took me in, like they did all wayward children of the arts, and I stayed almost a year and a half, longer than I had stayed anywhere else in the last decade; and, within their embrace, I probably could have learned enough to bury the old hate forever. I might have found a cure for the blackness in my heart; but that wasn't the way things turned out.

Someone had a different design in mind.

When we became initiates, we were taught the metaphor of the Weave. It's an inexact explanation for the way etheric energy works, but it suffices for newly opened minds. Even now, I still default to thinking of the morphological Akashic energy patterns that way. The world was a Weave, and each of us was a single thread woven through the complex canvas. The higher-ranked Watchers do more than Watch. They also twist and wind the threads, manipulating people to create new patterns in the Weave. The Old Man was the one who Saw more of the Weave than anyone else; his windings went deeper and further than the rest of us could imagine.

And some of us were a little overeager to begin twisting threads.

My stay in Paris started to unravel after a little collegiate-style hazing gone wrong. Someone died, someone got their feelings hurt, and Henri took a couple of bullets, one that had left a lasting impression on his left kneecap. I had been in a bit of a rush, and had only meant to slow him down. Not that, after all this time, he'd be interested in an apology. I had a suspicion his memory of that night in Béchenaux was permanently twisted around the bullet in his kneecap.

Silver will do that, silver and energized Will.

It had been his brother, Girard, who I had really wanted to put a bullet in, but he hadn't been available. It was probably a bit unfair that I had taken it out on Henri, but he had been an accomplice to the whole affair. Still, judging by the tension in his jaw and the way etheric lightning was arcing off his skull, he was looking forward to some closure.

I had taken that from him too, when I had fallen in the Seine six years ago. I hadn't come back up, not in Paris anyway, and to the organization, I had died. At least, that had been my hope: if I stayed invisible, they wouldn't have any reason to think otherwise. Sure, I had left a number of things unresolved, but I had made peace with that.

The Watchers, however, didn't like loose ends. Those were the threads that could create knots.

The disturbance around Henri's head was a halo of light. *"Venefice,"* he said, using the old term for a rogue magus. *"Adversarium te nomino."*

Marielle took a step forward, and my hand came into contact with her hip. The Chorus swirled in my arm, resisting the strong pull of her gravity.

Adversarius. Henri had just Witnessed me, labeling me in a way every Watcher would have to acknowledge. An enemy of the fraternity. The *Adversary*.

"I guess an apology is out of question now, isn't it?" I said.

Jerome and Charles weren't up on our history, and the sudden course of events was putting them off-guard, unsettled with the direction of the conversation. Henri was the ranking Watcher present, and they were beholden to his command, but the public nature of this confrontation was making them nervous. There were too many people, too many unsanctioned Witnesses who would remember what they might see. Not to mention the local law enforcement. The French took their terminal security a little more seriously than the Americans did.

It wasn't what they had been told to expect, the Chorus articulated.

"Step away from him," Henri said to Marielle.

"No," Marielle said, and the weight of her nexus increased. My fingers tingled with the tightening pulse of energy.

"With all due respect, Mlle. Emonet," he said. "He's—"

"I know who he is," she said, cutting Henri off. "And if I were beholden to your rules, I would question your summary judgment of his character. But—" Her voice got even harder, and I saw Jerome flinch. "Even if I were to find your pronouncement valid, this is neither the time nor the place to exercise your right of combat."

Henri hesitated for a second, caught by an old respect, but that was shoved aside by a stronger need. One that was quite plain in the smile that creased his mouth. "Of course," he said. "You are not beholden to our rules, and as such—your blood, notwithstanding—neither am I beholden to take orders from you." His lightning stormed. "Now, stand aside."

"I am staying," she said. *"Right here."* And I felt the emphasis of her words more than I heard them. I felt the strong lock she had on the flow of energy beneath. *Grounded.*

Jerome and Charles took half-steps back, violet light blooming in their eyes as currents of energy coursed through their bodies. A guttural noise started in Henri's chest, and in the frozen second that followed, I made a decision and reached toward the yawning pit of energy beneath Marielle. I felt it through her, as if she were suddenly not there, and I was teetering on the precipice of an endless drop, the vacuum of that infinite hole pulling at me. Like a black hole, sucking all light and energy into its maw.

Henri released his lightning and it arced across the space separating us, seeking the ground. The Chorus flexed, straining to build some sort of reflective shield, but I held them back. *Right here,* she had said. Marielle hadn't been talking to the Watchers.

She had been telling me where to find help.

The splash of lightning struck me squarely in the chest, and the front of my jacket smoked and flaked into ash. The electric touch of Henri's power raced through my nervous system, and as quickly as it bit, it was gone, racing down my arm and out through my fingers. Leaving me and going into Marielle. My palm burned and her flesh got hot, but the lightning passed through us, drawn down through Marielle's conduit to the ley energies.

Henri hesitated, confused by the lack of result from his lightning spell, and I leaped forward, driving the palm of my burned hand into his nose. Some of the residual energy on my skin was transformed by the impact, and I felt the cartilage splinter. Blood flowed.

The Chorus formed themselves into a six-inch psychic spike extending from my knuckles as I pivoted and hammered Charles in the sternum with my charged fist. His eyes went wide, and he lost his magick as his lungs seized up.

Jerome was frozen, transfixed by a vision behind me. I wanted to look, far more curious than I should have been, and as I started to turn my head, the Chorus seized my spine. All I could do was keep looking forward. Or up.

Up, along the curved ceiling of the terminal. I spotted several of the tiny metal spiders of the fire suppression system. Sprinkler heads. The kind that trigger in the presence of smoke. Or having their tips knocked off. As the Chorus released their hold on my neck, I squeezed them and flicked a drop of force toward the ceiling. A knot of Willful energy with a specific task to accomplish.

Keeping my gaze toward the floor, away from the fading edge of Marielle's glamour, I reached back and grabbed for her hand. She met me, and came easily when I pulled, no longer bound to the nexus of force.

The Chorus spark reached its target overhead and ignited,

a blip of energy unnoticed by everyone but me. Lights and sirens and water followed. The sound and fury and deluge of the Apocalypse, judging by the near-instant panic that flooded the terminal. Everyone was a little on edge in the airport these days.

"Your suitcase." Marielle tugged on my hand.

"Leave it," I shouted. "There's nothing important in there." *It's just baggage.* All I needed was in my pockets already.

We fell into the silver stream of souls, the suddenly torrential rush of lights for the exits. Marielle's hand was hot in my grip, and the Chorus buzzed at the touch. It felt like I had bees under my skin, racing up and down my arm. Behind us, I could sense Henri's outrage. His voice was lost in the noise and chaos of the terminal, but I could feel him pulling energy again. A broken nose wasn't going to stop him.

Marielle stopped suddenly, and her hand was nearly torn from my grip by the tide around us. Beyond the glass doors of the terminal, the flood of bodies became a swirling and disorganized mass, like river water that, having rushed thousands of miles through canyons and beds cut in the earth, suddenly spills into a delta at the sea. All the channeled energy suddenly finds itself no longer squeezed through a narrow passage and it spins out into a confusion of disparate currents. In these currents, uniformed officers were struggling to direct the flow, but they were like rocks in a river—obstacles more than channel markers.

My vision failed, a black curtain cutting everything off, and I couldn't breathe. The Chorus swarmed against the suffocation spell Henri had just hit me with. I had been less experienced the last time someone had tried this on me, and I hadn't known how to fight it. I had panicked, which was part of what made the spell effective. The lizard part of your brain kicks in, primordial survival instincts that spring to the surface. You can't see. You can't breathe. All that runs through your head is: *fly, fly, fly!*

The Chorus tore through the first layer of the spell, and like active sonar on a submarine, they pinged my surroundings and constructed an etheric overview: hot spots marking the three Watchers, starburst flare at my side, the ghostly streamers of the flood of people moving around us. Marielle supported me; slowly dragging me away from the door.

Henri tightened his Will, and my Chorus sight flickered. I flailed—physically and mentally—at the hood about my head, and failed to make any sort of contact. Henri, it seemed, had gotten better at this spell, too. I couldn't find a seam to force the Chorus into. If I could locate a crack in his magick, I could force my Will through. He was too far away to hit him effectively with the Chorus—not without more energy, and my reserves were already low.

The Chorus had another idea and they moved on their own, rushing through me like a rain of pebbles. They burst through my shell, extending on either side like a pair of butterfly wings. They bent themselves against the current, and I realized they weren't wings. They were nets, and as each spirit light moved past, the Chorus scooped off a little energy. Each pulse fed back to my central nervous system, keeping me alert. Keeping me from passing out.

Instead of pulling energy from the leys, I was pulling energy from the river of souls moving past me. Each scintilla of energy was clean and pure too; there wasn't any sort of spiritual ephemera attached to it: no memories, no histories, no emotional detritus. I wasn't stealing from their life force. I was harvesting the natural bleed of power.

What I know, I pass to you. Father. Son. Holy Spirit.

Henri's light flared, a split-second warning of a power spike, and as this energy was channeled by his Will into his spell, there was a tiny hiccup as the hood relaxed around me. Almost as if I could feel the difference between inhaling and exhaling. Time was getting sticky, and as I dove for that narrow gap, I had to keep my focus tight so as not to forget what I was trying to do. This entire exchange was happening on an ethereal level, outside the perceivable decay of the cesium atom, but it still felt like running the hundred-yard dash through three feet of mud.

I squeezed the Chorus into a knot, twisted it once, and when he squeezed again, the knot squirted through the hood, throwing a microdot of my perception on the other side. I could fight back now. I could touch him. *Sequere lucem.* Leaping through the conduit of power looped around my head, the Chorus arced back along the strand of energy for the steaming spark of his soul. I couldn't break his shell—too many layers of psychic armor—but I could break his concentration. I could deflect his Will. *On the nose. Like hitting a dog with a stick.*

The hood dissolved, and the air I sucked in was heavy with water. Staggering, finding and leaning on Marielle's arm, I tried to reconnect with my feet. The sprinkler system was doing a good job of reducing visibility as it reacted to the non-existent fire. The crowds were lessening, even though the doors were blocked with a confusion of bodies. The Watchers were still behind us, though Henri was trailing behind the other two. His nose was bleeding again, and steam rose from his head and shoulders.

"This way," Marielle shouted in my ear. She pulled me at an angle to the major flow. Moving like an elongated eel, we knifed through the press of bodies. Back into the terminal, parallel to the outer wall. It would take us too long to force our way through the crowd. We had to find a different way out. Marielle was more familiar with the terminal layout, and I let her lead.

"They're going to lock this place down," I Whispered to her. Making ourselves heard over the din would be too time consuming. Magi-speak was quicker, and more private as well. No point in revealing what our plan was to anyone close enough to hear us shouting. "If they haven't already. We need transportation."

"The train," she Whispered back.

"It won't be running," I countered. "They'll have shut it down."

She glanced at me, a tight smile on her shining face. "I hope so. That'll make it easy."

She was right. Getting the train moving was the easy part.

The RER-B train was in its bay beneath the central terminal, and though we had to force our way downstairs through a throng of confused people—the panic caused by the fire alarm was only now spreading to the other terminals—we managed to reach the landing beside the smooth bullet shape of the train.

The doors were closed, and the interior lights were dimmed; no one was in the front blister of the cockpit. De Gaulle security was already reacting to the fire alarm and the psychic confusion of our spells as if the airport was being subjected to a terrorist attack.

Marielle whispered a tiny invocation as she ran her fingers across the access panel beside the doors. With a sigh of compressed air, they slid open. Once I was inside, she pinched the loop of her magick, and the doors closed again with a tiny pop.

She went forward to get the train moving, and I stayed in the back to watch for the others. Shortly thereafter, the lights brightened and the train jerked forward a few feet. This aborted leap became a shuddering crawl that shook the whole car, and as the train picked up speed, the vibrations lessened. Archways and marbled partitions flashed past, followed by longer stretches of open sky as we left the terminal.

A nearby display showed the system map for this line. De Gaulle, past Parc des Expositions, Le Blanc-Mesnil, Le Bourget and Gare du Nord, to the central hub of Châtelet/Les Halles—Paris' nexus of subway lines. From there we could get a connection to anywhere else in the city. The crowds would help us again. A confusion of lights would make us impossible to track.

Of course, we'd be coming in on an empty train. One that had been hijacked from the airport. Somehow, I didn't think we'd make it that far before other forces than the Watchers would be surrounding us. We had to get off earlier. Somewhere in the suburbs.

As I started forward, I heard the rattling sound of a door being opened. The Chorus reacted as a spell ignited, spinning open into a rigid fan behind me. The air in the car crackled, and the windows on either side of the car blew out in a cough of shattered glass. My shoulder glanced off one of the upright metal bars of the seats as I was knocked forward, falling on my side and sliding across the floor. There was a black ring of scorched paint where I had been standing a moment before, and beyond, framed in the narrow door between cars, Charles and Henri.

Charles didn't hesitate this time. As he charged up the aisle, his right hand snapped down, telescoping out the metal wand in his fist. Violet light limned the shaft and a tiny spark flickered at the tip. I scrambled into a crouch, and dodged his first swing. He caught me on the side of the head with his left fist, and as I shook that hit off, he delivered a short backhand to my right knee with the stick.

My leg collapsed, nerves deadened and muscles short-circuited by the magickal discharge of his wand. I bounced off the hard plastic of the nearby seat, and barely rolled out of the way of another jab with the stick. I tried to connect with my left foot, but Charles swept the blow aside and I felt my foot go numb from contact with the wand.

Bad, getting worse. He was just going to keep whacking me with the stick, each shot taking out another body part. With one leg out of commission and the other one as functional as a peg-leg, I was already too slow to avoid him long. Piecemeal attrition. He was going to take me down.

Charles knew it too. His next swing was slow and clumsy. He didn't have to try too hard. What was I going to do?

Vis. I grabbed the end of the wand in my left hand, and as the jolt of magick deadened the arm, I pulled him forward. Storming at my command, the Chorus filled the muscles of my right hand as I reached for his wrist. His expression changed as my magick grip compressed the joint. I squeezed and twisted, breaking a few bones, and his grip faltered.

The spell flickered on his wand, and as it brushed my chest, all I felt was a light tingling on my skin. Clumsily, I swept at his legs with the dead weight of my own, and knocked him off balance. As he fell, Charles tried to catch himself with his bad hand—the instinctive reaction of the lizard brain—and he cried out as bone moved unnaturally in his wrist.

More importantly, he dropped the rod.

Falling onto my side, I reached for it, getting a finger on its handle. The Chorus bound the stick to me, and I poured my own magick into its shaft. *Ignis.*

Charles was bent over, cradling his wrist. Violet streamers were running along his shoulders and down his right arm. Armor magick. He didn't have time to rebuild the bones, but he could lock them into place so the injury wouldn't stop him. I cracked him on the cheekbone with the rod, and as he reared back, I drove the point into the base of his throat.

My spell was different, and he knew it as soon as the metal tip burned his flesh.

Gagging and flailing, he fell back against the edge of the bench seat behind him. I put as much pressure as I could manage against the rod, and he bent back along the bench, trying to get away from the smoldering tip of the metal wand.

Henri's spell split the light in the train car, fire splashing off the molded plastic and metal struts. The overhead lights exploded like tiny firecrackers, and the car was filled with smoke and flame. Charles was screaming and rolling, trying to put out the flames crawling all over his coat and head.

I lay still for a moment, still protected by the extended peacock tail of the Chorus. They had reacted before I had known the spell was coming, and as I struggled to sit up and pull myself toward the front of the car, I felt them extending the etheric nets. Harvesting energy from the chaotic spume of fire still howling around the car. I took in the light and heat of the fire, transformed it into a wind, and blew it out again. Fanning the flames, stirring the smoke.

The Chorus used the rest of the energy to break the deadening spell on my limbs. My arm and legs burned as the nerve endings woke up in a rush. I could stand, but barely, and working the heavy door between cars was almost more than I could do. I braced myself and, with one leg feeling like a piece of charred and smoldering oak and the other like a frozen steak, I heaved the door open. Gracelessly, I fell through the doorway, and stumbled against the outer door of the next car. When the door clicked shut behind me, I closed my eyes for a second and breathed air not tainted with the acrid taste of burned hair and melted plastic.

I could see the track racing by beneath my feet. The space between cars was a narrow platform, suspended inside an accordion of plastic and rubber. There were gaps and openings along the bottom, and I could see, in addition to the track, a variety of hoses and cables. There was probably an elegant way to separate the cars, but I didn't have time to figure it out. I had to keep moving. Fighting the neurological entropic lethargy that magick couldn't vanquish, I muscled the other door open and fell down in the next car. My numb leg—the one that felt like a burning piece of wood—didn't quite clear the threshold and the door banged against my ankle.

The Chorus swarmed again as Henri appeared in the window to the other car. His eyes blazed with violet light, and a storm of energy crackled and spat about his head. He had an open connection to the ley of the train track, and was marshaling energy as quickly as he could imagine his need. He blinked and the glass shattered in his door.

Pushing against the floor, I scuttled back, dragging my foot

free of the doorway. The metal door closed, and recalling a
protection seal, I threw the Chorus at the portal. *Confundantur
qui me persequuntur…* The Fourth Pentacle of the Moon, one
of Solomon's old seals. The Chorus spun around the rim of an
imaginary circle, activating the magick, and binding the door
shut. A barrier now, between me and Henri. *Pavascant illi, et
non ego.*

Henri threw his Will forward and his spell devoured the atmosphere between us. My protection spell wasn't all that strong,
and it wouldn't hold up to a concerted beating. Henri had more
than enough power at his command to chew through my spell,
but it would take a little while. He didn't want to wait, opting
for the brute-force solution.

I felt the backlash at the base of my skull, a psychic stab that
was going to turn into a raging headache. But it was better than
the alternative. My shield cracked, and for a second, it held.
Lightning snarled and stormed in the interstitial space between
the cars. Henri's Will couldn't go forward, so it splintered in a
compass rose against the flat plane of my shield.

The end of the car jerked and light flared out from either side
of the train. A screeching noise of metal against metal rose over
the regular rhythm of the train against the track, and the back
end of the car became bent and twisted. As if a giant hand had
reached out and crushed it like a beer can.

Henri and the other cars were gone.

No points for elegance; functional works. My shield had held
long enough for all of Henri's energy to be diverted in every
other direction. The couplings and the accordion between the
train cars had been vaporized, separating me and Marielle from
Henri and the others. Their car and the ones behind them were
no longer attached, and without the engine pulling them along,
the back portion of the train was slowing down, succumbing
to friction and gravity.

Bracing myself on a nearby bench seat, I dragged myself

upright, and realized the front part of the train was slowing down too. I had thought we'd be moving faster without the extra weight, but we weren't. The suburban landscape was rushing by slowly enough to read the graffiti sprayed along a stone wall adjacent to the track. High-rise apartment buildings, ugly remnants of utilitarian architecture banned from Paris proper, sprouted from the landscape beyond the wall.

Marielle pushed open the forward door of the car. "We're stopping," she said.

"Why?"

Her gaze lingered on the damage and lack of more cars behind me. "They've killed the power from the central switch. We're not going any further than Villepinte. We need to get off before we reach the station." Something like a smile touched the corners of her mouth as she turned her attention to the side doors of the train. "Can you walk?"

"Well enough," I said, leveraging myself to my feet and limping in her direction.

She invoked her opening spell again, and the wind rushed into the car as the doors slid back. She looked back at me, the wind throwing her hair across her face. "How about jumping?" And then she was gone.

"Shit."

From one threshold to another. No time to consider the possibilities. I limped to the doorway as fast as I could, and jumped after her.

I was committed now.

III

I landed badly, my right leg not up to supporting my full weight, and I tumbled across the rough ground. My palms were scraped raw, and a particularly sharp rock collided with my shoulder as I rolled. When I was done sliding across the ground, I lay still, staring up at the sky for a minute. Happy to be motionless.

Marielle's boot touched my shoulder, gently rocking me. "Get up, wolf," she said. "It isn't time to rest yet."

I squinted up at her, moving my head slightly so that I was in her shadow. The sun bled around her frame, lighting her up. Or maybe it was the glow of magick. I couldn't quite tell. Adrenaline and the flush of the Chorus were still ping-ponging through my bloodstream.

Wolf.

There was only one other person who referred to me by that term. Piotr Grieavik, a fortune teller based in Seattle, who had used it to remind me of the hunger that had driven me to his corner of the Pacific Northwest. Before that, it had been five years since the New Year's morning when Marielle and I had said goodbye. When she had last used that word to name me.

The morning of the duel beneath the bridge on the Seine. The morning I had supposedly died, falling into the Seine and vanishing from the Watcher fold, vanishing from her sight.

She retrieved her cell phone from a jacket pocket while I groaned and sat up. She speed-dialed a number, and didn't wait long for someone to pick up. "We need transport," she said. "No… there were… complications." She made a half-turn, her eyes partially closed, and the gravity well of her magick tugged at me. "Yes, I know. We were on that train, and now we need transportation. RATP cut the power to the rails." She glanced up, examining our surroundings. "West side of the tracks," she said. "Just outside of Villepinte. About a hundred meters from a crossing. I can see a billboard for Lagerfeld."

When I stood up, I could see the sign too. Rail-thin models draped in clothing that hung at weird angles. Everything was black and silver, monochromatic if there was any color at all. Must be the spring line. In the distance, I could also see the other part of the train, and the prismatic strands of Henri's magick.

"This way," Marielle said. "I have a car coming." She started walking toward the crossing.

I followed. The ground was rocky and unkempt, and my legs were still a bit rubbery. As I stumbled along, I did a quick visual check of my extremities. No unnoticed shrapnel, no smoldering edges, no numbed breaks in my skin. Other than some scrapes suffered in my headlong plummet from the train, I was doing pretty well.

My coat, on the other hand, was a lost cause. There was a large patch of charred fabric on the front, and a couple of the buttons had melted into soft watches. I checked the inner pockets. The key, the ring, and the cards were still there. All the important things.

A silver BMW sedan with smoked windows met us a half-block from the train tracks. Marielle opened the back door, and gestured for me to climb in. I paused, reading the energy signature in the car. My teeth involuntarily chattered.

The front passenger window slid down, and the blond-haired driver smiled at me. "Hello, *my friend*," Antoine said. "This is an unexpected surprise."

I started to shiver: partially from the adrenaline comedown of the last half-hour, partially from the presence of the man driving the car, and partially because of the tone of his voice. The Chorus thrashed along my spine, like a massive fish hooked on a line.

Marielle stepped back from the car, hearing the same thing. There was a quaver of excitement in Antoine's voice. He was usually able to hide his emotions extremely well. Part of his mystic armor was an unnerving inscrutability; this hint of delight was unlike him.

Was it the fact that I was still alive; that, like Henri, he had a chance to finish the business we started beneath the bridge five years ago? If so, he was acting out for her sake, as he had recently been in Portland. He already knew I was still alive, and we had put some of the past behind us. Because there was a bigger game afoot. One in which we had both been played like cheap pawns.

I waved a hand toward the track and the approaching storm of energy. Henri was walking along the track, drawing power from the ley beneath the rail, and with each step, his storm was growing wilder. "Can we do this later?" I asked. "I realize this isn't the reunion any of us expected, but can we—" I swallowed the acrid taste of the Chorus' concern. "—can we just get out of here?" I didn't want to get in the car either, but Henri's approach was reducing my options. Antoine was playing at something, and I needed a minute to figure it out, but right now, he wasn't the problem.

Where had he come from? Rapid-fire questions searing across my brain. *How did Marielle get to the airport in the first place? Had someone driven her? Was this the car?* The Chorus churned around these questions, seeking possible answers, seeking connections and patterns. You don't have to always read the future to understand the Weave. You can also examine where you've been, exploring the knots that lie in your past.

One scenario—a likely one: Antoine drove Marielle to the airport, ostensibly to meet her father, who was supposed to be returning from Seattle on an overnight flight. No one knew why he had gone, and he wasn't beholden to any of the others enough to tell them. But Antoine would have known because there was only one person in Seattle the Hierarch of *La Société Lumineuse* would visit. A visit we had been waiting for.

The larger canvas. Think beyond your narrow thread. The back of my tongue tingled with the frustration rising from the Chorus. *Why Antoine?*

Antoine ducked his head slightly and peered out the front windshield. Moving with the grace of a man with all the time in the world. "Who is it?" he asked. "Did they know you were coming?"

Marielle was looking at me too, the same question in her eyes.

"No," I said. "They didn't know. They were just there." As well as the man in the sweatshirt and sunglasses. He had been Watching too. *For the Hierarch,* I realized.

"Why?" Antoine asked.

Before I could respond, Marielle's face crumpled. "No…" she whispered.

I hadn't been ready with a good lie. Or even a bad one. I was still trying to figure out who all the players were, and as a result, I wasn't ready to distract her from the truth. The look on her face said she suspected, and in not leaping into the void following Antoine's question, I only fueled the fear starting in her heart. A spark of doubt became a conflagration of outright despair.

"No!" she howled, launching at me, her fists raised. I caught the first blow, but the second shot hit me square in the face. There wasn't much power in it—not yet, but she was pulling energy. My cheek stung, and the Chorus snarled at the psychic impact of the blow.

"I'm so—" I tried, and took a shot in the mouth for attempting to talk my way out of it. My head snapped back, and the Chorus coalesced between us. Their attempt to shield me wasn't enough, and she kept coming. Kept swinging. I had to retreat, or hurt her. I took one more step back and bumped against the car.

So much for the path of least resistance.

Catching her hand was like grabbing a red-hot poker, but I held on, and the Chorus slithered through my arm, redirecting the burning bleed of energy before my skin crisped and my blood vaporized. "Marielle. Stop. It's not like that."

"You son of a bitch," she spat. "You killed my father."

Okay, it was like that. Well, not entirely. Not that she was in the mood to listen to me split hairs.

Antoine grabbed her other hand and held her back. Neither of us had been aware of him getting out of the car, but there he was. He was radiant with magick, filled with all the power of the Protectorate, and his Will was stronger. She pulled at him once, and it was like trying to topple a mountain.

"Mari," he said, softly, his words cutting through the writhing haze of her anger. "It's done. You can't undo it."

She pulled out of my grip and clobbered Antoine, actually snapping his head around. "You knew," she snarled. "You knew what he was going to do."

Antoine shook his head, and though his expression was still serene and filled with empathy for her pain, there was a spark of anger in his eyes. "No," he said. "I wouldn't have let him go if I had known."

After the detonation of the Key in Portland, Antoine and I had talked. We had realized that the Hierarch was working on a design much larger than either of us had imagined. We had been twisted to be his agents, but to what end hadn't been clear. The only real way to find out was to ask the Old Man directly, and that task had fallen to me.

Our best guess was that he would, eventually, come to Seattle. All I had to do was stay put and wait him out. But, the Old Man had outfoxed us. He hadn't come to talk; he had come to die. At my hand, and in doing so, his problems became my problems. His wisdom became mine.

And what did that leave for the Protector to protect? came the whisper in my head.

Suddenly, I had a creeping suspicion who had tipped Henri off.

Antoine stared at me, trying to read what I was thinking. "Endgame," he Whispered via magi-speak so that Marielle couldn't hear. "The revolution is upon us."

I cleared my throat. *Sooner than you think,* I thought. "We need to go," I said aloud. "Henri and the others are coming. We can have this out, but let's not do it here." Marielle's face was taut with fury and sorrow, and I flinched at the sight of the hurt I had inflicted on her. *Not my intention,* I wanted to tell her. *It's not what I wanted.*

"I'm sorry," I said. The words couldn't heal the pain. Nor would they change what had been done, or absolve me of having done it. They were meaningless sounds, empty tokens that did nothing to wipe away my sin, but they were all I had to ease her despair.

She started to speak, and then shook her head. A tear tracked down her cheek and she slowly unclenched her fists. For a second, I thought my apology was actually going to be enough, but then her face hardened again. This time, I didn't even bother trying to block the punch.

I had earned it. *What is done is done, what is gone is gone.* I had earned her wrath. In so many ways. My knees buckled and I fell back against the car. Then everything went black.

In the weeks following the Ascension Event in Portland, I fell into a temporal loop when I closed my eyes. During the winter, a splinter group of magi had unleashed an experiment on the Rose City. Using a theurgic harvester, they had attempted to collect the living energy of every soul within reach. The device hadn't been properly prepared, and it didn't devour the entire city—just all of downtown. Everything between the bluffs and the river. More than fifty thousand souls.

When I tried to sleep, I snapped back to that night in a bad cosmological loop. Standing at the top of the tower built by Bernard du Guyon's hubris, and watching the dazzling un-light of the harvester. Even though the sphere of mirrors had been destroyed, I could still remember its hypnotic facets. I could still remember the device's hunger for all those souls. I could still remember the emptiness. The *Qliphotic* void.

The Chorus, as I had lived with them for a decade while I had chased my own ill-remembered history, had died that night. Detonated so I could escape the soul-dead of Portland, expelled from my broken shell to complete the purge of their poisonous taint. Spiritually naked, I had ascended to the top of the spire; there, given another chance to climb the mystic tree I had first seen at my initiation into magick, I had clawed my way to the top branches and touched the crown. *Kether*, the first Sphere of the Tree of the Sephiroth.

So far from mud-footed *Malkuth*. So far from that time of crawling on my belly among the roots of the trees. So far from who I was: a child, blind to the magick of the world; a pure soul, untouched by the corruption of the Weave.

Somewhere in the explosion of self and soul that followed, I found a new Chorus, a new collection of voices and personalities who were tasked with filling the cracks of my shell, who were meant to make me whole. A little bit of Bernard du Guyon was in there, a black coal sulking in the fiery pit of my heart. As were his Anointed, the psychoanimistic inner circle of the Hollow Men, the Seattle-based coven who had helped him build Thoth's Key. John Nicols, the Seattle detective who had fallen during the battle with Bernard's magus, was in my head too. Unlike the old collection of dead men, the new Chorus nearly had individual voices, soloists who occasionally rose out of the throng of voices.

You are different, they—*he*—had told me. *We are different.*

The experience at the peak of the tower had been one of the moments that Mircea Eliade, a twentieth-century Romanian mythology scholar, had quantified as a sacred epiphany, a cosmological instant of death and rebirth. At the *axis mundi,* the pillar of the world that reaches from our profane meat space into the sacred world of the spirit, a seeker is granted an audience with the Divine. Be it God, or Pure Ego, or Ptah, or Animal Spirits from Dogon: the name doesn't really matter, as they all fail to truly encompass the Infinite that breaches into the Finite. When the light goes out and the Ineffable retreats, the seeker is returned to his secular world, changed by his experience.

The Chorus wasn't the only thing I lost that night. I also lost that last part of my innocence. I had been clinging so tightly to it, to that tiny ego child of denial: I wasn't responsible for what had happened to me in the woods ten years ago when I had first seen magick; I wasn't responsible for the choices I made that night, or that I made over the successive years when I took lives. I did these things so that I might live, so that the hole in my soul might not devour me. All these lies over the years, wound around my frightened spirit like a security blanket. *It's not my fault.*

But it was. They were all my sins, and at the top of the tower, frozen in the eye of the Ineffable, I was judged and found wanting. I was thrown back, like a fish that was too small. *Rede, mi fili.* Go back, my son. Go back, and try again.

When I sleep, I dream of that night. I dream of throwing Julian, Bernard's insane right-hand man, out the window. I dream of the crown of stars I tore from his head; I dream of how it felt in my hand, the weight of those souls, and I imagine putting that crown on my head. Anointing myself, and fighting Bernard before he can trigger the device. I dream of rising and falling, over and over, as I try to understand the judgment delivered.

Go back.

But now—*nunc*—the dream changes. When I fail and fall, the tower exploding behind me, I fall through layers—concrete and timber and sheet rock—until I land in a library. In the dream, the fireplace is real, and the marble busts aren't medieval replicas but real heads, stuck on sharp sticks. And Philippe Emonet—the Old Man, the Hierarch of the Watchers, the Silent Guardian Who Waits, Marielle's father—is older and more decrepit, as if he had been wearing a glamour when I had last seen him—less than twenty-four hours ago—and now, in the True Seeing vision of my dream, the true extent of his illness was apparent.

His hair is gone, and black sores like weeping eyes cover his skull. His left leg is gone entirely, amputated just below his hip, and his left hand is reduced to a tiny claw like a dried chicken foot. He is blind in one eye, and he stutters fiercely when he speaks.

This is what would have happened if you had failed to stop him, he says. *This is the map of Portland, carved into my flesh.*

But, I remind him, *some did die. I didn't save them all.*

You can't, he says. *Every day, innocents die.* His voice beats against me. I am too soft in the dream, and his words are hard. *Most of them from stupid mistakes and misguided ventures of other mad visionaries whom they had the accident to touch. Most die in darkness and in pain, their minds filled with idle garbage about their bank accounts and whether or not they were loved by their children and respected by their friends. What do we gain by saving them? Do they recognize us for our efforts? Do they reward us by continuing their menial, grubby lives?*

We don't get to decide, I argue.

Of course we do. That is what we do; that is who we are. Every time you kill someone, Michael, you act like the Lord.

I contract at his words, at his blasphemous translation of my name. Like a slug pulling in on itself, I try to hide inside my soft shell, but he chases me, his claw digging into my flesh. *Those people in Portland died in an attempt to bring us knowledge of the Infinite, of the Creative Spirit that made everything. Those people didn't die in vain. They died for a cause. They died so that we could understand why we live, Michael. They died for knowledge.*

In ten years, there will be another million souls born on this planet. In ten years, Portland will be rebuilt and this will all be forgotten. We'll still be destroying the world as we refashion it with our limited bovine imaginations. Time slays us all, Michael, and the vast majority of people that it takes will never make any sort of positive impact on this planet. Why shouldn't they make an actual contribution in the search for knowledge? Why shouldn't they be allowed the opportunity to participate in a transmission to the other side? Bernard sought an audience with the Primal Agent of Reality. Those who sponsored him sought to Know the Divine. Can you damn them for the effort they made?

Yes, I shout at him. Over and over. *Yes, I can. Yes, I did.*

His claw stops digging. Milky tears drip from his good eye. *Yes,* he says, an echo taken up by the Chorus, who swoop around us in a rushing swirl of blank faces and hollow mouths. *Yes, you did.*

I weep in the dream, and maybe my body weeps outside the dream as well. I feel like I am starting to float. The library becomes transparent, and soon all that is left is the chair in which the Old Man has collapsed. He is getting smaller. *My body is a disease,* he whispers, *it can no longer support life. It must be slain.*

He is the organization, and the organization is the man. *What I see,* he says, *is the end. The end of this age, of this body. It is time for us all to be set free.*

Free. From ourselves. From our histories.

My legacy. He beckons to me with his claw hand, summoning me out of my soft shell. *You are my ultimate resolution. My panacea for this decay. You are the hand that will break this* corpus mundi. He bows his head, showing me the naked crown of his skull. All the black wounds on his skull stare at me.

In the dream, his request is not a request, but a command. And I balk, as I did in the flesh yesterday. I do not want to do this; I do not want to become what I was before—a devourer of souls, a breaker of the light.

I am dying anyway, a voice tells me, *you're doing me a favor.*

It is the voice of my shadow, the voice I thought I had destroyed. But, like Samael said, the shadow is never gone. Never completely forgotten. The stain will always remain.

For the last ten years, I'd been taking the souls of tainted men. To my own guilt, I had added the poison of psychopaths and deviants. At the unconscious bequest of the black seed I let root in my heart, I fed it all the rage and anger and bile the world could offer. That seed, that *Qliphotic* influence, had tried to make me over in its image.

In the end, I threw off that yoke, and found a path of forgiveness. Did it absolve my deeds? No. But it showed me the way out of the dark wood I had lost myself in. I saw the light, and earned... no, I *have not earned* this. I have not earned anything. I have only learned.

The stain cannot be removed. It is the shadow that defines us, because without it, we do not know who we are.

The Hierarch asks me to kill him. He asks me to stain the Chorus with the Willful Act of devouring a soul. Into the holy and cleansed core of my refreshed spirit, he asks me to bring a little darkness. Just a little bit.

Nunc. This is how it begins.

And I did it. In my dream, I watch Portland burn again, and I watch Philippe smile as I spike his soul. Light pours out of him: first from his eyes, then from his mouth and nose, and finally all the black sores on his skull open up and release his light. His spirit erupts in a brilliant geyser, and with the net of my Chorus extended, I catch it. A fisherman of souls, bringing in his harvest.

I am overwhelmed by the rush of Philippe's life: all that he knew, all that he was, all that he dreamed, all that he feared. It roars into me, threatening to drown my own identity under the tsunami weight of his existence. But, like with the others, I know how not to be drowned by the flood of another life. I know how to swim through it. How to separate the knowledge from the fantasy, the history from the speculation, the desires from the dreams. I know how to make the sound and fury of another life part of mine.

When I wake from this dream, I am clutching a memory of a little girl, chasing geese in a field by the river. *Marielle.* So small, so young. Her face, alight with laughter, shining like a morning sun. I remember that day as if it were part of my past, as if that sense of contentment and security were mine.

But it isn't. It belongs to Philippe, from a time before he was Hierarch, before he slew his predecessor, and took the ring as his own. Before he, too, took a little bit of darkness into him.

He's in me still. This is how fathers pass on their legacies to their sons. This is how sins are perpetuated across the generations. This is how the myths take root, and how they grow.

Our hands betray what we have done.

I'm sorry, Father.

And Aristotle Emonet grabs his son's blood-slicked hands as Philippe takes the ring. He can't speak, not with his throat cut, but he can still do magick. One last time. He grips my wrists, a phantom memory handed down to me, and I hear his final thought before he dies. *Te absolvo.* I forgive you.

The word was on my lips when I opened my eyes. *Absolvo.* I sighed, and it slipped out of me, like the Word that started the World. Not a shout, but a tiny whisper of sound.

IV

The ceiling was rough, unpainted stone mottled with age. A heavy blanket held me down, and as I moved my arms to push it back, the bed frame creaked. Lifting my head, I examined the room. The air was dry, with a hint of mold. I was in a basement somewhere, in a room made up as a guest room. Bed, dresser, floor lamp, chair.

Man in chair.

Antoine was reading *The Wall Street Journal*. The light from the lamp spilled out in a cone of yellow illumination, and it reflected from the silver fingers of his right hand. His blond hair was shaggy, a different style than I had seen on him a few months ago. He was still growing it back from when it had all been burned away. His face was smooth and unblemished, making him seem all the more like a teen pop star with his delicate cheekbones and narrow mouth, and there was no hint of bruising from when Marielle had tagged him. A wool jacket was carefully folded over the back of the chair, and his clothes were tailored and expensive. Dark colors: charcoal and black. His tie had a hint of red, threads that seemed wet in this light.

He deigned to notice that I was awake, and his lip curled in a hint of a smile.

"You look—" My voice broke, and I sat up to clear my throat. "—you look… well."

"A couple of months at a private spa in Sardinia," he said, lowering the paper. "Thalassotherapy. Very invigorating. All that seawater. For a little while, I thought I was going to grow gills along with all my new skin." He released the paper, and it floated in midair, shivering like a lover as he stroked it lightly with his silver fingers. With a gleam of violet light, it folded itself up and fell to the floor in a neat rectangle.

The Chorus backed up in my throat, making my mouth twitch with the acrid taste of ozone.

"You, on the other hand," he said. "You look a little haunted."

"I wonder why."

He smiled as he leaned back in the chair. He watched me for a minute, and I stared back, unwilling to give him anything else. *You two will always mirror each other.* The voice I heard in my head wasn't one of the Chorus; this was one of my own memories. Marielle, on the morning of the duel, acknowledging the eternal dichotomy of my relationship with Antoine.

"We've heard," he said finally. "A little over an hour ago. A call came in from the Consulate in Seattle. Our man there."

"I see," I said. An hour ago. I looked around for a clock. "How long have I been out?" The skin of my face still ached where Marielle had slugged me. A few times, if I remembered correctly. Somehow my arrival had gone horribly awry.

Par for the course these days. Things had certainly been easier when I had been hiding in my self-dug hole.

Had they? asked a familiar voice in the Chorus.

Denial is always easier, John, I told the spirit of Detective Nicols.

Antoine's mouth twitched, fighting to hide another smile. "You forgot her temper, didn't you?" He touched his cheek gently, and I knew I was supposed to notice his lack of bruising. "That was quite a punch," he said. "I *felt* it, and it wasn't even meant for me."

"Yeah," I said, gingerly touching my face and exploring the warm skin. I'm sure there was some nice color developing. Antoine would enjoy that. "She's gotten stronger."

The gravity well she carried with her was new. She certainly hadn't exhibited that sort of psychic pull the last time I had been here, and it felt… primal, for lack of a better world. Some sort of arcane magick that I didn't have any experience with.

"She's going to need it," Antoine said. "They're all going to be watching her now. Waiting to See."

"Where is she?"

He lifted his shoulders.

"Seriously."

"I don't know. She didn't come with us."

"What? You left her there?"

"She refused to get in the car, and I didn't want to deal with Henri. He was lost in his magick. He never would have listened."

"So you just—what? Threw me in the car and drove off?"

"Henri is not that stupid. He didn't want her."

I shook my head. "This wasn't what I planned. Not like this."

He laughed, and the Chorus slithered in my gut, feeding on the bubbling magma of my guilt and anger. He was goading me, hoping I would try to wipe that smug grin off his face.

He wants the excuse to hurt you, the snakes in my belly reminded me. *There is an imbalance of pain, a debt owed.*

I shook them off. "Yeah, well, okay. I guess it isn't my planning that brings us here anyway," I said. "Rough and tumble as it may be, we're still caught in the Hierarch's Weave."

Antoine leaned forward. "Are we?" His eyes glittered with violet light. "Did he tell you as much?"

I threw back the comforter and swung my legs out of bed so that I had something to do. Something other than lying there, looking at him. "Plainly? Of course not," I said. "It was like every other conversation with him. Soothsayer or Devil's Advocate: it changes with every sentence that comes out of his mouth."

"How could you expect anything less? But after you talked, what did he give you?" He paused, waiting for my answer, and when none was quick in forthcoming, he prodded me a bit more. "Other than his soul, of course."

I considered denying it, but realized there was no point. Antoine knew how the Chorus worked. He had killed Lt. Pender—the Hollow Man contact in the Seattle Police Department—so that I could have enough energy to face Bernard. He had offered me another man's soul. I had refused, because it wasn't so much an offering as a yoke. It would have made us complicit in the willful thievery of another person's light, and while I didn't have any illusions about being a lightbreaker, I wasn't a soul eater. Not like that.

"He gave me a lot of heartache," I said. "Philippe gave me nothing but pain, Antoine. His, and yours, and Marielle's."

His lips curled back from his teeth, a feral motion I had never seen on him before. More than a crack in his armor. This was Antoine, naked before me; before I could read him further, he disappeared, slipping beneath the ever-present layer of magickal distortion that wreathed him. Like a shark, always just under the surface.

"That's not completely true," I said, as if the thought had just occurred to me. "He did say you took credit for stopping Bernard. In your True Record, you were the one who destroyed the Key."

His gaze was hooded, the glint of magick in his eyes nearly invisible. That inscrutable exterior. That marble façade. I was starting to realize how much it revealed about him.

"I take it you're not going to disagree with him?" I asked as I stood up. I wasn't wearing socks or shoes. They were neatly piled on the dresser, along with my ruined coat and the contents of my pockets.

He shook his head. "I was protecting your anonymity," he said. "We had to discern the Hierarch's vision of the Weave. A global manhunt for you wasn't going to help us figure out what was going on."

"Of course not," I said, wandering toward the dresser. I was a little unsteady. Some lingering muscle twinges from Charles' magick wand. "That would have been distracting. And who knows how long it would have taken for them to track me down?"

"Yes," he said. "Exactly." A little too eager to agree with me.

"Though, with you being the True Witness to the event, and reaping the reward of being the badass who stopped their plan, you certainly got back in the Old Man's favor. All sins forgiven, perhaps?"

"Perhaps."

I tried to be casual about my inventory of the items on the dresser. New passport for Michael Dupont, my ready-made alias for this trip. Nearly empty wallet with one credit card, some business cards, and a couple hundred Euros. Velvet bag of tarot cards. A pack of spearmint gum I had bought in Heathrow, along with a page torn out of a magazine: a mention of the Archimedes Palimpsest. The conservation team had finished disbinding the manuscript a while back, and the news was finally getting out in the journals. I had a client who'd be disappointed; he had wanted access to it before they tore it apart.

What was missing from my personal effects was the key and the ring.

The key was old and made of iron. The ornamental bow had been smashed into an ugly lump, and the teeth had been slippery, wavering in and out of focus. A piece of paper had been previously attached with a loop of thin string, the word "Abbadon" written on the scrap, but I had ditched both the paper and the envelope the key had come in during my layover in England.

The ring was a platinum band, set with three opals. On the

inside of the ring were fine lines of arcane script, old magick I hadn't had a chance to decipher. The ring of a king, the circular seal of a thousand-plus years of history. It had gone on my finger quite easily and I had only taken it off and put it in my coat so as to not get comfortable wearing it.

"We had a deal," I said, picking up my coat and checking the pockets. Just in case. "We were going to work together."

"We are," Antoine said. There was nothing in his face but that placid serenity that challenged me to be the one to say otherwise.

Could I trust him? I wondered. All history between us aside, did we really have enough of a common enemy to work together? Or was everything he said on the riverbank in Portland just what I had wanted to hear? Was he manipulating me to his own end?

Ask him, the Chorus challenged. *Ask him for the ring and key back. Ask him as his liege. Ask him as is your right.*

"Is there something else?" Antoine asked, prodding me in my hesitation.

I wanted to know why. From Antoine as well as the Chorus. Why was it important that I force this issue? If he had the missing items—and I didn't see any reason why he hadn't taken them; they had been in my pocket when we had left the train—why would he give them back because I asked? He knew I couldn't take them from him. So why wouldn't he just deny having them?

"You're not telling me everything," I said, and I wasn't sure if I was talking exclusively to Antoine.

"Neither are you." He smiled. "But at least we're being honest about it. I'd call that progress."

Antoine and I have, at best, a tempestuous relationship. We were brothers in the Weave, fellow Watchers who came up through the ranks at the same time, a few years back. Though Antoine's family—like Philippe's—had been part of the organization for several generations. I was a recent recruit, a promising mutt found scrounging for scraps in the gutters of Paris. He and I and a few others made a little coterie of young turks.

Hermes Trismegistus, in one of the dialogues recorded with his son, Tat, spoke of a great basin lowered down from Heaven. It was filled with Mind—a word rife with many connotations that had occultists and philosophers arguing for centuries—and it was only through man's focus and will that he could achieve a purified state. One that allowed him to bathe in the basin and be covered with the luminous dew of God's Will. Or some such thing.

Metaphor aside (or not, depending on what you believed in), we sought the basin, whether the archaic artifact or some modern facsimile. That was our reason for seeking initiation into the inner mysteries of *La Société Lumineuse:* to be worthy of illumination. We had purpose and direction—for a little while—and then emotions got in the way.

Those basal desires that forever infect the flesh: lust, jealousy, fear, greed. Always fighting those demons that haunt our bodies, aren't we?

It was a combination of lust and jealously that did us in. Assisted by the vibrant presence of Marielle Emonet. Daughter of the Old Man. Which wasn't to say that there weren't others who were interested in Marielle. Her proximity to the Hierarch alone made her desirable. In an unenlightened throwback to our medieval roots, there was an unspoken belief that she was the prize. She would be given to whomever the Old Man selected as his successor, which failed to bring into consideration a number of things. Not the least of which were her temper and her willful independence.

I hesitate to say she enjoyed playing Antoine and me off one another, but it was such an ingrained response that it happened almost involuntarily. Clarity on the tangled trinity of our relationship came grudgingly in the years after I left Paris, and I realized I was a means to get under Antoine's skin. She liked me well enough, but in the end, I was a message sent to the other man: Marielle would make her own choice, and Antoine needed to respect her opinion if he ever hoped to have a future with her.

But outside the contest for Marielle's affection, Antoine and I had been friends. I seemed oblivious to the aristocratic heritage that the others deferred to, and the respect I had for him was that of a peer, of a fellow student of magick. He frightened me because of what he knew and what he could do, not because of the rich stock of his bloodline.

Who knows what he saw in me; maybe it was as simple as the fact that I didn't cater to him, that I asked him to earn the right of my respect. Once or twice, I had cracked that armor of his and Seen inside, and that I could—and had—may have been part of the reason he had adopted me into his little clan of magi. I was a wild card, and Antoine—like the Old Man—knew the best place for wild cards was at one's side. Who knew what mischief they could cause if they weren't Watched?

Well, sleeping with the girlfriend, for one.

Shortly after my Journeyman trial, Antoine and the others had tried to embarrass me. We took a little extra-curricular excursion to a tiny village near the Swiss border where the locals still believed in werewolves; I had thought it was to celebrate our initiation into the first circle of the society, but that wasn't the case. They had tried to frame me for the death of a local, setting me up to be a target of local superstitions. I went off-script, and left them with a mess to clean up, and during the course of that engagement, I stripped Antoine's shields and showed the rest of the gang that he was twisting all of us. All our threads.

No one was too happy about that.

Antoine and I were wary of each other for several months after that, finding excuses to dodge the other, but such denial didn't last. We had already eclipsed the other's orbit once, and it was just a matter of time before we came into conflict again. New Year's Eve, in fact, at a club near the Eiffel Tower. Tempers had run hot, and Antoine had ended up laying down the challenge.

Ritus concursus. The primal way of settling differences, man to man. Usually reserved for upstart magi who sought to get ahead on the rank ladder, ritual combat wasn't normally engaged between brethren of the same rank. But there wasn't any other way for Antoine to call me out without consequences. The rite of combat was recognized as a way of settling affairs that didn't require the same weight of evidence and prosecution that more modern methods had. Old school rules.

In our case: swords; under the Pont Alexandre bridge; at dawn, on New Year's Day.

It hadn't gone well. Antoine lost a hand. I got run through with his sword, after which I fell into the Seine. By the time I dragged myself out of the river, I was out of Paris. And staying out was the best solution to our problem. I went underground, and let them think the river had claimed me. Antoine was only too happy to consider me dead, and under the rules of combat, he was cleared of any transgression. It had been a fair fight, as far as those sorts of fights go.

And the status quo had been maintained for a few years. I went about my business: buying and selling black-market occult paraphernalia, sneaking into libraries and reading illegal texts, and looking for Kat. Five years later, I finally tracked her down in Seattle, where I found a group of magi involved in psycho-animism—the art of releasing the soul from the body. They were working on a secret project, one that had Watcher backing.

And the man sent to oversee the project was Protector Antoine Briande.

There are only twenty-one Protector-Witnesses at any time, and typically when one dies the election process is a long drawn-out affair. The same was true for Preceptor, the final *electable* rank beyond Protector, which was about as complicated and contentious as electing a new Pope. Mainly a series of political machinations and some ethically shaky tweaks to the Weave until a clear candidate could be identified. As for the Architects? They were Preceptors who were further elevated in ultra-secret ceremonies. We knew their titles, but none of us knew who they were. Part of the mystique of the *inner* Inner Circle. Even when you were on the inside, you were still outside: another one of those little reminders that each of us, regardless of our gained wisdom and knowledge, didn't know everything.

The rank was changing. Too many generations removed from their beginnings, the children forget the origin of a tradition; they forget the reasons for the old ways. Eager to get ahead, we eager youngsters think a title is a fancy word to impress the docile starfuckers, and we forget that it recognizes a body of experience and knowledge. We used to venerate our elders because they knew the secrets, because they'd taken the time to understand the inner workings of the universe.

Antoine defied history. He ran counter to the argument that, with age and experience, came understanding and mastery. He was, as far as I knew, the youngest man to ever hold the rank of Protector-Witness. Upstart, headstrong, and brilliant in his execution of magick and spellcraft, the man lived and breathed power. His connection to the leys—the energy lines, both natural and unnatural, that gave a magus access to power—was fundamentally instinctive. He didn't have to consciously think about connecting to the grid and drawing power. It was just *there* for him.

While the others were somewhat mystified by my lack of ability to tap the lines like other Journeymen and yet still do enough magick to pass the trials, Antoine suspected something like the Chorus. He knew why I couldn't ground myself well enough to draw power, just as he knew why that lack of egocentrism was also my ace. I took power from other souls, and I could even reach through them to the leys if they were connected.

My soul was broken enough that I couldn't ground myself, but I could draw power from a radiant conduit more readily than anyone else.

Pluses and minuses. These are the crosses we bear. The damage done, and the way we survive. *The knowledge of good bought dear by knowing ill.* John Milton, talking about the price of eating the fruit of the Tree of Knowledge. The price of what we became when we touched the other side and learned the magick arts.

Two months ago, Antoine and I had faced off over the experimental device built by the Hollow Men, who had been working off an ancient design, cobbled together from a variety of medieval-era sources—both European and Islamic. The Key of Thoth harvested souls, storing them in a reservoir that a schooled magus could then tap as an energy source. Bernard du Guyon, the grubby-fingered alchemist who had figured out the lost Key, had tried to breach the Veil and do something unsavory with the Divine. If there even was a Divine Presence waiting for us, on the other side. All in all, there had been a lot of theory and not a lot of practical knowledge at the basis of their plan.

I got ahead of Antoine by catapulting him across a parking lot, trying my best to remove him from the field. The only way I got the drop on him was that I had had a reservoir of power, a mass of energy taken from others earlier that day. I slowed him down enough that I could throw a wrench in Bernard's plan. I couldn't stop the harvest, but I did mitigate the scale. And, while waiting for dawn and the opportunity to stop the remainder of Bernard's experiment, Antoine and I realized we had both been played.

The Hierarch had been shaping a grander pattern. Antoine had thought *he* had been manipulating the Hollow Men to his design, but his actions were still within the parameters of a larger plan. And it went back further than that: our duel under the bridge in Paris five years earlier had been part of that design as well, as had my subsequent exile. It hadn't been chance that we had found each other again in the Pacific Northwest. There, on the river's edge, Antoine had glimpsed the larger Weave and realized it wasn't his place to stop Bernard. It was mine. As a *Qliphotic*-damaged soul eater, I knew better than he did what the device was and how to destroy it.

And if I died in the attempt? Well, that would have solved the other nagging problem for Antoine.

Seeing the Weave isn't the same as scrying the future. It's more like seeing the complex combinations and permutations of possibilities. Manipulating the threads of the Weave is like using your hip to influence the ball on a pinball table. Just the right amount of force at the right time will cause a ripple in the fabric. You can't always control how the ripple spreads, but as you get better at it, you learn how much influence—how much pressure—you should bring to bear.

But there are always spots where there is too much interference. There are too many possibilities to consider, or the outcome of a situation is so radical and catastrophic that seeing behind the knot is too difficult. Maybe it was easier for the Old Man. Maybe he could see further than any of us.

But Antoine and I couldn't see beyond dawn. We didn't know what was going to happen when I returned to face Bernard in the tower.

And Antoine had been a little disappointed when I came back. It would have been easier if I had fallen—I didn't necessarily disagree with that assessment—but in the end, I hadn't been ready to be unraveled. When I returned from the tower, having broken the Key and liberated the captive souls, he and I had talked about the problem we had in common. A rebellion was forming in the rank, a schism that was going to have far-reaching repercussions, and based on what we had Seen of the Hierarch's hand in the Weave, he wasn't entirely unaware of the mutiny that was coming.

The rebellion would have a contingency plan in place, a

secondary course of action to depose the Old Man, and the question we had wrestled with that morning was where would we be in the coming war. Which side would we support? Antoine had argued for signing up with the New Guard, and I had sided with the Old Man. Why? To be contrary to Antoine, partially, and partially because I still believed in the Hierarch, even though he had played us both. Somewhere in the discussion, Antoine changed his mind and, grudgingly, agreed that the Old Man's camp was the better place to be.

Or, at least, that had been the plan. But Antoine had come back to Paris and taken full responsibility for throwing Bernard's plan into disarray. While his argument that he did so to keep me hidden was sound, it wasn't the truth. It was a smoke screen, a subtle twist to the Weave that could draw my thread out of the pattern. If I didn't exist to the rest—if they didn't know about me enough to care that I was a wild card—then I wasn't necessary for this pattern. I had stopped Bernard, and taken away his toy. I had done the job I had been set up to do, and there was nothing else I could offer to the Hierarch. I could safely be removed from the pattern. That had been Antoine's take on my place in the Weave. I was a piece used, now useless, and easily discarded, and even though we had decided to wait for the Old Man's call, Antoine had been hoping that it would never come. That the Old Man would have no more use for me.

Philippe's visit to Seattle must have been a surprise to those around him. So close to the spring equinox. I had been wondering how he had managed to slip away from Paris without the entire rank knowing that he was gone, but then, he was the Hierarch. Misdirection and obfuscation were so ingrained in his psyche that he was probably incapable of not contorting and complicating everything.

But there was indeed more to his visit—again, part and parcel of his methodology—and I hadn't understood why he had come all the way out to Seattle to activate me for his final solution. I had had no idea how integral I was to be in his final hours.

The Hierarch had come to show me his cancer. He had come as close as he could to the place where his wounds had been inflicted upon him. The deaths in Portland had wounded him. Deeply. His power was fading, and his mind was starting to go too. He wouldn't survive long, especially if the Opposition discovered the extent of the blight laid upon him by the Key's detonation. He hadn't called me to his side. He had come to me instead, not to pass judgment on past transgressions against the family, but to ask a favor.

Ritus concursus. To the victor go the spoils.

His ring, and his mind.

There were a couple of other party gifts which he hadn't explained, and the Chorus had been maddeningly unable to discern any concrete details about them. The key, an old twisted thing that was half-melted but resonant with magick. The tag, which read "Abbadon," I had long discarded. His deck of tarot cards—the Marseille pattern—and more than one card had notes scrawled in the margins. They were his private journal of occult knowledge. The High Priestess had Marielle's name written on it, and a cell phone number I assumed was hers.

What was I supposed to do with all this? Go to Paris. That was clear. Get under Antoine's skin. That was a happy by-product. Stay alive? Obviously.

The Hierarch had wanted me to be his harbinger, his angel of vengeance, and I had politely refused. But I hadn't walked away from him when he asked me to take his soul. I hadn't said no, which made me complicit in his design.

But I already was. That was the trap into which I had been forced. I was the outsider, the quintessential village idiot who had undertaken the great quest into the world of sacred darkness and who had returned. I was Campbell's Monomyth Hero: chosen against my will, imbued with the knowledge that would save or damn the kingdom, and destined to be cast out again in the end when the cycle spun to its inevitable conclusion.

Hurray for me. Last time I had thought this was the part I was playing too, and that hadn't turned out to be the case. Misguided and befuddled like the tarot's Fool, I had danced my way off the cliff.

I wasn't going to be *that guy* this time.

But Philippe knew that, which is why he offered me everything. He knew this was a carrot that would entice me.

There were two carrots, actually. And the combination of both would make me overlook the danger of returning to Paris. We make our own traps. Philippe was well aware of how readily we would walk into disasters we knew we should avoid. He knew, better than any of us, how little effort it took to sway us onto a different path than the one we meant to follow.

Here, little one, take my hand. I will show you the way.

He knew. He knew, beneath all my bluster and outrage, I had wanted this. I had wanted a focus. That was the way my thread was wound. It wouldn't take much to twist me to his plan, and it hadn't.

V

"Stay here." Antoine admonished me as he put on his coat.

"And do what?" I asked. "Meditate?"

"If it helps."

"Where are you going?"

"I am a Protector, Michael. I have responsibilities. The Hierarch is dead. The rank will react, especially this close to spring, and I must be visible. We need to know what the rest will do, how much they will panic." He looked at me, his eyes guarded. "A lot of them will be thinking about it."

The Crown.

Each spring the Hierarch underwent a ceremonial renewal, a Coronation that was part pomp and circumstance and part cosmological rebirth. With Philippe gone, the question was: Who was to fill that void?

Without a clearly designated heir—me notwithstanding—the rank was going to turn into a chaotic mess of egos and agendas. Antoine was right. We needed information. Who was going to make a play for the Crown? Who had the resources to take it? *Who wanted it?*

"How long?" I asked.

He shrugged, adjusting the cuffs of his coat. "I don't know."

An honest answer, but one that made the Chorus tighten against my spine. Too much uncertainty. Too much waiting. Too many things out of my control.

Antoine wasn't about to tie me down; he was, after all, leaving me on my own recognizance, which meant one of two things: a) he expected me to stay like a good house pet; or b) he expected me to bolt.

"I'll be here," I said as he walked toward the front of the narrow apartment.

He paused at the base of the stairs that led up to the street level and looked back, his eyes violet with light.

We both knew I was lying.

I remained in the single hallway of the apartment, listening to the sound of his boots against the stairs. The basement apartment wasn't much more than a trio of rooms off a central hallway, and it must have been in the center of the block as there were no windows. Not in the bedroom; not in the tiny kitchenette; not in the bathroom. It was a box, hidden away from the world. Good, if you wanted to be invisible; bad, if you were worried about someone coming after you.

A door at the top of stairs opened, spilling light down the wooden steps. For a second, the noisy sounds of Paris tumbled down into the basement, but then Antoine shut the door, and everything became quiet again. Muted and distant. Separated from the world. Isolated in this boxlike prison.

If he had wanted to kill me, he would have done so while I was unconscious, or he would have left me in the road near the train tracks. A gift for Henri. But he hadn't. He had ditched his ex-girlfriend, and spirited me away to this safe house. For which I was supposed to be grateful. I was supposed to sit tight and wait.

Didn't he know better by now?

He does, the Chorus whispered.

My head was starting to throb, a massive headache sneaking into the forebrain. I was wound tight, and the screws had only been tightening since I had gotten on the plane in Seattle.

I will not be your agent of vengeance.

That is all you will ever be, an echo of Philippe, twisting through the Chorus.

The images cycled through my head as I rubbed my face: Philippe, sitting in the chair; the flickering streamers of light caught in the fireplace; the suppurating blackness of his leg; the pale skin of the crown of his head; his pupils, dilating as the spike of the Chorus split his heart. These were my memories, and while my rank was no longer recognized by the society, these images were a True Record. I was the sole Witness to the Hierarch's death, and even though the rites of combat said I took the spoils, no one would believe me. Which meant that the body politic was headless, and like Antoine had said, who knew how stable that body was going to be.

The Coronation. Via the network of bound memory, I knew what happened after the death of the Hierarch. There was a resurrection, a ceremonial recognition where the new leader was Crowned. Recognized by both the rank and by some external agency. Some sort of institutional memory, a historical legacy that was passed on to each new Hierarch. The Spirit of the Land. The Secrets of the Ages. The Truth to the Inner Mystery. The combination to the safe in the back room where all the deadly occult paraphernalia was held. Or some such thing.

There were other secrets too, hidden by the noise of the Chorus. The *Qliphoth* had hidden in that confusion and darkness; after I had scoured them out, it was as if I had driven the rats out of the basement, but the room was still there. Dark, inviting, and who knew how far back it went. All I did know was that Philippe was in there, and he had locked the door shut from the inside. I didn't have the strength to force my way in, nor did I have a key.

That damn key. Did Antoine know what it was for?

I showered, discovered there was nothing edible in the refrigerator, and used that as a convenient excuse to walk away from the safe house. Pants, shoes, shirt, wallet, tarot deck, crawling paranoia about being in the heart of the enemy's empire: everything I needed. I left the passport—no point in carrying the false identity anymore; not when they knew I was here—and my jacket. The burn pattern on the front would draw too much attention. I could pick up another at a shop somewhere. I went up the stairs, out the front door, and found myself in a narrow alley.

Residential neighborhood. The surrounding buildings were gray concrete, the sort of invisible architecture thrown up during the bleaker part of the Cold War. Windows, placed in precise rows, were afterthoughts, squares cut out of the foreboding walls. The accreted history of the lower classes, packed tightly together in little boxes. The Chorus didn't sense any danger, nor any watchers behind the curtains of the numerous dull windows along the alley. I turned left and started walking.

Eventually, I'd spot a landmark. This was Paris, after all. You're never far from a picturesque monument or historical landmark.

In this case, the Père Lachaise Cemetery. One of the world's largest cemeteries, Père Lachaise was a nineteenth-century solution to the problem of overflowing churchyards, and had become a status symbol in the subsequent centuries. You weren't somebody until you were buried at Père Lachaise.

I followed the old stone wall, tracing the rectangular shape of the city of the dead until I found the collection of shops clustered around one of the cemetery's entrances. I needed a few things. Coffee, coat, cell phone: Maslow mapped to the twenty-first century. Start at the bottom, work up.

After procuring the items on my list, I settled at a sidewalk table, outside the Brasserie du Père Lachaise. The wind was light, from the north, and the sun was out, so it wasn't too cold. Winter was dying; spring was coming.

The Chorus reminded me of the field beyond Philippe's

farmhouse. In the spring, it exploded with wild flowers.

In the spring…

The cell phone I picked up at the shop was a pay-as-you-go type and I had put a couple hundred minutes on it while at the store. It included, among what seemed like a dozen other functions I'd never need, a calendar that informed my jet-lagged body that today was March 19. The spring equinox was tomorrow.

The Coronation.

Not much time.

Antoine hadn't taken Philippe's tarot deck, and I emptied the cards out of the velvet bag and shuffled them. The Marseille deck was the oldest design, light and precise with the symbolism as opposed to the flood of versions that came out of the nineteenth and twentieth centuries, and on some of the cards Philippe had written tiny marginalia. Marielle's phone number was written in an arc over the head of the High Priestess, and I transferred the number to my new phone.

I dialed, and while I was waiting for her to answer, I shuffled the cards together and cut the deck.

Nine of Swords.

I almost hung up the phone, not wanting to bridge a connection between this card and Marielle, but the call went to voice mail immediately. "It's me," I said. "I have a local number. Call me when you can."

The Nine was a piece of work. The swords, hanging behind the figure on the card. The imminent approach of doom. Pain and suffering, not just the physical kind. There was mental anguish associated with the Nine. Someone else's physical pain, resulting in your mental agony. As I tried to decipher Philippe's notes, scrawled along the left edge near the hilts of the swords, the letters twisted. The words lost their shape, bleeding and writhing into echoes of Philippe's history.

When I absorbed another soul, in addition to the raw energy of that light, I also took on various other aspects of that personality. A lot of it faded over time, mental detritus that I didn't have any way to anchor, but some of it stuck. Memory is extremely subjective, nothing more than a collection of biochemical impulses, and what keeps it vivid and intact for a person is how well it connects with other clusters. "Mental scaffolding" is the term a Boston-based psychologist I knew had told me once. Like the sort of thing you see on the side of a building that is being retrofitted. A jumble of ladders and metal pipes, somehow staying together while simultaneously affording easy access to every floor and every window of the building.

We are nothing more than the aggregate of our experiences, and if you tear the scaffolding down, the rest falls apart in rather short order. I was the dominant personality in my head, and everything ultimately found some place in my ego personality. Everything became part of my memory, but I had learned how to reconcile absorbed memory with my history.

The memory of Marielle playing in the field, for example, and others like it were memories that didn't match my personal history. They stemmed from a time before I was in Paris, before I knew her. Things from her childhood: picking at the seams of the school uniform from when she was a small girl, the one forced upon her by the rigors of private education; standing before the Nike of Samothrace and staring up in open-mouthed wonder at the headless, winged woman; laughing at the expressions on the gargoyles atop Notre-Dame, the wind blowing her hair—worn long and black during this period. These memories clumped in my head, attaching themselves to my history of her. In this way, the history of the Chorus became my own: I knew what they knew, learned what they learned, feared and loved what moved them as well. I became more than the individual parts.

However, this behavior with the cards was new, a vestige of Philippe's connection with the deck. When I put the card down, the writing slowed and became fixed; when I touched a hilt of one of the swords, the words started crawling again. Flowing into the hilts and up through the blades until each of the nine swords was awash with text. My fingertip started burning, but I didn't move it. The swords filled with black ink, more than there had been in the margins originally, as if it was being sucked out of my finger, a vampiric leech drawing out my blood.

The Chorus stormed, strands of white fog twisting into a tight nexus. The sound of their voices climbed in volume and pitch, growing louder until I was sure the sound was leaking out my ears. Without warning, the balloon of noise popped.

Splitting like a piece of rotten fruit, the Chorus vomited a flood of images. My headache increased, as if all of these memory shards had weight and presence. As if they were cutting and slicing their way through my gray matter. I ripped my finger off the card, and the external world went fluid on me, receding like a camera lens pulling back. Everything became distant and indistinct. Contrails like stretched taffy hung in the wake of all moving objects, as if I were slowly falling through time. In my mind's eye, I was under assault by a barrage of images, a viral download of sensations from Philippe's memory. Nothing visual; this was all emotional and tactile memory. In that burst of data, I learned the extent of his pain, and not only did my head ache, but my left leg did as well. It felt like I had been burned.

Philippe's cancer.

We all have a part to play in this. His voice drifted past me, like a satellite orbiting my head. Yesterday seemed like such a long time ago. Already the memory—bifurcated by his point of view overlapping my own—seemed distant, as if it were already crossing the horizon. Every point between now and then seemed to be both equidistant and part of the present. *There are no Witnesses,* he sighed. *There are only participants. We are all part of the design.*

I saw him holding up his hands, nine fingers raised. Like the Nine of Swords. *We are all part of the same pain. We all pass through Yesod.*

With a physical pop, I snapped out of this vision. The liquid in my coffee cup quivered, and a bus coughed as it crossed the nearby intersection. A bird flew in front of the sun, and I was dazzled by the flicker of shadow and light.

The Nine of Swords lay on the ground, face-down, and without turning it over, I picked it up and shuffled it back into the deck. The back of my neck was cool with sweat, and my hands shook slightly.

While in Seattle, I had become friends with Piotr Grieavik, an old Georgian seaman who had floated into the Puget Sound region a few decades ago. He did tarot readings out of his Airstream, and his silver trailer moved in concert with the flow of energy in the city. He was good, a True Seeing reader, and he saw the cards as a means to clarify our location and vector on the morphic fields. I wasn't sure if the fluidity of Philippe's cards would fascinate or terrify him. There was a difference, he had told me once, between interpreting the future and influencing the future.

When my hands stopped fluttering and my heart calmed down, I cut the deck and looked at the two cards. The Fool and the Magician. "You're funny, Old Man," I muttered, and the Chorus slithered through my brain like oil across water. I put these two on the table, face up, and then buried them beneath the rest of the deck, like a layer of fall leaves covering the seeds planted for spring.

I took a sip from my cup, and glanced at the traffic and people walking along the sidewalk. All so normal. All so mundane. A normal day, late in the season; life moving toward spring again, getting ready to bud and grow another year.

When I dug up the Fool and the Magician, they had changed into the Ten of Pentacles and Ace of Cups.

The Marseille Ten only shows the coins, and there is no background on it like the gate and magician that crops up in the Rider-Waite deck. Nor is there the re-arrangement of the coins into the positions of the Tree of the Sephiroth. The Marseille Ten is just a field of coins, but the meaning is the same. This is the realization of spiritual wealth in the death of the gross body. This is the breath of resurrection that is the reward for those who have prepared themselves for the next realm, the world of light and wind that lies just beyond the arch (or, in the case of the Marseille deck, that lies beyond this field of coins, round-headed disks covered with ornamentation so that they almost seem like flowers).

The Ace of Cups is the Grail, of course, but in the Marseille deck, it is a miniature castle resting on top of a golden base. A chapel perilously perched above the firmament.

When I touched both cards, they merged into a single image: a chapel with stained-glass windows. *Not far,* a voice in the Chorus whispered. *Close enough to touch.*

The image vanished when I took my hands off the cards, and they stayed quiescent as I re-assembled the deck and put it away. I sat in the sun, drinking my coffee, until the cup was empty and my bones were warm.

Close enough to touch. The same thing the Chorus had told me over and over again when I had gotten close to Kat in Seattle last fall.

Very funny indeed, Old Man.

He had been pushing me for a long time. How much longer was I going to let him manipulate me?

We all pass through Yesod, he had said. The Ninth Sephirotic globe, one step up from the fleshy death of *Malkuth.* Knowledge realized. Wisdom gained. One step closer to God.

Maybe I was asking the wrong question. How much longer was I going to let *anyone* manipulate me?

VI

From the outside, the building was a nondescript rectangle, but inside, the walls came in, forming a shallow transept. The nave was obviously more narrow than the width of the building proper, an architectural illusion so as to provide a sense of depth to the shallow indentations of the transept. Tiny niches along the outer edges formed a blister of bubbles, filled with stained glass. As the church was sequestered between other buildings on the street, the stained glass wasn't windows, but panels that were lit from behind.

The church was a small chapel, tucked down an alley about a mile from the cemetery. A sort of locals-only church that wasn't on any of the tourist maps, nor were there any indications on the street that a place of worship existed down in the alley. I found it because the leys converged on it, currents arcing off the main flow into this nondescript alley.

The place was lit by soft lights, recessed in the floor behind the row of column arches set off a few feet from the walls. Mounted to the western wall was a massive cross of wood, and hanging peacefully, as if asleep, was an equally enormous Christ figure. Tall candelabras stood in attendance on either side of his nailed feet, and light from the candle flames danced on his skin.

He was made from glass.

I knelt on a prie-dieu in the front, resting my forearms on

the padding rail, so as to get a better look at him. The work was clever in that the scrap of cloth covering his waist was real as was the crown of thorns on his head, and his features and hair were a mix of paint and colored glass. Unless you had some experience with the luminous qualities of glass, you wouldn't realize what the material was. It would be easy to leap to the conclusion that the way the light reflected off his skin was from a divine influence, that God Himself blessed this church and this idol of His son.

I hadn't been in a church in several years, as I typically didn't have much reason to traffic in their sort of communal psychosis. Like all modern religious spaces, they are a confusion of profane noise and sacred reverberations. It is difficult to find a space that is pure in its harmonic resonance with the energy flow, as most secular-based religions have spent centuries codifying their blindness. Occasionally, you could still find a place that wasn't completely moribund—the Grotto, outside of downtown Portland, for example—but most of the nexus points are no longer located beneath the old holy stomping grounds.

Our temperament shifts, over generations, and while we never lose our fear of the unknown, we hide from it in different temples now.

At least, that had been my experience with churches in the United States. Some of the older places, ones that had history going back a hundred years or more, still had the magick in their bones. Too many years of regular service, too many penitents praying for guidance, too many dreamers asking for some sign of the Divine. These sorts of echoes permeate stone after a while, and the stone never quite lets go.

This church had some history in its bones. The building was clearly the oldest structure in the alley, and while the inside looked like it had been made over in the last hundred years, the leys still converged on it as if they had been redirected by several generations of foot traffic. Or maybe it was something else.

What do you want me to See, Old Man? There was no answer from the Chorus. I was going to have to figure this out myself. Even in death, he was still teaching.

Like all new students, I had struggled with the semantic distinctions the Watchers placed on certain words: seeing and Seeing; knowing and Knowing; Witnessing. This uppercase emphasis like we were reenacting one of Byron's Romantic epics. But, gradually, like all initiates, I came to understand the subtleties of our discourse. Language is an imperfect system, more so when you start working in several tongues at once (cultural mores start to become an issue; more than once I felt like I needed advanced degrees in history and cultural anthropology to understand the lessons given to us). Almost like Platonic Ideals, some words were echoes of older, more enlightened, concepts. An extra stress on the initial syllable (a capitalization, if you will) implied the higher meaning of the word.

The distinction between seeing and Seeing, for example. I could describe the physical attributes and placement of all the objects in this church, but such a passive description failed to explain why they had been placed the way they had. Such mundane objectivity couldn't encompass the movement of energy and Will required to make this scene the way it was. Who made the Christ? Why had they chosen glass as their medium? What effect did that have on the congregation? Or on the energy patterns?

Glass could distort or mirror, affording the viewer either a filtered view of reality or a reflection. It didn't have any identity of its own, forever slippery to the viewer. A perfect vehicle for inspiring meditation and personal reflection. *Look upon my face, my children, look up and tell me what you see?* asked the face of the glass Christ. *What pains you?*

The echoes in my head.

During the decade I had been running from my shadow, I had been using the energies of stolen souls to complete myself. I was whole with them, and while I couldn't quite ground myself like other magi and open myself up as a conduit point, I could still exert my Will on the world around me. I was a schizophrenic with a dominant personality matrix, and that ego consciousness was the singular point around which my world spun. The rest were echoes, trailing ghosts caught in orbit. But the spirit of Philippe seemed like it had its own satellites.

Like looking in a mirror and seeing another mirror. And the more you compare that reflection to the endless parade of fainter reflections, you realize each one is subtly different.

Could an organization have memory? Could it have the same sort of eternal life that a pile of old stones did? I didn't really know what it meant to be Hierarch of the Watchers, but the echoes of Philippe's history in my head had a peculiar edge that wasn't like other lives that I had absorbed. Granted, the Chorus was different since I had been changed by the explosion of souls in Portland, but my relationship with the memories—with the other personalities—was still the same.

Each soul that has passed through me changed me. I was no longer who I was prior to being initiated into the mysteries, which isn't to deny the fact that all experience changes us. But profane experience builds upon the history that has gone before. We remember things because they remind us of other events and sensations, and the strength of any given memory is commensurate with the amount of like material it can bind itself to. Our ego identities are raised up by this tower of memory, but when I examine the stones of my memory, I find them strange and alien. I do not know where they came from, or how they came to be lodged in my mind, but time and energy has welded them to the foundation. I was the sum of the history of all those who have been touched by the Chorus, and as my shadow was intent on poisoning me for a long time, a lot of this history was black and vile. Fear, loathing, hate, sexual release.

If a core sample were taken from this pillar of rock, like a geologist examining strata of stone, the bottom layers would be akin to compressed layers of black shale and the topmost layers would be lighter. More porous, like sandstone. In there were untainted memories: Marielle as a child; an auburn-haired woman who I knew without knowing was Detective John Nicols' wife; and cathedrals, lots and lots of cathedrals. St. Mark's in Venice, the Basilica in Rome, the cathedral at Ulm, Sacré-Cœur, Saint-Sulpice, Mont-Saint Michel, Notre-Dame.

And this tiny church, nearly lost in the shadow of the surrounding tenements. Nearly lost in the relentless progress of modernity.

Was it the solemn serenity of this place that I was supposed to See? The glass Christ. The Chorus kaleidoscoped under my pressure, splintering into a rain of colored glass. Some of the shards formed pictures, panels that turned toward me for an instant before shattering again. I stood, and wandered over to the mounted stained-glass panels. Yes, some of those images were here. The north side detailed the Stations of the Cross. But there were subtle differences: the inclusion of extra figures, not typical of the iconography; alchemical symbols, inscribed on clothing and floating in space above characters; and the expressions of the figures weren't as traditionally sorrowful.

Not these, the Chorus sighed. They drifted across the glass, making the white cloaks glow so that the soldiers of Christ became floating ghosts. *Not here.*

I prowled further, investigating all the tiny niches. The rain in my head had stopped, and the only image left was a Christ figure, floating on the cross, his heart a flaming ball in his chest. Like Dali's hypercube Christ, but without the geometric overtones. The picture was there in my memory, but I couldn't find it in any of the panels.

"Can I help you?" The priest was dressed in gray—pants, jacket, t-shirt—and his white collar seemed more like a nod to couture than a religious vestment. He was a head taller than me, and clearly in shape. The loose cut of the jacket couldn't hide the breadth of his shoulders. His eyes focused on a spot beyond my left shoulder, and his face, though weathered, was calm. His right eye was surprisingly green, a vibrant emerald, in contrast with the empty whiteness in the center of his left. He stood quietly, hands clasped like he was holding a small moth, waiting for me to find my tongue. His hands were harder than his expression. He hadn't always been a priest.

"*Salve, Pater,*" I said. "I am a weary *traveler,* seeking guidance." Seeking a sign.

"*In corde prudentis requiescit sapienti,*" he said, nodding.

Wisdom lies in the heart of one who has foresight. One of the Old Man's favorite lessons.

The priest had just offered me a countersign to my mention of "traveler."

"I have lost my faith, Father," I said, as the Chorus swirled in response to his phrase. It wasn't the church itself I was here to see, but the man inside it. "I wonder if you might have a place where a *frater* such as myself could pray, where I might receive such wisdom."

"Of course," he nodded, acknowledging my recognition of his countersign. "I have a private study. Let us adjourn there. Please, follow me."

He led me to a narrow panel set in the wall on the left side of the sanctuary. It turned out to be a door with no knob. I felt a brief whisper of magick and the door opened, swinging silently inward, and after we passed through, it clicked shut as quietly as it had opened.

No knob on this side either, the spirit of Detective John Nicols acknowledged.

I had thought the priest was leading me into a sacristy, one of those tiny rooms off the main area of the church, where the priests usually stored all of the mundane tools of their profession. But this was a hallway, a narrow, low-ceilinged corridor that inclined downward. Tiny paintings hung along the walls. Watercolors. They were lit by tiny spotlights that ran along a strand of fine wire. I was about to ask who the artist was, when I realized why they seemed so familiar.

In the converted studio at the farmhouse, along the Aude. Where Marielle chased the geese. *I painted them. No,* I corrected that thought. *Philippe* painted them. That was his memory, tying itself to my soul.

The paintings weren't copies; they were studies, preliminary versions of the stained glass in the church, and in them, the differences from canon were even more pronounced. Especially when I examined them with Chorus-sight. The silver symbols filling the open spaces became sea creatures floating on vibrant waters.

The last painting was the truly radical departure: Mary Magdalene, accepting Christ's flaming heart. It was close to the one I had been looking for, but broader in scope, and I wondered if what was in my head was a detail, a small scrap of this picture.

At the end of the hall, there was another door—one with a knob this time—and it opened into a long, narrow room. High windows, narrow slits in the stone, ran along one wall, providing pale and indirect light for the room. Bookcases filled most of the wall space, and along the wall opposite the windows were a rectangular desk and two chairs. A single book lay on the table, open, and its page was covered with tight rows of dots. Past the table, a woolen screen afforded a little privacy for a small niche, complete with a narrow cot, neatly made, and an unremarkable wooden wardrobe.

In the far end, beneath a large oak cross mounted on the wall, was a kitchenette. Hot plate, microwave, refrigerator, sink, freestanding pantry. Another table—this one more square—was pushed into the corner, and two more chairs—matching the pair next to the reading table—were loosely arranged at the table.

The priest waved a hand toward nearby chairs as he walked

over to the pantry cabinet. "Tea?" he asked as he got out a battered metal pot and filled it from the tap.

"Please," I said. I ran a finger along the spines of the nearest row of books, and selected one at random. It was written in the same patterned script as the book on the table. I ran my fingers lightly across the page and felt the raised bumps.

He didn't watch me put the book back, but I could tell he heard me replace the volume. I went to the table and sat in one of the chairs, waiting quietly for the water to boil. Watching him as he performed the ritual task of measuring loose tea into two tea strainers by touch. He was quite practiced and conscious of putting me at ease. He looked down at the tea as he measured it, though I noticed that his head was cocked a little to the right—much like he had when we had first spoken in the church. He favored one ear.

"There," he said, as he put the two covered porcelain cups on the table. "We will let it steep for a few minutes."

The clock on the microwave was flashing "12:00." As if it had never been set.

Up close, I could see that it was a piece of glass that gave his right eye its bright color. Faint scars ran along his cheek and neck, and part of his right ear was gone. The right eye watered, a perpetual tear forming in the corner of his distressed socket.

"I was prepping a chandelier," he said, innately aware of the question on my mind. "At Versailles. The studio I was working for had been commissioned to provide art for a centennial celebration. We were behind schedule and were overtaxing our hot shop. Too much heat, too much glass, too many of us—tired and exhausted—and there was an accident. Some of it I stopped," he said, showing me his hand. Knots of scar tissue roped across his palm, and more curled around to the back. "Some of it grazed me," he continued, "taking nothing but skin, but one piece stuck. The doctors thought they got all of it out, but it had broken off in my head. Grazed the inside of my eye socket as it had gone in.

It didn't show on the X-rays, and several months later, it was just there, caught in my eye." He shrugged. "And there it stays."

"And the left?" I asked.

He smiled. "I stared too long at the sun of the forge."

"Before or after you became a priest?"

He lifted the covers from the teacups and removed the tea strainers. "Milk or sugar?" he asked. His smile was all the answer I was going to get to my previous question.

"Both," I said.

Once we had both doctored our tea to our satisfaction, he sat across from me, silently, staring at nothing in particular, and sipped his tea. He gave no indication that he was in a rush to talk, and—gradually, grudgingly—I became aware of how noisy I was on the inside.

The Chorus was buzzing in my spine, electric sparks of memory and energy that I couldn't quite control. I wanted to move; I wanted to lay the deck of cards on the table and put the priest's hands on them. I wanted to ask him questions, so many of them fighting for position against my tongue. And part of me still wanted to flee, wanted to run and hide from the magick storm brewing across the leys of the city.

But I sat there, instead, with a modicum of patience, and listened to the micro-ambience of this inner sanctum. I *was* a weary traveler, and without speaking a word, he gave me the space to find some wisdom.

VII

Eventually, the priest gave a small nod, and pushed his cup aside. The sound of the china moving across the laminate surface of the table dispersed the meditative ambience of the tiny apartment.

"It is not an easy task to quiet oneself," he said. "Many of us forget. Your energy is still much too quick, but I can see the impression of its orbit now. There is a lot of history bound to your light."

"I'm impressed," I said. "Most can't see me at all."

He snorted. "Most are blinded by their own light. Too caught up with the glitter of their own thread. All they see is the surface, the forward and backward of their lives."

"But you see deeper than that, don't you? Beneath the Weave."

His hands moved on the table, as if he were re-arranging pieces of a game. "We teach the new ones to call it the 'Weave,' because that is a concept they can readily understand, but it is like teaching a child to play checkers. It's a simple game, two-dimensional really. Only later are they ready to play a richer game on the same board."

"Chess."

He nodded. "The Akashic Weave extends in every direction, and when I gave up my sight, I was to see it more properly. I was able to understand the true nature of how the threads bind together."

"The big picture."

"Yes. There is a balance to all things, and we are too small and mean to want to believe such universal hegemony exists, but that is part of what we must strive toward. An understanding of the reflections and shadows that the unconscious symbols of the Divine leave in their wake. So that we, too, may be creators."

The Chorus caught a slice of memory, and turned it over, spinning it like a coin; it opened up. A small burst of memories exploded: the fiery eye of the glass furnace; the priest pulling and stretching a piece of red glass into a flat sheet; on a nearby table, a rack of colored sheets—green, blue, yellow, white—cooling. The priest wore a modified pair of goggles. Only the left eye was protected from the light of the forge.

"You made all the glass," I said, answering my previous question about his vocation. "From his designs."

The Chorus twisted the images in my head, turning them inside out so as to see a different perspective. A different time, in the same place. The priest, now kneeling before the furnace, sweat and grime staining his naked torso. A pair of hands entered the frame—my hands—and removed his protective goggles so as to firmly grasp his head. I held his face still as he opened the blast cover of the furnace. Tears started from his eyes, droplets like molten glass streaming down his cheeks. In his right eye, the emerald shard of glass glittered; in his left, a howling whiteness devoured his cornea. I could feel the heat from the forge on my hands.

The priest was unafraid, and the expression on his face held no pain.

This was not punishment. This was a reward.

"And when you were done," I said, slowly, the words shivering up from the snarled core of the Chorus, "I took your other eye and gave you your new name: the Visionary."

In speaking those words, in being Philippe for a brief second, a cascade of the Old Man's history fell into place, now anchored by my act of speaking aloud. I knew the priest's name, how Philippe recruited him, his secret training and preparation for the task of making the stained-glass panels, the title given to him by Philippe; all that and more were known to me as if I had always known them. It was a disconcerting moment of vertigo as I flickered between my identity and Philippe's before returning to my—now altered—self.

His name was David Cristobel. Once: an itinerant laborer; a student of the arts; a glass-blower. Now: parish priest, and one of the secret masters of the society. The Architect known as the Visionary.

Father Cristobel bowed his head. "Our Father," he whispered, "who art in—"

I stopped him. "No, not yet."

He hesitated for a moment, and then nodded. "Yes, of course." He raised his head and looked directly at me, Seeing me. "It is a bold binding, and he hides you well." He wasn't speaking to me; he was talking to the spirit of the Old Man, as if he was—

"He isn't hiding," I said. "Philippe is dead, but some of his... personality hasn't faded yet."

He stared at me more, and the ever-present tear finally slipped from the corner of his right eye. "The Lightbreaker," he said. It was his turn to name me. "You knew all along, didn't you?"

"Knew what?"

A small laugh jerked free of his chest. "You are far more trusting than I, old friend. Your vision is, indeed, deep and distant."

"Father Cristobel," I said. "You and the Hierarch had an understanding of the threads that defies my feeble grasp, and I'm glad you're impressed with the Old Man's plotting, but he told me very little. And he's gone. All I have left are fragments of his memory, and I can't control how and when they offer themselves to me. I am, for lack of a better word, a bit *blind* here."

He smiled at that, but the motion quickly died on his face. "Yes," he said, staring at a point behind me. "There are many knots in the fabric itself, and much… that obscures the Record. It is difficult to see very far. Or very clearly." A shake of his head wiped the rest of the humor from his face. "The Hierarch wound tight and far, Lightbreaker, and trusted—perhaps too much—that the threads would move in the manner of his suggestion."

"Endgame," I said. "All the knots, coming undone."

"But will they unravel to his design, or someone else's?" Father Cristobel wondered. "How strong was his Vision?"

"That's the big question, isn't it?"

Father Cristobel stood and retrieved a bottle of whisky from the cupboard. He got two more glasses and filled each with a finger of liquor, nudged one toward me, and raised the other one. "Now is not the time for tea," he said, raising his glass. "To Philippe Emonet. My father, in spirit and in my heart."

Our Father. Holy Spirit. My Son. A confusion of histories overwhelmed my tongue and I settled for tapping my glass against his. The whisky was heavy, filled with the earthy taste of peat, and it went down like a hot coal.

Father Cristobel coughed. "Ah," he said, after taking a second sip. "It has been a while."

I turned the bottle so I could see the label. "A Lagavulin 16," I said. "It's a little mean when you first come back."

"Most things are," he said, pouring another portion for himself. "How long have you been away from the family?"

"A while." There was no point in denying it. I was starting to See how far back Philippe's planning went. "A little over five years."

"Ah, yes," he said, nodding. "Before the Upheaval." He set his glass down. "I know you. You are the rogue who left us, taking a hand and a heart with you."

I knocked back the whisky in my glass, the peaty burn killing the words in my throat. The fire of the scotch rose up from my stomach and inflamed my lungs.

"Markham," he said. "Yes, that is who you are. 'Michael,' she called you, but it isn't your Christian name."

"Landis," I said, my tongue burning. *She.* Such familiarity. I exhaled, fiery exhaust from the whisky, and memory turned in my head.

A small baby, wrapped in white linen. *Marielle.* A nocturnal baptism, here in this church, the glass Christ hovering overhead like a watchful angel. A younger Cristobel and Philippe, their hands suspending the tiny child over the basin of purified water. The glistening stroke of a wet finger across the child's forehead.

Cristobel was Marielle's godfather.

She watched them, unafraid. Aware of what they were doing. Aware of the pulsating energy emanating from both men. The flow of life moving into the basin and then into her body. A secret ritual, hidden away from other witnesses.

Father Cristobel seemed unaware of my sudden realization, the tumult of memory happening in the blink of an eye. "You were a useful tool," he continued, "hidden away before the fracture made itself known. You didn't know your part to play in his grand game, did you?"

I shook my head. "No. I thought I was... free." That was a lie, but I had thought I was free of Paris. *Evidently not.* "But that's not the case, and I need to know what my role truly is."

Because Philippe won't tell me, and that's part of his design too. That's the difference between knowing and Knowing, and when the hard choice comes, he's going to want me to truly Know.

"Yes." Father Cristobel sighed, and seemed to weigh some decision for a few moments. "I will assume that your blindness extends to the events of the last few years within the family. You wouldn't—" He hesitated, as if he were mentally preparing himself for a task, one he knew had been coming, but hadn't expected it to arrive today. Hadn't expected it to ever come, but here it was.

"It has been... a few years now," he continued, sliding into the role he knew was his. "Call them the 'Opposition,' for lack of a better term. They've been plotting a long time, but it was only recently we realized they were more than a bunch of idle dreamers.

"U.S. foreign policy had become even more of a disaster than we anticipated. Washington's cadre of radical capitalists had gutted their own economy and were turning their greedy eyes toward the EU. With this attention came a legion of tin-star despots who wreaked havoc at a bureaucratic level. Our influence in the U.S. became problematic. Every effort we made to control affairs vanished into a black hole, this vortex of uncertainty. Then, shortly after the last U.S. election, we lost an Architect."

Emile Frobai-Cantouard, the Chorus offered, having just come up from the basement with this nugget of information. The Cantouards had ties to the vineyards of Champagne, and Emile had fought in the Foreign Legion. Sub-Sahara revolutions. His magick came from the desert. Most of the memories of the man were dim and distorted, like film that had been rescued from a fire. Philippe was much younger in these memories, a time before he became Hierarch. Distant memories that were starting to fade, history being subsumed into the muck of my soul.

"The Hermit," I said, recalling Emile's Architect title.

"Yes," Cristobel said. "Emile Frobai-Cantouard. Do you know him?"

I shook my head. "No. I have some recollection of the rank, almost like a dossier on some members, but I don't know which ones or how much data there is to be gleaned until I actually need it. It's a frustrating side effect of the process."

"Do you know the others?" The question was casual, but the Chorus reacted to an underlying tension in his words.

"Who?" I asked.

"There are nine Architects, and I know the identity of three. I assume the others are equally—if not more so—ignorant of the others."

"What do you mean?"

"Each of the nine has a distinct title, separate from his rank. Some of them recognize specialization, some of them are historical titles that bind them to a specific aspect of the Akashic Weave. As an organization, we have been consumed with secrecy for so long that the true masters have become faceless. We are just names, no longer real flesh and blood. The Architects cannot be held responsible for their actions and directives because they cannot be found."

"Like… the Secret Masters of the Illuminati," I said.

He smiled. "That is one of our names."

In my gut, something twisted, and the Chorus dove after the elusive strand of thought. But they couldn't catch it, and any sense I had of Philippe floating near the surface of their boiling energy vanished. Something was wrong; something Cristobel had said wasn't true. Was he lying to me? The Chorus flexed, and strands of memory flared into arrays of white light. No, Cristobel was telling me what he thought was true.

"Someone knows," I said. "Someone knows who all of the Architects are."

"Of course. The one who chose them. The Hierarch."

And those names were hidden. I had a feeling they were there, down in the bowels of my subconscious, locked away in the secret vault Philippe had inserted in my head. A vault to which I had no key.

"What happened to Frobai-Cantouard?" I asked. The Chorus kept digging, sifting through uncatalogued memory.

Father Cristobel chewed on the inside of his cheek for a moment. He couldn't see my face, but he could read my confusion. My energy signature was in flux. "He vanished. When Philippe could not find the end of his thread, he came to me. I can't wind the threads like he can, but I can chart them better. Over the next few weeks, as I searched for signs of Emile's thread, I noticed his history was being dissolved. Somehow, the morphic fields were breaking down his thread, almost as if there was some sort of unnatural decay devouring his presence. He couldn't be removed from the Akashic Record, but it was becoming more and more difficult to discern his history."

"He wasn't dead?" I asked.

"No, in death, a thread withers, but it remains in the Weave. The next generation is laid on top of the last. In that way, the Weave is organic, a field that never becomes fallow. Each death provides nutrients from which new threads emerge.

"What was happening with Emile's thread was an obscuration, the like of which I had never seen before. He was hiding himself not only from us, but from history as well." He touched the table, his fingers idly tracing a pattern on the laminate. "In the course of searching for him, I learned the identity of two of the other Architects. They were searching for him too."

"And they didn't have any more luck than you?"

He shook his head. "The rest of the rank knew something was amiss, even if the Preceptors weren't passing the news along their chains. You can't See and not have noticed the abnormal shifts in the etheric flow across the Weave. This chaotic movement was interpreted by the younger rank as an opportunity for change."

"Personal advancement," I said. "The old-fashioned way."

"Yes. *Ritus concursus*. The old ways are so ingrained in us, aren't they?"

The old ways. I couldn't help but think of Antoine and our duel under the bridge.

"Protector Briande," I asked. "Do you know him?"

"Of course."

"Whom did he kill to get his rank?"

When he came to Seattle last fall he was a Protector-Witness, a full rank higher than he should have been. Most likely, Antoine had taken Traveler in the year after our duel and, given the normal schedule for advancement, he should now have been an early-stage Viator—a couple degrees ahead of Henri. There were seven sub-degrees in Viator, and the trial for each one required—typically—a year of intense preparation. Somehow Antoine had managed to leap all of that, as well as whatever degrees of Traveler that he hadn't finished, in a single fight.

The identity of who he had killed for the rank was in my head somewhere, somewhere in the vast roster Philippe had kept of the rank—names, titles, allegiances, faces even—but they were all jumbled, as if they had been all tossed in a sack and shaken. *Which one?* I just needed a little hint.

"Protector Hieron."

There. One of the names came into focus, and I could now bind his history to my memory of Antoine. Yves Hieron. Originally from Brussels; took his oath during the '70s; one of the Renaissance alchemists. Never married; dedicated to his research. Unremarkable trials. One of those who stay with a company for so long they become management by sheer weight of their organizational history.

Antoine's choice was, as ever, a tactical one. He took out an old scholar, a man who made safe, dependable choices, and who preferred to stay on the fringe. He had arbitrated more than a dozen disputes over the years, acted as a Witness to even more duels. Hieron had been a centrist, one who could be counted upon to hold the line. In a time of upheaval and crisis, Hieron would have been a steadfast soldier of the status quo.

The rest of the fights were small advancements, magi leap-frogging each other up the ladder, but probably nothing of any consequence in the long term. Old rivalries were settled and some narrow-minded bitterness about perceived slights were probably worked out, but nothing dramatic. Except for Antoine, who had stepped in and snatched a position of historical responsibility. Regardless of Protector Hieron's working knowledge of combat magick, he should have been able to withstand the assault of a gifted, yet nominally ranked Traveler. And yet, Antoine had won and in doing so transformed a resolute and steadfast Protectorate into a wildcard, a position held by an enigma whose allegiances and motivations were unknown.

I had thought I understood Antoine's motivations after Portland, and for a moment or two, when we had been talking earlier this morning, I thought I had a handle on what he wanted. But now, with the ring and key missing, I wasn't sure. I wasn't sure Antoine wasn't pulling threads at a deeper level. He was slipping away from me, disappearing into that inscrutable void that no one could penetrate.

Not only did I not know the inner workings of Philippe's grand design, I was starting to realize Antoine's confusion and dismay at being played may have been an act. While he had professed to not be privy to Philippe's design, I was starting to wonder if the Old Man had underestimated his star student, if he had failed to penetrate Antoine's mask and See the naked Machiavellian desire in his heart.

Maybe it wasn't a matter of who had the best insight, but who could hide their true intent. Who could guard their heart best.

VIII

"We've come to call it the Upheaval." Cristobel brought the conversation back on track. "Once the challenges started, the trickle became a flood. More duels were fought over the next twelve months than had been—cumulatively—over the last decade. There were two immediate results of this conflict: the rank was thinned, and those who survived were more inclined to be a fighting force than a group of scholars. The upwardly mobile brought with them a skewed morality. They didn't have any issue with using magick for personal gain; that was the underlying conceit in their intent. The theorists and the philosophers were cast aside, and what was left had a taste for blood. A taste that ran counter to Philippe's leadership."

"They'd lost their taste for Watching, hadn't they?"

The body must die. No wonder the Old Man had considered a scorched-earth solution. It was like God throwing up His hands and crying "Do over!" with the Flood.

"Precisely. A new direction that could come to fruition under new leadership." Father Cristobel's lips twisted downward. "I Saw the shape of it in the Weave, but thought it would only be a passing ripple. I didn't realize how much of an endemic change it would be until Philippe admitted he was ill."

"The cancer," I said. "I saw his leg."

Cristobel shook his head. "That came later, when he wasn't

strong enough to repel it."

The black sores on his spirit, the darkness eating his brain.

"He was losing his mind," I said. I had felt it in my head, that cold touch, and I had mistaken it for a resurgence of the old *Qliphotic* hunger that had lain in my soul for so long. That ugly, gnawing hunger. I pushed the Chorus aside, and took a long hard look *down there* and considered the blackness.

No, this wasn't the same. Philippe's hurt was more of a void, an emptiness so much more terrifying for its alien silence. "Alzheimer's," I realized. "I thought there were therapies now. Stem cell treatments."

"They slow, but they don't cure," Cristobel said. "The decay is, ultimately, inevitable, an untenable condition for the Hierarch. He has to renew his Promise each spring, and if he isn't healthy, then he is... rejected... he is—"

"What?"

The priest was looking at me, Seeing through my skin. "You don't understand this, do you? You don't know."

"Know what?"

"Certain details of Philippe's history are clear to you—facts only he would know—and yet other aspects of being Hierarch are hidden."

"Maybe because I'm not the Hierarch."

"But you—" His brow furrowed, and I felt a tension in his energy field. A narrowing of focus as his magick intensified. As his Vision deepened. "You and he overlap. Your threads are intertwined to a point of being one, but you are still distinct souls. How—" Cristobel didn't finish his question.

Not that I had an answer to it anyway. The Chorus used to be echoes of the old souls I had taken, nothing more, but since Portland, they had changed. They were still bound to me, snared by Reija's white braid, but they weren't a collective mass of unconscious desires any longer. Could Philippe still be "alive" in some spiritual sense, riding me like a psychic leech? I had broken him, and absorbed his essence, and in the past, that would have been spirit death. His personality—his spark—would have been torn apart.

Yet, Cristobel thought he could still See Philippe's thread.

"Is it like Frobai-Cantouard's thread?" I asked.

"No. This is almost an optical illusion, the sort of glimmer on a mirage that becomes less visible the more you examine it. Philippe vanishes when I really look at your thread, but when I pull back and try to see the surrounding Weave, his *touch* becomes evident."

"His touch? You mean the fact that he has twisted me into this design of his?"

"No. Your thread shows definite signs of having been twisted. But this is deeper. Intertwined." Putting his hands together, he tried to demonstrate with his fingers. "This is your thread," he said, holding up his right index finger. "This is Philippe's." The matching finger on his left hand. He tried to wind his left finger around his right. "This is still your thread," he said, wiggling the pair of entwined fingers. "This is clumsy, I know, but you can see there is another thread wrapped around your thread. Like a—"

I swallowed past the braid of white hair around my throat. "I know how a braid works," I said hoarsely.

"Ah, okay," he said, dropping his hands.

"So what does that make me? Some sort of hybrid soul?"

Cristobel looked past me, toward the church, and appeared to be Seeing somewhere else entirely. His eyes tracked back and forth. "This is it, isn't it?" he mused. "This death that isn't Death. Are you testing me, old friend? Is this what you meant with those cards?"

"What cards?" I interjected.

His blind eyes tracked back to me and the Chorus reacted to his magick again. "You aren't him, even though, on a certain level, you are. You and I can tell the difference, but other…

entities may not."

"What sort of entities?" I asked, trying to keep his focus. Trying to keep Cristobel from losing himself to an old conversation with a man who wasn't here. Philippe had obviously pushed me toward the priest, but I had to keep him focused on talking to *me* and not to the spirit he saw in my head.

"Every year, the Hierarch renews the Promise extracted from him at his Crowning. Every year, he is vetted as being suitable for the role."

"By whom?" I prompted.

"By the Land."

"Which land?"

"All of it."

"Gaia? What? Some sort of earth spirit?"

Cristobel shook his head. "No, the Land itself. The Hierarch is bonded to the leys. What they feel, he feels; he becomes one with the energy patterns of the morphic fields."

I was going to argue the point, but then I flashed on the cancerous decay of Philippe's leg. The sympathetic destruction wrought on his flesh by the event in Portland. "Their fall-back plan," I breathed. "Even if the Ascension failed in Portland, they knew the devastation would reflect on him. They couldn't touch him, but they could touch the Land."

Cristobel nodded soberly as he picked up the bottle of whisky. I pushed my glass toward his open hand.

The old vegetable rituals: the Corn King slain in winter, resurrected in spring. Like all pervasive mythological structures, they were reflections of old sympathetic, magico-religious rites. What happens down here is reflected up above.

Dumbly, I watched as Cristobel, having poured an inch in my glass, guided the mouth of the bottle to his own glass with a finger, and then poured. And missed, the whisky splashing on the tabletop.

The flashing display on the microwave went dark. I may have

blinked, or perhaps time simply started again, but the green numbers came back, blinking "12:00" as they always had.

The Chorus prickled up my spine, like ice crystals forming on an exposed rib of stone. Something had just happened, a subtle twist to the ley grid, but it had been enough to trigger their defensive reflexes.

Father Cristobel ignored the spill of whisky. "The chapel grid has been compromised," he said as he stood and moved toward the cupboard.

The Chorus poured out of my fingers, streaking for the ley energy surrounding us. They had to go far, as they only found a thin trickle running beneath us. When I squeezed them, sending them deeper, they found no sign of a natural etheric stream. Nothing but blank space, a void that reminded me of the yawning darkness in Philippe's head.

"We've been caged," Father Cristobel said, sensitive to the radiating confusion in the Chorus. "This is a nexus, but you can't See that now, can you? We've been placed in an *oubliette.*"

He returned to the table with a small mahogany box. It had no hinges or visible lock, and his fingers danced across the tight pattern of raised dots on the surface. A latch clicked, and the top twisted to the right, revealing a hidden cavity inside. He lifted out a long strand of dark beads, a strand longer than the space available within the box. They were black glass—obsidian, perhaps—and of two sizes. "My rosary," he explained as he slipped the chain of beads over his wrist. It was meant to go around his waist, a loop of glass with a long tail. A silver disk, inscribed with a magick circle, terminated the loop and the tail, and when he put it on his palm, the wide chain of beads slid around his arm like a serpent. The loop tightened, and the tail became longer. At the end of the dangling strand was a metal sphere, inlaid with black and white script.

"Why did they cut us off?" I asked, reeling the Chorus back in just as they were starting to read bright spots beyond the walls of the church. *Oubliette.* A prison within a prison, cut off from the rest of the world in every way possible. Like being cast out into the void before creation.

"This is holy ground," Father Cristobel said. "The circles and sigils are mine. But without access to the energy grid, they're just writing on the wall."

I nodded. The Chorus sizzled in my fingertips as I touched the puddle of spilled whisky. The alcohol reacted to the energy beneath my skin, bursting into a blue flame that crawled up to my knuckles. "They're taking away your advantage."

"Yes, it is not an unexpected move on their part."

Visionary. He was the one who had made the stained-glass panels, who Philippe used to track missing magi in the fields. Regardless of their secret names, the Architects were still thread winders, long-term plotters and manipulators. "You played war games, didn't you?" I asked. "Contingency planning. 'What if?' scenarios, disaster planning, tactical mapping—"

Thread winding, the Chorus supplied. *Our oldest art.* They had a secret in their mouths, like a grouse brought back from the field by an eager retriever. Each thread had a unique tension, a special vibration that, if you knew how to read it, made it stand out against the noise and chaos of the Weave. When a thread was tightened—pulled, plucked, wound—it reacted, generating a sub-psychic pulse through the surrounding threads. Reading this vibration was how the Architects built their machinations. They considered the possibilities and permutations, winding threads until they had the right tension. Until they twisted and bent in the direction of their choosing.

"Which one?" I asked. "Which *winding* is this?"

"A variant of the Blitzkrieg, most likely."

Germany's rapid assault of Eastern European targets in World War II. An overnight deployment and seizure of targets, effectively immobilizing the enemy before they know the fight has begun. So soon after the news of the Hierarch's death. *Yes, this is the way I'd do it. Quickly, while everyone is still in shock.*

"Multiple targets?"

"I would assume so. We don't know who leads the Opposition. But they know their targets, and will move swiftly against us. I have some suspicions as to who they are, but it is a Vision only truly realized in hindsight." He picked up his cup and hesitated for a second, as if mentally preparing himself for this last sip. "If my Vision is True," he whispered, and then he drank the rest of the whisky in his cup.

The Chorus registered the presence of souls in the church, spirit lights moving within the empty confines of our prison. They weren't radiating magick, but they were still brighter than the surroundings. Raised heart rates, elevated adrenaline levels. Men with guns. I counted six, and said as much to Cristobel.

He nodded. "As I suspected."

"How does this gambit play out?" The alcoholic fire danced along the ridges of my knuckles, spreading to my other hand as I bumped my fists. *Manus ignis, manus animi.* I felt the circuit connect through my chest, and the air popped and sizzled over my hands.

"Statistically, the odds favor them. Especially with six."

"There isn't a way to improve these odds?"

He cocked his head, listening to an echo I couldn't hear. "That depends."

"On what?"

He smiled, an old motion of his lips that spoke of a different time, of a different life. "On you, *Lightbreaker*. You are a blind man, stumbling through the fields. You do not know where the path is. I can help you."

"How?"

"Anamnesis," he said. "Remembering what you have forgotten. I can guide you. But we need to escape this trap."

"Yes," I said, the Chorus singing in my voice. "We need to find a way out." And then, a phrase I knew was right, that I Knew was required of me. *"Duc me, Pater."*

He clenched his fist and his Will activated the sphere at the end of his rosary. The sphere became a heavy, four-bladed cross. "I will, my son."

Father Cristobel disabled the power in the church with a thought as we came through the door with no knob. The church was dim, lit by flickering fingers of light from the tall candles in the sanctuary and from the sea of votive candles in the transepts. Shadows clung to the columns along the outer edge of the church, shadows deep enough for us to play hide-and-seek with our attackers.

The strike squad had split into two teams of three, and they moved in tight triangular formations. They were dressed in nondescript clothes: muted colors, some jackets, some sweaters—nothing that would seem like a shared uniform among them, but the sort of outfits that afforded places to hide guns. On that front, they were unified: compact machine guns. Heckler & Koch MP5s. I recognized the weapon's distinctive rattling burp as one of the assassins opened fire. Chips of stone cracked off the pillar I was hiding behind.

The Chorus filled my eyes, and I saw silver motes dancing over a glowing outline of the church's layout. The first team was in the central aisle, scattering for cover among the wooden pews; the second trio was in the rear of the church, sheltered by the pillars at the back. They were going to flank us along the outer wall. Father Cristobel was on my left, closer to the main altar.

I heard the whirling sound of his rosary, and he grunted as he cast the heavy end. Lit by his magick, it curved in a long arc from behind his hidden position. The glass beads separated, an elastic line of fire stretching across the church, and the spiked ball clipped the edge of a pew. Someone cried out and the snake of glassine fire whipped back.

First blood for us. The Chorus marked the cut on the man's

shoulder with a glittering line, and they vibrated in my fingers. While they weren't the same group of souls I had before Portland, there was emotional memory there. A resonance of their predecessors. Angels of vengeance, singing a song of violence.

I moved toward the back of the church, leaping between pillars in random hops. When I was close to the narrow shrines with the glass and the candles, I lifted one of the stubs of wax with the Chorus, infused it with my Will, and flipped it toward the center of the church. The candle, a squat block of wax with a tiny flame, morphed into a ball of fire as the energized Chorus realized my spell. The makeshift fireball bounced across the pews, scattering a trail of fire, and exploded with a dull pop a few rows over from the assassins. I threw two more in quick succession, giving little thought to where they landed. Just as long as they were noisy and bright.

Tiny noisemakers, distractions meant to afford me some cover as I sprinted for the back.

The trio at the rear heard me coming, as I wasn't making any effort to be silent, and the point man thought he was going to surprise me. He was stationed on the far side of the last pillar, waiting for me to run right into him. He thought I would hesitate when I saw him, that little moment of surprise that would make me freeze. He was the one who froze though, transfixed by the sight of the Chorus rising off my head and shoulders like a rampant phoenix, by the fire burning on my knuckles. I grabbed the barrel of his gun with one hand, and his throat with the other. I squeezed, and when he opened his mouth to scream, I could see the light of my fire at the back of his throat.

The other two started firing as the first gunman and I wrestled with his gun. Getting close and twisting him around, I felt him twitch and jerk as he took the brunt of their fusillade. Something raked my left shoulder and side, leaving tracks that burned. My hand shifted on his weapon as his grip loosened, forcing his arm away from his body, and I got a finger inside the trigger guard.

I squeezed, firing the gun. The shots were wild, but the others scattered anyway, seeking cover behind the pillars.

The gunman leaned against me, gasping like an asphyxiating fish. Smoke leaked from his mouth and nostrils, and when he coughed, blood spattered my coat. *He should be dead,* Nicols whispered, his homicide experience providing commentary. *Multiple hits at close range from 9mm ammunition.* The Chorus was already in the gunman's throat, but they refused to go any deeper. There was something wrong, something buried in him that the Chorus didn't want to touch.

I had read the assassins wrong, assuming the light coming from them was being thrown off by their overly active Wills. But the glow wasn't the concentrated gleam of actualized Will, it was stemming from a hard knot in their chests.

I fired a couple more bursts from the pistol to keep the others at bay while I struggled to hold the wounded gunman upright. His eyes were glazing over, and each time his mouth flopped open, blood ran out, streaming down his chin. Definitely mortal wounds, so why wasn't he dead? Why wasn't his soul disassociating from his flesh?

Slightly more worryingly, why didn't the Chorus want it?

My finger brushed something hard on his chest. Some sort of raised shape, and as I was trying to discern what it was, a metal canister rattled across the floor at our feet.

Flashbang, Nicols noted, the only one in my head with the requisite experience.

I ducked, pulling the gasping gunman with me. The inner wall of the church bumped against my back and I buried my face against his bloody chest. Even with my eyes shut, the world went white as the flash grenade went off. Sound vanished in an imploding thump, and the ground moved sideways as my internal gyroscope was beaten back and forth by each successive burst of the grenade. Sound and fury, leaving me with nothing. The chapel wall kept me from completely falling, and I slid to the ground, the dying gunman sprawling across me. My head and neck were splashed with hot blood, and I couldn't see or hear anything.

The Chorus wasn't affected by the flash grenade, and they tracked the other two assassins. They also spotted the thin strands of etheric energy rising off each man. Anchors. The filaments, like spider silk fluttering in the wind, trailed behind them, back through the wall of the church to their magi controller outside.

The Chorus roared down my arm, through the metal of the pistol, and kissed the remaining bullets in the gun. *Linguae ignis,* was the thought I had, but I couldn't recall the conscious decision to use that spell. The Chorus moved anyway, following a definite course of action. Popping across the tips of the bullets, they laid their trap. *Seven,* they reported.

More than enough, I thought. My wrist moved, and the gun left my hand. It was like throwing a coin into a bottomless well: I let go, and it vanished; I never heard it hit bottom.

The Chorus swirled down into my chest, building a thunderhead of energy. Lightning streaked off their cloud, and the charge rejuvenated my stunned flesh. Like getting zapped with a car battery. Everything felt a little more alive. Everything became a little sharper.

I could hear a little now, and some of the flashes of light in my vision weren't retinal burns.

The other two gunmen approached. Keeping their distance, their weapons raised and ready. While they weren't magi—they didn't have any magick of their own—they were familiar with the occult practices, a familiarity that kept their fear mostly in check. Still, the sight of their buddy, who was vomiting more and more blood as he tried to get up, was starting to fracture their resolve. An animalistic thread of terror twisted in the gut of one, a familiar taste the Chorus read easily, and the other was a dense mass of chaotic thought. Some of it concerned the thread connecting him and his master.

The pair got close enough, and the Chorus darted out—a tongue of flame—and touched the pistol I had thrown. Their fire ignited the magick on the bullets, and the gun exploded.

When the gunmen reacted, I shoved the not-dead man off me and rolled forward, grabbing the foot of the thinking assassin. The Chorus found a nerve cluster in his ankle, and unleashed a furious lightning bolt from their energy cloud. The psychic energy pulse went up his leg, found his spine, raced up his back like a rocket launching, and exploded out the top of his head. His nervous system short-circuited, he dropped like a sack of rocks.

The other gunman reacted poorly, immobilized by the fear bubbling in his gut. The Chorus unleashed the rest of their storm, and the shockwave lifted him off his feet and hurled him across the width of the church. The psychic backlash from the spell upgraded my headache into migraine territory. Add to that the confusion from the flashbang and the Chorus' instinctive defense, and my circulatory system took up this internal pulse and echoed it all the way down to my toes. Pain, pain, pain.

Moving like a myopic sloth, I pulled the nerve-stunned gunman closer, pawing at his coat and shirt. He had the same hard ring on his chest, right over his heart. It was a ring of gray stone, cold to the touch, and my Chorus-bruised fingers traced the markings running along its surface. I couldn't make any sense of the script. Arcane shorthand, more symbolic than actualized.

What the hell was it? Not a protection sigil. My fiery hands had touched the first man easily enough. Yet the Chorus refused to get any closer, balking at my command to investigate the knot of energy held beneath the ring. The stone was filled with magick.

I started to reach for the silver strand rising off him, but stopped shy of actually touching it on the etheric layer. It was a conduit. I had seen them before. Magi used them to channel power to each other. To do remote viewing. In some extreme cases, they were used as a leash, a means of animating and controlling an otherwise reluctant host. In theory, it could be used to keep them alive. Energy flowed to them instead of the other direction.

But that didn't make much sense. To effectively transform that incoming energy, they had to know how to use it. They couldn't be passive receptors. They had to have some training. Otherwise it was just an open line, an unattended hose flooding the garden.

The Chorus boiled in frustration. There wasn't any energy flowing through the line, at least not an appreciable amount. A single pulse, rhythmic and steady, almost like a... heartbeat.

Dead man switch. The Chorus finally spelled it out for me.

The strand was more than a conduit; it also monitored his body and soul. There was enough Will burned into the sigil that the conduit superseded the psychic link between flesh and spirit. As long as the conduit persisted, the soul couldn't leave the body. He couldn't die. Not until his master said so. *Soul lock.*

And when the signal came, the knot of power lodged in the gunman's chest would be released. In all of them. The assassination squad was on a suicide mission. They were a massive bomb, with linked detonators.

The mortally wounded gunman had rolled onto his back, and though my vision was still blurry, I could see that he was looking at me. He coughed, and his mouth moved into a smile. His eyes glittered with silver light, and I knew someone else was Watching.

The gunman coughed once more, and the breath that came out was his last one. His face spasmed once as all the pain he'd been carrying the last few minutes suddenly lit up his brain, and then the muscles in his face went slack. The silver light in his eyes intensified.

I scrambled to my feet, ignoring the pain in my shoulder and hip. My feet slid on the blood-slick floor as I tried to get as far away as possible from the downed gunmen before they died. Before the sigils on their stone rings activated.

The air in the church was thick, and I felt like I was swimming in water. My ears, still ringing and throbbing from the flash grenade, popped as the pressure in the room changed. The Chorus flexed, hardening against the explosion of the soul locks.

The psychic detonation hammered the room on multiple levels. My flesh frayed as fléchettes of etheric energy sprayed from the nexus point of the explosion. The Chorus howled as the shards cut through them, tearing out slivers of their history.

Knocked sprawling against the pews, I held on as the ground rolled and undulated. Several of the nearby pillars cracked, disgorging clouds of granite dust from their peaks. In the transept, stained-glass panels exploded, flinging shards of glass across the central nave like flights of frightened birds. The glass Christ swayed on his wooden cross, the psychic light of the explosion lighting up his painted skin.

Beneath him, braced against the altar, Father Cristobel struggled to stay upright. There was blood on his face, and his right arm flapped loosely at his side. His rosary beads were wrapped around his left arm, and they bounced off the side of the altar, sparks dancing off the magicked beads.

In the wake of the explosion, my stomach continued to flip back and forth, caught on a rollercoaster of muscle spasms. There was blood in my mouth—most of it mine this time—and the stains on my clothes were a combination of my wounds and blood from the gunshot assassin. I pried my clawed hands off the pew and staggered, drunkenly, toward the front of the church.

The Chorus still howled, their noise cutting through the blasting percussion of the headache. They were shouting something about the Abyss and I didn't understand what they were talking about for a second, and then I felt it too. Rather, I felt the void.

All of the gunmen had detonated, and the concussion of

those souls going off had created a void in the church. Suddenly I realized why we had been cut off from the ley grid, why an oubliette had been erected around us: nature abhors a vacuum. The walls of the prison were gone, and all the channels that met in this church, all the natural confluence of energies that had been directed here to give Cristobel a nexus of power, were suddenly open again.

The soul locks were only meant to loosen everything, what came after was the etheric quake meant to tear us apart, like a thresher separating the grain from the chaff.

"We need shelter," I Whispered to Father Cristobel.

"Here," he Whispered back, and I realized he wasn't trying to support himself against the altar. He was trying to move it.

I stumbled toward the front of the church, moving as quickly as I could in my vertiginous state. I half-fell, half-knelt next to the altar and put my good shoulder against the marble stand. It moved, slowly, turning on some hidden pivot. A hinge that hadn't been used in a very long time.

The Chorus started keening, a rising crescendo of psychic terror. I couldn't tune them out. They were down there in my soul, their screams vibrating me like a tuning fork.

The altar moved aside, revealing a black hole down into the subbasement of the church. Father Cristobel's hand fell upon my back, and he pushed me forward. "Go," he Whispered. "I will follow you." With nothing to brace myself against but the side of the altar, I slipped and pitched forward into the hole.

The ley flood hit, and the etheric implosion lit up the inside of the church. Father Cristobel looked back at the burst of psychic light, and it must have been like looking at the sun going supernova. His Vision couldn't protect him from this psychic detonation; if anything, it would only magnify the spiritual impact of what he saw.

Tears streaming from his right eye, he smiled.

Unafraid. Without pain. *Do not be afraid; this is your*

reward.

I fell, the world bleaching to empty whiteness in my wake. The wave of the quake hurled me away from the church, and my vertebrae started to separate. Like a leaf in a hurricane, I was blown away, falling further and farther than the ground beneath the church.

THE SECOND WORK

"For the present it is enough to have told you these two stories which seem to confirm two things in particular. First, that the souls of men which are almost separated from their bodies because of a temperate disposition and a pure life may in the abstraction of sleep divine many things, for they are divine by nature; and whenever they return to themselves, they realize this divinity. The second thing these stories confirm is that the souls of the dead, freed from the chains of the body, can influence us, and care about human affairs."

— Marsilio Ficino, in a letter to philosopher Matteo Corsini (c. 1465)

IX

A montage of memories flickered, a greatest hits collection: David Cristobel as a young man, standing beside the raised canvas of a boxing ring, intently watching a pair of fighters, soaking up every jab and swing; Cristobel, sunbrowned and glistening with sweat, breaking up stumps with an ax; behind him, the brick farmhouse and a river I knew to be the Audle, in the ring, in a different time and place, fighting a lean Filipino man; the glowing heat of the hot shop furnace, rods of colored glass jutting from its mouth.

I lay in a field of glass, silver light caught in the fragments. I lay on this glassine ocean, a sea that chimed as I moved. There were no stars overhead, and the air was heavy and musty, filled with a fetid dryness. The sort of dead atmosphere found underground.

Memories of Cristobel's life continued to flicker past like images projected on clouds scuttling across a black sky: the gilded ostentation of Versailles; a chandelier, glistening with emerald drops of frozen light; a ladder, collapsing, and the chandelier falling; an explosion of green fire, a coal lodged in the left eye socket. I felt sympathetic pain, as if a poker had been shoved into my brain.

I blinked, unable to move any other part of my body—caught in some sort of sleep paralysis. I blinked again, and again, and kept on doing so until the green fire winked out, its light draining away into the churning depths of the Chorus.

I could hear him praying, as if he were kneeling beside me. His voice gave me strength, enough to break the lassitude holding me down, and I sat up slowly. Shards of glass fell from my limbs, tinkling into the surrounding sea.

Father Cristobel floated on the glittering surface. His rosary was looped around his fingers, the silver and black cross glittering with spectral light. His eyes were closed, and he was intently reciting an old Latin prayer. The whisper of his words had no echo, as if we were lost in a place that had no horizon.

The Chorus moved slowly, turning like frozen gears, and eventually they generated a spark. This tiny spark escaped my mouth as I sighed, and it floated up, casting its glow across the floating surface of the ocean.

Underground. Not on a sea. Walls of ragged, unfinished stone. A hard floor covered with sand and glass. The subbasement beneath the chapel. I hadn't fallen all that far, regardless of the prior, endless sensation I had experienced.

I sent the light higher, trying to find the hole through which I had dropped, and found a ragged tear in the ceiling plugged by wood and a long piece of glass. The Christ figure had come off the wall, smashing the altar and sealing the hole. Parts of the sculpture were scattered across the floor of the subbasement, scattered across my body. Shortly after Cristobel had shoved me, the cross and Christ had fallen.

I glanced at him again, and realized he wasn't really there. Just a retinal afterimage of a strong memory.

The Chorus light floated through Cristobel's ghostly shape. He raised his head as the light moved through his chest, but he didn't open his eyes. The beads of his rosary reflected the spirit light, tiny sigils dancing along the curve of the beads.

The catacombs, he said, his voice a phantasmal echo in my head. *One of the old ossuaries that riddle the underground. A remnant of the Resistance.*

That explained the smell.

I glanced up at the dark ceiling once more. "Why didn't you jump?" I asked.

I did, he pointed out.

"No," I argued. "Not like that."

Father Cristobel was dead, crushed beneath the cross and glass first, and then the rest of the chapel as it had come down. The etheric implosion had brought the walls in too, the whole building crumbling in on itself. The Chorus had reached back for his soul as it had fled his crushed body, and apparently, he had come willingly.

I can guide you.

"When I said yes," I pointed out as I slowly got to my feet, "I thought you were talking about doing so while alive." More glass fell from my frame and I carefully shook out my coat and pants to divest myself of the tiny shards clinging to my clothing.

Cristobel didn't answer, and when I glanced around, his phantom was gone.

The rosary was in my coat pocket, coiled pleasantly like it had always been there. Right next to Philippe's tarot deck.

In law enforcement circles, the Chorus hinted, drawing on Nicols' memory, *this would be classified as keeping souvenirs.*

As Cristobel intimated with subtle shifts in the mood of the Chorus, there was a way out—*there's always a way out*—but it was a complicated route through a maze of unmarked passages. He might have known the route once, but all of his sensory data was aural and not visual, which meant it was next to useless for me. I didn't have enough experience to know what to do with the collection of clicks and bumps. The Chorus built a mental map as we progressed, supplemented by their reading of the spaces just beyond the nearest wall. My reserves were low, and I was tired; focusing the Chorus to extend them further would sap my remaining strength. Following Cristobel's hints was a slow process, but it was the most effective use of my resources. Frustratingly slow, but at the same time, I had to remember I was in enemy territory, and they had agents out hunting. I had to be careful.

I also needed some time to think, to sort through the chaotic swirl of emotional feedback from the last few hours. Cristobel had sacrificed himself to get into my head, as if being there would be a better place from which to direct me. But it wasn't, because while his soul energy was permanently part of the Chorus now, his personality wasn't fixed. Some of it would last, like the others, but not enough. Yet, there was no regret on his part, no sense of failure in doing what he did. It was as if his death and transference was part of the grand design.

If my Vision is True.

First, Philippe, and now Cristobel. What the hell were they doing? They were taking advantage of the psychic nature of the Chorus, of the manner in which I leeched knowledge from those I broke, but it was a fatal choice. Why couldn't they have just written down what I had needed to know? Or told me over coffee? Why the need to die to pass along their knowledge?

The body must die, the Chorus reminded me.

"I'm getting tired of that answer," I muttered.

Cristobel nudged me at the next split in the tunnel, and the Chorus added a marker to their map of the underground. I took the left fork—as directed—and stumbled slightly as the floor dipped downward.

"I realize this is a matter of interpretation," I said, "but this eagerness to jump into my head is starting to feel a little bit fanatical. Like you guys are trying to start a cult or something." Making light of the situation, trying to get some sort of reaction from my spirits. Some hint of why *two* Architects were co-habiting my head-space now.

Was I an easy escape hatch? The assassins in the church had

been primed to take out Father Cristobel. A surgical strike against an Architect. Cristobel had expected them to show up—eventually—but he couldn't have anticipated my arrival. Nor the opportunity I presented him.

What about the assassins? They had been unwitting pawns, unaware of the nature of the stone ring affixed to their chests. Whoever was running them had been remote viewing through their eyes, and once their master ascertained the situation was properly engaged, he had sent the mental command to detonate the rings.

Who? I wondered.

Images of sigils flashed before my eyes, an encyclopedic catalogue of magick circles. Keys from Solomonic lore, Enochian matrices, others I didn't recognize. Geomancy. I knew the word, knew the style of magick, but had never seen it other than a neat parlor trick of spotting and tapping ley lines. Some of the magick circles stayed in focus long enough for me to begin to understand their construction and purpose. Geomancy went much deeper than that. A properly schooled geomancer could redirect ley flow; he could build the sort of oubliette that had been erected around the chapel.

The stone rings on the assassins. Soul lock, conduit window, magick bomb: all wrapped up in one simple ring.

Who was the geomancer in the society? Which one was he? I ran through the list of secret names for the Architects: Visionary, Hermit, Crusader, Navigator, Thaumaturge, Mason…

Jacob Spiertz, Cristobel provided.

"Where is he?" I asked. And, equally important: Why him? What was his rationale for wanting Cristobel dead? Was he the Architect of the original plan as well? The man who had given the go-ahead for Bernard and the Hollow Men's experiment with the theurgic Key?

Cristobel didn't answer, and the Chorus shied away as I grabbed at them. "Tell me," I growled, and when the Chorus darted away from me again, I froze them with an angry explosion of Will. They shivered and whimpered as I tore at them, ripping through them like I was swatting a frozen cobweb with a stick. Their strands shattered and melted, dissolving into white smoke that curled backward into the pit in my soul. I hacked and hacked, looking for Philippe in the strands, looking for the source of the glitter of amusement I still felt. "Tell me, you son of a bitch."

Telling you won't help. Cristobel manifested on my visual field, floating beside the wall of the passage. His serene face puckered with a hint of apprehension. *The knowledge isn't enough. You have to understand what it means. You have to Know what has happened, and in doing so, you will See what is to come.*

I went physical, flailing at him, even though it was a pointless effort. You can't hit a spirit. You can't touch a phantom of your own imagination. Not with your fists. All I did was scrape my knuckles on the wall, which didn't give me any of the satisfaction I wanted.

You can't fight him, Cristobel said, floating just out of reach now. My own brain taunting me with the immaterial nature of the spirits in my head.

"I don't want to fight him," I said, trying to catch my breath. "I just want him gone. I'm done with his games."

My left shoulder ached, and my hip was on fire. The bullet wounds from earlier. Surface wounds that weren't fatal, but all this exertion was tearing the scabs open. The rest of my exposed skin had suffered as well, tiny scabs from all the flying shards of glass. Trying to punch out a spirit and tearing up my hands was only compounding the trauma suffered by my flesh. I needed to get out of these tunnels and find a sanctuary. Somewhere where I could get some help. I needed to find someone I could trust in the midst of all this chaos.

The Watchers were all insane, and I was caught in the middle.

I could burn the Architects out of my head. I had done it before, when I had ascended the spire and faced Bernard. I had detonated the Chorus so as to drive back the soul-dead who had surrounded me. Samael's children. The zombies of Portland who had wanted to devour my light. I had driven them back by sacrificing the Chorus. I could do it again.

A spike of pain went through the base of my spine, and my legs gave way. I banged my face against the floor, and lay there, squirming like a stuck bug. The spike reversed, coming back up and exploding in my brain, and I cried out. My vision flared white, and in the stark emptiness that the ossuary became, I saw a negative man seated on a black throne. Black flames licked from his naked skull, and his chest was a ferocious storm of black smoke. *You cannot be rid of us,* Philippe said. *That is not the way.*

"I… am… not your pawn," I gasped through the pain.

We are all pawns, he reminded me. *There is always a grander game than the one we control.*

I don't want control," I said. "I just want to be free."

You always have been, he said, leaning forward. *You are free to make your own choice. That is why I cannot tell you what you must do.* His eyes glittered with black tears. *Do you understand, my son?*

When I reached for him, the vision vanished, and I was left groping for nothing in the dark. In my head, I could still see him sitting on that chair—the colors all normal now—the memory of those last few moments in the library before I spiked him. The expression in his eyes.

Philippe knew what he had been doing; he knew the pain his death would bring to those he considered his children, but he also knew the alternative was much worse. He chose his own fate, willingly, because that was the right path. The hard path, but the right one.

You are free to make your own choice.

In that conundrum lay the obstinate madness of his actions, of his long manipulation of his fellow Watchers. He couldn't tell us what his plan was, because to know of it would be a temptation. What if we could change it? What if we thought we could make a better choice?

But we couldn't. He was Hierarch. His understanding of the Weave was deeper and wider than any vision we would have. He Knew, and had twisted the threads so as to bring about the end he had already Witnessed. Did it mean we were on predetermined paths that we couldn't change? Probably. But to walk those paths meant we had to chose them ourselves. I was in the thick of a war for the succession of the Hierarch that had its roots nearly a decade back, and in the midst of all the coming conflict, I didn't know who I could trust. I didn't know who wanted what, and from that ignorance, Philippe knew I would have to make my own decisions.

He knew I would be loath to participate in this game of vengeance—if that is, indeed, what it truly was—but if I didn't know the rules of the game or what my designated role was, then I couldn't act counter to it. I couldn't try to extricate myself from this pattern.

Besides, there was a carrot. *Make it personal,* Philippe had said to me one night, back when I had been a young student, craving any bit of knowledge he deigned to give me. *Always make any conflict personal. That way they hand you their thread and ask you to twist it.*

I couldn't trust any of the Watchers. But there was one person whom I could trust.

Marielle.

It couldn't get much more personal.

I started crawling. I had a long way to go.

X

Eventually, my cell phone chirped, and the tiny signal meter climbed to two bars. I was close to the surface. Another icon appeared in the menu. Voice mail. I dropped the phone back in my pocket. It could wait a few minutes; I was almost there.

The dry smell of the dead had gotten more pervasive in the last half-hour, and the texture of the walls had started to even out. Several of the rooms I had passed through had niches in the walls, and the floors were polished by the tread of many years. This area was more recently used.

My internal compass had been thoroughly fucked by the soulquake, and even though the ley energy had gotten progressively stronger as I had made my way through the tunnels, I hadn't been able to sync myself to the natural grid. There was too much noise, both in my head and from my surroundings, which led me to think I was moving through sections of the Parisian underground that had been heavily used to inter bodies. The only thing that leaves more psychic history than the bones of a church are the bones of people.

I thought I was under Père Lachaise, and the heavy iron gate barring my further progress confirmed that suspicion. I was on the wrong side, though, as the location of the lock proved. The keyhole had been filled in and the mechanism had been welded together. Parisian officials didn't want to fill in the tunnels, but they certainly didn't want anyone to think going further into the old tunnels was an option. Nothing short of an acetylene torch or some C-4 was going to open this gate. Or magick—the occult key of blunt force. When subtlety wasn't an issue.

The bars were cold and hard and I was more tired than I realized; it took me a while to bend the Chorus to the task.

On the other side of the gate, the tunnels were clearly marked and I soon found a metal door. With a handle, even. It led me into the cramped basement of a maintenance shed, and at a desk near the ground-floor door, I sat down and checked my voice mail.

Marielle, returning my call. She was clinical and precise in her message. She didn't explicitly tell me to crawl off and die, but the sentiment was clear in her tone. She ended it with a long sigh, silence, and then, in a quieter voice: "Call me back."

I did, and she answered it on the second ring. "I got your message," I said.

She was quiet for a moment. "I probably wouldn't have said what I said if you had answered."

"Well, it was good that I didn't. It needed to be said."

"It didn't. I—I know you, Michael. I know you well enough. You didn't do any of it to hurt me. It's just…"

"I have a crappy way of showing affection," I provided for her.

She laughed, and it sounded like something came loose in her chest when she did. "Yes," she said, "Yes, you do. You're like a cat who kills birds and leaves them in my shoes because you want to give me a gift."

"I am sorry."

"I know." She exhaled noisily.

"I kept the message," I said. "So I can play it back later, when I'm tempted to do something nice for you."

"You think that'll be enough to stop you?"

"I hope so."

"Me too. Though, there isn't much else that you could—"

"I could burn your house down."

"I've moved since the last time you were here, and no, I'm not taking you to the new place." There was some levity in her voice now, the pain of our history fading away into the endless well of memory. The imprint of my actions and the consequences would always be there, but we were moving past the recent incident. They wouldn't be forgotten—like all sins, they never are—but the other reasons we were bound to each other were reasserting themselves.

I glanced around the shed. "How about you come to my place?" I said. "It's a little small and smells funny, but it's cozy."

"Where?"

"Père Lachaise."

She didn't answer right away, and I thought I had lost her.

"Were you there?" she asked finally.

Father Cristobel spun in the Chorus, a tiny knot of light sparking within their serpentine fog. She knew what had happened at the Chapel of Glass. She hadn't known I was there, but news of the chapel's destruction would have certainly been heard by the Watchers by now. My being at the cemetery—in relative proximity to the church—couldn't be a coincidence.

"I was," I said. "I'm so—"

"No." She cut me off. "You can't have been responsible."

"No, I wasn't. Well—"

"You're not at fault, Michael. You can't take that weight, nor will I accept it from you."

"He—" I tried again.

"Tell me later," she said. "It doesn't matter right now. You are safe. That is good enough."

My chest tightened, the Chorus grabbing my heart. I tried to speak, and found myself as tongue-tied as a ten-year-old boy with a crush on his babysitter.

"Can you find the grave of the painter?" she asked. "The one who shares a name with my godfather?"

David. Jacques-Louis David, the late-eighteenth/early-nineteenth-century painter who had been the herald of a new neoclassical style. He had a tendency to pick the wrong team politically, first Robespierre and then Napoleon, which made him rather unpopular in his death. Still, art was art and a number of his paintings hung in prominent places in the Louvre.

"Yes, I think so." I glanced around the shed. There had to be some sort of reference chart. If not here, then near any of the entrances. Through the tiny window of the shed, the light was russet and gold. Sunset already. The gates were closing soon, if not already.

"Meet me at the entrance nearest his grave," she said, reading my thoughts. "Half-hour."

On a shelf near the door, I found a dog-eared guidebook to the cemetery. Once I figured out where I was, finding David's grave and the nearest entrance was easy.

The guidebook offered the trivia that David's grave only held his heart. The rest of him was buried in Brussels. I knew how that felt.

Marielle showed up in one of the ubiquitous smart cars that were everywhere in Paris. A tiny two-seater that wasn't much more than a bubble of glass and aluminum lashed on top of an engine and drive chain. We rubbed shoulders, and every time the car went over a bump or a hole in the road, I nearly fell into her lap. In other circumstances, I would have found the constant physical contact terribly distracting, but as it was, I kept feeling like I should apologize.

"You need to stop that," she said while we waited for a light to change.

"What?" I asked.

She was wearing Escada. It was a scent I would always associate with her, and trapped in the tiny cab of the car, it became a narcotic. She was wearing a sienna-colored v-neck sweater beneath her long coat, and a slender strand of pearls lay across her clavicle and the hollow of her throat like a chain of moonlight. "That hangdog expression," she said. "It's like you've got more bad news."

"Sorry," I said.

"That too." She glanced at me, light dancing in her eyes. "I'm a big girl, Michael. I'm not a glass figurine." The light changed and she took her foot off the brake. "I'm going to need your strength. Not your sympathy."

"Okay." I swallowed heavily, pushing down the weight of the—*call it what it is*—the guilt. The Chorus took the weight in, swallowing it as easily as they swallowed the dreams and fears of other souls. "Did you know," I said, changing the subject, "David's body isn't buried in Père Lachaise?"

"I know," she said. Glancing over her shoulder, she changed lanes. I shifted my gaze to the steering wheel, but not before she caught me looking at her throat. "He was declared a revolutionary after his death. He wasn't allowed back in France."

The car slowed and she turned a corner, slipping off the main road onto one of the tiny side streets of Paris. In the smart car, the road seemed wide enough, but with the two rows of parked cars it would have been a tight fit for any American-sized car. I was always amazed at how much denser the cities were in Europe, especially after spending a few months in Seattle. It was a constant topic of conversation in that city about the tight navigation of the hilly streets, but they were wide open compared to Parisian streets.

"There's a regulation actually," Marielle continued, "concerning the distribution of body parts in Père Lachaise. Since David's heart is buried there, they had to remove the heart of another person."

"Seriously?"

"Chopin's. His heart is buried in a church in Poland."

"But his body is here? Because David's isn't?"

She laughed at my expression, and after a moment, I joined her. "I can't believe I fell for that." The laugh knocked something loose in me. Like ice falling off a roof in early spring. A thaw coming to the old, cold country.

"It's true," she said. "About Chopin."

"But there isn't a law."

"No," she admitted. "But some say the heart is the seat of the soul, and that the rest of the flesh is just raw meat." There was still a mischievous note in her voice, but the Chorus felt an echo beneath it, a sub-harmonic tone that reminded me of the psychic pulse she had manifested earlier.

The Chorus resurrected a memory of the painting in the narrow hall at the Chapel of Glass, the watercolor study of Christ and the flaming heart. The gift to Mary.

"Do they?" I said cautiously. "Well, *they* say a lot of things. In fact, *they* are always talking. Mostly gossip and innuendo, really."

"Is that so?"

"Absolutely. You can't trust them. Nothing but conjecture and speculation. Internet forum talk. All baseless."

"Really? What if they said you and I were sleeping together?"

"That was a long time ago, and no one knew."

She looked at me.

"Okay, Antoine knew. But he's not the gossipy type."

She turned the wheel and the tiny car slid through a gap between two parked cars. A narrow gate blocked our path, and with a mental command much like the opening spell she had used on the train, she exerted her Will on the barrier. It responded, rolling back on tiny wheels, and she eased the tiny car through the portal into the inner courtyard of the building. There were several other cars parked in the octagonal courtyard and she backed into an open space. The front pointed toward the gate. Quick escape, if we needed it.

Switching off the engine, she leaned toward me as she opened her door. Her eyes were dark pools, and the Chorus pulsated in time with her heartbeat. "It wasn't that long ago," she said quietly.

She led me up a flight of stairs to a tiny second-floor apartment. The living room looked out over the courtyard, and judging by the lack of a television and how empty the pair of bookcases were, as well as the position of the only comfortable chair in the room, watching the neighbors was the primary source of entertainment. A stub of a hallway led to a bathroom and a single bedroom. Around the corner from the door was a tiny nook and kitchen.

Marielle filled a teapot from the tap and put it on the stove. "There should be fresh clothes in the wardrobe," she said. "You can take a shower too, if you'd like."

I nodded. "Where are we?"

"Somewhere safe. A friend's." She nodded toward the picture window. "The others are across the courtyard. We'll join them when you're ready."

"The others?"

"Loyalists. People who we can trust."

I wandered over to the window and lifted the edge of the curtain. The window of the second-floor apartment across the way was lit, though the curtains were drawn. "How many?" I asked.

"Eight."

"That's all?"

"Here, yes. Things have gotten bad, and we don't know who we can trust. We can't afford to meet openly." She opened the cupboard and took down two plastic mugs with lids.

"How bad?" I asked.

"We're not sure. It has been difficult to get accurate information. Some of the rank have just gone into hiding—we hope—and they're waiting out this whole affair. The rest—" She didn't finish, and she didn't need to. The rest were ending up like Father Cristobel.

"What are they doing?" I nodded toward the other apartment

Marielle snorted. "Talking, mostly."

I let the curtain drop. "I guess I'll go get cleaned up."

She nodded distractedly, busy spooning loose tea into each of the two mugs.

I didn't think much about the war council going on in the other apartment while I showered. Instead, my mind kept wandering back to what she had said just before getting out of the car.

It hadn't been that long, nor had there been any sort of serious relationship in between. Granted, what Marielle and I had shared during my time in Paris couldn't be considered serious, as the specter of whether or not she was still dating Antoine hovered over us. She had said it was over, but I had always suspected she had neglected to tell Antoine that fact. Or, if she had, neither of them had really believed their separation was permanent. I wasn't Rebound Guy, more the Transient Mysterious Stranger. Not the healthiest of relationships, but compared to the others I'd had, it was pretty cut-and-dried. We liked each other—a lot—and knowing that circumstances were going to doom us at some point, we simply lived in the moment. The arrangement worked until the duel on New Year's Day.

The Chorus had been obsessed with Katarina, and so I had never been fully able to commit my heart to Marielle, and she had a connection to Antoine that remained steadfast throughout our relationship. We were both bound to others, but that hadn't diminished the intensity of our attraction to each other. You can love more than one person—the human heart has such capacity—but you will never be completely resolute in your attention. There will always be the distraction of that other person in your mind.

Even with Reija—and Rose, too—there had been the ghost of Katarina. But now that the *Qliphotic* shadow was gone, I was no longer as divided as I had been. I could give my full attention to Marielle.

There was only one annoying detail: the spirit of her father floating in my head. Kind of a mood killer. Unless I could figure a way to lock him out.

I gave that some thought while I stood in the shower. It kept me from thinking of other things. Like the slope of her neck, and the way a pearl kept nestling in the hollow of her throat. Like a soap bubble, a tiny moment of time caught in a sphere of magick.

On the morning of the new year, the city slept, exhausted from the midnight revelry of the new aeon. We had survived the millennial change, regardless of how you counted the first year of the next century, and the parties had been flush with the release of all the pent-up panic and apprehension that had unconsciously filled our hearts during the last years of the old world. It was a new world—this shiny twenty-first century, this third millennium—and while everyone slept off the hangover of the old, the new was still too young to be fully aware. We were outside of time for a few hours, between midnight and daybreak, where nothing mattered. Where nothing was true but the breathless promises exchanged during the ebb and flow of our rhythm. For a few hours, wrapped in the midnight cloak of cosmological renewal, we could pretend the past and the future weren't connected. We could close our eyes and forget our fears, thinking such elective blindness did, indeed, wash away the stains of our history. We could forget our petty jealousies and febrile paranoia. For a few hours.

Paris slept, wrapped in heavy blankets against the winter chill, and no one saw the sun's light splash across the white walls of Sacré-Cœur but Marielle and I.

She leaned against the railing of the apartment balcony. Her dark hair was a tangled mass of curls, and she wore an old anorak, threadbare at the left elbow and unraveling along the top of the right shoulder in a way that made it slip down on her arm, revealing the base of her neck. It was too long, coming down to mid-thigh, and her bare legs and feet seemed unaware of the chill air. She held a bottle of soapy water in her left hand and, plastic wand held close to her lips with her right, she blew a stream of bubbles out across the rooftops of the sleeping city.

The clothes weren't hers, nor was the apartment. A friend of Marielle's—a flash of blonde hair in the lights of the club and a husky voice in my ear—had pressed herself up against me shortly after midnight. "She has the key," the friend had said. "Take her away from here." She gave me the passcode to the security system, and thus armed—key and code—we had vanished from the world. Anonymous and lost to everyone but each other. Suspended between midnight and dawn, between the last and the next, we could come together one final time.

I sat on the edge of the bed and watched Marielle blow soap bubbles, my left hand covering the ugly scabs on my right knuckles. There was no disguising the black stain of the bruise forming under my left eye, yet she hadn't said anything about it other than to brush the tender skin once with her lips during our out-of-time excursion.

She dipped the wand into the bottle and glanced back into the shadows of the apartment, her hair falling across her face. "Come outside," she said. "Watch the dawn with me."

Pont Alexandre. At daybreak.

I was already late.

I shook my head. "I have to go," I said.

She looked across the rooftops and lifted the wand to her

lips. A mist of soap bubbles streamed away into the world. "What would you do for love?" she asked. "Anything?" The tiny bubbles—slippery with gold and green light—spun and turned, caught in the eddies of air rising from the street.

"'Anything' is a dangerous word," I said, recalling the taste of her finger in my mouth, of the bone beneath the skin; her pinkie digging into my cheek as I bit her ring finger. *Mark me as yours, wolf, so that we never forget. Let us choose this.*

She walked to the balcony door, framed by the white light reflecting off Sacré-Cœur. "So is 'love.'" She blew a large bubble, a swirling globe of iridescence, and with a tiny flick of her wrist, she set it free.

It floated toward me, a sphere of rainbow light. I was afraid to catch it, as if there might be too much electrical tension in my skin. As long as it didn't break, I didn't have to answer her question. I didn't have to look past her and recognize the dawn.

"What are you afraid of, my wolf?"

"I don't want to break it."

It wasn't tomorrow. Not yet. Like this bubble, we were still caught outside of time.

"I can blow another one." She dipped the wand in the bottle slowly, her pinkie finger delicately raised from the end of the wand as if she were using a silver spoon to stir tea. She watched me, her eyes in shadow, the light making a halo in her hair. "But it won't be the same."

The bubble landed on my naked thigh, and for a second, it hung there, quivering and swirling like a gaseous world, then it popped with a tiny noise like the death of a star. Perhaps the noise came from me. The memory was filled with the striated noise of the Chorus.

"You can't save them," she said gently. "They will all fall, and they will all vanish. Just like every minute of our lives. What is done is done, and what is gone is gone."

"I know." I touched the damp spot on my leg. "It's just—I

wish…"

She came into the room, and straddled me, her naked body pressing against my groin. The fabric of the anorak tickled my chest and arms. Looking down, she dipped the wand into the bottle and blew a stream of bubbles into my face. "I'm sorry," she said. "I never thought it would come to this. I thought you two would be stronger, but you are too polarized. Antoine is your opposite, I see that now; he is like you and yet so different. He knows his heart intimately; he takes it out and scrutinizes it every day, trying to understand what makes it work. Yet, he will never understand the passion that pumps through it."

My face was wet with exploded soap bubbles, and she lowered her head to kiss me. Her lips brushed and caressed each damp splash of soap. "And you, my wolf, refuse to look at your heart for fear of being overwhelmed by the passion therein."

We are all bound to something, be it darkness or light; sometimes we choose which, and sometimes it is chosen for us.

A bubble caught in my throat, one of my own creation, and I couldn't get it out. I couldn't find the breath or the energy to make it rise. My heart, cold and frozen, was a stone in my chest. The Chorus lay about it, a writhing mass of black serpents.

Let us choose this.

"He will kill you," she whispered, "because that is the only way he understands how to ease the pain in his heart. If he does, he will lose me, and he knows this, but he doesn't know any other way." Her lips moved to mine and lingered there. My hands held her waist, and she leaned against me, the bottle of soap bubbles crushed between us.

"If you kill him," she whispered, her voice all but lost in the noise of my pulse, "do it because your heart wants such an end, and not because you think I do. And, if you do, you, too, will break my heart."

She plucked my left hand from her hip and slipped it under the anorak, up between her breasts so I could feel the heat of her skin, so I could feel the pulse of her heart. One last time.

"The old world is gone," she said with a sad smile. "The new one begins today, when my heart stops."

What is done is done, what is gone is gone.

XI

A barrel-chested man with a bushy beard answered the door of the apartment on the other side of the courtyard. His face lit up as he saw Marielle, but when he glanced at our hands and realized they were empty, the light faded. "I thought you were getting food."

"No," Marielle said. "I went to pick up my friend."

The bearded man examined me, and the Chorus held still, letting his magick wash over me. "Do I know you?" He moved behind the door, closing it slightly. Behind him, I could hear strident voices.

Hubert Lafoutain, the Chorus reminded me, tagging old memories with new details. *Protector of the Archives. He Witnessed your trial.*

I put out my hand. "M. Lafoutain," I said. "It has been some time. I never properly thanked you for putting your name on the Record on my behalf. My initiation to the rank."

The Bear, we called him. Gregarious, slow to anger, easily distracted when food was involved. An old friend of the family, Lafoutain had studied with Marielle's father. He had been an adjunct professor at the University of Paris in the late part of the twentieth century, before retiring to devote his attention to the Archives, though I wondered if he still taught a class here and there. Once a teacher, always a teacher.

"Ah, yes," Lafoutain said after a moment of searching his own memory. "I do recall an earnest student who didn't have the common sense God gave goats. The straddler. Caught between two worlds. What was it? 'Markham.' That's right. Landis Markham, yes?"

"That would be me, sir," I admitted. "Call me Michael." I hadn't been the most adept of adepts; my pre-Watcher education was full of holes. A flush crawled up into my hair, and I resisted the temptation to check the expression on Marielle's face.

"Michael it is." Lafoutain looked past us, his magick fading into the ambient etheric vibrations surrounding the doorway. "No one else with you?"

The courtyard was empty and quiet; there were no souls for the Chorus to mark.

"Damn their eyes," Lafoutain sighed as he stepped back from the door, opening it further. "I told them to just go down to the corner." He shut the door after we entered the apartment, and traced a finger between two lumps of silver stuck to the back of the door. Activation nodes for a magick circle, his touch completed the circuit again and the magick engaged. My ears popped with the sudden change in air pressure. "There's no food left," he explained. "There wasn't much to begin with, and they've had nothing to do but bitch and eat."

"No news, then?" Marielle asked, the tone of her voice suggesting she already knew the answer.

Lafoutain squeezed past me, shaking his head. "Nothing good."

This apartment was much bigger than the one across the courtyard. A central hall ran from the front door back to the long rectangular space of the kitchen. A large living room opened to our right, off the main hall, and from there another hallway led back to bedrooms. On our left was a narrow sitting room, filled with bookcases, and beyond that was a large dining room that had been turned into the war council chamber. The lights were bright in there, and men clustered around the central table, arguing.

Sitting in an overstuffed chair near the inner wall of the sitting room was a man with a face like a long knife. Propped against the wall was a Mossberg shotgun. His clothes were dark and he sat in half-shadow, almost blending into the fabric of the chair. His eyes were dots of violet light, and being subject to his magickal scrutiny was much more intense than Lafoutain's cursory examination. The Chorus played a short game of dodge and redirect with his magick for a moment. Just long enough for us both to know the score.

Robert Vraillet, the Chorus said, licking the taste of the man's magick off their claws. *Lafoutain's man. A Viator.*

Ignoring the dick-measuring moment between his bodyguard and me, Lafoutain led us back to the kitchen, sparing a single glance and a rueful shake of his head toward the dining room. "Still too much speculation," he said. "They don't know anything, and it makes them afraid."

The kitchen was filled with chrome-plated appliances. Dishes and the detritus from a serious pantry raid were scattered on the counter and center island, along with more than a few empty bottles of wine. Lafoutain picked up a cheese knife and attacked a quarter wheel of an aromatic hard cheese as he nodded toward the cupboards on the right-hand wall. "Get yourself a glass. There should be a few bottles of that Spanish excuse for a table wine still."

He flipped the knife over, sliding a piece of cheese into his mouth. "I sent Moreau and Tevvys out for more food, and they're backtracking to check for Watchers on their trail, or some other nonsense."

Marielle opened the cabinet behind us, and got down two glasses. I had just had tea, and wasn't all that thirsty, and I didn't think she was either, but this looked like a social nicety. After I took the offered glasses, she opened the cabinet below the stemware and revealed a temperature-controlled wine rack. "Nice setup," I observed. "Well, except for the sparse pantry, of course."

"Thank you," Lafoutain said. "But it's not mine." He pointed the knife at Marielle. "Friend of hers."

"Really?"

Marielle glanced back at me, hair falling across her face. She tried to read my expression, but I kept my face neutral.

Lafoutain was watching me, a half-smile sliding across his mouth. "She has a lot of friends," he teased.

I was thinking about the blonde woman's apartment, the one we ran off to on New Year's Day, and about the somewhat vacant apartment on the other side of the courtyard. *Where are we? Somewhere safe; a friend's.*

Marielle brought a bottle to the table, and Lafoutain fumbled through the mess on the counter for the bottle opener. "God help me, but I'm developing a taste for it," he said as she started to open the wine. "That's a sure sign of the Apocalypse."

"Or desperation," Marielle offered.

"Most assuredly," he said. He tapped the remnants of the cheese wheel. "Rioja and an Appenzeller." He shuddered. "That's the first sign, you know. When our standards start slipping. Next time, though, could you find a place with a decent liquor cabinet?"

"You wanted something defensible," she countered.

"True," he sighed. "See what I mean about standards?" He cut a slice of cheese and offered it to me.

It was softer than I expected, and had a fruity taste, like it had been soaked in apple cider. "This is good," I said.

Lafoutain snorted. "It's not even French," he said. "You are a philistine." His eyes flicked toward Marielle, who appeared to be concentrating on opening the bottle of wine. "In matters of food, of course," he amended.

My tongue was thick in my mouth. "Of course," I muttered.

The Chorus chattered in my ear, the laughter of raucous birds. You can take the boy off the farm, but you can't take the farm out of the boy. The pretty things would always entrance the son of a potato farmer.

Marielle pulled the cork with a single, fluid motion, poured an inch in our glasses, and when Lafoutain nodded at the offered bottle without an ounce of irony in his expression, filled the empty glass next to him as well. She raised her glass, and we followed suit. "To fallen friends," she said quietly, reminding us why we were hiding out in an apartment that didn't belong to any of us. Lafoutain and I, for separate but not entirely unrelated reasons, leaped at the opportunity to change the topic, and we raised our glasses as well.

The wine was a little young, but not that bad. Good enough for the palette of a potato farmer.

Lafoutain set his glass down with a sigh that had nothing to do with the pairing of the wine and cheese. "Who?"

"Father Cristobel," I said.

"You are the Witness?"

I nodded. "At the Chapel of Glass. They cut us off from the ley and sent in a suicide squad."

"Guns and explosives? Against the priest? That seems ill-prepared on their part."

"Guns, yes; but they had locks on their souls with some sort of remote conduit. They blew the cage out from within and the subsequent implosion was… partly an etheric quake. It brought the place down."

Lafoutain and Marielle exchanged a meaningful glance, and when she nodded, he continued the questions. "And you?" he asked. "How did you escape?"

"There's a tunnel beneath the chapel. Eventually it comes up in a maintenance shack in Père Lachaise. Cristobel sacrificed himself so that…" I trailed off with a wince as the Chorus pinned Cristobel's last memory into my mental scaffolding. A crushing sensation of an enormous weight. The cross and the glass. Bones shattering. The air being forced out of my lungs, along with what felt like every other organ in my body.

Lafoutain cut another slice of cheese and chewed it noisily while Marielle finished her first glass of wine and poured another. "That's ten," he said.

"Ten?" Marielle asked.

"We heard from Byatt in Amsterdam while you were out," Lafoutain said. "He says, on good authority, that Lysenski is gone. Rudolph Lysenski, Preceptor of the Northern Ice. Master of the temple up in Tromsø, Norway," he added for my benefit.

"Are we sure he wasn't an Architect?"

Lafoutain shrugged. "Byatt won't Witness that fact, but he's pretty confident that Lysenski wasn't the Thaumaturge. He's too remote up there…" Lafoutain's tongue touched the inside of his cheek as his voice drifted into silence. His expression was thoughtful, and he wasn't looking at me. He was looking through me, to an indistinct point beyond.

"I was one of the Witnesses at your trial for Journeyman," he said, as a different train of thought came to his attention.

"You were," I said.

"I was never called to Witness your trial for Traveler."

"No, sir."

"Why is that?"

I swallowed half of the rest of the wine in my glass. "I never took the trial."

Lafoutain raised an eyebrow, and cocked his head toward Marielle. "A Journeyman? Does your other boyfriend know?"

"He's not my boyfriend."

"Which one? Him, or the other?" A smile tugged at Lafoutain's mouth.

Marielle's answer was interrupted by the sudden appearance of a slender man with closely cropped brown hair. He stormed into the kitchen, arms raised in exasperation. Spotting us, he halted and realized he was in mid-gesture. "Ah, you've returned," he said to Marielle. Then his attention turned to me. "With a friend." We all heard the stress on the last word.

"Not a boyfriend," Lafoutain clarified.

"He's not—" Marielle started, and then stopped with a shake of her head. "Jean-Pierre Delacroix," she said, indicating the brown-haired guy. "Michael Markham."

Delacroix came forward, turning his awkward gesture into an outstretched hand. "M. Markham," he said. "A pleasure." His grip was firmer than I thought his frame could muster, and the Chorus chattered at the power humming in his palm. "Where have you come from?" he asked.

"Overseas," I said. "Just arrived."

"Oh, really?" Delacroix couldn't decide whose expression could tell him more, and he looked back and forth between Lafoutain and Marielle for a few moments. "Recently?"

"Yesterday," I said, aware that Lafoutain, for all his feigned indifference as he cut another slice of cheese, was paying close attention to my answer. His previous train of thought was still uppermost in his mind.

"Am I missing something?" Delacroix asked.

"I think we all are," Lafoutain said.

"Markham flew in from Seattle," Marielle supplied. "Where—"

"Portland, actually," I interjected.

That distinction went over like someone had just discovered a dead body in one of the cupboards.

"Interesting," Lafoutain said finally. He turned to Delacroix, as if that was all that needed to be said at this time. "What can we do for you, Jean-Pierre?" The dismissal was inherent in his words, a steely command given by a man who, for all his bluster and outward-facing gastronomical zeal, was still a high-ranking officer in the organization.

The younger man waved a hand toward the dining room.

"They're chasing ghosts. They're actually listening to Chieradeen now. I needed a drink more than I needed to hear his theory about the Bavarian Conspiracy again." His tone was slightly petulant, as if he knew he was intruding on a private conversation, but wanted us to know that he didn't care much for the snubbing.

"We've lost Cristobel," Lafoutain said.

"Oh," Delacroix said. "Damn." His smooth face went through a gamut of emotions, and he suddenly looked much older than the thirty-odd years I guessed him to be. "If he was the Visionary, that's four."

Lafoutain nodded. "Yes. What about the other possibilities?"

"Nothing concrete." Delacroix shook his head, trying to hide his exhaustion. "All his paranoid bullshit aside, it's looking like Chieradeen's suggestion about the Mason might actually be solid. No one has been able to confirm contact with him for several weeks now. The scryers have all vanished along with their master, and the Thaumaturge is still…" He stopped and shrugged.

Lafoutain tapped the newly opened bottle with the cheese knife. "Tell them the news about Cristobel. Assume he was the Visionary, and redo the charts. It'll distract the others from Chieradeen," he said. Delacroix nodded absently, and took the bottle with him as he went back to the dining room to relay the news.

Without a word, I went to the wine cabinet for another bottle. Mainly to give myself a chance to process these conversational scraps. They thought the Mason was out of the picture, and had been since before Philippe came to Seattle. Yet Cristobel had said they'd only lost one Architect previously. The Hermit. Not the Mason.

If he was the Visionary, that's four.

They didn't know Cristobel's secret, and for the time being,

I was going to keep it to myself. Until I had a chance to figure out the field.

The Mason was a master at geomancy, the sort of art that could create the oubliette around the chapel. And the soulquake as well. That wasn't the sort of artificing done in a minute. The whole assault was meticulously planned, well in advance. Move quickly, neutralize your opponent's home base advantages, and deliver a killing blow that didn't deplete any of your own special assets. Contrary to Lafoutain's belief, it could be done with conventional weaponry. Quite handily.

It was a raid that gave its planner deniability, provided no one survived, and the fact that non-magi were used for the strike team implied a scorched-earth sort of end result. Everyone dies, the strike team included.

But such deniability wasn't all that useful to a man who wasn't there. If the Mason had been gone for some time, then who had called for the strike? And why make it look like he was involved?

Unless, the Chorus suggested with a sly whisper, *he went underground. Before the killing started.*

Pulling out a bottle of wine from the severely depleted rack, I returned to the counter, mulling over that option. The strike was pre-planned, and if it was set to go with a phone call, then it could have been triggered by a blind relay: someone who didn't know who or why they were calling.

But someone had been Watching through at least one of the assassins. A remote viewer. Someone who had triggered the spell when they were sure of maximum yield. Was it more than one Architect? Was the Mason supplying the tools and the men, and someone else was providing the insight into the remote locations?

That question suggested some organization to the Opposition, and with organization came some sort of planning. I may not know who the Opposition was entirely, but I did know they were operating—even in their own limited cells—under orders. And those orders had to come from some sort of hierarchical structure.

Intuitively, I knew I was on the right track with this line of thought, and while the presence of the Chorus increased my reliance on intuition and whispered suggestion, I felt there was a very definite hand working behind the scenes. Someone who could twist thread as easily as the Old Man could. Someone—or some cadre of like-minded peers—was making us dance to a tune of their making.

And we were. While I trusted Marielle, and her relationship with Lafoutain was relaxed enough that it seemed like we were with the good guys, this ad-hoc safe house seemed like an act of desperation, a plan that was thrown together at the last minute. The sort of decision made in the heat of the moment, without proper consideration for all the ways it could go wrong. There was something amiss in this place, but I couldn't quite put my finger on it.

Four Architects dead. *How many left?* The Chorus twisted around the question. *Three*, I thought. Delacroix had mentioned them a few minutes ago: the Mason, the Scryer, and the Thaumaturge. Was the Mason working alone, or was the conspiracy broader than that?

Who stood to gain the most?

La Société Lumineuse had a pyramid-shaped hierarchical organization. One man at the top, hundreds at the bottom, and each layer fed into the one above it. One Hierarch, supported by seven Architects who were drawn from a field of twenty-one Preceptors. Each Preceptor sponsored a Protector-Witness—his eyes on the ground, so to speak—in addition to having a coterie of Viators—warriors well-versed in the way of magick. Below the Viators were the Travelers and Journeymen. Seven ranks, each of the lower rank having seven sub-degrees within it. Highly ordered, highly stratified, and everyone knew their place within the structure of the pyramid. Power flowed up, and the bottom rank was constantly jostling against their betters in an effort to make room for one of them to advance.

The way to force the issue was ritual combat. Properly declared and Witnessed, it was an acknowledged power grab, a calling out by juniors of their betters, and other than the standardized trials for rank and degree, it was the only way to advance in the organization. *Ritus concursus*. The right of might to declare itself.

However, this sort of willy-nilly leapfrogging wasn't the way the top of the pyramid was organized. The Architects, secretly chosen by the Hierarch, were his named successors. Cristobel's flip response to my jibe about the Secret Masters of the Illuminati aside, the identity of the Architects was protected so that they weren't targets for the overly eager and impetuous. If the Hierarch grew too ill to fulfill his duties as the Silent Guardian Who Waits, then he was replaced by one of his Architects. They, in turn, elevated a fellow Preceptor into the power vacuum of the empty Architect spot. And so on down the pyramid.

Cristobel had likened the assault on the chapel to the Blitzkrieg of Nazi Germany, that swift and decisive surgical strike into the enemy's heartland before they knew it was coming. If the Opposition had known who Cristobel was, then it followed that they knew the identity of the others as well. Send out synchronized strike teams, hit all your targets at one time, and you ended up with a situation much like the one we were currently in.

Lafoutain scratched his beard. "You're thinking awfully hard over there, M. Markham. I can smell the neurons burning."

If the Architects were supposed to fill in for the Hierarch, and were his chosen ones, then why had Philippe come to me? Why had the pyramid been shattered? *Why me, Old Man?*

The doorbell chimed, splintering the swirling mass of the Chorus. What had been forming in them—that niggling detail so frustratingly elusive—vanished. Gone, like a curl of cigarette smoke into the evening air.

Lafoutain wiped his hands on the nearest suitable cloth, which happened to be his shirt. "Finally." He strode into the hallway.

"Must be the food," I said.

Marielle nodded absently. She picked up the discarded knife and hacked off a corner of the shrinking block of cheese. "You know who attacked the chapel." It wasn't a question.

"Yes, Cristobel—" I caught myself. "The first thing they did was shut down access to the grid. Cristobel couldn't draw any power. Then, they sent in their goons. Redirecting energy flow like that is geomantic magick. There's only one Architect who specializes in that school of thought."

"And you think he's hiding himself to confuse us? If we can't reach him, we assume he's dead like the others."

"If you were taking on an opposing force that was probably—at least in raw numbers—larger than yours, yeah, I would. It'd be the tactically smart thing to do."

Lafoutain bustled back into the kitchen with a clutch of plastic bags in either hand. Two more men trailed behind him, carrying more of the same. They swarmed around us, clearing space on all available surfaces to lay out take-out containers. Marielle and I grabbed our wine glasses, the wine pull, and the unopened bottle, and got out of the way.

The newcomers were young—early twenties, wet-behind-the-ears Journeymen, still eager to do the menial tasks. They had been sent out on a quick food run, but it was clear they had over-compensated. The counters were filling fast with a variety of exotic choices. Thai, Chinese, Vietnamese, Italian: the mix of curries, spices, and sauces made my head spin and my mouth water.

Lafoutain didn't even bother with a plate. He dumped half of one container into another and then filled the space with vegetables and meat from the next two boxes. "Eat," he said, waving a pair of chopsticks at us. "Help us make some room. This may be the last hot meal any of us has for a long time."

"Fatalist," Marielle said, but she went to the cabinets and found a pair of plates.

"Pragmatist," he replied, shoving an egg roll in his mouth.

My stomach agreed with him.

XII

While the others came down to the kitchen to mob the take-out, Lafoutain led Marielle and me into the dining room. Delacroix glared at me as we passed in the hall, and judging by the expression on a few other faces, no one was terribly pleased to meet Marielle's new friend.

I could imagine their reaction if they knew the rest of it.

The dining room was in disarray. Chairs were scattered around the table, a collection of energy drink cans were piled in the corner of the room, and the top of the table was covered with newspaper effigies, sigil pages (scraps of paper covered with symbolic script done in heavy permanent marker), cheap tourist trinkets and other pewter icons used in warding, the stubs of a few candles: the signs of many hours of occult work. At the far end of the table, written out across several pages taped together, was a series of concentric circles, covered with handwritten scrawl and a scattering of black dots.

The working model of the society's network reminded me of a two-dimensional representation of the Tree of the Sephiroth, circles within circles. In the middle—*Ain Soph Aur,* the central point from which all light emanated—was the Hierarch, and floating throughout the concentric rings were small circles marked with names. The twenty-one Preceptors. More than half of them were filled in, and beside four of them were their

Architect titles, written in all caps.

THE VISIONARY: Father David Cristobel. *Dead.*

THE HERMIT: Emile Frobai-Cantouard. *Dead.*

THE CRUSADER: Matthew Wincott. *Dead.*

THE NAVIGATOR: Pierre Juneaux. *Dead.*

I found Jacob Spiertz on the map. There was no title next to his name. *They didn't know.*

"It doesn't look good." Lafoutain gave voice to what we were all thinking.

I put my half-empty plate down and leaned over the diagram, reading some of the notes scrawled across the page. Names of the rank, with lines connecting them in a desperate attempt to chart allegiances. This wasn't all of them, not by a long shot, just the names of Watchers who could be clearly identified as belonging to one school of thought or another.

Once a magus reached Viator, a choice was declared—a rubric of occult study that took one under the aegis of one of the Architects. I had always thought it was an educational and vocational choice, but looking at the tangle of lines, I began to see the hierarchy in a different light. Given the circumstances and rampant paranoia now sweeping the rank, suddenly the distinction between schools of thought looked a lot like battle lines.

Is this what you wanted? I asked the spirit hiding in the Chorus. *Is this your master plan? To force everyone to chose a side?*

A dark whirlpool swirled in my skull, and the Chorus vanished like smoke into the yawning mouth. Lightning arced from my anger, lighting the mouth of the hole, and the outline of old spirits lit up in the smoke. I reached for them, my current electrifying their shapes. They whined and tried to slip down the hole faster, but I had a chain now. One and another and then another. Like tiny cut-outs for a Christmas tree, little children all holding hands.

Tell me. I need to know. Tell me what you want from me.

The whirlpool shivered and white ice formed on the rim of

its lip. The hole closed and opened again, a parody of a mouth. *Tell me what you want,* it parroted back at me.

You came to me. You wanted me to kill you. In a time and place of your choosing. Away from their eyes.

The body must be destroyed, the whirlpool hummed.

Is this your answer? I demanded. *Your Architects were supposed to Witness your death. They were supposed to be on hand to elect a successor. By dying out of sight, did you bring on this chaos?*

Opportunity, Philippe whispered through the swirling motion of the Chorus. *I gave them opportunity.*

"Opportunity," I whispered, the word slipping out of me.

"Pardon," Lafoutain said, reminding me I wasn't alone.

The Upheaval, Cristobel reminded me, flitting across my perception like a ghost of a hummingbird. *A trickle that became a flood. A crack in a dike means the wall is no longer strong; time becomes its greatest enemy.*

"It was just a matter of time," I said.

"What was?" Lafoutain glanced at Marielle, who was toying with her food, not really eating much. "What does he know?"

"More than he realizes," she said. There was a strange expression on her face, a mixture of confusion, fascination, and a glimmer of something else. Revulsion?

Lafoutain stepped closer, his voice dropping into a near whisper. "Who is he? He said he came from Portland. We didn't have anyone in Portland." He looked at me. "Not anyone we could trust."

Marielle laughed, a hard bark of sound ripping out of her chest. I flinched at the sound, and Lafoutain grew more agitated. "What is going on?" he demanded. He blinked heavily, and his forehead was shiny with sweat.

I put my finger on Spiertz's name. "The Mason," I said. My hand drifted on its own accord across the map. *Ulrich Husserl.* "The Scryer." *R. A. Kircherus.* "The Thaumaturge." And three makes seven. Seven Architects.

But my hand kept moving, sliding across the page until it landed on Lafoutain's name. "The Sch—"

Lafoutain stepped forward and slapped my hand away from the map. He threw a nervous glance at the kitchen. "Enough," he hissed.

The Scholar. The whirlpool broke, scattering like snow in the mind.

Each of the nine has a distinct title, Cristobel's voice echoed in the fading spray of snow.

"There are nine," I said, staring at Lafoutain. "Not seven." The Chorus darted around the implications of the number nine. The rank was organized on the mystic resonance of sevens and threes. Seven ranks, seven sub-degrees. The higher ranks contained three times seven members. A third of the Preceptors were Architects. Threes and sevens. Nine was the cube of three, but it was an anomaly in the structure. It didn't seem to fit.

And Lafoutain wasn't a Preceptor. He was a rank below. A Protector of the Archives. But he was the Scholar. I knew it as concretely as I did the other names. I knew it because Philippe had known it, and that made it true.

"Your father named nine men as Architects," I said to Marielle. "Not the traditional seven. He built his own secret within the secrets." I indicated the map. "Visionary, Mason, Hermit, Scryer, Navigator, Crusader, and Thaumaturge. Those are the seven. But Philippe had two more." I looked at Lafoutain. "The Scholar. And the Shepherd. Who weren't Preceptors."

Lafoutain made a shushing motion with his hands. "Okay, okay. I hear you. Now shut up about it." He glanced toward the kitchen again. He was sweating clearly now. "They don't know." He glared at me. "No one knows."

"Except the three of us," Marielle said. I tried to get a read on her as something in her voice had made the Chorus shiver, but her expression was unreadable. *She hadn't known,* the Chorus hinted, *not until you just told her. She didn't know about either of them.*

But why did that matter? I asked the spirits in my head.

"Let's keep it that way." Lafoutain raised his eyes toward Heaven. "Let's keep it a secret. For now. Okay?" He swiped a hand across his forehead and when it came away wet, he looked at it dumbly as if he didn't know how that moisture had gotten there. He wobbled for a second, leaning forward against the table. "That panang." His mouth crooked into an awkward smile. "Spicier than I thought."

I pulled a chair closer and he sat down. His face was red, and his breath rasped in his throat. "Maybe some water," he said, tugging on Marielle's arm. "Could you get me a glass of water?"

She nodded, her face clearly showing concern now, and went to fetch the Bear a glass.

As soon as she was gone, Lafoutain grabbed my arm and pulled me close, his face next to mine. His eyes were clouded with pain, but they cleared for a second, filling with violet light. "Quickly," he said. "There isn't time."

"It's just a curry—"

He shook his head, sweat flying off his brow. "No, it's something else. Damnit. Undone by my stomach." A spasm of pain ran through his frame, and I felt his hand tremble on my arm. "Those little pricks betrayed us. I knew they were gone too long." He shivered. "They dosed the food, probably all of it."

I stared at the plates on the table. How much had I eaten? Had Marielle?

Lafoutain leaned heavily against me, his hand moving to my shirt so that he could bring my head close to his mouth. "The Shepherd," he hissed. "Do you know who the Shepherd is?"

The memory was there. Now that I knew what to look for. The burned face upraised, the eyes closed. The skull showing through the ravaged flesh. My hands touching his eyes and lips, delivering the benediction of rank. After the fall. So recently elevated, as if, in having survived being burned, he had proven himself capable.

I nodded. "I do."

"Does she?"

I shook my head. "I don't think so." The Chorus crawled under my skin. "She didn't know about you."

A crash of falling china came from the kitchen, followed by shouts. The Chorus flared into the peacock shield as they felt magick blossom in the other room. Instinctively, I moved toward the fight, toward Marielle, but Lafoutain held me tight.

"No man is an island," he whispered. "Not even Philippe." His grip faltered, and I nearly tore out of it, but he summoned strength from some reservoir and held me tight. "Do you trust her?"

I hesitated for a second, all this secrecy about the hidden Architects giving me a moment of pause. But only a moment. *Speak what lies in your heart, wolf. Be true to me, and to yourself.*

"Why shouldn't I?"

A spasm of pain wracked his face. "Don't be obtuse, Michael. Answer my question."

"Yes," I said. Committing myself. Making a choice. *Be true.*

He tried to nod his head, and only managed a slight tremor of his neck muscles. " 'It is more difficult to live with a woman without danger than to raise the dead to life.' Do you know who said that?" His voice was fading in and out, like the fluttering edge of foam on a wave, as his life ebbed. "Bernard of Clairvaux." He managed to tilt his head to the side enough to look up at me. The light glittering in his eyes gave his face some of its old humor back. "So very medieval of him, and yet so…" The light faded, taking with it most of his remaining strength. His head fell forward again, and his voice was almost lost in his throat. "…daughters, not our sons that will… Oh, *my little chicken.* I am so sorry…"

I knelt beside him, so that he could look at me without having to lift his head. "I know who she is." Ex-lover of my old rival.

The prize, as far as many of the Watchers were concerned. The woman whose heart I had broken. More than once. Daughter of the Hierarch.

He stared at me as long as he could, blinking through his pain. "I hope so," he murmured. "I truly do." A low moan started in his belly, and it occluded his throat. His grip on my hand loosened, and his shoulders slumped.

"Goodbye, old friend." The voice rising from my throat wasn't mine, and the impulse that moved my hand belonged to the spirit as well. "I'm sorry." My hand lifted his head, and even though the light was almost out in his eyes, he was still there. When the Chorus flared, the shadows fled from his face, and in his final moment, he could see again. He gazed at the light of the rampant Chorus, gazed at a face he no longer knew, and then closed his eyes as the light overwhelmed him.

I took his soul before it could escape.

The two who had gone for food were down, one of them permanently. Delacroix was still standing, his shirt and pants covered with a brown smear of sauce and noodles. Marielle was examining three others, all of whom were pale and sweating and looking like they were fighting losing battles with their stomachs. The Chorus found Vraillet in the front sitting room, all his wards extended, and tagged a couple more soul lights in the rest of the apartment—one in the bathroom just off the kitchen, throwing up as if his life depended on it. Which it probably did.

The room felt hot, and my palms were slick. The energy from Lafoutain's soul coursed through me, burning my veins. I had been poisoned too, though not as bad as some of the others. Given time, the Chorus could probably burn it out.

Lafoutain had been brought down by his appetite. He had eaten more than any of us, the nervous rapaciousness of a gourmand. Whatever the two had dosed the food with was quick-acting.

Delacroix put up his hand in a warding gesture, fingers splayed, when he saw me. "You," he said. "Who are you working for?" His magick changed, growing into a fiery halo around his head.

"Stop it," Marielle said. "He's with me." She gave the other magus a fierce stare.

Delacroix didn't drop his spell, nor the sneer that slid across his lips. "Who is he?" he asked as if I wasn't standing right there. "Being your fucktoy isn't enough of a seal of approval. Not anymore. Not after Briande sold us all out."

She reacted as if he had slapped her. The Chorus flinched at the sudden pulse of the ley beneath us, a heartbeat echoing through all of us, resonating off our bones. She moved during the echo, nothing more than a blur as I blinked, and Delacroix stepped back in surprise. Before my blink, she was kneeling beside one of the sick Watchers; after, she was holding the cheese knife to Delacroix's throat, forcing him back.

He was still blinking, trying to figure out how she had moved so quickly. "Say that again," she said in a quiet voice that cut through the tense atmosphere in the kitchen, "and I will cut your throat."

The cheese knife wasn't that sharp, but Delacroix and I both knew it had enough of an edge for her needs.

He swallowed heavily, pulling his head back from the small knife. There was a lump in his throat, and no matter how many times he swallowed, it wasn't going away.

"Markham is the only *man* you can be sure isn't trying to kill you," she said. "Unless you piss him off by being a *child* about things. And I won't stop him if he changes his mind, because you will, undoubtedly, have done something to deserve it." She pressed the knife against his throat. "Are we clear?"

Delacroix thought about it. Marielle was more patient than I would have been. I would have dropped him after about five seconds of this passive-aggressive sort of bullshit, but she waited him out. Never faltering. Never doubting he'd actually do it. Maybe she could read his heartbeat. Maybe she knew his heart better than he did, or maybe it was the shallow depth of his courage that she knew. But she waited, and after what seemed like an hour, Delacroix nodded. Only after he dropped his magick did she lower the knife.

Vraillet cleared his throat, drawing our attention toward the front hallway. "They're coming," was all he said. He had the shotgun in his right hand, and I noticed it was casually pointed in my direction. His eyes flicked toward the barrel of the gun as he felt my focus shift toward him, and he turned his wrist, moving the gun aside.

Marielle stuck the knife in the tiny slab of leftover Appenzeller on the center island. "We can't stay here," she said. "It's not a matter of defensibility anymore. They'll bring the whole building down." She glanced at me, pushing her hair back from her face. "It'd be easier."

"There's no back door," Vraillet said. He pointed the shotgun at the ceiling. "Two floors above us."

"One below," she said. "But that puts us closer to them."

"True," Vraillet said. His Will shrank to a shiny dot in the middle of his forehead, and then exploded outward in a thousand psychic lines. Each line snapped out a few dozen yards and then came back, flush with physical details of the materials it had just touched. Like a three-dimensional sonar that read through everything. The Chorus did something similar when they mapped lights for me, but Vraillet was doing a full scan.

His etheric sonar ping read the dining room too, and his Will wavered as he picked up the empty shell of Lafoutain. He took a half-step in that direction, but stopped himself. "Is he?" he asked.

"He's gone," I said.

His hands whitened around the stock and barrel of the shotgun, and his face tightened into an uncharacteristic display of emotion, an expression that was both monstrous and awkward on his face. When he exhaled, all the rage flowed out of him, and his Will tightened again. He looked at me once more, his eyes bright with violet light, and then he nodded. He touched his fingers to his lips and then pressed them against the barrel of the shotgun, and his Will bubbled around the mouth of the weapon, wrapping it in silence.

All business, that one. None of us would ever know how much the loss of his mentor meant. Lafoutain was gone; we had to get out: he knew what to do next. Armed with an etheric map of our surroundings, he was going to make an escape hatch. Up and out. The shotgun would make nice big holes for us to travel through, and the silence spell wreathing the weapon would keep our enemies from knowing what we were doing.

He was the sort of inhumanly focused magus that made me nervous. The kind whose Will couldn't be broken. I was glad he was on our side.

Marielle looked at the three incapacitated Watchers. "Walk out or die," she said. "We're not carrying any of you."

"What about Moreau?" Delacroix asked, pointing at the remaining Watcher who had brought the food. Moreau, a narrow-faced guy with a stylish haircut that probably looked better when he wasn't sweating profusely, had been sitting very quietly next to the wine cabinet, trying to be invisible through strength of Will.

"He's already chosen sides," she said coldly.

"No, wait," he whined. "It wasn't my choice." The other Watcher who had gone for food with him lay in a heap nearby, a red and gray stain leaking out from beneath his head. Moreau was trying not to look at him.

"You spineless fuck," Delacroix spat, a knot of hot magick sparking in his fist. "You just carried the food, is that it?"

My gut tightened as a psychic pulse blipped through the room. Vraillet had found a good spot in the ceiling and was making a hole with the shotgun. Moreau felt the psychic boom of the shotgun too, and the sound startled him. "I didn't know," he squeaked, his tongue loosened by the psychic noise. "Tevvys got a phone call. He wanted to make an extra stop."

"Where?" Delacroix asked.

"A Thai place. Over near Place de la Nation. He sent me in to get the food. It was already waiting for us." He held up his hands. "That's all I did. I just got the food. I had no idea it was poisoned." Moreau shook his head, his face crumbling into a shivering hole. "We came right back from there."

"Where was Tevvys when you went into the restaurant?" I asked.

Moreau's eyes widened. "In the car." He sat up a little straighter. "I thought he was in the car."

Delacroix glanced at me, and I shrugged. "It's deniability," I said. "But it doesn't mean anything."

"You're not listening to me," Moreau shouted, seizing the line of reasoning I had given him. "Tevvys was in the car by himself for a good five minutes while I was getting the food. He dosed it then. The Thai place was the last stop."

Marielle exhaled, and the ley pulsed with her. "The Thai food was poisoned too."

"No," Moreau wailed. "I didn't do it. I didn't do anything. Tevvys took a call. It was all Tevvys." His eyes darted toward the dead man.

"Tevvys can't help you," Marielle said. As if punctuating the seriousness of her tone, Vraillet's shotgun ruffled the ether again. A mundane-sounding cascade of plaster and wood rattled against the hallway floor.

"I didn't do anything." Moreau's voice shrank to a whimper.

"And your brothers are dead because you failed to act," Marielle snapped. "Which is worse? That you failed to save them, or that you participated—willingly or unwillingly—in an action that killed them?"

"That's not true." Moreau forced himself to move, scrambling to grab his dead partner. "His phone. Check his phone." He dug through the dead man's coat, rolling him over to do so. The front of Tevvys' head was gone, and it came away from the tile floor with a sucking noise. Moreau found the other man's phone and juggled it badly as we felt Vraillet put one more round into the ceiling in the hallway.

Marielle took the phone from Moreau's outstretched hand, and she went to thumb through the call log. She paused, and her expression went even colder than it already was. "It's locked. He's got it password protected."

Moreau's mouth moved, but nothing came out but a wordless sound like air leaking from a balloon.

Delacroix stepped forward, his magick swarming through his hair. Marielle stopped him and shook her head. "Get the others. Those who are mobile." Delacroix hesitated again and when she spoke again, her voice was like a whip on his naked flesh. "Now. Go follow Vraillet." Delacroix moved with some haste, and one of the Watchers on the floor staggered to his feet, swept up in the suggestion of Marielle's voice. He tottered into the hall.

Marielle knelt beside the other two. Only one of them was coherent. Barely. She kissed them both on the forehead, smoothing the tension and fright in their faces. "I'm sorry," she said. "Make them feel your pain."

Incredibly, the half-dead one came back from the brink of the Abyss with that.

Marielle stood up and walked over to me. She stared at Moreau until Delacroix came back from the rest of the apartment with one more Watcher in tow, and she kept staring until they went into the hallway. "My benevolence is boundless," she said. "But not infinite."

"You have to believe me," Moreau tried one more time, "I didn't know what was happening."

"You are lying," Marielle said, and Moreau's entire body tensed with a shock of realization. She knew, without a doubt; she wasn't calling his bluff, she was ripping it aside and looking right into his heart. She touched my wrist, and her fingertips vibrated with the echo of Moreau's jackhammer heartbeat.

"Tell me what he knows," she said to me, and with that, she was done with him. She removed her fingers, and the sudden void of the man's heartbeat was like he had ceased to exist. She left the kitchen, left me to ask Moreau in my special way.

Moreau's gaze darted after her, and then toward the hallway to the bedrooms. Gauging his chances.

I lit the Chorus up, and his attention snapped back toward me. The other two Watchers looked away as he started screaming.

XIII

The last time I had looked over the rooftops of Paris, the view had been colored by the glitter of soap bubbles and the golden light of morning. Now, as I joined Delacroix and Marielle on the fourth-floor balcony, I looked out on a nighttime view of Paris. The glow of lights from the surrounding Marais, and further on, the Right Bank, was a hint of civilization beyond the stiff line of the apartments across the street, and the sky, dark with clouds, threw back the light from the city. The shadows were deep and rich enough to hold many things.

Delacroix was scribbling glowing script on the rough balcony; it looked like a variant of a Solomonic Key—one of the Pentacles of the Sun. Some sort of flight circle or focus for making a long jump. As much as part of me wanted to peer over his shoulder and take notes, I joined Marielle at the railing. We were on the outer edge of the building, the central courtyard behind us. All we had to do was clear the buildings across the street, and we'd be gone from this place.

The wind played with Marielle's hair, and I could smell her scent, heavy on the light breeze. Her heartbeat was a slow, solid pulse, its gravitational attraction strong but not irresistible. "I don't See anyone," she said.

With some effort, I tore my attention away from the rhythm of her heart. Faint sparks danced at the edge of my vision, and my head was half-empty and yet overly full. The poison, working on me; the Chorus, fighting it. My concentration was off-kilter; it felt like I was both winding up for an all-night rave and coming down off a bad dose of LSD. What had Moreau and Tevvys dosed the food with?

"They may think the poison has incapacitated us," I offered.

"But you'd think they'd have at least one spotter."

"They should," I said. I remembered the guy from the airport and how he had blended into the background. I hadn't had a chance to look for him again after Henri and the others showed up, but I wondered if he was part of a splinter group too. Forward observers or scouts or some such thing.

She pushed her hair back from her face, and the ambient light reflected off her cheeks and throat. Darkness smeared in a half-moon beneath each eye. "Did Moreau tell you who his master was?"

"No, he didn't."

She looked at me, searching my face for some inkling of the subtext of my reply. Had I not done what she had asked, or had Moreau truly not known?

Delacroix clapped his hands, and his magick circle came to life. The wind shifted, tugging us away from the edge, and half of Marielle's face became obscured by her hair. She pushed it back, but I had already turned away, shielding my eyes from her. She'd have to read me a different way.

"It won't last long," Delacroix said. "And it isn't very strong. You'll have to generate your own wind if you want to go far."

"It'll do," Marielle said. "Clearing the next block might be enough."

It might. The Chorus twisted up my neck. Was she voicing a positive opinion to buoy their confidence or did she know something about the men coming to kill us?

The building shivered, and the tremor in the walls made the balcony sway unnervingly. The Chorus, noting the stress fractures in the masonry of the building, observed that the architecture of this block wasn't very earthquake-proof. The leys were being warped, coerced into a volcanic nexus that was coming up through the foundation and lower floors. Inside the fourth-floor apartment, several of the lights guttered out as the next tremor ran through the structure, and two floors below, the windows in the kitchen where several Watchers lay dying, blew out, raining flowers of glass down on the sidewalk.

Vraillet came out onto the balcony, still carrying the shotgun. "Time to go," he said. "They've breached the apartment below." He thrust the weapon into Delacroix's hand, and stepped into the circle of violet and blue light. He pointed east, toward the white cathedral of Sacré-Cœur, and jumped. Delacroix's magick circle popped beneath him, a magick spring throwing him into the air, and his own magick bloomed like a tiny sun sparking. Then he was gone, a shadow streaking across the roofs of Paris.

One of the two ailing Watchers followed, though his concentration was bad enough that he only managed a long jump, across the street and onto the roof of the building opposite. His landing was rough too. If he was smart, he'd just lie there, below the roof line, and wait for all the dust to settle. Eventually he'd be able to walk out. If the poison didn't kill him first.

The other guy demurred. "I don't care for heights," he stammered. "And… and I haven't mastered flight." He was standing inside the apartment, nervously shuffling back and forth. As close as he dared to the open sky.

The building groaned again, shaking more violently, and in the kitchen behind the scared magus, glassware rolled out of a cupboard and shattered on the floor. Somewhere, distantly, someone started screaming, a thin siren of sound like a teakettle boiling in the next apartment over.

Steadying myself against the outer wall, I reached in and caught the reluctant magus' jacket, yanking him onto the balcony. "You're coming with us," I said, wrapping him in long ribbons of the Chorus. Delacroix's circle gave off a huge flash of blue sparks when I hit it with the other man in tow, but it still worked. The ground flexed beneath us, and we were suddenly thrown aloft.

The building growled, and it seemed to lean forward as if it were going to swat us out of the sky. The balcony cracked, part of the railing breaking away and falling. The sliding glass door shattered, glass sliding like water across the angled floor of the balcony. I twisted around, trying to catch sight of Marielle and Delacroix. As if I could carry more weight than I already was.

There were two more flashes of blue light, and then the circle disintegrated along with the rest of the balcony. The whole side of the building started to come apart.

The psychic wings of the Chorus unfurled and we caught an updraft of hot air.

Back in college, I had been an avid outdoorsman. Even worked at REI part-time. I had grown up in the shadow of the Grand Tetons, and getting out into the mountains surrounding Seattle had been a vital part of the weekends. I had started with rock climbing, but had graduated to BASE jumping a year or so before that night in the woods up north, when everything changed.

One of my fellow jumpers said it best: "Jumping off a rock isn't crazy. It's the most controlled expression of freedom you can achieve. It's just you, your gear, and gravity; and gravity never lets go." We jumped off cliffs, bridges, antenna, and the occasional half-completed building in Bellevue, and every time, we were in complete control of our descent. You never *fell*, you always *managed a controlled descent;* we were very particular about the distinction. You climbed to a high spot, found your landing spot on the ground (pre-scouted, of course), gave the wind the middle finger (because the wind, unlike gravity, was a capricious bitch), and jumped. Everything else was just a matter of focus and control.

Much like magick.

Jumping from buildings was tougher, only because the winds were more chaotic, and stronger too. In Seattle, some nights they'd howl in off the Sound, like alienated djinn exiled from the desert, and the buildings would creak and groan under their pressure. Only those eager to die talked about jumping from a structure downtown on those nights. The wind was too strong, and it would grab a jumper like a leaf and shake him until he was nothing but pulp and bone caught in the tattered remnants of his 'chute.

Towing another man was a bit like falling with a torn parachute. Control was sluggish, the drag unnatural, and gravity was an issue. I wasn't so much an owl as a clumsy bat, struggling to stay in the air. The magus and I scraped the side of a building, nearly collided with a black metal railing—invisible in the shadows of the alley into which we were falling—and then bounced off the pavement.

My cargo—who, the Chorus informed me, was the conspiracy theorist Chieradeen—groaned loudly. I sat up, checking for anything worse than a bruised rib and scraped palms. "Any landing you walk away from is a good one," I told Chieradeen, whose only response was a grunting noise. My center of gravity rolled once as I got to my feet, and the Chorus was heavy in the base of my head. They shifted like a pool of mercury and my balance settled.

A pair of shadows eclipsed the ambient light pollution trickling down from the roof line. I glanced up as Marielle and Delacroix glided down and landed with much more grace. Delacroix had left the shotgun behind.

I eased Chieradeen over, and when he opened his eyes and looked at me, I helped him sit up. He was like me, bruised and a little battered but alive, and the realization that he wasn't going to die from falling was starting to sink in. Chorus-sight lit up his skin and revealed the chaotic insanity still in his veins.

I checked Marielle and Delacroix too. We were all still poisoned to varying degrees. No wonder I had flown like a wounded duck. Half my mind was busy fighting a chemical war in my bloodstream. I had been able to ignore it so far because of the heightened energy state of the Chorus, but I was going to have to do something about it soon.

Marielle knelt beside Chieradeen, and in a quick motion, stripped off her sweater. Underneath, she was wearing a tight black tank top. Motioning for the Watcher to lie down on his back, she bunched the sweater under his head as a makeshift pillow. "He's going to need a hospital," she said, looking up at Delacroix. "We need a car."

Delacroix's mouth compressed to a fine line, and he stared at the pair of them for a long moment. The muscles in his jaw worked, chewing on an idea that none of us wanted him to articulate, and then he nodded finally.

"Keep it simple," Marielle admonished to his back as he strode off toward the street.

When he was out of earshot, she bent over Chieradeen. "How can it be that you don't know how to fly?" she asked him, her voice gentle. "It's the quickest way to get out of a bad situation. I figured you'd be good at escape routes."

He tried to smile, and managed a weak grin. "Long story," he croaked. "And stupid too. It's better—" He coughed wetly.

Marielle pressed a hand against his shoulder as he tried to continue. "It can wait," she said. She bent closer to him. "But you have to live to tell me."

He nodded, his hand stealing up to hold on to hers.

"Your fight is not with us," she said. "We can't stay together. You must find your own path."

He looked at me, and the fervor in his gaze made the Chorus churn in my gut. "Is he—" he started.

Marielle shook her head. "Do not allow yourself to be distracted, Traveler. Not with the poison that is eating your heart."

She caught his chin and pulled his attention back to her face. "*Vide te animum, frater.*"

Watch your spirit, brother.

"Ye-yes," he said, and the spinning confusion of his soul lost some of its chaotic motion. "Yes, I can do that." He let go of Marielle's hand.

I helped her up, and we faded into the shadows of the alley, heading for the other end. I glanced back once, when we reached the street, and Chieradeen was just a misshapen heap on the ground, a huddled shape like a solitary rock on a wet beach. One man, trying to hold his own against chaos—within and without.

"We're going to need a hospital too," I pointed out.

"I know," she said. Shivering slightly in the night air, she pointed toward the nearest intersection. A pair of cabs were parked next to an open brasserie. We went to the closer of the two, and she bent over next to the driver's window, making sure the guy inside the warm car got a nice view of her breasts.

The cab window scrolled down a few inches. Sweet-smelling smoke and French hip-hop rolled out of the car. "Pitié-Salpêtrière," she said. "Please."

The cab driver, a huge, bearded man who barely seemed to fit behind the wheel, stared for a second, and then nodded. The back doors unlocked and we got in. Inside, the music and cigarette smoke were even stronger. We were barely seated when the driver put the car into gear and mashed the accelerator. Marielle fell against me, her arm and shoulder across my body. Her skin was hot.

I was feverish too, and the secondhand smoke wasn't helping. Whatever the guy was smoking, it was strong and exotic, and he was using it to hide the smell of a recently smoked joint. The combination made me dizzy, and the stop-start motion of the cab wasn't helping either.

Marielle repositioned herself a little less awkwardly, though she didn't move that far away from me. She rubbed her up-per arms, mainly—I thought—as an excuse to do something with her hands. "Moreau," she Whispered instead of trying to make herself heard over the banging hip-hop. "What did he tell you?"

"He didn't know who called Tevvys," I sent back.

She glanced at me sharply. "He was lying to us."

"I know." The cab dashed through a changing light, bouncing hard on the street, and I waited for my stomach to stop com-plaining before continuing. "But not about that."

She glanced at the driver, who was oblivious to our magi-speak conversation. "What about, then?"

I shrugged. I looked out the window instead of looking at her. Her neck was exposed, as were her shoulders, clavicle, and a bit more. I didn't fault the driver for staring when he had the chance. "He didn't say."

"I told you to find out what he knew."

The Chorus bristled at her tone, but I kept them in check. "And I did."

She didn't say anything, and implicit in that silence was the accusation that I had disobeyed her, that I had failed to follow through with her intent.

But it was her intent. Not mine. I had no reason to kill him, nor any desire to do so. The sight of the Chorus had been enough to reduce Moreau to tears. He had told me everything he thought he knew, and the Chorus had easily read his earnest desire to be believed.

"I am not your instrument." I told Marielle as gently as I could, but I couldn't keep the echo of my voice, the buzzing noise of the Chorus, snarling through a ripple of memory. We had been here before, and the sentiment had been the same then. *I am not your angel of vengeance.*

"We don't know anything," she said, vibrating with a quiet fury. She couldn't know what the Chorus was reacting to, but she could read the underlying bite in my words. "We lost more men and learned nothing. What was the point of all that, Michael?"

I shook my head. "What would killing Moreau have gained us? The satisfaction of Old Testament-style retribution? Is that what this has come to already? Besides, killing Moreau would have been a waste of a useful tool. I shouldn't have to tell you that, Marielle. Alive, Moreau can still be twisted to our design. He can still perform a useful service."

"What service is that?"

"We have Tevvys' phone," I Whispered. "I told Moreau that the only way he could redeem himself was make contact with whoever was coordinating the attack and have them call us."

"I don't—" She stopped and shook her head. After taking a few deep breaths, she changed direction. "He'll turn on us the moment he has a chance. Provided he actually lives long enough."

"I guess he has some incentive then."

"Michael—" She sighed, and a bitter laugh got caught in her throat. "You are such a fo—"

"I'm not." I spoke out loud, biting the words off more firmly than I intended, the Chorus sparking behind my anger. "I used him, Marielle, instead of throwing him away."

"What if he doesn't survive? How is that useful to us?"

"It tells us they don't care who they hurt." I reached out for her leg, and she moved away from me. I dropped my hand to the seat. "If they did bring the building down, it'll take them too long to dig out anything useful. They don't have that kind of time. They need to either find us or make a deal. As long as we can stay a few steps ahead of them, they'll have to keep flailing away at us. Wasting resources and energy trying to find us."

I glanced out the window again. Through a break in the buildings, I could see the black shape of the trees along the Seine. Beyond their silhouettes, I could see the lit buttresses of Notre-Dame. My vision swam suddenly, a disorienting pressure inside my brain. The lights around Notre-Dame changed, lengthening into tall shapes. The crown of the church looked like it was swarming with phantom gargoyles, all struggling to take flight. "Meanwhile," I offered. "We've got a head start."

"Yes, but a head start to where?"

"One thing at a time," I said. "Let's take care of this poison first."

This time, the laugh didn't get caught in her throat. I tried not to react, but it was like getting hit in the face again. She knew I had no idea.

The Chorus read a haze of magick coming off Marielle as she stood next to the car and leaned over to talk to the driver again. The driver smiled, welcoming her suggestion and letting it smooth his memory. His window scrolled shut and the vehicle slid away slowly from the curb. Marielle didn't look at me until she had walked a few paces and realized I wasn't following her. The wind pulled at her hair, winding it about her face and neck.

I pointed across the street at the massive shape of the one-time gunpowder factory, now a celebrity hospital. "Uh, the hospital is over there." I could have said it a hundred different ways, but my tone was nothing but petulant attitude.

"Too many eyes." Marielle said it like she was talking to a child.

"We don't have much choice," I pointed out. "I don't know how you're doing, but this thing is eating me." I tried to be a little more conciliatory, assuming that part of our crankiness toward each other was due to the twisting spikes in our guts and not the petty argument we had had in the cab. "I'm not going to be able to hold it off for much longer."

"Then you have some incentive to follow me, don't you?" She didn't wait for me to answer.

I sighed. Obviously the disagreement about Moreau was going to hang on a bit longer. *Ride it out.* Within an arc of steady light floating in my head, the spirit of Detective Nicols exuded a calming influence. *Hold on to what matters; let the rest go.* And, a second later, when I hadn't moved: *Follow her.* My legs started kicking on their own accord, and I stumbled into a steady trot, jogging to catch up with her.

We didn't go far, just a block or two further along the road, and when she turned toward the river, I saw our destination. I would have had to be blind to miss it. It was anchored at a quay on the river, and lit up with a thousand strands of red lights.

"Batofar," she said.

We could hear the music from here, and at quayside, there was a line waiting to get in. Batofar was an old lighthouse boat, Marielle explained as we walked over. Moored on the Left Bank since the turn of the century, it was a progressive nightclub catering to the electronic and industrial crowd. Small and intimate, it had several bars onboard as well as a dance floor below deck.

"And why would we want to go inside?" I asked. "There's not a lot of advantages in a cramped space with no escape route."

"It's not on land," she said. "And they have absinthe."

I swallowed a scathing comeback. *Ride it out.* But she read the annoyance and disbelief in my face. Somewhat surprisingly, she didn't bite back.

"I can mix a drink with absinthe that'll take care of the poison," she explained. "And it'll be harder for the geomancers to read us if we're not in direct contact with the leys."

Now those were two reasons I could get behind.

Dockside, there was a narrow gate with a temporary shelter that looked like a good breeze would tear it off the quay. Three blocky men in dark trench coats were slowly processing people through a security checkpoint. Everyone going through the gate was decked out in their best gothic and industrial gear: helmets and headpieces studded with rivets and chains; piercings through every visible (and invisible, I'm sure) body part; gas masks and insectoid goggles; black jackboots and long trench coats with sinister authoritarian logos; vampire teeth peeking out from black-stained mouths; Victorian-era clothing, decked out with steampunk accessories.

I hesitated as we approached the dock. Marielle could get away with the minimalist goth look in her black top and pants, but I was looking like a country hick in town for a weekend while my uncle took the pigs to market. Even with the cool pockets on my jacket.

"We're not going to be conspicuous in this crowd?" I asked.

"Eccentric," Marielle corrected. "There's always a couple."

"Couldn't we find someplace where we could be invisible instead?"

"We will be." She softened, shedding more of the black mood that we had brought from the cab. "Trust me."

I did, and when my hand started to reach for her, she met me halfway, wrapping her fingers around mine. Turning my hand up, she pressed her lips against my palm. I cupped her face in my hand, and didn't want to let go.

She lowered my hand, gave me a sad little smile, and led me toward the boat. Nothing more was said. Nothing more needed to be said.

The security detail took one look at me, and tripled the cover charge. Because I looked like that sort of sucker. They would have considered rolling me for my wallet and dumping my body in the river, if it hadn't been for the unconscious glitter of the Chorus under my skin which gave them pause.

On board, the red lights strung along every surface made everything appear as if covered in blood. Through Chorus-sight, I could see sigils woven everywhere: across the bulkheads, around the metal pipes, crawling across the hinges and locks of sealed doors. The lighthouse stack was a confusion of arcane script that seemed to tell some sort of story about ascending angels and Enochian watchtowers. The bar in the front prow of the boat was lit by black light, and most of the drinks were glowing green and yellow. As were the fangs of more than one patron milling around in their best gothic finery.

The entire structure shook with the music. Most of the upper register was a mess of echoes, too many metal surfaces that broke everything above subsonic into shards of noise. The lower registers, though, reverberated through the frame of the boat; the rhythm pushed at me from every direction, like being caught in the crush of a midnight rave. The beat echoed in my lower back and groin, a steady thrum that was creating a bit of stir.

Piotr had once told me that the engines on old boats—like the rusty freighters on which he had shipped around the world during his time in the Merchant Marines—would sometimes vibrate at a frequency that drove the sailors nuts. *You stay at sea too long,* he had said, *and it doesn't take much to get you off. The ship takes care of her own.*

"What?" Marielle asked, noticing my expression.

"Nothing," I said. "Something a friend once told me about boats."

Her naked arm brushed against my hand. Instinctively, I stroked her skin, a motion of old familiarity. A shiver ran through her frame, and she turned slightly, moving closer to me. She put her mouth next to my ear, and my hand grabbed her waist. Comfortably, as if we did this every day. She exhaled for a minute, sorting through some response in her head, before she settled on a string of words. "The poison," she said. "We need to deal with it. First."

When she turned away, most of her body slid across mine. Hip, breast, shoulder. It was the sort of broad stroke a painter used to cover as much of the canvas as possible. It was the sort of motion that made it clear what was on her mind.

The poison. The Chorus wound into an ever-tightening knot in my groin. *Focus.*

She led me toward the door that would take us down to the lower bar and the dance floor. Inscribed on the door in ink that glowed white in Chorus-sight was a magick circle, calling for protection against spirits and possession. It didn't flair as we passed.

One of the pentacles of Saturn. *Constitue super eum peccatorem, et diabolus stet a dextris ejus.* Protecting the innocent from possession and the influence of foul spirits.

Not much help for those already lost.

XIV

Below deck, the light was purple and crimson, splashing off metal surfaces so as to create a play of shadows and reflections that made the hallway seem wider, the ceiling higher, and the dance floor cavernous. The DJ booth looked like it was a half-mile away, and the intervening space was filled with a crush of gyrating bodies. Whatever gothic aloofness or mechanical inflexibility was adopted by the patrons of the club above ground was abandoned down here, laid aside for a feverish exultation of the music.

The bar, a long slab of shiny steel, was near the door, and Marielle dove into the surging crowd like a championship swimmer vying for a channel crossing. I stayed near the wall, feeling a little more grounded with a steel bulkhead at my back. Colorful flashes of light were bursting at the periphery of my vision, and I was pretty sure they weren't the club's light show. Sweat ran down my back, and the Chorus was moving uncontrollably in my head.

I was running out of time. My reserves were dwindling quickly. The energy I had acquired from taking Lafoutain was going too fast, eaten up in a losing battle with the poison in my system. I had lasted longer than the others, but that was a small comfort in the long run.

A woman bumped into me. Hooded and wrapped in translucent latex, she was anonymous but for the swirl of her tattoos visible through the sheer material. Flaming snakes crawled up her belly, and ravens with lightning clutched in their talons rode her shoulders. She groped me like an old friend, and laughed as I responded to her eager fingers. Her tongue was pierced with a star, and the light behind her eyes was entirely unworldly.

Her companion, a sleek dominatrix with bloodied lips and too-pale skin, pulled her away from me. The shining one, still laughing, waved to me as they dissolved in the sea of bodies, and for a second, it looked as if she were carrying the disembodied head of her stern friend on a platter.

Behind them, flickering in the crowd like a reflection caused by something in the corner of my eye that was catching the light from the DJ booth, was Antoine. My teeth chattered as a cold draft snaked down my collar, and my vision washed out with too many colors as I started blinking uncontrollably. He was suddenly everywhere, hiding behind every face, and the more I tried to find him in the crowd, the more I wasn't sure which face was truly his and not some illusion. I spotted the woman in latex again, still laughing with the star in her mouth, and when I tore my eyes away from her dancing light, Antoine's face was gone.

But the sensation that he was watching me was still there.

Tremors ran through my legs, vibrations that increased in amplitude as they moved to my chest. Pressing my back against the wall for support, I scanned the crowd near the bar for Marielle. The Chorus reached out, flicking from light to light, trying to find her psychic signature. I needed something familiar. Something I could trust. *My anchor. Where had my anchor gone?*

A centurion stood near the bar. I blinked, and he remained. Out of time and place. Glistening as if he had just stepped in from the rain. Over his head, a bronze fish was attached to the wall. The ostrich plumes of his headdress were crimson and black. He held a pole in his right hand, and the top was ragged as if several inches of the stick had been crudely snapped off.

The shaft was stained black, as if it had been dipped in oil, and some of the blackness was on his hand too. He wore mirrored sunglasses, an incongruity that made him more like a costumed patron than a vision.

Something burned my side, and when I slapped at my coat, my hand hit the pack of tarot cards in one of the inner pockets. Like a detoxing alcoholic who finds a tiny bottle of vodka in the sofa cushions, I dug for the bag and fumbled with the strings. The cards spilled out, and I frantically grabbed at them, trying not to lose any.

Death. The Tower. Lots of swords. The Eight of Cups. The Moon. The High Priestess. Too many. Too many possibilities. I couldn't focus, and I felt like I was drowning. The beats were waves, battering me against an unyielding shore. Too… many… choices.

It was the Chorus, flush with a cacophony of voices. Too many willful souls so recently taken. I couldn't control them, not in my current state. Their histories and personalities were overwhelming me—still too vibrant—and I was vanishing. Struggling to block out the sensory tumult of the dance floor, I tried to relax. *Don't force it,* I thought. *Don't try so hard.* My hands knew what to do. They could master the deck, and I wouldn't drop any of the cards; and if I could hold the cards, I could hold my thread. I could find myself again.

Somewhere in the rush of noise in my head and the pounding waves of sounds, I found shelter. I imagined a tiny alcove, almost like a monk's cell, tucked away in the bowels of an unknown monastery. No light. No windows. Just a space large enough for a man to kneel and consider his own fate. His own choices, and the paths granted to him. A quiet place, where I could sift through the detritus and the dross of my being and ascertain what had been lost. Where I could remember who *I* was.

This tiny place was like the altar I had visited. Not in any profane church, not in any physical building. The one surrounded by wind and light, though when I realized the stone was there beside me, there was neither wind nor light. Just an empty void, a vacuum without life or spark.

The stone was bare, unmarked by Bernard's water. This place was untouched, unmarked by sacrifice. I hadn't come here yet. No one had. It didn't exist. Not yet. It was just an idea in my head.

There was something in my hands, and I thought it was the deck of cards, but it wasn't. The cards were gone, gone with the rest of the real. I was somewhere else, hidden away in this wilderness of the mind. The object in my hand was luminous, twitching and squirming in my grasp as if it were alive. My fingers were translucent from its light.

There was a wound in my side, a long rip weeping slow tears. Dried on my naked skin, in a track running down to my waist and thigh, was a line of rose petals.

If I opened my hands, would the light go out? There was no answer to my question, not even from my own spirit, and so I kept my hands pressed together tightly. I was afraid to find out what happened next.

I do not Know the course of the future. I cannot See what comes next.

In the darkness before the world began, I hugged my warm hands to my bare chest and wept.

Drink, my lord. Drink from this vessel.

Marielle put the cup to my lips, and I coughed as the acidic vapors burned my nose. I recoiled and my head banged against the bulkhead. My lips refused to cooperate.

"Michael," she said. "Drink it. It smells worse than it is."

The fumes seared my nose and eyes badly enough that I gasped in pain, and Marielle forced the cup between my teeth and tipped it up. The fluid moved like half-frozen sludge and tasted like motor oil mixed with battery acid and putrid fruit. I choked on the first sip, nearly spit it out, but managed to keep my lips pressed together. It went down like you'd expect that combination to, burning all the way, and the explosion it caused in my stomach forced all the air out of my lungs. My vision went white, and I felt electricity spark from my fingers and toes.

The second sip went down more easily. By the third, I could feel my arms again, and after that, I held the cup myself. Drinking the potion greedily as if it were nectar squeezed from a half-dozen exotic fruit.

At least, that's what I told myself. It still tasted like rotten apples coated in axle grease and bile, but I knew it wasn't going to kill me. On the contrary, it was cleaning me out. Of a lot of things. The magickal purge. One potion washes away all manner of sin and poisons.

"God, that's toxic," I managed when my throat worked well enough for words.

"Whatever doesn't kill you makes you stronger," she said.

"Fuck Nietzsche. He never had to drink that stuff."

She patted me on the chest and then left her hand there. "And look. Your mood has improved too."

I nodded at the battered cup. "Where did you get that? From the engine room? They didn't have something cleaner?"

"The cocktail would have melted anything else," she said.

I ran my tongue over my teeth. "I think it stripped off a layer of enamel." My stomach still boiled, but the prickling fire in my joints was gone, and the noise in my head had fallen to a dull roar. The normal sort of roar. The music, while still a pervasive pressure, wasn't as bowel-rattling as it had been a few minutes earlier.

She was right: I was stronger.

A man in black leather and a mask that blocked all his peripheral vision bumped into Marielle and she pressed more firmly against me. Her fingers started tapping on my chest. "You need to move around," she said, her mouth close to my ear. Her breath was hot on my neck, and I felt a welcome flush of blood move through my skin. "Get your blood circulating. Make sure all the toxins are burned out."

"What do you suggest?"

She nodded toward the crush of bodies on the dance floor, and her hair brushed the side of my face.

"Strictly for medical reasons?" I asked.

"Of course." She nipped my earlobe.

I looked toward the bar. Beneath the metal fish on the wall, a pair of young women dressed as goth Lolitas were busy texting on their mobile phones. Probably to each other. There was no sign of the centurion. Nor was there any sensation from the reinvigorated Chorus that Antoine was still in the crowd somewhere. If he ever had been.

"Come on." She dragged me into the mass of dancers, and I gave up looking for something that wasn't there. Her hand was hot and real, and the rest faded away. It was all a dream, and what I held was what mattered. It might be enough, I told myself.

The last time we had danced in public had been the New Year's party/millennium celebration at a place simply known by a Greek symbol. I had no idea if Omega was still there, though I doubted it; the party that night had had a vibrant fatalism about it, as if either we or the place itself wouldn't survive past dawn.

There had been Watchers there—Bento, the last one from our little coterie who was still speaking with me, and a number of others—and the mood, while celebratory, had been slightly tense. Ever since the game of Hunt the Werewolf had gone badly in Béchenaux, Antoine and I had been circling each other, waiting for an opportunity. In the months and years since that night, I had come to realize that it wasn't that Marielle had been blind to our antagonism, she had simply expected us to behave better. The question never satisfactorily answered was who had been the most naive that night: Antoine and I, or her.

In that moment, during those few hours before New Year's Day, I hadn't cared. The world shrank to her and me; everything else was hidden behind a barrier of rhythm and light. She and I moved against one another, breathing in time. Her hands against my chest. My mouth on hers. My hands in her hair. Our breath, moving back and forth. Her voice, Whispering in my head in a way that made the Chorus jealous.

We had been this intimate prior, but not like this in public. Not in front of Witnesses. Let the Record show that the Daughter of the Hierarch chose to end the last century in the arms of the Outcast—*solūte frater, veneficus*. The one named *Adversarius*.

The Record also contained the death of the adversary at the hand and sword of her champion, a man who later became Protector-Witness—one of the chosen soldiers of the society. Such was the cost of sinning against the fraternity, of a brother transgressing against brother, and while Marielle would argue that she was not a possession—not something that could be bought or traded or kept—the simple fact was: I fucked Antoine's girlfriend—more than once—and then celebrated such intimate knowledge with her in public.

Sins of the flesh. Though, while I harbored a few regrets from the last decade of learning magick, Marielle was not one of them. She was a ruinous complication; the sort of entanglement which everyone involved knew was going to end badly, but which no one shied away from. We were hedonistic children of an age which had no use for the morality of our forefathers. We believed we were stronger than the desires rooted in the flesh, that we were more emotionally evolved. We were domesticated creatures, no longer obsessed with the basal elements in the hierarchy of needs. We could—and did—concern ourselves with the eternal riddles of philosophy and consciousness. We knew the flesh was mutable, fallible, and would ultimately betray us without reservation. Why would we not enjoy the sensory opportunities it afforded us while it was healthy and strong? Why not?

The ecstatic ceremonies of ancient cults involved rituals of the body. Whether it was physical contact with another or the ingestion of pharmaceuticals or narcotics or the deprivation of sensation, the secret rites took advantage of the body's limitations. Overload the body, a machine that operates via a systematic structure of patterned responses, and it doesn't stop functioning, it stops following those preset patterns. It loses control, and turns to the mind for help. Freedom is the drunkard's waltz, the doper's irrepressible stream of consciousness, and the hedonist's climactic shiver. In these moments, the body is gone, and the mind is free to venture beyond the shell of meat that holds it.

I know what it is like to occupy the life of another, to experience their sense of taste, touch, and smell. To see and feel what they do. To know their fear and desire. While the Chorus is the fractured history of a dozen or more lives, it is not the chaos of schizophrenia. I never switch places with them; my Identity is always the strongest, for it is in contrast to them that I am defined.

I am not the man I was ten years ago, but then who of us is?

And yet, validating that nexus of our cosmology, I gravitated toward Marielle once more, drawn to her in this enclosed space. She was a spark without shadows, and her pure light pulsed with the rhythm of the world around us. A moth flings itself at a light, Icarus flung himself at the sun, and I clutched Marielle tight, more desirous of that heat and light than any prior seeker of illumination. The crowd moved with us, a whirlpool cycle that ebbed and strained against the walls of the boat. Sensing the change in the crowd, the DJ flipped on a record with a lock groove, an endless loop disguised as a piece of vinyl, and no one cared. We were a primordial sea of flesh, electrified cells circling a central star.

This is how life began, a hundred million years ago. Tiny

lights swirling tighter and tighter until all the gross materials caught in the whirlpool of energy fused into the primal gases and fluids of existence. The soup kept spinning, following the rhythmic cycle of God's heartbeat, and each rotation compressed everything a little more.

With each cycle—life, death, life again—we got a little closer, and eventually I kissed her. Her lips were hot and real, and they, too, might have been enough.

In an alcove that barely qualified to be called such, on a shelf that wasn't much more than a steel bump on the bulkhead, wreathed in shadows of our making, Marielle braced herself with one foot on the floor. Our pants were already undone; mine bunched around my ankles like a pair of short-chain manacles. With one hand supporting her raised leg, I fumbled with the edge of her panties.

The beat shook the boat, a subsonic rumble that shivered the rivets. My fillings vibrated, making my mouth tingle with electricity, and her tongue carried the same current. She opened her mouth wide against my lips as I pushed her back against the wall, and her lips curled into a smile as I slid into her. Arms wrapped around me as if I were saving her from drowning, Marielle held on tight as our rhythm became a counterpoint to the pulse beating through the bulkhead.

The song became stronger, the beat more insistent and violent as if the river was being bombarded. A knot of white-hot heat flooded my groin, a pressure that wouldn't release, no matter how hard I thrust. No matter how hard the walls shook against us. Marielle strained and pulled at me, her fingers raking through the fabric of my jacket. At some point, she bit me and blood smeared across her lower lip. Her teeth were shining blades of ivory, eagerly poised to bite me again.

The knot of our bodies tightened, cinching into an impossible tangle of desire and restraint. I thought my body was going to rupture, an explosion of bone and blood, before I could climax. She pulled harder, the tendons in her neck and shoulders standing out. When she cried out in frustration, I couldn't hear her voice, so loud was the feedback of my pulse jackhammering in time with the staccato climax of the drum and bass track.

I must have blacked out for a few seconds because, when I became aware that the knot was gone, I had no recollection of when or how it vanished. The song had changed too, and the walls only shivered quietly now, a distant buzz that was like a vibrating cell phone in a coat pocket. My face lay against the cold wall, and Marielle lay nestled against me, her face buried next to my throat.

Reluctant to let go, to let this moment of stolen intimacy end, I stroked her hair gently as I tried to burn all the tiny details into memory.

The trembling pulse beneath her skin. The tender brush of her fingers against my lips. The hint of her breath against my neck. A tear, sliding down my throat and melting into the braid of the Chorus. Ephemeral relics of her presence. All so fragile that, were I to move, they would vanish. All tiny fragments that would be lost in a moment.

I would keep them; when everything else became confused and tangled in my head, when my memories became twisted with the dreams and recollections of others, I would still have these tiny treasures. They would last, unlike the dreams.

They would be enough.

XV

The wind had died during the last hour, and as we sat on a narrow bench near the terrace bar, we weren't cold. Winter had died, and the land was thawing once again toward the season of rebirth.

Marielle was thawing too. The sweat-soaked atmosphere of the boat's interior had melted the icy crust of her opinion of me. The kiss had unlocked both of us, and in the crowd, we had shed some of our old skins. In the sweat thrown from our brows and arms were the liquefied remnants of old habits and old hesitations. All of us gathered in that tiny space gave up something we had been carrying for far too long, and we came out of the metal cocoon wearing new skins, moist with the perspiration of our rebirths.

She stared out at the river, watching the lights of a boat drift by, and while I should have been looking and thinking about other things, I examined her face. My memories were a mess now with Philippe's constantly folding into my own, and my recollection of her went back much further than it should. I could remember her face when she was a tiny baby, and looking at her now, a procession of images strung themselves in my head. A time-lapse vision of Marielle growing from baby to girl to woman.

I reached for her hand and raised it to my lips. I kissed the back of her hand, and her lips quirked into a tiny smile. I kissed her ring finger, and the white marks of my teeth became visible on her skin. The hidden tattoo of our stolen morning together. She turned her hand over so that I might kiss her lifeline, and I did, inhaling her scent.

Philippe's memories were very visual—he didn't store olfactory and auditory triggers—and the memory of Marielle's scent was mine. It had been the same way with Kat; what had survived during the years of trauma was the smell of burning lilacs. Marielle, on the other hand, had an ephemeral scent that was like nightfall in early April, as the ground starts to cool after the sun has gone down, and all the nocturnal flowers are opening. It was a scent that remained indescribable, and I could never quite recall it with confidence, but I always knew it the moment I was in its presence again.

It's a funny way to remember someone: as a sensory phantom haunting you when they are gone. They become a collection of elusive details; you cannot remember them completely, and the more you struggle to put the puzzle together, the more you obsess about the gaps between the pieces. But, when you find these people again, when you crush them to you and inhale their smell, when you hear their voice, when you feel their touch, the pieces arrange themselves and you can't fathom how you didn't see the whole picture before.

Being with her made my heart ache as much as it healed the rifts, for it reminded me of what I had lost in the wood, of what I had let into my soul, and even though I had burned out that disease, there was always going to be a stain. A permanent mark where my humanity had been scarred by the *Qliphoth*. No matter how much my memory felt whole and complete when I was with Marielle, I was never going to be that way myself. I would always be a patchwork man, no matter how much her presence made me feel otherwise. Because when she was gone, all I would have would be memory, and my memory was far from perfect.

"I dreamt about you a lot after the duel," she said, as if she knew what I was thinking. "Antoine claimed victory and his second Witnessed the event, and that was the official Record. But I kept dreaming about you, as if part of me didn't believe you were truly gone.

"Water dreams. You were drowning, and I would try to save you. At first, I was in a boat and you'd be floating out of reach, and no matter how much I rowed or bailed or tried to raise a sail, I could never reach you in time. You always sank before I could touch you. Later—eight or nine months after the duel—I would find myself on a bridge and you would float by underneath. Like Ophelia, after she drowned herself. It was always a different bridge, as if I was searching for the right one, the one that was low enough that I could lean over the railing and grab you as you went past." She looked at me, and her eyes were bright. "The Record said you fought beneath a bridge, but it didn't say which one, and Antoine would never tell me."

"Pont Alexandre," I said.

She nodded, and seemed to notice I was still holding her hand. She moved her fingers so she could grip mine. "When I was in the boat, your eyes would be open and you would watch me try to reach you, but when the dreams shifted to the bridge, your eyes were always closed. And you started to sink. Each time, you were a little further underwater, until one night, I dreamed of the river and I wasn't on the bridge anymore. I stood on the bank, watching the boats move on the water, and I never saw you again. You were gone, finally, and all that was left was memory."

What is done is done, what is gone is gone.

She opened my hand and examined the lines on my palm. The jagged arc of my love line, the broken strand of my lifeline with its tiny hook near the top and the deep groove it cut into the heel of my thumb. The tiny scars that bit and chewed at the line, never breaking it but transforming it into a spiky branch.

On the night before the duel, the night we had taken for ourselves, she had read my palm. We lay in the large four-poster bed, a king-sized king, surrounded by bolsters and comforters and pillows. We could have been disembodied spirits, lost in a sea of smoke. Like the pair in Toulouse-Lautrec's painting that hangs in the Musée d'Orsay. Marielle had put her hand next to mine, and we had compared lifelines. Hers was smooth and it wrapped all the way around the base of her thumb, seeming to go on forever. I traced it over and over again, like I was following the course of a great river on a map. All the way to its source. *Yes, this is where we will go. All the way to where it begins.*

The Chorus tickled my spine, and something Philippe had whispered to me floated up again. *Nunc.* Latin for "now." Both Bernard and Philippe had referenced it, both had said the word as if it was a marker, denoting a separation between the past and the present. *This is how it begins.*

This is where we will go.

What is done is done.

But that which is gone didn't stay gone. The world rotated, and the cycle bent back on itself. The world ended and began again. *Nunc.* The word spoken at the beginning, when the cycle starts anew. And where we stood was where it began.

The airport. Marielle had been surprised to see me there. But not in the way you'd expect when someone you thought dead showed up.

"You knew," I said. "You knew I hadn't died under the bridge."

Her lips tightened to a thin line, and she looked out at the river again.

I took her silence as confirmation. "You weren't *that* surprised to see me at the airport. You weren't expecting me. Not there. Not then. But, you knew I would be back. Almost as if, when I did turn up, you could stop wondering when I was going to. You could stop pretending I was dead."

"I thought you were," she said, and there was venom in her voice. "For a long time."

"Did Antoine tell you?"

She laughed. I had pricked an old wound in her heart, and what was leaking out was bilious and vile. "Why would he do that?" she asked. "That would be tantamount to admitting that he lied. That he *failed*."

"Failed to do what?"

She ignored my question. "When he came back from his trip to the States, he refused to see me. Father mentioned he had seen Antoine, in passing, as if it was nothing remarkable." Her voice thickened. "But, then, nothing Father ever said wasn't calculated. I knew he wanted me to see Antoine, just as he knew Antoine would refuse. When I called him, he brushed me off. 'I have something to do for your father, my dear'—you know that condescending tone of his—'I have to leave tonight. There isn't any time.' As if he could hide from me, as if I didn't know him well enough to know when he was lying, only because he was so bad at it. He wasn't working for my father. He was going into hiding, until he healed enough that no one would know what had happened to him."

"He went to a spa," I said. "Down in Sardinia, I think."

She nodded as I confirmed what she had suspected. "I could hear it in his voice, and not just because his throat was burned. He had been beaten, and he was going to crawl off and lick his wounds like an injured dog. And I knew there was only one person who could force him to run and hide like that, who could hurt him that badly."

"No," I argued. "There are others—many others—who could have done that."

"But he would have reported the fight; and whatever they had done to him, he would have done worse to them. And he would have been proud of his injuries, because it meant he was stronger. But he didn't. He crept off and hid, which meant he hadn't won. And whoever had bested him had shown him mercy and let him live."

"It wasn't like that."

She laughed again, and the venom bubbled in her throat. "Michael, however you see it doesn't matter. All that matters to Antoine is that you defeated him."

"No, I—"

"Just like you had at the bridge."

"No, he won. That's what the Record—"

She put her hand on my mouth and looked at me intently. "Michael, the Record is wrong. Don't you see? You being alive means Antoine is a liar, and no matter what your intent was or is, his actions are his alone. He has to bear responsibility for them."

My argument fell down through the empty hole that opened in my stomach—a bottomless pit—and I stood very near the rim. Like the Fool, dancing along the cliff's edge, unaware of the danger in front of him. One more step meant disaster.

Was I too late to stop myself? Was I already making that fatal misstep? Philippe had twisted me deep into his design, and Antoine had talked me into believing that he and I had a common goal: after the destruction of Portland, we were no longer enemies, but allies. But could I trust him? Were his actions altruistic or was he simply using me?

Show me altruistic occultism. After what happened in Ravensdale, John Nicols had asked me to show him that we weren't all seeking answers for our own ends, that we were conscious of and capable of a higher morality. Having seen the handiwork of the theurgic mirror, Nicols had wanted to know where he could hope to find a spark of decency. Some sign that mankind wasn't entirely fixated on fucking itself into oblivion. Did such a spark exist, or was belief in it simply an illusion of my own naiveté?

What did Antoine want? What did I want, for that matter? Or Marielle?

The spirit of John Nicols morphed into another voice, a more recent addition to the echoes of the Chorus. Lafoutain and his skepticism. Did I trust her? Or was I blinded by the devotion I had inherited from her father? Or my own desire, even? Just as capable, if not more so, in misguiding me.

It is more difficult to live with a woman without danger than to raise the dead to life. Lafoutain had said that pithy aphorism belonged to Bernard of Clairvaux, the twelfth-century Cistercian monk who had helped guide the Templars to their glory against the bloody backdrop of the Crusades. Having raised the dead, I was inclined to agree with him, medieval morality aside.

"This isn't your fault," Marielle said, misreading my confusion and silence, and for once, I kept my mouth shut. She removed her hand from my mouth and let it fall to her lap. A shiver ran through her that had nothing to do with the ambient temperature on the exposed deck.

"My father had been sick for a long time." She started again. "Or maybe not that long at all. No one can be sure, really, because he kept it secret. He didn't trust anyone with the bad news. The only one who might have known would have been my mother…" Something akin to a smile moved across her face and she was much younger for a second. So much like the little girl in the field. "…She was the only one he could never hide from. Not completely."

The tiny girl was replaced by an older woman, one filled with a yearning hunger. "That is why he liked you, Michael, you know. Why he took you in so readily. You were like him: bound to none, hidden to all."

That is all you will ever be.

"I was—" She drew in a long breath. "Not an accident. No, he wouldn't like me to call it that. I was *unexpected*. I wasn't—" She let the breath out in a noisy rush. "—I wasn't a boy. And that complicated things for him. Especially after my mother died. He didn't have a *male* heir. He didn't have someone he could readily groom to take his place. Whatever vision he had of the organization, of the future, was complicated by the fact that he had to turn it over to someone else. Someone who wasn't his offspring.

"Every father wants to know that his legacy is going to persevere. It isn't just a matter of propagating the species, but a matter of passing along an imprint of what you are and believe. Every parent wants to die knowing that their efforts are growing in the next generation, stronger and richer than they could ever imagine. The society was given a mandate to protect and secure, and Father had to find someone he could trust with this mandate. Really trust. Since it couldn't be his flesh and blood, he had to find someone else."

Her eyes were bright and wet. I reached for her hand and she let me take it. Her skin was getting cold, and I could feel her pulse racing.

"I was—I still am—the Daughter of the Hierarch, and whether I like it or not, I am the prize. Father left everything to me. Material-wise. His villa. His apartments. His library. Everything. He didn't leave it to the society, and whoever becomes Hierarch is going to assume that the way he gets access to my father's legacy is by marrying me. To the victor go the spoils.

"But, the choice is mine. I can't be forced. Father made it very clear—many times over the years—that if I was to… take up… with any of the magi in the society, it was because I wanted it, not because I thought he would approve, or because I felt it was the right thing to do for the organization. I was free to choose. Anyone I wanted."

"And you picked Antoine." I hadn't meant to interrupt, but I couldn't stop myself. It came out somewhat sulkily and I wanted to take back the words the moment they left my mouth, but I couldn't. It was the way I felt, even after all this time. Even though I had been the one who had driven the wedge between them in the first place.

It still hurt, deep down in the black loam where the Chorus hid, and it wasn't the rejection, but the fact that Antoine had been right. She would choose him, in the end, because I would break her heart. I hated to admit that he had been right.

A tear tracked down her cheek. "No," she said. "Antoine loves me as best he can, and he would move the world for me. But he—" She stopped, a sad smile moving across her lips.

My heart was pounding in my chest, a noise so loud I was sure she could hear it. I was sure the sudden flush of blood through my veins gave away my every secret. I felt like a fool for reacting to the barest hint in her voice, the tiniest possibility that—

"These last few weeks have been hard. Knowing that the spring renewal was coming, wondering what my father was thinking after what happened in Portland. Wondering what the rest of the organization was going to do," she said. "And when he disappeared two days ago, I knew the time had come. I knew that whatever weight we had been carrying—by virtue of being family and friends—was going to get heavier…"

—that this whole affair wouldn't end badly for all of us.

"…and I fear the weight will be harder to bear still."

She moved her hands around mine, and gave my fingers a squeeze. "You make such a mess of things, my wolf. You always do."

I flinched, but her grip was stronger than I expected, and I couldn't pull away.

"You throw yourself headlong into everything. You don't know any other way. You don't know what it is to act without passion. Do you remember that night we rode the Ferris wheel at the Tuileries?"

"Of course." My voice cracked.

"We got stuck at the top and it started to rain. You tried to turn it into something else. What was it?"

"Flowers," I said.

"Flowers?" A smile lit her face. "But what did you make instead? What was that?"

I had tried some spell of my own devising. One I had made up on the spot, trying to throw my Will against the elements. I had failed. Badly. "Something else," I said. A smile pulled at my mouth. "Something shit out of the Abyss, probably." It had smelled very foul, and had been sticky, coating us and the wheel and the carriage. There had been no way to gracefully recover. We had sat in the ecto-shit for a half-hour and then calmly walked away from the wheel when it brought us to the ground again as if nothing had happened. I recalled throwing some manner of misdirection glamour on us as we left. Something that had made the experience truly ridiculous enough—more than it was already—that we ended up laughing about the whole thing.

It had always been easy to make her laugh. Back then. I seemed to have lost the knack in the interim.

"My father would have approved," she said, switching gears. She turned my wrist and brushed my fingers open.

"Approved of what?" I asked.

One of her father's tarot cards rested on my palm. I had no idea how it got there. I thought they were all still in my coat pocket. Even after my envenomed vision on the boat where I had spilled them all on the floor. They hadn't left my pocket.

She picked up the card before I could close my hand. "I know you did not kill him because you wanted to."

I started to interrupt her, but she quieted me with a shake of her head. A glance that said, *If you don't let me say this, it will never be said.*

"I know you did it because he asked you to. I know you did it because it was the only way to heal that which had been broken, to repair the damage done."

What is done is done.

The card was Strength. A woman holds open the mouth of a lion, and as I glanced at the card, the faces changed. Me, holding open Philippe's mouth, his soul streaming out of his body and fusing into an infinity halo over my head.

"I believe you cannot turn away, Michael," she whispered. "I believe in my father's trust in you."

Strength. Philippe's soul flowing into my body, merging with my spirit. His fight becoming mine. His wounds becoming mine. His legacy, becoming mine.

"Okay?" she asked. "No lies between us."

Strength.

"Okay."

I wanted to kiss her then. To pretend it was five years ago and we were still innocent and unaware of the future. That we were still in that other bedroom, flush with the fantasy of New Year's Eve and living on the cusp of something new. It hadn't happened yet, and as long as we didn't move, as long as we didn't leave that bed, nothing would happen. We would stay safe, and the future would never come. Or that we were still on the dance floor, caught in the lock groove, circling one another as if we were the only two bodies in the entire galaxy. Exerting an inexorable pull on one another.

But there was a fire in my head. Furious sparks that weren't mine. I couldn't put them out, as much as I wanted to. They were the present and the future, and the past was getting more distant and more muddled with every hour. I couldn't go back, not without losing my mind. I had to go forward. I had to accept what I had become.

Strength.

I told Marielle how her father died and what happened to him afterward. To her credit, she took it really well.

But, then, I was pretty sure she already knew.

THE THIRD WORK

"As a first step towards the successful prosecution of an investigation into the true nature and character of the mysterious object we know as the Grail it will be well to ask ourselves whether any light may be thrown upon the subject by examining more closely the details of the Quest in its varying forms; i.e., what was the precise character of the task undertaken by, or imposed upon, the Grail hero, whether that hero were Gawain, Perceval, or Galahad, and what the results were to be expected from a successful achievement of the task."

– Jessie L. Weston, *From Ritual to Romance*

XVI

Light reflected off a mirror, a flash like a flare of flame from a newly woken fire. The Chorus exploded out of me, a flock of startled birds, and they rose overhead into a swarming mass. Near the gangway, a man stepped onto the walkway—leaving the boat—and the light off his glasses was lessened by the fact that he was turning away from us, but the flare was still there.

I was off the bench before Marielle could say anything, and by the time I reached the railing, the gangway was empty. The Chorus fell back into a defensive perimeter, their astral wings collapsing about me, but there was no threat. Just the queasy uneasiness of having been spotted.

Down on the dock, a figure separated himself from the crowd and approached a black car idling nearby. He looked back once more before he got in, and I saw the sunglasses again. He wasn't wearing the centurion uniform, but the glasses were the same.

"There." I pointed him out to Marielle, but by the time she looked, he was already in the car.

"Who was it?" she asked as the car drove away.

"I don't know." He seemed familiar, beyond being the man from before, but not so familiar that I could place him. What with the poison-inspired visions, the wealth of knowledge hidden within me by the Architects, and my own history with the

Watchers, it was difficult to pinpoint why he had been familiar. Or, even, could he have been the man at the airport? "He was wearing sunglasses."

"At night?" She drew me away from the edge of the boat. "Were they polished? The kind that are like mirrors?"

"Yeah. They were."

"A scryer." Seeing my expression, she explained. "They see the future in reflective surfaces. They don't need water anymore. Mirrors work well too."

"The glasses are mirrored on both sides?"

"Yes. Mirroring the outside protects them. Makes it easier for them to be invisible."

"This is the second time I've seen him," I said. "Earlier, he was downstairs."

"Why didn't you tell me?"

"I thought he was a hallucination." I decided not to mention the illusion of having seen Antoine. "He wasn't dressed like all the others. He had this faux Roman centurion outfit on. With a big plumed headdress and a broken staff."

"Broken? Are you sure? Was it a spear without a point or a broken staff?"

I tried to remember. "It was just a stick with the top broken off. But, if it was part of his costume, then it might have been a spear, but it seemed wrong. Why would you go to all the effort with the rest of the costume and then not have a real spear?"

And the oil on the shaft too. What had that been about? I couldn't place the symbolism, even though I should have known. It kept slipping away from me.

"For the same reason you'd go to the trouble of imagining him wearing the costume in the first place," she said.

"And why would I do that?"

She stared at me. "You're kidding me, right?"

"No. I don't know what you're talking about." *I should know.*

"How can you have my father in your head and not know what you saw?"

"He's not sitting in his favorite chair by the fire, doling out arcane secrets on demand. He's this... sort of persistent sense of déjà vu that comes and goes. Sometimes, I know exactly what he knew, and other times—most of the time—there's only a nagging sense that I'm missing something. It's like when you forget where you put your car keys. You know they exist, and you know you had them, but you can't figure out where you left them. But, abstract it one layer up. I don't even know that it is the car keys that I'm looking for."

I realized I was still holding the tarot card, but it wasn't Strength anymore. The lines had twisted, changing the image from a woman holding open a lion's mouth to a pair of cherubic children on the back of a draft horse. A pair of apple-cheeked, blonde-haired babies basking in the glow of the sun. I handed Marielle the card while I dug for the bag in my pocket. "How did you do that magic trick?" I asked.

"With the card?" She glanced at it. "I was going to ask you. It was an eerie bit of sleight-of-hand."

"I didn't." I pulled open the strings of the bag and reached in for a handful of cards. They were slippery—mischievous and intent on getting away from me—but I grabbed them quick and held tight. "It's your father's deck, and it seems to miss him." I nodded toward the card in her hand. "What card is that?"

She held it up. "Strength."

I shook my head, and shuffled through the cards until I found the one I was looking for. "This is Strength." My fingers tingled when I named the card, and from the way the Chorus churned, I knew that it wasn't, even though my eyes told me otherwise.

"It's the Fool, Michael," Marielle said. "You're holding the Fool."

Of course I was.

"No, I'm holding Strength, and you're holding the Sun. What

you see is the Fool and Strength," I said, pointing to each of the cards.

"I don't understand this game," she said.

I took the card from her, and as I touched it, the lines started to squirm and change. I shuffled it back into the deck, along with the card I had picked out. "They keep changing on me. Sometimes into other cards, sometimes into weird amalgamations of multiple cards. I cut the deck in half and showed her. "See? Strength and the Fool." I waited until she nodded in agreement and then I put my hands back together, and without changing their position, split the deck in the same place again. "Now what do you see?"

"The same thing."

I looked. "I see the Sun and the High Priestess."

"How is that possible?" she asked.

"I don't know if it has something to do with your father or if I'm just losing my mind from all the recent activity in my brain, but the lines don't stay in place. The cards keep shifting, as if he's using them to communicate. Not very clearly, mind you. But when he wants to tell me something, he manipulates the cards."

In spite of the implication of her father being un-dead, Marielle stepped closer and grabbed my arm. "What are they telling you?" Her grip was tighter than necessary, and her body was uncharacteristically rigid.

"The Sun and the High Priestess," I said, putting the deck back together and taking advantage of that motion to drag my arm out of her grasp. Shuffling the deck a few more times, I cut it, reversed the halves, and went to flip over the top card.

"Stop." Marielle covered the deck with her hand. "No, I believe you."

"It's just a card," I said. "It's all in my head."

"It isn't," she said. Her tongue touched her lip nervously. "Leave it alone. Don't invite anything in. Not with those cards.

Let them be."

"You have a better idea?" I asked as the Chorus slid around my spine and squeezed. What was it about the Sun and the High Priestess that had her so agitated?

She hesitated, caught by some internal argument.

"We've been spotted. We need to go somewhere else."

Marielle's gravity well fluttered. For a second, she almost seemed to be a little girl again, and then the weight of her Will came down and the image vanished.

"What about Tevvys' phone?" I suggested, trying to jostle her out of her mental peregrinations. "We could try to crack his passcode."

"I don't have it."

"What? Moreau gave it to you."

"He did, but I don't have it anymore. I left it back at the apartment."

"Why didn't you say so in the car?"

"I was—" She took a deep breath. "It doesn't matter."

"It does. I told Moreau—"

She cut me off. "It doesn't matter. It was a dumb idea."

"No, it wasn't."

"It was. For a number of reasons. Besides, if they wanted to call us, they'd call my phone. I'm sure someone has the number."

I wanted to argue the point, but before the words got all the way out of my throat, I realized she was right. If they wanted to talk, they'd be able to figure out how to reach us. No one knew my number but Marielle, but I'm sure a lot of the Watchers knew her number. The Chorus chattered, admonishing me too, and I bristled more at their umbrage than Marielle's comments. *What was the other choice?* I asked them. *Killing Moreau?*

I blocked their response, as the question had been rhetorical. It was so easy to find that path again, wasn't it? And what had I gained from going that route previously? Walking the dark path in the wood had only brought me and others pain. That wasn't the way. Regardless of what others wanted me to do.

"Don't worry about it," she said, filling my silence. "I'm sure Moreau took you seriously when you told him. And he might even have tried to follow your—"

"Don't," I said. "I get it. I fucked up."

She ran her hands through her hair, brushing it back from her face. "I'm sure the building collapsed on him," she said finally. "Squashed him flat."

"I'm sure he sold us out the first chance he got," I said, nearly at the same time.

We paused, waiting for the other to speak, and when neither of us leaped into the gap, she smiled. "What is done is done. Let's move on."

"Agreed." I waited for a second before asking. "The cards."

Her smile faded, but she nodded.

I turned over the top card of the deck. The Sun. The twins on horseback. Lafoutain moved in the cloud of the Chorus, and one word escaped from the vortex of their noise. *Daughters.*

Marielle eyed the card with some trepidation, and when I tapped it, she looked away somewhat nervously. The Chorus couldn't read her: her pulse was gone, and the swirling energy caught beneath the boat dispersed into the general stream of psychic force that ran through Paris.

"Daughters." When she appeared to not hear me, I said it again. "Tell me about the daughters, Marielle."

She searched my face for some sign that I knew what I was talking about, and the Chorus slapped away her subtle attempt to read my aura. I locked myself off as completely as she had—*two can play this game*—and stared back at her. Willing to wait her out.

When I had started to explain to her how her father moved in the cards, she had been nervous. Anxious, as if her father could tell me something she didn't want me to know. Like father, like daughter: the family couldn't help but keep secrets. Was that what Lafoutain was talking about? The age-old argument that men are transparent, unable to keep a secret to save their lives, but it is women who are impossible to read. If you want any secret to be truly kept confidential, you tell your daughter and not your son.

"All right," Marielle said. She nodded toward the quay. "Find us a cab. I'll call ahead and let them know we're coming. They can tell you themselves."

She seemed relieved that I hadn't asked about the High Priestess.

Tour Montparnasse stuck out of the glittering landscape of Paris like a bruised middle finger. The skyscraper was one of those concessions to modernity that was immediately regretted as soon as it was finished; shortly after the building was done, Paris outlawed any further skyscrapers within the central part of the city. One of those rare moments of humility from a civic government, and some believe the building remains so that no one ever forgets. You can kill the magic of a city by changing it too much.

It reminded me of the Eglanteria Terrace, the building in Portland where Bernard took the theurgic mirror and launched his assault on humanity. A spire to Heaven, drenched in darkness.

. At the tower, Marielle typed a security code into the pad in the elevator, and we ascended to an unmarked floor. The doors opened onto a simple foyer, with a rose marble floor and pale green walls. There was no other exit, just a small marble plaque—the same sort of rose stone like the floor—with the letters "l F d M" engraved in it and another security keypad.

Mounted in each of the four corners of the room were tiny blisters of security monitors. Discrete enough to be easily missed, but not so invisible that you didn't see them if you were looking.

Marielle entered another passcode and the light on the pad

flashed green, but nothing happened. In response to my raised eyebrow, she nodded toward one of the security cameras. "Entering the right code only announces you," she said. "You still have to be invited in."

"In where?" I touched the plaque, tracing the letters, hoping the Chorus would provide some clue as to what they meant.

"*Les Filles de Mnémosyne*," Marielle said.

The daughters of Mnemosyne, who, according to Greek legend, lived on Mount Parnassus. The nine Muses.

The Chorus registered the magickal release of a seal, and the walls of the anteroom flickered out of existence, leaving us standing at the edge of an immense room, filled with rows upon rows of tall bookcases. The marble floor around the elevator remained, as did the elevator column itself, and Marielle stepped across the line separating the marble from the warm polish of the library's wooden floors.

I followed, and the Chorus shivered as we crossed over, an animalistic twitch that ran through my veins. The seal activated as I crossed, binding the walls solid again, and on the inside, layers and layers of magickal script vibrated with activity. The wards of *Les Filles de Mnémosyne*.

"Welcome to the Archives," Marielle said. "Don't touch anything."

I snatched my hand back. The case next to me was devoted to books, and as I looked more closely at the nearby shelves, I noted that some of them held display cases of varying size. Most of them weren't lit with any sort of track lighting—this wasn't a public museum after all, and long-term exposure to artificial light could very well damage some of the artifacts held here. The ambient lighting of the grand chamber was purposefully restrained, leaving the contents of the cases in mysterious—and tantalizing—shadows.

"That's a copy of the *Secretum Secretorum*," I said, indicating the book I had almost touched. "One of the Tulbriss editions."

Only fourteen were reputed to have been made, and they were a facsimile of the original translation done by John of Seville back in the twelfth century. There were English translations readily available—some of them even on the Internet—but they were very literal, and a great deal of the symbolic richness—the magick bound into the text—had been stripped out. This edition had been commissioned to re-create the arts lost in the mundane translations, and before I could stop myself, I found the catalog description on my lips, the words nearly falling out of my mouth like money out of the wallet of a drunken old bookseller: Roxburghe-style binding, lambskin leather, gold stamp lettering, Fabriano Ingres endpapers, an oyster paper interior—

"You know the Tulbriss?" The speaker was a robust woman, dressed in a charcoal suit that managed to be corporately stylish and haute couture at the same time. Her blonde hair was pulled back from her round face and plaited in a long strand down to her mid-back. Perched on the peak of her forehead was a pair of red-rimmed glasses. Definitely going for the sexy academic look, and succeeding very well, though the arch of her eyebrow at my expression suggested she had heard enough variants of "hot librarian!" over the years that for me to mention it out loud now would be as banal as pointing out that she was wearing shoes.

And they were pretty great shoes too.

"Yes," I said, with no small amount of clumsiness. My chest was tight, and it took me a minute to realize the sensation wasn't some schoolboy reaction (you never forget your first librarian crush), but a spirit sensation from the Chorus, an agonizing pang of loneliness. I knew why she looked familiar. "You're—"

"Vivienne Lafoutain," Marielle said.

Lafoutain's daughter.

Stricken, I looked at Marielle for help. The pain in my chest increased, and my heart skipped. *Once was enough. Don't make me do this again.* "I can't," I whispered. Don't make me tell another daughter that her father is gone. That I've taken the soul of someone they love.

Marielle's face softened. "I'll tell her."

"Tell me what?" Vivienne asked.

"Your father is gone, Viv. I'm sorry."

Vivienne took her glasses off her head, glanced at the lenses for a second, and then settled them on her face. "The Tulbriss," she said, after clearing her throat, "how familiar are you with the edition? Have you actually handled one?" Behind her glasses, her eyes were shiny, the only outward sign that she had heard Marielle.

"Yes," I said, feeling incredibly awkward, even more than I had a moment before. *Little chicken,* a voice cried from the Chorus, *don't hold it back.* "I, uh, acquired a copy once. For a private collector."

"One in Hong Kong?" She touched the corner of an eye, wiping at something so faint neither Marielle or I could attest that it had ever been there.

"I can't say."

She favored me with a tiny curl of her lips, an expression so haunted with a different emotion entirely that the Chorus nearly exploded in my chest. "You don't have to. Aleister Forge is the only collector who knew there were copies still out there."

"Viv—" Marielle took a step forward.

Vivienne shook her head, and her face hardened. "No, *sister.*" Her hands clenched into fists. "I won't share this with you." Her anger shook a tear loose and it slid down her cheek. Her hand still balled tight, she swiped the tear away. "So, you're the one."

"Yes," I said, knowing without knowing why that I was.

"Come with me," she said, turning and walking further into the stacks. She hadn't glanced at Marielle. "*She* said earlier that you two needed some guidance. An understanding of the process by which the Coronation is completed. Yes?"

"Yes," I said, sticking with the safe answer.

"There is an artifact that must be retrieved. The Hierarch had a key. I can tell you where the lock is."

And there went sticking with the safe answer. "I…" *The key.* "I don't have it."

Vivienne stopped, reversed her direction, and walked close enough to me that I could see the cracks in her emotional armor. "What do you mean?"

"Philippe had a key—one with a smashed top and magicked teeth. 'Abbadon' he called it. That one?" When she nodded, I reiterated the bad news. "I don't have it anymore."

"Who does?"

"Antoine." I swallowed, stealing a glance toward Marielle. "I think."

When Vivienne finally looked at Marielle, her gaze was filled with such fury that I expected Marielle to burst into flames from the intensity of the glare. "Of course," Vivienne said. "Why does that not surprise me?"

XVII

Vivienne left me in a room with a window while she and Marielle had it out. It might have been a conference room if someone had brought in a table and more chairs. There was a single desk, on which a fairly generic-looking computer and monitor sat, and a larger flat screen mounted on the wall opposite. The lack of other ephemera of occupancy made it hard to classify the room as an office either.

I stared out at the Parisian landscape and did some deep breathing techniques, calming and re-centering my spirit. In the distance lay the lights of the Louvre, the Ferris wheel near the Tuileries, and the gold spire of the Place de la Concorde. The Great Meridian that ran east to west through the center of Paris, all the way out to La Defénse. To my left, the Eiffel Tower, glittering yellow diamonds lighting up the night. I couldn't see the blocky structure of La Defénse as it was hidden by the Eiffel Tower; there was another meridian running from La Defénse, through the Eiffel Tower, to Montparnasse.

The Chorus thrilled at such architecturally precise geometry; it appealed to their nature, all the monuments built to facilitate the flow of energy. The natural course of the leys in this region followed the Seine, but occultists from the Renaissance onward had consciously strived to bend the leys to their Wills. All of the great cities of Europe were built—to some degree or another—in a way to maximize the flow of energy through specific points. You didn't build a city without giving some thought and effort to making it both defensible and a conduit of power to a central seat. Paris had always been one of the greater achievements of civic planning from an occult perspective. Louis XIV's sobriquet of "Sun King" was well earned. A tad overreaching, much like Crowley's self-chosen title of "The Great Beast," but power has a tendency to dull one's sense of humility.

Like a worm wiggling back in the ground when you turn over a rock, a tiny thread twisted in the dark depths of the Chorus. They boiled over the memory of Bernard du Guyon, but I already noticed that tiny shard of him moving in my mind. I couldn't look out over the nocturnal glow of a city landscape and not think of him, standing at the top of that tower in Portland, incanting the culmination of his great work. He had tried so hard to unmake everything, a petulant child who believed destruction came from the same divine urge as creation. Every inhalation is but a prelude to a *Hallelujah!*; all life rushes back on itself so that it can be born again.

The only trouble with that theory is the assumption that the universe will eventually contract as God finishes exhaling. To believe that He mirrors us—inverting the supposition that we have been built in His image—is to conflate our ability to dream with His creativity.

Thus it always has been with power. With knowledge. With the truths we conceal. We harbor the keys to these occult secrets and think ourselves greater than the rest, scurrying about in these jeweled landscapes. We stand above them, in great towers raised by sweat and blood and sacrifice, and think we are closer to Heaven. We think we are closer to God from this height because we can See all the way to the edge of the world.

A phone rang somewhere and I turned, confused, as I hadn't remembered seeing one on the desk. When it rang again, it also vibrated. Against my side. Because it was my cell phone ringing.

Making a mental note to change the ringtone to something other than the stock ring, I fumbled the phone out of the inside pocket of my coat.

My phone didn't recognize the number, which meant it wasn't Marielle.

"Hello?"

"Hello, M. Markham." The voice was clipped and precise. Each word afforded just enough breath to form all the letters, and each word was equally spaced from the others. It would have been easy to think it was computer-modified in some way so as to disguise the speaker, but there was more of that old analog warmth of a human throat behind it than the cold sterility of a vibrating speaker. "Enjoying the view?"

I glanced around, and didn't see any obvious cameras, and I was too high up to be clearly seen from the street. The windows were polarized too, so even if someone down on the street level was watching me with binoculars, they shouldn't be able to distinguish features enough to recognize me.

"I am," I said. "You?"

"It is a bit voyeuristic, I admit, but I like to See."

" 'Seeing.' Interesting word choice. Most voyeurs are 'Watchers.' " It was a cheap shot, but I might as well see what sort of man I was talking to.

His laugh had none of the characteristics of human warmth, though. Like a loop of sound that wasn't cut quite right, and there was a jagged hiccup at the end as it leaped back to the beginning again. I had mental images of steel jaws opening and closing in a parody of amusement. "Not tonight, M. Markham. I am not bearing witness. Not now."

I shivered involuntarily, and tried to pretend it was a reaction to the dry air of the office. I stopped trying to find the camera pinhole, because even if there was one, he wasn't watching me through it. *Not bearing witness.* Whoever he was, he was using remote viewing, astral magick to See me from afar.

"Do they know you can peer into the Archives?" I asked.

"Only the outer ring," he said. "They're fastidious with their security."

"I'm sure they are." I looked out at the flickering lights of Paris. "So, other than this demonstration of power, what else would you like *me* to Witness this evening?" It was an old distinction, one coded very specifically into the rules of *La Société Lumineuse*. Remote viewing wasn't recognized as a means of Witnessing—the official manner in which history is marked and recorded by the Watchers—unless it was grounded first by another Watcher. Someone had to verify the remote viewer was, indeed, viewing the proper location and event before the Viewer could enter a True Record.

There were a couple of moments in history that needed a Witness but were problematic in the matter of the on-site witness surviving. Setting up a remote view prior and then extracting the Watcher on the ground was a concession to the alternative of losing the magus and the Record.

"You asked me to call," the voice said.

"I did?"

"Yes. You spared the Journeyman's life in hopes that he would carry a message for you."

I actually looked at the phone to make sure it was mine and not Tevvys'. "I believe I told him that we'd be reachable on Tevvys' phone."

"Ah, my apologies. I was under the impression you wanted me to call you from it. Why else would you have left it behind?"

"Why else?" I tried to be nonchalant in my response. Tevvys had never known my phone number, nor had there been any reason for Marielle—the only person who knew it—to give it to him. Before the others realized the food had been poisoned and had bashed his skull in. *Don't let him rattle you,* the Chorus murmured, *it's a display of power. "We think we are closer to God…" Remember?*

I remembered that I had been thinking that thought just before the phone rang, which made it all even less of a coincidence. *Pointing that out was supposed to make me feel better?*

"Talking with the spirits?" the voice asked.

"Fuck." I hadn't meant to let it out, but what was the point of trying to keep it in? The guy was nearly in my head already. "Yes." I took a moment to control my breathing. "Okay, I get the point..." I made an intuitive leap. "M. Husserl."

"Yes." He sibilated the "s." "Very good."

The Architect known as the Scryer. Remote viewing. Forward looking. Physiology scanning. The legacy of Dr. Dee and Edward Kelly, scrying was a way of interpreting the Weave, though it wasn't the same inexact science as it had been in the sixteenth century. While tarot was a means by which one's part in the Weave could be comprehended, scrying was a tool by which the Weave itself was illuminated. Kelly hadn't been able to control his sight all that well, and he and Dr. Dee squabbled too much about the interpretation of what Kelly saw. But we had gotten better about understanding the Akashic Weave, and what lay there. We had become better readers. Scrying, unlike the sort of postulating and calculating that Father Cristobel did as Visionary, adhered more to the core principle of Witnessing. One could look ahead as a scryer; the trick was knowing what you were seeing, and Ulrich Husserl was, evidently, the best at Knowing and Seeing.

"Is this a social call? Just calling because you can," I asked, my voice no longer unsteady, "or is there a specific detail of my future you wish to impart?"

"The spirits will not be able to aid you forever. They will leave you."

"I'm sure they will. Probably when I'm dead."

"Assuredly."

"But I don't need you to tell me that."

"No, of course not. What you do need me for is to tell you

when they abandon you. Prior to your death."

"And in return for this piece of trivia, I'll grant you…"

"Nothing, M. Markham. Any promise you give me is hollow. We both know that."

"So this one is free."

"The first one always is." He laughed again, and my skin crawled even more this time. The Chorus swarmed like someone had just poked them with a hot stick, and the ripples of their unease went all the way down my spine.

I walked over to the desk and emptied out my pockets. I needed a way to get this guy out of my head. There had to be some way to shield myself or divert his astral eye. Wallet. Still had that pack of gum. Folded pages of the hand-drawn org chart. Cristobel's rosary. Philippe's deck of cards. Holding the phone between my cheek and shoulder, I upended the bag and spilled the cards out on the desk.

"What are you looking for, M. Markham?" Husserl asked. "Some sort of ward against me?"

"Something like that." For a moment, I considered Cristobel's rosary. It might protect me if I wrapped it around my head, but that's not what I needed right now. I needed something to cloud Husserl's vision.

"The first card you turn over will be the Four of Pentacles," he said.

I slid the rosary off the table and put it back in my pocket, and then I flipped over the closest card. The way the Chorus was churning in my stomach suggested that Husserl was going to be right.

Four of Pentacles.

My hand drifted toward the next closest card. "Eight of Swords." He was right again. "I could do this all night," he pointed out. "But we don't have that much time."

I stopped flipping cards over and glanced toward the door. Marielle and Vivienne. Neither of whom would be terribly pleased to know I was talking with the man who had ordered the death of Vivienne's father.

"What do you want?" I asked. *We don't have much time.* He wasn't toying with me; there was an underlying reason for this conversation.

"I want you to understand the power that I have. The power I have given to the men who believe, like I do, in the future we've Seen."

"Doesn't that kill the adventure?" I wondered. "Seeing the future? You know all the conversations you're going to have tomorrow. What you're going to eat. What you're going to wear. Doesn't it make the future somewhat… dull?"

I was stalling, and we both knew it, but if he had already Seen this conversation, then he wouldn't mind. Or it wouldn't matter. Whatever he wanted to tell me would come out. *Wouldn't it?* The advanced practices of astral magick and accessing the whole time/space continuum were the sort of theoretical occultism I had never managed to wrap my head around. You had to sit down and sort out the Free Will/Determinism argument with yourself before you could even begin to consider bending light into a cone through which you could See a different time; and I had been too much of a proponent of Free Will to get far in that discussion.

"That isn't the sort of thing we tend to focus on," Husserl said.

"Yeah, I probably wouldn't either. Just the big picture, right? But once you See the future, doesn't that violate it? How can you Witness something and not have it be changed by the act of Witnessing."

"Is light a wave or a particle?" he asked. "It all depends on who is looking, doesn't it? The future is nothing more than a frozen collection of light, one of many million possible permutations that these particles can combine in." Husserl laughed. "But who's to say that my efforts to change them aren't the catalysts that bring them about? Witnessing the future is an act of creation."

"So the future is set when you look at it?"

"Yes. There. That wasn't as hard as you thought, was it?"

What I was thinking was how terrifying a concept that was. You look at the future and see yourself getting hit by a bus in the next fifteen minutes. Now that you've seen it, it is going to happen; whereas if you had kept your curiosity under control, that bus might have missed you. Piotr always referred to reading the cards as akin to listening to echoes of people moving in the next room. There was room for interpretation, and with that uncertainty, you were never sure.

No wonder fortune tellers were happy to be listening from the other side of a wall. The possibility of being wrong left us with the illusion of Free Will. Without that illusion, what were we?

"So each scryer fixes the future a little when he looks forward? What happens when a room full of scryers all look?" I didn't really want to know, but I had a feeling he needed to tell me. We were building an aspect of the future he had already Seen.

"We build the future, M. Markham."

"And if there were enough of you—?" I got it. "Oh." That's how the universe had been created. God looked forward. All the way to infinity, and thus was existence born.

And here we are. Right where he Saw us. Me, getting a sense of the big picture; him, giving me the nudge that made me See it.

"So what do you want with me?" I asked, more than a little shaken by the implications of what was coming.

"You are a singularity," he said.

The Chorus erupted into a frenzy of light, thrilled by the arrival of the moment they had been waiting for. The moment where I was allowed to understand why I had been chosen. Why Philippe had come to me, given me his soul, dumping this whole shitty mess in my lap.

His enemies couldn't See past me. They were blinded by the divergence of souls in my head. They couldn't anticipate or See what lay beyond me. *Therefore he doesn't Know the future.*

I felt more of the veil fall from my mind. Philippe could undo what Husserl and the other scryers Saw. That was the balance that Cristobel mentioned. There was a change coming. They all saw it in their own way, and none of them could be sure what happened beyond it. But they wanted to be the ones who were in charge when it passed. Just like Bernard had tried with the theurgic mirror in Portland. He had wanted to be the one talking to God when the world started anew. And now, with Philippe gone, the question of who was going to stand at the Coronation was completely... unknown.

In a stroke, I understood the brutal genius of Philippe's grand plan. It was all about Free Will, in a world that had been atrophying into Determinism. They all thought they Knew enough, they thought they Saw the whole of human existence and could—and would—take a grander role in directing it. But that wasn't the mission of the Watchers. It never had been. It had been to Watch, and to keep safe the mysteries. In order to keep his mission safe, Philippe had hidden everything from them.

By giving it all to me.

Whether or not that was a wise move was still up for discussion.

"You'd like me to remove myself," I said to Husserl. "You want me to be your noble sacrifice, and clear the way so that you can look ahead again."

"Yes," Husserl said.

"What do the other Architects think about this plan? The ones still alive," I asked, shooting blind, but hoping to hit something. "The Mason, perhaps?"

Husserl didn't answer, and that was answer enough.

"I wonder what he'd think about this phone call, and what you've asked me to do."

"You aren't going to call him."

"No," I said. "I'm not." I wandered back to the window, and

looked out at Paris. I looked beyond the frozen lights of the streets and buildings, down the energy layer and the flood of power moving there. The Chorus swirled, and like water clinging to a cobweb, they flung themselves into a mental gridwork of the etheric lines. I still wanted to call it the "Weave," but I was starting to see Cristobel's point, that the word failed to properly encapsulate what it really was.

"You're guessing," I told Husserl. My other hand slipped in my pocket and I felt the warm stones of Cristobel's rosary. I rubbed a bead between my fingers, becoming familiar with its smooth surface. Anchoring myself. "You haven't Seen whether or not I call Spiertz. You can't be sure."

"I am," he said. *Was that a note of defiance in his voice?*

I concentrated on the grid of lines, and my consciousness felt the scattered droplets of the upper layer, shooting down into the squirming mass of the luminous threads that ran along the surface of each drop. The Chorus hissed with white noise as I found the twisted mass of threads that corresponded to the tower where I stood. My light was a dot of swarming fury, too many lights collapsed into a single point, and around it were several luminous threads. One, more faint than the rest, twisted away at a strange angle from the others. I touched it, felt its tension, and plucked it like a harp string.

On the phone, I heard Husserl make an involuntary noise. It wasn't much more than a sudden intake of air, but it was enough.

"You can't See all of the future," I whispered. The Chorus plucked the astral thread of his remote viewer. "This I Know."

When he spoke, the mechanical precision of his voice was gone. There was nothing left but a guttural bark of anger. "I See enough."

The thread broke, vanishing in a mist of light and static. The phone line was dead too. He was no longer there. Gone, just another phantom haunting me.

XVIII

"Am I interrupting?"

I turned from the window at the intrusion of Vivienne's voice. I hadn't heard her come in, nor had the Chorus warned me. "No," I said, closing the phone and dropping it back into my pocket. I didn't offer any more of an explanation, nor did she ask. She also noticed the scattered cards on the desk as she walked past, but didn't comment on them.

"It's a spectacular view, isn't it?" She was an inch taller than me, her mother's Nordic heritage making up for her father's gastronomic disposition. His face had been rounder, but his humor was clear in the fine lines at the corners of her eyes and in the natural curve of her mouth. All of which only highlighted the fact that she had been crying.

"I'm sorry," I said. "I didn't get much of a chance to know your father, but he seemed both kind and generous. A fortunate man, both in family and in affection."

"Thank you," Vivienne said. Her throat worked on more words, and they came out slowly. "You can never prepare yourself for this hole, can you? You could be with someone constantly, watching every minute twitch of their eyes or mouths, listening to every breath they take in, recording every moment of their lives so as to not forget anything, but…"

She approached the window with heavy steps, and with some

effort, she looked down at the darker patch of ground to our right where there was few lights. Lamps along paths guide the living through the maze of headstones and mausoleums of the cemetery grounds. Much like Père Lachaise, the cemetery at Montparnasse was a remnant of Old Paris, a plot of cultural heritage made over into a tourist attraction. Pilgrimage sites for lovers and artists and obsessive idolizers.

"It doesn't matter when they're gone," she continued. Her voice was even softer now, and I had to quiet the Chorus in order to hear her. "All that remains is memory, and you don't understand how completely inadequate memory is until that is all you have. My father and I had our share of... differences, but he was still my father, the flesh and spirit that molded me. He—" Her voice faltered for a moment. "He was like the sun rising in the east—that one inviolate thing in my world—and I would always see him again. I could refresh that inadequate thing that is memory, but now..."

Lafoutain would be buried in the cemetery at Montparnasse, I thought. Close by where his daughter could keep an eye on him. Close enough to touch. *Almost.*

I cleared my throat. "I chased a memory of a woman for ten years. She wasn't dead; she didn't know I was still alive. I tracked her across half the world, and when I did find her, I discovered what I remembered wasn't the truth. I had invented a fiction to sustain me." I looked at Vivienne. "It's not the same sort of hole at all, but I think I know what you mean."

"Is your father still alive?"

"No. He died a few years ago. Cancer. It wasn't terribly—"

No, I pushed the Chorus away, *that wasn't the way it had happened.* My father had had a heart attack during a lecture. Philippe had the cancer. My father was the university professor, a second career after we had lost the farm in Idaho. His leg had never turned black. I had never—

"I'm sorry." She misunderstood the sudden violence of my

silence. "Is that better or worse? Did it—" Her throat worked, but nothing came out.

"No," I ground out, fighting to keep the memories of my father separate from the bleed-through of Philippe's death. *Stop confusing my past.* I wanted to call a time-out and back the conversation up. Start over, and tell her the truth.

What truth? Philippe asked. *That it took your sister a week to find you and tell you? That you went to the funeral and stared at the picture of the man who was being buried and realized you didn't know who he was? That you had been so consumed by the darkness in your soul that you didn't understand the pain your sister was feeling? That you have no idea what it feels like?*

"You develop scar tissue," I said, finding something akin to honesty. Something I understood. "Which only means you feel the loss less, and in some ways, that means everything else is lessened too. Is it better? I don't know. I wish none of us had to find out…."

The tiny lines around her eyes deepened as her face tightened. "Marielle is… well, let me be blunt: she is a cold-hearted bitch. And while it feels good to know she has lost someone as well, it's a hollow feeling. You know? It doesn't fill the void in *my* heart. Because I know she feels it less than I do. She knew her father was going to die. She's known ever since she was old enough to understand what it meant to be Hierarch. One day, he would be killed so that another could lead. She's had a long time to grow all the scar tissue she might need." Her eyes were bright as she fought to keep the tears away. "Better to feel something than nothing. Right?"

An old memory, poisonous in its clarity and single-mindedness, pushed through the Chorus. That old focus, dripping with pain and anger. *Find Katarina; take back what she stole from you.* How it had sustained me for so long. It had been something. "Right," I said softly. "Better than nothing."

Vivienne shivered, and hugged herself, rubbing her upper

arms. "As smart as we are, we are still afraid of the dark. Afraid of what happens when the sun goes away, and the light dies. What do moths do when there is no bulb to gravitate to? Flutter aimlessly in the dark with no purpose—no desire—until they die? Is that better than being burned alive for trying to touch the light?"

"I don't know."

She wiped at the corner of one eye and offered me a sad smile that nearly broke my heart. *Little chicken,* Lafoutain cried from an impossible distance, *I am so sorry to give you this pain.* The rest of the Chorus was a veil of silence, ghosts of ghosts.

While I cleaned up the disarray of tarot cards, Vivienne discovered the pieces of paper I had taken from the apartment. The cards were cold to the touch, and none of the figures twitched or exploded into fragments. Philippe and the rest were keeping their distance.

"This is my father's handwriting," Vivienne said, pointing to a scrawl of marginalia on one of the pages. Realizing each page was a fragment, she spread them out on the desk. Putting the puzzle together. Making sense out of nonsense. Re-creating the world.

"It's the org chart they were working on. At the safe house." I glanced at the pages. I hadn't really paid attention to all the details when I had first seen them. There hadn't been any time. The majority of the notes were in the same precise block characters, but there was scattered notation done by someone else. Hubert Lafoutain, apparently. "They were trying to sort out who they could trust. I showed up late, and they were mostly done."

"Figuring out who the Architects were," she said, quickly divining the purpose of the pages. She spotted her father's name, and involuntarily looked up to see if I was paying attention.

"I know," I said. "He was the Scholar."

"There are nine," she said, nodding. "Just like Mnemosyne

had nine daughters."

"Is Marielle one of your number?"

"No, she is the Daughter of the Hierarch. Though, like he is sometimes considered a peer of his Architects, she is often mistaken as one of us."

"The tenth Muse."

Her lips curled back from her teeth. "Everyone feels better when there are ten. Nine seems unfinished, especially in our metric world."

"Only if you start from one."

"So few think otherwise."

"We're all so concrete-sequential. Zero makes things complicated."

She gave me an odd look, a laugh rising in her throat. "Ah, Monsieur…" She caught herself, and let the rest of the sentence go unfinished, busying herself with lining up the pages. I didn't press her, and quietly finished ordering and putting the cards away.

When the chart was laid out again, she looked at it for some time, reading all the notes. "The Tulbriss," she said absently, as she traced her finger along an arc connecting the Crusader and the Navigator. "Do you know how many copies were actually made?"

"Fourteen, I heard."

She nodded, still looking at the chart. "We have six of them. Three more were destroyed during the occult purges of World War II. One is buried in the archives of the British Museum—" She glanced up, a twinkle in her eye. "Misfiled in a crate catalogued as 'Miscellaneous Texts Damaged in the Great Fire.' And another is in a private collection in Massachusetts. That leaves three."

"It does."

"Forge has tried to buy one of ours. Many times. He's a sanctioned collector, and he's got far more dangerous things in his library, so why can't he have a copy of the Tulbriss edition of the *Secretum Secretorum?* This is his argument, you understand."

"Of course."

"I think my father liked saying no, frankly. There wasn't any strong reason Forge couldn't have one, other than the basic policy that things come into the Archives, they don't go out. But Father always said he liked listening to Forge rant: that English accent, those rigorously exotic Chinese curses, how he'd go on for minutes at a time.

"Though, more pragmatically, if we denied Forge what he wanted, he would obsess about it. He'd not stop until he found one, and in doing so, might actually scare up one of the remaining three copies. We'd probably have let him keep it, if a copy did surface, but that was dependent upon whether or not we got to it first."

I recalled the meeting in Bangkok where I had taken receipt of the book, and the ensuing fracas that had left my Thai contact dead and me on the run from several of my black market competitors. It hadn't been my first brush with the seedier side of underground occult artifact trafficking; just the first where I realized how difficult it was going to be to stay off the Watcher radar and continue doing what I had been doing.

"You were the Weatherstones' client," I said. Thomas and Rebecca Weatherstone. English antiques dealers who also moved occult artifacts. One of my main competitors, and over the years, we had had a reasonably friendly rivalry. Until Bangkok, where their field agents had killed Kraisingha and tried to do the same to me. I still had the scars—a couple of knots of hard flesh on my chest from the bullet holes.

Vivienne nodded. "We were."

Rebecca had been sleeping with the magus I had killed. Thomas hadn't known, and probably still didn't. Rebecca didn't know I knew, but that's only because she didn't know what I had done to her man. I knew a lot of things about Rebecca and

Thomas, enough to have made it easy for me to avoid them ever since. They didn't need to know what I had in my head about them.

"What were you offering them?" I asked, professionally curious.

"Finder's fee of twenty-five percent."

"Twenty-five percent of what? There isn't an open market on these."

She shrugged as if that was a minor detail. "What did Forge pay you?"

"Two hundred thousand."

"Dollars? He got quite a deal."

He had paid me in Euros actually. At the time, I hadn't been too happy about it, but recently, the United States dollar had been taking a beating in the world market. But, even in Euros, she was right. He had gotten a deal.

He had also given me a few other things. Objects I had leveraged for other deals I had had in the works. The two hundred thousand had been for "operational expenses." The rest had been a much quieter—and less violent—transaction. Two men, exchanging briefcases during an intimate and private dinner at a very exclusive club in Hong Kong.

But I didn't see the point in bringing that up with Vivienne. I had probably already said too much. The rest was sure to cause me grief.

Especially if it got back to the Weatherstones.

I smiled at that thought. Worrying about next week, when tomorrow was the bigger problem. Classic sign of denial.

XIX

"**H**ow much do you know?" I asked Vivienne, indicating the chart on the desk. "Did Marielle tell you what happened?" Who lived, who died, who was left. The litany of wounds sustained so far in this war.

"She did." Vivienne sighed, reluctant to engage on the present. "Most of the secret masters are dead. Are the remaining Architects working in concert to remove the rest, or are they still targeted? Is there some unknown party behind the whole affair?"

"The guys who hit the Chapel of Glass came with soul locks and whoever was running them put an oubliette around the chapel. And, when we were fleeing the apartment, they were doing some heavy-duty structural assault on the building. Trying to bring the whole thing down."

"Geomancy."

"Certainly a step up from reading the pattern of leaves and arrangement of stones, but that'd be my guess."

"So, the Mason. Is he working alone?" She sighed as she looked at the wealth of names on the page. "Impossible to know, isn't it? He could be any one of the remaining Preceptors. Any number of them could be working together too, removing opposition to their own advancement. And what of the other Architects who aren't accounted for?"

"The Mason is Jacob Spiertz," I pointed out, touching his name on the chart. "The Scryer is Ulrich Husserl, and he's still out there too. The Thaumaturge is... missing. The impression I got was that he was unaccounted for, but not dead. What that means I don't really know. And the Shepherd is..."

My gaze wandered along the lines connecting Spiertz to the other Watchers, and I spotted a pair I knew. The brothers Vaschax: Henri and Girard. Henri had a tiny symbol next to his name: a "v" in a tight box. Interesting. They had drifted apart in the last few years. No longer matching each other, step for step. Henri had made Viator; Girard hadn't.

Trying to recall the names of the two men who had been with Henri at the airport, I checked the desk drawer for a pen. *Jerome Theirault and Charles Lentier,* Cristobel reminded me. I found a black ballpoint in the top drawer and added their names under Henri's.

"You know Vaschax?" Vivienne asked.

"I'm the reason he limps."

"You do leave an impression on people, don't you?"

"Not intentionally," I argued. "It just... that's the way situations turn out. Sometimes."

"I'm sure they do."

I let that slide, and continued to make notes: labeling Husserl as the Scryer, drawing a line connecting Father Cristobel and Vivienne's father (if there wasn't a connection before, there certainly was now), and putting a thick box around Antoine's name. He was way out on the edge of the chart, as if they couldn't decide what to do about him. He'd like that placement.

Next to his name was a small lowercase "p" within a circle with tiny lines radiating from the circle like eyelashes. Protector-Witness. I started to cross the symbol out and write his new title, but a spasm in my arm sent the pen sliding away.

It's his secret; let him keep it awhile yet.

Vivienne misread my hesitation. "You and he have fought

over Marielle, haven't you?"

"It was a long time ago," I said.

"But these things are never really forgotten, are they?"

"No," I admitted, thinking more about why the Chorus didn't want me to reveal Antoine's secret. There was the obvious reason: I didn't know Vivienne all that well, and she clearly had some history with both Antoine and Marielle. Who knew what she would do with the information should I give it to her.

I was starting to see some of the paranoia that Delacroix had disliked about Chieradeen. You started to not trust anyone whom you didn't know intimately. And even those people could have motives they weren't being clear about.

"He has the key."

"What?" I asked, jerked back to the present.

Vivienne tapped Antoine's name. "You said he has the key."

"Yes," I said, catching up with the conversation. "Well, I think he has it. I'm not entirely sure. Well, almost one hundred percent. But—" I glanced around the room. There was no one there but the two of us, yet the sensation was strong that we weren't alone. The spirits in the Chorus, notwithstanding.

Paranoia. Another symptom of schizophrenia.

"He had the opportunity—" The words slid out of me almost unconsciously, distracted as I was by the thoughts in my head.

"When was this?"

I blushed. "When I first arrived yesterday morning. Marielle met me at the airport and—"

"Just Marielle? Not her and Antoine?"

"No. Just her. Antoine showed up later, when we were in trouble."

Vivienne nodded. "The incident at the airport. Terrorists supposedly hijacked a train and tried to deliver a bomb to Gare du Nord."

"It wasn't a bomb. It was me and Henri. And…" I tapped the pen on the page. "…some friends of his."

"So you called in the big guns."

"No, she did."

Vivienne spread her hands. "She did. Okay. What happened next?"

"I… uh—" The Chorus sparked, and I felt the sharp spike of their energy down in my hips. "I told Marielle that her father was dead."

A smile that gave me goose bumps rose on Vivienne's lips. "Was it an accident?"

"Yes. I hadn't meant to tell her. Not then."

"No. The Hierarch's death."

I stared at Vivienne, trying to read the light in her eyes. "No," I said, finally.

"Did you kill him?"

I nodded. "At his request."

"Are you sure?"

I cast back to that final conversation with Philippe. *I am beginning to forget things,* he had said. *I've Seen too many springs.*

Is the organization supposed to die with you? I had asked, and he hadn't answered that question. Not then. But earlier, he equated himself with the organization, and the organization had become diseased. It could no longer support life, and it had to die. Vivienne's point was well taken. Philippe had never said it outright—*kill me, Michael*—but the inference had been clear, and he had let me touch him with the Chorus.

Though, in hindsight, I wasn't sure the Chorus had harvested him properly. In the past, they had been a voracious hunger, driven by the *Qliphoth* to harvest darkness so as to keep the lies intact. Philippe had been the first soul I had taken since that night, and it was like the new voices didn't know how to do it correctly. Thinking about it now, though, I wondered if the problem wasn't that the Chorus was doing it wrong—that I had somehow forgotten how to break a soul—but that the Hierarch had leveraged some loophole in my mind. Some trick by which he could remain a separate personality within my patchwork soul, and now that he had friends, they were building a separate community within my brain. Kind of like a rogue state inside your national boundaries.

"No," I told Vivienne. "I'm… not sure."

Nothing is ever lost; it is simply transformed. The memories kept overlapping. Mine and Philippe's and Cristobel's and Lafoutain's. More so than the old Chorus had ever been, these new additions complicated my identity, confusing my self with this scattershot amalgamation of past experiences. The Chorus had been my psychic anchor, a nexus through which I drew power that sustained me as I did magick, and I no longer needed them for that. The upside of the Ascension Event had been a healing of the split in my psyche. I no longer believed in the hole in my soul, and as a result, I had been more able to actualize energy from the leys.

The Chorus was still my conduit, though, an old habit that was integral to my understanding of how magick worked. But they had changed too, and their new formation had new secrets. Nothing approaching the *Qliphotic* agenda that had driven me back to Seattle, but a subtle influence on me nonetheless.

You will be your own agent. That is all you will ever be.

"I'm sorry." I shook off the echo of the Old Man's suggestion. "I don't mean to be difficult. It's difficult to explain what happened…"

"Why don't you try?" She glanced at the table, and saw something there that caused a momentary hesitation. She touched my wrist, and through the contact, I felt the warmth of her pulse. "Tell me what ails you," she Whispered, and the words remained in my head, a glowing script floating in the cavern of my brain.

My hand had been fidgeting with the pen, and the touch of her fingers stilled that energy in my hand. I had been doodling on the page. Tiny strokes, over and over, blackening a tiny spot in the margins. A curve, two lines, a third perpendicular to the two. A curve, two lines, a third. Over and over again.

The shape of a cup, like the Ace of Cups.

The glowing words compressed into an ornate key that dove into the shadows of my skull, finding a lock. The one that, apparently, controlled my tongue. Almost without realizing I was doing so, I started telling her the truth.

"Philippe… bequeathed me certain gifts when he died. The key, his ring, and his deck of cards. Those were the physical artifacts I got, but there was something else too."

I set the pen down and moved away from the table. I was full of nervous energy all of a sudden, and I wanted to move about. To not be caged. It was like going to confessional and finding the small box too crowded, too full of your guilt and need to talk to someone about what you had done. I had had a long time to live with my guilt, and until now, I had never been overtaken with such a need to talk about it. And yet, in this room with Vivienne, I wanted to tell her what had happened. I wanted someone to know my side of the story, before it got lost in the noise of the Chorus.

"He gave me the symbols of his office because I was an outsider, because I had no stake in the outcome of the contest for the Crown. I didn't care who wore it next; it wasn't my fight. But I was uniquely positioned to be an…" I searched for the right word, falling through a sudden tear in the nebulous veil of the Chorus. Falling and finding myself in a place without shadows, a place of clarity. "…arbiter, I suppose, an arbiter of the ultimate selection for leadership of the organization."

I started pacing, my legs working off some of the energy coursing through my nervous system. I had been unlocked, and Vivienne's key had unleashed a torrent of words and thoughts. The Ace of Cups, spilling its water. The flood of life, unrestrained. I didn't want to think about where this desire was coming from; I wanted to let it all out.

"Philippe knew there were members of the organization who were actively plotting to remove him. But as long as he remained bound to his office, they were forced to skulk in the shadows and attack his power in an indirect way. When their effort to create a new Hierarch failed, they fell back to a secondary position: mortally wounding him by wounding the Land. His strength reduced, they could more readily best him physically. If it came to that."

"Did it?"

I shook my head. "No, he beat them to it. He died before they could take his Crown."

"Giving it to you."

"Yes."

"And it isn't a physical gift."

"No. It is his…"

"Essence?"

"Essentially."

"And what are you supposed to do with it?"

I stopped pacing. "I don't know."

She nodded. "No wonder Marielle brought you to see me."

"Excuse me?"

She closed her eyes for a moment, and the room felt darker. All the exhaustion of the day came racing back to the forefront of my brain. On the desk, the tiny drawing I had scribbled no longer looked like anything important. It didn't look like the Ace of Cups at all, and a tiny part of me wondered what I had been thinking.

Something had definitely changed in the last moment, but I didn't feel like I had been conned, or that the words had been taken against my will. Quite the opposite. It had felt liberating to tell her, and now that it was done, I was glad to be rid of the weight. But whatever glamour had been on me, it was gone now. In the back of my throat, something clicked shut and my tongue felt heavy in my mouth again.

She sat down at the desk and laid her hand on what I had thought was the mouse pad beside the keyboard. It glowed beneath her fingers, a green light outlining her hand.

"What rank did you achieve when you were actively part of the fraternity, M. Markham?"

"Please, Michael." We might as well be on first name basis, after that confession I had unleashed. My tongue still felt a bit wooden. "I made Journeyman."

"Seventh Degree?"

I flushed. "No. Only Third."

"And how long have you been gone?" The computer came out of sleep mode, and the light from the LCD screen illuminated her face, highlighting the shadows under her eyes. "Did you study during that time?"

"Five, no, six years now. I've been teaching myself since then."

"Ah. *Venefice.*"

"I wish you wouldn't put it that way."

"You were—are—an unrecognized and self-taught magus, who was given access to the teachings of the society and who, while retaining those teachings, no longer answers to the hierarchy to which you once swore an oath. I don't know; what name would you give to that sort of person if not 'traitor'?"

"How about 'free radical'?"

"All right, *solūte frater.*" With just a touch of sarcasm in her voice. "Let me ask you a few questions."

She moved her hand across the pad, mousing with her fingers, and the flat screen on the wall came to life, displaying a line drawing of a human figure, but overlaid with the ten spheres of the Tree of the Sephiroth. The sphere at the top of the tree floated over the figure's head. This was *Kether,* the holy crown at the apex, and it wasn't by accident that it appeared to be a halo. Much like the representation of saints in medieval art and iconography.

Like the saints in the watercolors and stained glass at the Chapel of Glass.

"What's this?" I asked.

"You tell me," she said. "What does it look like to you?"

"It looks like an overlay of the Sephiroth on an anatomical drawing. Like da Vinci's Vitruvian Man without all the geometric distractions. It looks modern though, like some aspiring occult student did some sketching and didn't bother with doodling a bunch of commentary around the margins."

"Very likely," she acknowledged. "But what does it represent?"

"It's the symbolic representation of mankind. Rather, humanity, if you prefer a more gender-neutral word. We stand upon the globe of *Malkuth,* and the forces and energies of the Sephirotic realm travel up through our bodies so that we may attain the enlightened awareness of *Kether.*"

She selected an icon on her screen and the picture changed. The figure was no longer standing with its arms outstretched over the Sephiroth of *Geburah* and *Chesed* – Strength and Mercy. Now, the figure was in the traditional crucifixion pose, and resting in his open and upturned palms were the globes of *Binah* and *Chokhmah,* the spheres of Understanding and Wisdom. His head was bent at an angle, and the sphere of *Kether* was a solar disk pressing down on his neck, like a vast weight.

A dim line went through the man's neck, separating the head from the body. It was the line on the tree between *Binah* and *Chokhmah,* and the center of the line corresponded to the base of the man's throat. Right where *Daäth* lay, the entrance to the nightside of the tree. The Abyss where the *Qliphoth* dwelt, where they waited for the innocent to call them forth.

"And this one?" she asked.

I swallowed the lump forming in my throat, a sympathetic memory of the night in the Pacific Northwest woods where I was initiated into magick and touched the Tree of the Sephiroth.

I made the mistake of touching that dark spot between *Binah* and *Chokhmah*. "The ascended martyr," I croaked, as I turned away from the screen. "The one who knows he cannot sustain the weight of the tree. But he bears it anyway, and so it crushes him."

I closed my eyes, but the image was still there, and the similarities between Vivienne's picture and the enormous Christ figure in the Chapel of Glass were readily apparent. Head bowed by the weight of the crown, no longer supported by Strength and Mercy, but holding Understanding and Wisdom in his bloodied hands. This was the magus who Knew, who had Seen beyond the veil and understood the nature of the Divine. This was the man who died, knowing who he was and what he would become. I had thought the figure had been sleeping, but there wasn't much distinction between sleep and understanding.

Philippe Emonet understood. Hierarch of the Watchers, Architect of Architects. *I am the Silent Guardian Who Waits.* In that down-turned face, in the serenity that wreathed the slumbering visage, was peace.

When I had killed him, when I reached into his heart and broke his soul, he had smiled.

"I am the daughter of the Scholar," Vivienne said after a moment. She spoke quietly enough that I had to come away from my own thoughts to hear her. "I am the chief librarian of the Archives. I have devoted my life to the illumination of knowledge. I don't like questions that appear to have no answer." She waited for me to look at her before she continued. "Like: Why did the Hierarch choose to give an untested, untrained, and uninformed magus—a dumb courier, at best—the symbols of his office? So that you could arbitrate?" She shook her head. "I don't think so."

Peace is not for us, Michael. Responsibility yes, but not peace.

Something popped in my chest. A reaction to those words, to this question. "It's a perfectly valid answer," I snapped. "You just don't care for the inference that it carries. Philippe wanted someone untested, untrained, and uninformed in the ways of the organization because that would be someone he could trust. Not the rest of you.

"I am supposed to seem like a clueless monkey sent to deliver a message, and fortunately enough, I am pretty good at that sort of charade. But I'm not, and while this game of rubbing my nose in my lack of formal training might be fun for you, it's the very sort of self-righteous and sanctimonious attitude that has poisoned—"

She stiffened. "I'm not—" With an angry swipe of her hand, she blanked the screen. "You think this is about power? About me not being happy that after a lifetime of service to these Archives I'm supposed to eagerly welcome some rogue magus into my sanctum? 'Oh, sure, come in. No, I don't mind that you've thieved two of our more prized artifacts from us. No, not at all. I don't mind that you're a fucking clueless idiot who has no idea what is going on. It's okay. I'll wipe your ass and hold your hand.'"

Her vehemence surprised me, and I fumbled for a minute, trying to figure out where this came from. Okay, so maybe I had come on a little strong, but I was getting tired of everyone wondering how in the world I had managed to get the keys to the kingdom. "It's not like that," I said. "I didn't ask for ——"

"Oh, with all due respect, go fuck yourself." She put her hands in her lap and sat rigid. Her eyes were moist, and she took several slow, deep breaths.

This isn't about you, Lafoutain murmured, and Nicols reminded me of the pain one takes on when death comes close to you.

"I'm sorry," I said after a time with a voice that wasn't entirely mine.

"For what?" she asked sharply. "You killed her father, not mine."

I took a deep breath and pushed the Chorus away so that I

could speak without their influence. "I'm sorry," I said, "that your father isn't here to tell you himself how much he loves you, *little chicken*. I'm sorry that, in *this* instance, I am just a dumb courier, because it is no substitute for the real thing."

A tear slid down her right cheek. When it fell onto her clasped hands, she became aware of it, and she came out of her mental trance. She sniffed once, and pushed the next tear back with a knuckle. " 'Little chicken.' " She shook her head. "He hasn't called me that in… a very long time."

Her hands fell back into her lap and she stared out the window. "My father and mother haven't spoken since I was seven. The last time I saw her was the summer of my twelfth year, when I visited her in Tromsø. I didn't want to come back to Paris. My father had to send someone to come get me, and I hated him for a very long time for that. I didn't want to be his daughter; I didn't want to serve. I wanted to be my own person, to not be anyone's 'little' anything."

When she paused, it would have been polite for me to ask what changed, what happened to make her feel differently about her father, but I couldn't find the words. My chest was tight, and the Chorus was a heavy weight, pulling me down.

"It doesn't matter what we think, does it?" she said. "We can't control how other people love us, can we? Eventually we recognize that they do."

With some awkwardness, I became fascinated with my shoes. And the carpet.

"Goddess help you, Michael Markham," she said after an excruciating pause, "if you are that alone."

I chuckled. "Far from it." To lend the statement some weight, I met her gaze and dared her to call me a liar.

She looked away. "Of course. How silly of me."

Which only cut worse. To be so summarily dismissed.

She smoothed her hair, even though not a strand was out of place, and swiped her hand across the pad once more. The computer came out of sleep, and she found another icon. "Is this the key you lost to Protector Briande?" she asked as another image came up on the flat screen.

We were done sharing, it seemed. Back to the business at hand.

On the slowly rotating image, the bow was intact, and I examined the intricate carving and scrollwork. "Yes, though the top had been smashed." It appeared to be a three-dimensional combination of several pentacles.

"Before or after you received it?"

"Before."

"By Philippe?"

I searched my memory, and the Chorus swirled around my effort, both aiding and confusing my attempt. Philippe's spirit remained elusive, unwilling to come forward and offer a helpful hint. "I don't know." I wandered over to the screen to get a better look. "Can you freeze it?"

She did, and I peered at the symbols. "What are they?"

"We're not sure, and these are, at any rate, only a best guess. But we believe they are binding talismans."

"And the blade is wrong," I pointed out. "The teeth were… elusive. You couldn't focus on them. They kept changing."

"I know. It's not possible to show that readily in this program," she said. She was actually warming to me a little now, almost as if we had gotten past that awkward dance of verifying each other's credentials and were now talking as peers. Or almost peers. "Even though the program used to draw this is a modified auto-CAD, it doesn't lend itself well to animated loops."

"A loop? Not an endlessly random sequence?"

"Perhaps," she shrugged. "I've never actually seen the key. This graphic is an amalgamation of several sources."

"What does it open?"

She selected another image from the computer and sent it to the remote screen. A still photograph of a castle on a rocky promontory. A rounded dome with a tiny gold figure mounted on the top stood at the peak of the hill. Around the base of the cliffs was an endless expanse of blue water. "Do you know this place?"

"Mont-Saint-Michel," I replied. "On the coast."

"Have you been there? Recently?"

"No," I said, and then: "Yes." A flash of memory. The green grass of a cloistered space, surrounded by the peaked arches of a sanctuary. Then: vaulted ceilings with exposed ribs; an underground space, barely a niche, hidden behind one of the oldest walls. The floor before the small stone altar was covered in script, radial arms spiraling outward from a central starburst. Closer to the altar, there was a smaller starburst of script, and when I put the key in the center of the smaller image, all of the script—both sections—flashed white and violet, a series of wards coming to life.

The memory fled quickly as I tried to anchor it, and all I was left with was a smoldering sensation in my palm as if I had briefly held a warm stone.

"Which is it?" Vivienne asked.

"I'm having trouble with my memory. It's not all… linear, and—" I searched for a good way to describe what it was like to have memories of a time prior to my birth. How could I tell her without going into an extensive discussion about what the Chorus was and what I did with it?

You can't. So keep it simple. Tell her a version of the truth. Something you can believe.

"No," I said firmly. "I visited once, many years ago. But *I* haven't been recently. What's there?"

"One of the two artifacts necessary for the Coronation."

"Which one?" I asked, as if I knew what they both were.

"The Spear of Longinus."

The air fled from my lungs, and I mentally counted to ten as the pressure on my chest began to ease. The Chorus buzzed in my ears and my skin tingled with all the excitement normally reserved for the minute and a half before the first item went up for bid at a Sothby's antiquarian auction.

If the Spear was one part of the tools needed for the Coronation, what was the other? The answer floated in my head, an image almost teasingly offered by the Chorus—the tarot suits: Wand, Disk, Sword, and Cup—and I couldn't quite believe it.

I realized Philippe had given me his tarot deck, not just as a means to communicate with me, but also as a symbolic representation of the mystery of his office. If the Spear of Longinus mapped to the suit of swords, then what would map to the other suits? There was an obvious answer, when I thought about it, and while I couldn't quite believe, the Chorus simply countered with a simple question: *Why wouldn't they have it?* This was the archives of the *La Société Lumineuse,* after all. If there was any place where such artifacts would reside, it would be here.

Which posed an interesting question.

The Chorus released their hold on my chest finally and I could draw air. "Why isn't the Spear here?" I asked.

Vivienne favored me with a withering look.

XX

While Vivienne and I had been talking, Marielle had been arranging transportation, anticipating the need for a vehicle of our own. Too keyed up by my conversation with Vivienne, I offered to drive, and the dashboard GPS directed me to the A13, heading toward Mont-Saint-Michel. Traffic was light at this time of night, and within a half-hour, I was far enough from Paris that the flow was barely a trickle, and most of it was heading back toward Paris.

Marielle was curled up in the back seat, my bunched up jacket a pillow beneath her head. I resisted the temptation to tilt the rear-view mirror enough so that I could keep an eye on her. I had enough on my mind already; I didn't need the extra distraction of watching her sleep. Of wondering what she was dreaming about.

One of two.

Vivienne said there were two artifacts necessary for the Coronation ceremony. While I had managed to eke out the identity of one—the Spear of Longinus—my gut told me the other one was the Grail. The Grail was stored at the Archives—it had to be—and, for no reason other than perhaps the danger of having two such artifacts in constant proximity to each other, the Watchers didn't store the Spear in the same location.

My brain couldn't stop repeating the words: *the Holy Grail;*

the Cup of Christ.

Every child knows at least one version of the Grail story—the Roman Catholic version, at the least. The Grail was the cup Jesus Christ drank from at the Last Supper, and, in all probability, was the one he offered to his Disciples when he asked them to drink the wine that was his blood. Other Christian versions say that the cup was received by Joseph of Arimathea when he interred Jesus' body in the tomb—kind of a party gift from a ghost of the Messiah.

Pagan mythology claimed the Grail was Celtic in origin, maybe even Bran the Blessed's cauldron of mighty resurrections; or that it was a curved plate used to carry the head of a king through the phantasmal halls of the Chapel Perilous. Chrétrien de Troyes' final romantic poem of the twelfth century was all about the Grail, and though never finished, it was the symbol by which the questing knight was to be recognized. When the seeker was pure enough, the Grail would come to him, and he would be able to heal the king, thereby restoring the land.

It was the holy fucking grail—literally—of Western esoteric artifacts. The thing that every occult relic hunter and alchemy-obsessed magus spent their lives searching for. The Nazis had come close to finding it during WWII; at least, that was the persistent myth that refused to be easily debunked. Where had the Archives been before Tour Montparnasse had been built? Was that part of the reason Hitler occupied Paris? To find the Grail?

The Nazis had the Spear of Longinus, but hadn't known how to use it. The Gospel of John reports that Romans wanted to break Jesus' legs in order to quicken his death—nothing makes an occupying army more nervous than a martyr who refuses to die quickly. Before they could do so, an unnamed soldier stuck Jesus in the side with his lance. Whatever came out—blood, water, or both—convinced the soldiers that the Messiah was dead, and they went away to conquer the rest of Europe, thinking they had squashed the local groundswell of mysticism.

The point of the lance, covered with the blood of Christ, passed into legend as an artifact of mystical power. Along with nearly every other trinket from that day on Golgotha. What made the lance valuable to any earnest megalomaniac was that it was supposed to grant invincibility to any army that you lead. As a mechanism for propping up one's psychoses, the Spear was hard to beat. Though, having the Spear didn't work out all that well for Hitler.

There was another version of the story of Joseph of Arimathea, one where he already had the cup—before Christ died—and when the soldier stabbed the Messiah, Joseph held up the cup and caught the falling blood. Was that the story that bound these two artifacts together? Could you only work the Spear if you had the Grail? Was that the trick?

There are no tricks, Father Cristobel pointed out. *There is only belief.*

"Belief in what?" I muttered, glancing back at Marielle. She didn't seem to hear me; I could probably have a conversation with the spirits and not disturb her. "That Christ was more than a magus with a flair for dramatic presentation?"

Maybe they are symbols. Representations that bind the mind. Is the Coronation a reenactment of the Crucifixion and Ascension of Christ? And if so, what is accomplished with this Passion play of death and resurrection?

"You tell me. Is that what the ceremony is all about?"

What are you willing to believe?

"No," I said. "It is what I Know that matters. Not what I believe."

Is it? Faith gave me back my sight. It gave Lafoutain the strength to face his destiny. It gave Philippe the insight necessary to wield his power. Why do you believe it has failed you?

"I don't—" I struggled to find an answer that wasn't an hour-long diatribe. An answer that was also honest, to both him and me. When I had been at the top of the tower, facing Bernard and his Key, I had been sustained by faith. I didn't Know what would happen after I gave up the Chorus and faced the Key. I didn't know what my sacrifice would give me.

I still didn't know. I could remember what happened after the Key detonated, but it was like someone else's dream. I had enough of those sorts of things in my head to know the difference between my own memories and those I collected. My memory of the palace of wind had two perspectives, and I wasn't sure which one was true. Or if they both were. Or if they were both nothing more than a dream.

But what isn't a dream? Life is nothing more than a series of wakeful and dreaming states. States that, in retrospect, the mind transforms into some allegorical and mythological justification for existence. Descartes said *"Cogito, ergo sum,"* but that only provides for a singular point of existence. What makes us human is the order offered by sequential history. Thinking and learning and thinking again.

But that was still a linear, nearly mechanistic existence. Simple computation. The type that we can replicate with a computer. Computers could, with extensive enough programming, argue that they, too, could pass the *cogito, ergo sum* test, but that only meant they were highly functional.

How do we become nonlinear? How do we learn to consider the possibility of consciousness and knowledge beyond what our brains currently hold? With the act of dreaming; the act of faith. Free Will was the ultimate expression of faith, wasn't it?

That was the crux of Cristobel's question, really. Did I Know the Cup of Christ and the Spear of Longinus existed, or was I willing to believe in them? If they existed, they were incredibly valuable historical commodities, so valuable as to be worthless on the open market. Considering them as religious artifacts, they would validate several thousand years of Church doctrine, and probably cause all manner of self-fulfilling prophetic apocalyptic reactions. As objects with mystical powers? Well, that was a bit trickier.

Prior to two months ago, I would have doubted the last. I would have acknowledged the first two and that would have been enough. But, having experienced the power of *The Book of Thoth*, I suddenly wasn't so able to dismiss the possibility anymore.

That was the trouble with questions of faith.

Perhaps, Cristobel offered as he faded back into the phantasmal body of the Chorus, *the Cup and the Spear aren't important. Perhaps they are simply tools for a ritual.* His voice faded into a crackling storm of noise, a tempest of memory and emotion stirred up by the Chorus. *Rituals are the chains that bind us together.*

And through the storm of the Chorus, there came a bolt of clarity, like sunlight piercing a dense layer of rain clouds. I almost slammed on the brakes and stopped the car as I lost track of what was real and what was in my head. The vision passed in a second, but in its wake, there was a lingering strand of light, a flickering series of loops that I could follow back through the noise. Like a chain, or the stones of a rosary.

Anamnesis. Remembering what you have forgotten.

All the memories in my head, all those echoes of other men and other times, they were a chain. I hadn't been able to make sense of them because I hadn't any sense of context. But there was a way to understand them, to see how they all fit together. I had been confused by their overlap, by how they seemed to be variations of the same event, and in many ways they were. They were all celebrations of the same event: the same classic cosmological rebirth sequence. You celebrate the beginning of the world by re-creating that moment of Divine Birth. Each Hierarch came into power through this same ritual. Over and over again. Across several centuries. That was the chain that bound them all together.

When I grabbed the chain of light, the storm of the Chorus broke, splitting open like an enormous sunflower blooming, and its petals stretched all the way to the edge of my vision. I fell into the sunlit embrace of the petals, tumbling through a haze of light and dust, and I passed through a veil and out the other side where I saw the living pattern of the Weave. And I Knew what it was.

The Weave was a tapestry, a mass of threads woven together into a complex pattern too vast to comprehend. It was the Akashic Record of our souls, the threads that bind us to each other and to the world. We are who we are because of the passage of our threads through the Weave. It is. It was. It will be. Everything. All laid out in an infinite tapestry of existence. This was the body of God.

As I floated over the infinite canvas, I realized it was three-dimensional as well, having a depth that I could now perceive. This was how the Hierarch saw it; this was why Cristobel insisted that it wasn't a weave at all. Beneath the surface, the threads were tangled and knotted in unceremonious clusters and clumps; they were folds and ripples across time and space. I felt a whisper, a silent exhalation of agreement. Yes, these were the loops created by each Hierarch during his reign. The visible record of their manipulation of the threads—the cutting, the splicing, the severing: all the marks of their secret touch upon the world. And *there*, a clustered knot larger than any others. That was the knot through which all the Hierarchs passed. That was the knot where they were born and died.

The Cup and the Spear were, like all things man creates, nothing more than symbols. Tools by which the world can be re-created. But there is a difference between normal rituals, like the ones we do every day or even once a week in the sanctity of our churches, and sacred rites. That difference is magick. And magick comes from Will. And Presence.

I carried Philippe Emonet's presence in my head. Parts of his soul were still here, trapped in the web of the Chorus.

It didn't matter if I believed that the Watchers had the Grail and the Spear, there were others in the organization who did, and they believed in their ritual. They Knew of the power behind the rite. They knew someone got to be Crowned, and in doing so, would become the Hierarch. They wanted to Know the future, because it would be the one they imagined. The one they could manipulate into existence.

They wanted to Know the secret of the Body of God, and they would spill blood in order to achieve that vision because that was the way the ritual worked. *This is my body. This is my blood.*

That was the way they knew how to transfer the spirit from one body to another, and the spirit they wanted was Philippe's because he knew the secrets. He Knew.

I blinked, snapping back to the car and the road, and the image of the Akashic Weave vanished. With the reduction back to the microcosm of my own head, I found some clarity as well, a focus consumed by one question.

"Who does Philippe want to be King?" I said it out loud, thereby anchoring myself in the flesh again. Anchoring myself with the basic question that simplified all of the confusion of histories in my brain.

Not only could he See all the threads, but he could twist them as well, and he had been. But to what end?

Why had Philippe given me the key and the ring, and his soul? While Vivienne had posed the question that was bothering her in those words, that wasn't what she really wanted to know. It wasn't the *why* that troubled her, but *to what end?*

My history of Paris—the unfinished business between myself and Antoine, between Marielle and me—had been blinding me. I hadn't been thinking about the bigger picture. About the real reasons why Philippe came to Seattle. It wasn't to look me in the eye and try to justify Bernard's actions—or even the actions of the other Watchers. He knew what my reaction was going to be to his justification for their massacre. He knew I would be angry, prone to the violent nature which haunted me. He knew he could goad me into killing him.

I told myself it was doing him a favor, just as I told him I wasn't going to be his agent of vengeance upon the others. I told these lies, and then acted differently. Just as he knew I would. Because that was the way my thread was wound. A thread he had been twisting for a long time.

Was I his candidate for the Coronation? No. Vivienne was right: I was the wrong guy for that thankless job. However, was I his stand-in, his psychic avatar in the twilight of this era? Was this my penance to be paid for my flight five years ago: to die in the service of the organization that I had abandoned?

That question aside, if it wasn't me, then who was it? Like the slow collapse of a lengthy chain of dominos, a carefully constructed plan was coming to fruition. But, was this still his game, or had it been co-opted by someone else? Had things gotten out of hand, moved far beyond even his undead reach, or were we still beholden to his vision?

Who was it, then? Who had he envisioned as standing at the nexus of this coming era? Who was supposed to be Crowned?

I twisted around in the seat and looked in the back. I wasn't sure, but I thought I saw shadows squirm across Marielle's face. As if she had just closed her eyes.

Sometime after 4:00 A.M., when I had switched over to the A84 and put Caen behind me, the road vanished. The headlights still worked, but they revealed nothing. I glanced further afield and saw no lights either. In the distance, on either side of the road, there had been an irregular stream of lights from farms and tiny clusters of houses, but those were gone as well. Everything was gone; it was like the light of the world had been extinguished.

In the back seat, Marielle whimpered in her sleep. A sublimated cry of suffering that couldn't be held back.

I stopped the car, and twisted around in my seat to touch her. She was shivering, curled up into a fetal position—as much as the seat belt would allow—and when I touched her leg, she spasmed. Her head snapped back, bouncing off the headrest, and her eyes shot open. Wide and staring. Not seeing me. I grabbed at her knee as she started to thrash like she was having an epileptic fit, and when my touch didn't calm her, I bore down harder on her knee.

Her hands shot forward, her fingers wrapping around my wrist, and the Chorus shrieked. The psychic whirlpool was there, but it was a ravenous void now, a sucking hunger greedily pulling at them.

Vis, I told them. Be strong. They held on to the anchor I offered them, and we became like a turtle caught in the path of a tornado: armor up, make as small a target as possible, and ride it out. All storms pass, eventually, and this one did too. Gradually, Marielle's eyes changed: no longer staring unseeingly, filled with stormy fury and blind panic; she came back to herself and knew me again.

"Goddess," she whispered. The white band of teeth marks on her ring finger were bright and visible, as were the bones of her knuckles, stark beneath her skin. She finally realized how tight she was squeezing me and let go. "What was that?"

"I don't know." I rubbed the skin of my wrist, trying to get the blood moving again through the mottled flesh. Part of me was wondering what I had seen in that naked terror in her eyes. *We are all bound to something, be it darkness or light,* the Chorus whispered, recalling the New Year's Day morning and the promises offered and taken between us. *Sometimes we choose which, and sometimes it is chosen for us.*

She fumbled with her seat belt suddenly, struggling to get out of the confines of the car. She was halfway out when she threw up. I rooted around in the bag of processed food I had gotten at an all-night stop a few hours ago for something resembling a clean napkin, and when I got out of the car and offered it to her, she had finished heaving up the contents of her stomach. She accepted the cheap napkin and wiped her mouth.

There were stars in the sky. Orion looked down on us, and I felt less frightened knowing the heavens were still there. Whatever had happened could be more mundane than the terrifying cosmological possibilities of the onset of darkness if the stars were still in the sky. I knew their light was an echo, a stream of electrons that had been traveling for years and years, but my tiny human brain clung to them. *Let us choose this.*

"Can you feel it?" Marielle asked, and when I shook my head, she grabbed my arm. The Chorus flowed down and leaped across the connection of our flesh, and I felt the sucking emptiness again. We were standing on the lip of the Abyss, its yawning need a persistent whisper in our heads. *Give of yourself. Give everything. Feed us; we are so hungry.*

Like the circadian buzz of the soul-dead in Portland, their psychic chatter burrowing into my head as I had walked back to the tower and the unholy theurgic mirror.

"The leys are gone."

My eyes grew accustomed to the low gleam of starlight. The road was there, under our feet and the wheels of the car; a thin breeze, barely a whisper of breath, touched my face when I looked around; but, other than the hum of the car engine and the repeating warning bell of an open door, there was no other sound. The world was still there; it was just a dead zone.

"Look," she said, pointing. Instinctively, I tried to orient myself on the compass points, but without the ley energies, I couldn't tell what direction she was pointing. *Over there* was the best I could do.

A nearly invisible scatter of light clung to the horizon, like a dying searchlight that wasn't strong enough to penetrate a damp coastal fog. Too many shadows. *Too many echoes.*

"How close are we to Mont-Saint-Michel?" she asked.

"I'm not sure. Fifty kilometers maybe. We passed Caen a while back."

I looked toward the other horizon as if I could see the invisible wall of force that had blown through the leys and scattered them. They hadn't been consumed; they had been driven away, and in the absence of that force, they would come back. All things return to fill a vacuum.

"We need to go," I said.

The oubliette at the Chapel of Glass. When the spell holding the grid at bay came down, the psychic energy came back, rushing to fill the void.

I realized how Marielle had been able to pinpoint the light on the horizon. The sucking vacuum wasn't coming from her; she was too attuned to the leys not to feel the hunger of a land bereft of its natural energies, and it was hungriest at the epicenter of the blast.

Beneath Mont-Saint-Michel.

XXI

There was a warehouse fire raging in the industrial district of Avranches. The rest of the city was dark but for isolated pockets of generator-powered illumination, and the fire was a vibrant spectacle of orange and yellow. Beyond the fire, we could see the psychic glow surrounding Mont-Saint-Michel.

Still a ways off, floating in a sea of darkness, the fortified island and cathedral were covered in a haze of sparkling motes. The void at the island was nearly palpable, and the ambient glitter of distressed energy was a pervasive cloud surrounding the rocky spire. Somewhere between ash and snow, the bleak cloud made Mont-Saint-Michel seem like it was caught in a localized snow storm. Fog and ice, filled with glittering reflections of moonlight. A storm made visible only because of the pure darkness beneath it.

Marielle hadn't said a word ever since we had first spotted the island, but I knew what she was thinking. *Antoine*. He had the ring and the key, and Vivienne had been certain that he knew what to do with them. He had come to fetch the Spear before us, and had triggered some sort of psychic trap.

Though to call it a "trap" was to categorize it as the same sort of thing one used to catch rabbits or squirrels or even a bear; this was on a different scale entirely. But the principle was the same: put your hand in for the prize, trigger the snare, and it all comes down on you. In this case, it was like yanking a lever and having a small-yield nuclear warhead drop on you.

Every kilometer we drove got us closer to the island, but it wasn't fast enough for Marielle. The Chorus was turning in an ever-tightening gyre, feeding off her tension. It wasn't just concern for Antoine, there was another, deeper, panic surging in her chest as well. A paralyzing fear, the sort you never thought possible, but which was caught in your chest now as if it had always been there, as if it had been lurking for a long time, waiting to squeeze your heart. The Chorus knew that sensation, and we circled each other, memory and instinct spinning in frenzied orbits.

The GPS guided me to the frontage road that ran along the tide flats, and I ignored the water on the road as best I could, drifting and praying through each turn that the wheels would find dry pavement again. This close, there was physical damage, evidence that the leys had been scattered from their regular paths. The pavement was cracked in places, jarring edges that slammed against the wheels as I drove over them. The tide was in too, further than it had been in years, and sections of the road were under black water. Fortunately, none of it deep enough to swamp the car engine. Yet. I fully expected each puddle to be the big one that would drown the car, but our luck held.

Until we reached the causeway out to the island. Here the ash was thicker, and my lower spine started to ache.

An SUV with its emergency lights flashing blocked the road, and though Marielle wanted me to drive around it, I slowed to a stop. The gendarme who had been waving us off ran over to my side of the car.

"What the hell are you doing?" he shouted at us as I rolled down the window. "There's no road ahead. Where are you going?" His voice was high and strained. However long he had been positioned here had been too long for his nervous system. His face was white with stress, and his eyeballs twitched back and forth like a meth addict going into withdrawal. The ash fell on his cap and melted, white going dark.

Lights going out…

Marielle was out of the car before I could shake off the memory, and the gendarme straightened up to admonish her. She got in close, grappling for his keys, and for a moment, he didn't understand why. It was enough of a pause for her to find what she was looking for and to get her other hand on his face. A small star flared in the palm of her hand and he went down, his fingers digging at his eyes.

"Marielle." I tried to not hit the gendarme with the car door, and by the time I got to the SUV, she was already behind the wheel. I banged on the driver's window as she started the car. "Where are you going to go?" I shouted. "The tide is in too far, and the road is out. You heard him. You can't get there by car."

She slammed her foot down on the accelerator, and the SUV's tires screamed on the pavement. The car fishtailed, nearly clipping me as I leaped back, and shot off down the empty causeway. I had no idea how much of the road was gone, or how far away the break was, and even though I had no hope of catching the car on foot, I ran after her.

Winded, my side burning, I reached the first break in the road. Chorus-sight showed the other side, and it wasn't far—probably not more than fifteen feet—but it was far enough. Chest heaving, I glanced about for some sign of Marielle or the SUV. There were no marks on the pavement as if she had tried to stop, no sign of the car in the partially submerged wreckage of the road in the bay. Even with all the residual etheric dust in the air, the Chorus could still read a faint glimmer trail, almost an afterimage of a heat disturbance, and I wondered what it had cost her to hold the vehicle up across the gap.

Too bad I hadn't taken better notes when Delacroix had been

building the flight circle back at the apartment. Solomon's Pentacles of the Sun were devoted to binding angels to the magi's Will, and the one Delacroix had been working from was specifically tuned to flight. There was a spell we learned as Journeymen, most likely some sort of sub-invocation of the Pentacles drawing, that was useful for making long jumps. Marielle had probably wrapped her magick around the car and hauled it along with her.

I was carrying less weight and the Chorus readily followed my instruction. *Resuscita me.* The etheric net of my spirits unfolded and smashed down like a giant bat wing against the pavement. I popped across the gap, flying clumsily from lack of practice and general lack of aerodynamics, stumbled a few steps on the other side, and caught my footing.

More tracks on the road, a shine of violet light like a slug track across a black streak on the pavement. Where the SUV had landed. Further than my puny leap. *Wasteful,* the Chorus chided with the voice of her father, *such a poor use of resources.*

With him and the other Architects watching over me, I tried not to embarrass myself. I leaped over a few more gaps in the road, and I was starting to think that the first had been the worse, when I came to the big one. The one that killed any question of whether or not we could get a car out to Mont-Saint-Michel. The Chorus flared, extending my visible range, but I couldn't see any sign on the other side that Marielle had even tried this huge jump. It had to be more than double the first one. There was no way she could have hurled both herself and the car that distance.

The Chorus spotted the SUV in the water. It was stuck in the mud, nose-first, and the water barely covered its back bumper. The residual magick on it from Marielle's spells was a thin slick of luminescence in the water. There was no sign of Marielle.

I leaned over, catching my breath. The running and jumping was wearing me out, and I could only imagine how exhausted

Marielle must be. She didn't have the luxury of pulling energy from the leys, and so she was running on sheer willpower alone. How long would that last?

Not long enough, the Chorus whispered. And for what? The car in the bay aggravated my spirits. She had dragged it out this far, and then ditched it. So why bother hauling it along in the first place if it was going to be discarded?

How about some help with my predicament? The gap was too far. I couldn't jump it. Not now, not on my own. *Anyone want to offer a suggestion?*

A phantom—Lafoutain's—intruded into my consciousness, and the Chorus snapped into a spark at my fingertip. The flight circle Delacroix had drawn was suddenly there in my head, and somewhat unconsciously, I started drawing on the ground. Automatic writing, my Will leaving luminous tracks on the pavement. With the leys gone, the circle would lack a proper power source, but it would give me focus. Like the difference between a trampoline and a cannon. The cannon doesn't need the input of your kinetic energy to function; whereas the trampoline is a rubber matt on springs and it only serves its purpose when you jump on it.

A grating noise echoed along the road as I finished the circle, and as intent as I was on the drawing, I hadn't realized this wasn't the first echo. Glancing up, I saw the headlights coming toward me. Two pair. They rose up from ground height and came back down, and the crunching sound of the impact of rubber and metal against concrete rang again.

Someone else was brute forcing cars across the gaps.

I know a trick, I thought, shuffling off the spectral touch of Lafoutain. I snapped fingers of both hands now, raising the Chorus to the tips of every finger. They whined, straining at my control, wanting to trigger the flight circle. I knew I shouldn't wait around—there was almost no chance the approaching cars held friends—but I wanted to see who it was. I wanted to know who was hot on our tail. Following my directive, the Chorus crackled out in spider lines of violet energy, carving lines and script in the pavement. There wasn't time to go all the way to the edges of the road, so I settled for carving deep with my intent, hoping that gravity would do the rest.

I probably couldn't stop them here, but I could make them work harder to cross this final gap. Wear them down a little more, so that when they did catch up with us, they'd be more tired. A little slower. The Chorus chewed across the pavement, writing out the spell, and when I snapped them back, they bound my incantation to the circle. One little hop would set off both.

The first sedan hit its brakes and slid to a stop as I stepped into the circle. Bending my knees slightly, I prepared to jump. The Chorus stroked the car, waiting for the chance to read the astral auras of the men inside.

The second sedan came to a halt too, and a figure quickly tumbled out of the driver side. "No, wait," he shouted as the doors of the lead car opened. I caught a glint of light from polished mirrors.

Henri Vaschax stepped out of the lead car, a nimbus of furious magick flickering about his head.

I threw him a salute—middle finger extended—and lit the circle, leaping away from the blast like a quail startling from the brush. Violet light coruscated behind me, breaking the pavement across the bridge, burning down through the man-made causeway. There was a clap of thunder, followed by a rolling avalanche of concrete falling.

The Archives had a series of maps of Mont-Saint-Michel, plastic overlays charting the centuries of construction and deconstruction of the island. The nineteenth-century modifications when the island was used as a prison. The fortifications erected during the fourteenth century which successfully held the English at bay during the Hundred Years' War. The gothic cathedral, rebuilt after the fire in the early thirteenth century which took most of the village surrounding the peak. The Carolingian chapel built by the Benedictines upon the very spot where St. Aubert supposedly was visited by the Archangel and told to build a church. It was in this crypt, the Chapelle Notre-Dame-sous-Terre, that Vivienne believed I would find the lock which Philippe's key would open.

My magick-fueled jump carried me far, and when I landed on the causeway again, I was within sight of the outer battlements. A pair of old bombards, huge cannons that threw immense slugs of stone or metal, still sat atop the wall. *Les Michelettes,* Lafoutain provided, *left behind by the English when they were driven off from their final siege at the end of the Hundred Years' War.*

This close to the island, the spectral haze made my skin itch. It was like inhaling fine dust, silica that scratched and crackled in my lungs. There were no lights on the island, and Chorus-sight made the etheric snowfall glitter violently. The shadows I saw weren't natural. Too many echoes of death and pain. The island, for all of its quaint tourism, was the site of a great deal of violence over the centuries. The sort of death that didn't fade quickly. Too many souls smeared across the stones.

There was no quick way to the top, not without expending a lot of energy and Will to leap buildings, and as the streets were empty, there was no impediment to the tried and true method of walking. Henri and the others would be on foot too, when they arrived, so as long as I kept moving, I could hang on to the lead I had gained by bombing the bridge.

I jogged up the road, listening to the grating sound of magick and granite dust in my lungs, to the sound of my feet slapping against the cold pavement, to the distant hiss of the ocean beating against the rocky edges of the shoreline; listening for some indication that there was someone else on the island. The desolate silence wasn't the same as that emptiness in Portland following the implosion of the theurgic mirror, but it was close enough that the Chorus moved uneasily in my spine as I ran. If there were still people in the buildings around me, they wouldn't be soul-dead, but they would be on the edge of the void, sliding toward that maddening hunger for light. They would be hiding in their beds, the covers pulled up over their heads, reduced to being children again, afraid of the darkness.

The ground felt sterile and cold beneath my feet. You don't realize how vibrant—how warm—the earth is with all the energy constantly flowing through it. You live with it for so long that you take it for granted. Like the sun. It has always been there, ever since our birth and the birth of all our ancestors. We know—with the certainty afforded us by the rigors of scientific faith—that our planet rotates about its axis, and the presence of the sun is an irrefutable fact of existence. We don't wonder—not anymore, at least—about whether or not the sun will come back.

For a magus, an awareness of the natural flow of energy is the same sort of instinctual belief. It is always there—nourishing us, guiding us, giving us extra-physical aid. When it is gone, when there is no power to draw on beyond your own reservoirs, you realize how tenuous and infinitesimal your Will is compared to the enormity of the Akashic Weave. The land and sea and sky around Mont-Saint-Michel had been stripped of their natural resources, and all that remained was etheric decay. This land was dead, and would remain so until enough light came back. When the light of the sun gave the world its psychic charge again.

The Universe operated as a closed system—and there was no reason to think otherwise—and this void wouldn't last. All vacuums are filled—the first law of *Qliphotic* possession—and having been in the Chapel of Glass when the oubliette fell, I had a pretty good idea of the cataclysmic repercussions the sudden return of the ley energies would bring.

At the top of the road, I reached the base of the Merveille, the three-story structure that ringed the top of the mount. The main cathedral of Mont-Saint-Michel was built across the top of the island, and the surrounding buildings were nothing more than the exposed sub-structure that held the long cross of the church in place. Vivienne's quick history lesson of the buildings flashed through my head. Once past the first gate and the Almonry, I wound around the rock to the first of two staircases that would lead me to the top—the External Grand Degré. The stone steps led to the Châtelet, the narrow spire of stone that was like the long finger of a giant, blocking access to the Abbey proper. Past the defensible cut of the Châtelet, it was the Interior Grand Degré and a maze of vaulted chapels, leading me—eventually—to the open air again with the Cloister and the main cathedral. But Vivienne hadn't thought I needed to go that far. I was looking for the Chapelle Notre-Dame-sous-Terre, one of the oldest chapels.

Every door was already open, a sure sign of Marielle's passage, and I followed the obvious trail: around the rock and up the stairs. Philippe's memories—and the memories of Hierarchs before him—caught up with my feet and the rough stone of the interior passages took on familiar character. The arches and vaulted ceilings were a honeycomb where angels lived.

The wide-eyed look on Marielle's face when Philippe first told her that explanation for church ceilings nearly broke my heart. We had been so innocent once. All of us.

The Chapelle Notre-Dame-sous-Terre had all the unfinished aspects of the original Carolingian architecture: rough blocks of stone held together more by gravity than mortar, window niches cut whenever someone remembered that the human heart needed light, rough arches with none of the ornate finery that would become such *de rigueur* during the Gothic era. The chapel had two sanctuaries, and the northern one was dedicated to the Virgin Mary. Vivienne had noted that during the reconstruction effort of the 1960s, workers had discovered an older wall behind the sanctuary, a wall that was most likely the original wall of St. Aubert's oratory. As I stood in the narrow chapel, I realized they had uncovered more than the first wall.

There was a hole in the middle of the sanctuary floor, and the rim of it crawled with sigils of old ward magick. On the other side of the hole was the mandala and starburst of magick I had picked up from Philippe's memory, filling the space between the hole and the niche where the wall was cut to show St. Aubert's original wall. In the heart of the squirming magick was the flickering knob of the key.

I edged close to the hole and peered down. The script on the walls of the well went down a long way, deep into old rock of Mont Tombe, like veins running through marble, and I cautiously reached out and touched the cold stone. The Chorus skipped off the spell holding the rock back; it was like touching hot glass. There was a breeze coming up from the hole, carrying a whiff of that familiar salty smell.

The Chorus couldn't penetrate the surrounding rock, and all they told me about the hole was that it was deep. There was no sign of Marielle, and while she could have kept on going up to the top level of the Merveille, I had no doubt she was down in the hole.

I kept my arms close to my sides and stepped off the edge of the pit. The Chorus ballooned out in a teardrop shape around me, a long strand running in my wake as if they were reluctant to let go of the surface world. I didn't blame them, but there wasn't any other way down. *Descende*. Gravity pulled my teardrop down and my skin erupted with goose bumps as I passed the rim of the hole. My vision went white with the warding magick for an instant, an overwhelming rush of the legacy of Philippe's memory and the active magick of his wards, and as my ears popped, the white went away.

The well opened up. It was nothing more than a narrow throat through the massive stone block of Mont Tombe that led to a large grotto. The bottom was further away than I had expected, and at first, I thought the warding magick was written on the walls down here too, but when the Chorus tightened my focus, I realized the flickering motion on the walls wasn't thousands of lines of script, but worms of ambient energy boiling through the stone of the grotto. The effect of the energy glow was to fill the chamber with a sourceless luminescence. There were still shadows, but they were out-of-focus shapes that capered madly at the periphery of my vision.

The leys might be gone, but down here, something else was filling that void. The squirming energy was an optical illusion, sort of a heat mirage, and it was more of an echo of history than an actual presence. But something had been here once upon a time, something big enough to fill this space, and it had left an impression upon the stone of this chamber.

The Chorus felt like a very tiny light in my head, and I flashed on a memory of cupping my hands around a flickering heart. Shivering on a cold stone that floated in an infinite emptiness, trying to preserve the infinitesimal spark of their heat. It was cold in the grotto; the constant fluctuation of energy greedily fed on any available source and our lights were not spared.

A tiny stream ran across the floor of the cavern, a rut carved in the rock by centuries of slow, steady flow. The smell of blood was stronger as I floated closer to the flow of water and it wasn't clear if there was something in the water or if it was the water itself that was the source of the smell. The stream came out of the wall below the hole to the chapel and flowed in a looping, curving path across the slope of the floor until it reached a pool at the farthest, lowest corner of the chamber. Standing in the pool, the water halfway up its chest, was a statue.

The most disconcerting thing about the statue wasn't the elongated shape of its head or the vaguely serpentine cords coming off its skull; no, what made me shiver when I looked at the statue was its lack of a face. There was nothing there. Just a ragged blankness, as if someone had come along after the sculptor had finished and had taken a chisel to its features. Stripping it down to a blank slate. But there was still a hint of a face, a patina of shadows that—like the rest of the fluid darkness in the grotto—refused to stay still. It reminded me of Samael and the *Qliphoth*. There was a hole in the statue's chest, right at the water line of the pool. A narrow incision that looked suspiciously like the sort of wound a spear blade would leave.

Marielle crouched on the floor near the edge of the pool, bent over a sprawled figure. Reluctantly, the Chorus let me touch the ground, and the soles of my feet tingled at the contact with the energized stone.

"Is he dead?" I asked, half-hoping.

She shook her head.

Caught in Antoine's metal fist, seemingly fused to the silver, was the long blade of the Spear of Longinus.

XXII

L ike all relics, there's more than one contender for the title, and the Spear was no different. I've seen several over the years, including the spear in Vienna and the one the Vatican keeps in St. Peter's, and while both are imbued with enough history to be effective foci, there's never been any doubt in my mind that all of them are copies. Looking at the object in Antoine's hand now, it would appear that the one on display in the *Schatzkammer* of Vienna was the most representative copy. Though the Vienna lance had the nail bound to it and the wrap of silver and gold.

Often the addition of another holy relic made up for one's lack of possessing the real thing. *Lancea et clavus Domini.* If you repeat a lie long enough, it may become true.

The blade in Antoine's hand had no adornment, and no nail bound to its side with wire. It was a piece of metal forged for functionality: a narrow shape streamlined to slice, with a tapered point that was long enough to reach all the way to the back of a man's chest cavity. The blade was permanently etched with a black stain, and the discoloration made the head of the spear appear to have a shadow, as if there was a light side and a dark side that one could be cut with.

It appeared that the one thing the Vatican lance had right, though, was the broken tip. One of the competing myths about the Spear was that the broken tip was part of another relic (a crown of thorns that had been lost since the French Revolution).

Antoine must have made fingers to grasp the blade, but his magick had evidently started to slip and, as if he were trying to hang on desperately to a slick surface, his fingers had become a slurred mess of ridges and bumps.

The Spear radiated heat, like a hot stone pulled out of a fire, and when I looked at it with Chorus-sight, it was nothing more than a series of flickering shadows—the two edges sliding in and out of focus. As if it were constantly moving, always slicing the world around it. Never standing still. Always seeking a target. Always seeking to draw blood.

It wasn't an evil weapon—that would imply some consciousness residing in the blade—but it had one purpose, and it afforded that purpose to its wielder with all the force and energy it had at its disposal. It was a tool; a tool that, once you put your hand on it, made its intent known to you. Very clearly.

I wondered at the psychic cost of physically binding yourself to the blade. I noticed Marielle was careful to keep as far away from it as possible.

Cradling his face in her hands, she continued to whisper to him, calling him back from the Abyss. The Chorus felt a strong pulse in his body still; his soul was still anchored in his flesh. He was in there somewhere, and I had no doubt Marielle knew how to coax him out.

I walked to the edge of the pool and looked at the blank-faced statue. I didn't have any memory of it; there was nothing in Philippe's history of this sculpture and I couldn't place the style. There wasn't enough of it exposed to be really sure of the physiology, which made dating it difficult, but the work was too smooth—too precise—to be something from as far back as Greek antiquity. Even with a few thousand years of exposure, a statue wouldn't acquire the smooth surface that more modern tools provided. And yet, it still had that patina of age that typi-fied the High Classical Period.

"I don't like this," I said, the Chorus echoing in my voice. "Why was the Spear here?"

This is where it is kept, Cristobel offered, his presence rising out of the squirming storm of the Chorus. *The heart of the rock.*

I looked at the hole in the statue's chest again. The little rivulet of fresh water fed the pool, and yet the water level remained constant, so there must be a drain somewhere. I crouched, and touched the rock. *Still damp.* My finger came away with a delicate rose color, a stain that wiped away easily enough. But a stain nonetheless.

Behind me, Antoine made a noise deep in his throat, and Marielle's whispering stopped. He moved slightly, pulled back to this world by her voice, and the tip of the Spear dragged across the rock. The sound was like nails on a chalkboard, and all the fine hairs on my neck stood up.

"Help me carry him," she said, looking up at me.

"Why was the Spear here?" I repeated, not moving.

"We can talk about it later," she said. "We need to be out of here before the leys come back."

"Why?"

"Michael—" She reconsidered her tone, and her voice soft-ened. "There isn't much time. Please."

I considered arguing with her. Playing hardball and seeing what it got me, but I saw something in her eyes which made me reconsider. It wasn't fear—she had too much armor up for me to see that deeply—but it was something akin to affection. Hiding beneath the exhaustion that dimmed her eyes was a recognition of the pain we were all carrying. The heavy bag-gage that had brought us here, and that we were going to carry with us for some time yet. What stole a little more light from her face was the tired acknowledgement that it wasn't Antoine that we were going to carry out of here, but the weight of some decision as well.

We were already too late to stop whatever had been set in motion. Even if we wanted to. It was like our tumultuous ride on the RER-B train, only this time RATP wasn't pulling the plug. They were giving us more power to hurl ourselves along the track. We couldn't stop the train. Our only hope lay in riding it out and hoping we could get off before it crashed at the end of the line.

Nodding curtly, I helped her get Antoine upright. We did an awkward dance for a moment, trying to figure out how to carry him and keep the Spear away from our bodies, and I ended up dumping him over my shoulder like a sack of grain while she held his arm out. Staggering and slipping occasionally, I made my way back toward the hole.

Ascende. The Chorus formed a lattice beneath us, tightening into a disk of force that I could use to lift all three of us back up to the basement of the cathedral. Marielle stood close, wrapping an arm around my waist; and the Chorus struck sparks from the floor as they became solid and pushed away from the ground.

Antoine flinched and his legs kicked. I tightened my hold on him, and Marielle's hand disappeared from my waist. "No," he groaned, kicking again, and this time his foot caught me on the hip. My hold on the Chorus flickered, and the disk wavered. Antoine flailed in my arms, and I tucked my shoulder down and threw him off.

He sprawled on the ground, and the Spear cut across the rock with a high-pitched whine. A line of fire burned on my upper arm, right below the shoulder, and as I fell the short distance back to the grotto when the Chorus' elevator disk vanished, I noticed the thin slice through my jacket and shirt.

I put a finger in the hole and touched the cut. The Chorus sizzled in my fingertip as I felt blood.

Antoine struggled to sit up, and Marielle knelt beside him, keeping a wary eye on his right arm. "No," he muttered again, his eyes half-open. "We need to leave it here." He dragged the Spear across the ground again, the stone shrieking at the touch of the cold weapon.

I was about to point out the basic problem when the Chorus flooded my spine and skull, erupting into full defensive mode. "Magi." I looked up as if I could see something beyond the noisy haze of ward light. "We've got company coming."

She pushed her hair back. "Can you deal with them?" she asked. "They don't have access to the grid; you should be strong enough." The commanding tone was back in her voice. That tenor of a woman who expected her words to be obeyed.

I hesitated. *I am not your agent.* "What are you going to do about the Spear?" I asked. Her teeth were starting to chatter. She had used up too much of her reserves getting here, and this chamber was leaching her core temperature too fast. Mine too, for that matter, but I was better equipped to keep the suction at bay. Without the leys to bolster her resources, she was fading quickly.

"There isn't time to argue," she said, biting off the end of her words. She grabbed Antoine's shoulders and sat him up. *There isn't time.* She was berating both of us. "Go, wolf. Show no mercy."

I was going to object, but the Chorus blossomed into a stalk of energy, lifting me away from the ground.

She Whispered one last command to me. In case I hadn't gotten the hint clearly enough. "Kill them all."

The Chorus sang in reply, and I shot up faster toward the chapel.

I had some vain hope that the Chorus had warned me early enough I could get back to the Châtelet as it was a nicely defensible position, but I wasn't going to get that lucky. I got as far as the large chamber known as the Ossuary before I met the Watchers.

There were five of them, clustered near the far end of the Ossuary, and for a moment, we froze, staring at one another. Familiar faces—some of them going back a few days, the rest going back a few years: Charles and Jerome, the two Watchers who had accompanied Henri at the airport; Charles looked pleased to have an opportunity to finish our tête-à-tête from the train car; Henri, of course; and the somewhat expected presence of his twin brother, Girard.

Prior to getting shot in the leg and gaining the limp, Henri and his brother had been nearly identical. Physically, they were mirror images of each other, and like most identical twins, the divergence lay in temperament and character. Henri was the more empathic of the two. I should have shot Girard as he had been the one who had done more of the bloody work back in Béchenaux. He had been the one who had really deserved a couple of steel-jacketed rounds, but as I had given him over to the enraged villagers as one of the architects of the werewolf plot against them, there hadn't been time or opportunity to put a bullet in him.

The last man wore a pair of wraparound sunglasses, and now that I got a good look at him, I knew him.

"Hello, René." René Bataillard had been in Béchenaux too. I hadn't shot him, but I had put a shotgun round through the engine block of his car. He had loved that car, so it had almost been worse that putting a bullet in him. I hadn't recognized him earlier because he had been wearing less flashy clothing. As much a clothes horse as a whore for his car, the best disguise he could wear was simply generic clothing—nondescript grays and black. Not only had I spotted him on Batofar, where he had been the man I had mistaken for a centurion, but he had been at the airport too. He'd been Watching, like a true brother. At least, until he'd tried to warn Henri on the bridge. "You their hunting dog?" I asked.

Trying to charm your way out of trouble again, aren't you?

Lafoutain noted dryly as the Chorus rippled through my skin, rising to the willful challenges evident in their auras. There was another tension in the air too as if each inhalation drew in a denser atmosphere.

The leys, coming back.

René ignored my jibe. "They're back there," he said, pointing with his chin. "In the next chapel."

Girard cracked his knuckles, an ugly smile splitting his face. "Henri said you were back," he said. "I'm glad he didn't kill you. I wanted that pleasure for myself."

There was some new scar tissue around his right eye, and the iris canted inward. I caught myself wondering if he had gotten that from the mob at Béchenaux. I had gone to ground for some time after Béchenaux, staying away from the old haunts, so I wouldn't *accidentally* run into the Vaschax brothers. Of the five who stood against me that night, Bento had been the only one willing to let it all go. I had said my piece on the bluff, calling Antoine to task for winding *all* of our threads, and that had been enough for me. But for Henri and Girard—and to a lesser extent, René—the matter hadn't been satisfactorily resolved.

Nor for Antoine, really. But, then, I had been specifically targeting him. The rest got caught in the middle of our pissing match.

"You sure you boys want to do this?" I asked. The Chorus danced on my fingertips, energy angels ready to strike. "Here. Now. You think you have enough strength?"

Jerome and Charles had come prepared. They side-stepped around the brothers, pulling guns from beneath their coats.

The Ossuary wasn't laid out like a regular chapel space. Not so much as an afterthought, but more from the long period over which most of the buildings on the mount were raised, the Ossuary became a hodge-podge of pillars and vaults. Nothing really matched, and other than the space along the inside wall, there weren't very good sightlines. Which made it easier for me to raise the Chorus' peacock shield and get behind a pillar without taking a bullet.

The report of their firearms was close thunder in the room, and the bullets whined as they ricocheted off the walls.

Karma, I thought, *the circle always closes.* Last time, I had been the one with the gun.

The Chorus had already put together an overlay of the Ossuary, marking each of the Watchers for me. The Vaschax brothers, for all their bluster, knew I was a distraction, and under the cover of the Travelers' guns, were making a move toward the Chapelle Notre-Dame-sous-Terre. René wasn't hanging back like I expected him to; he was creeping along the eastern wall, trying to surprise me from the other side. I couldn't really afford to play cat and mouse among the bays and niches of the Ossuary. There were too many of them. I needed to take the fight to them, and quickly. Jerome and Charles had the only guns—so far—and they were semi-automatic hand cannons from the sound, but the others would be able to do some magick. Nothing big and dramatic. Just the quick and dirty sort of spells that had been my bailiwick for years.

I went to my right, toward René, and nearly took a barrage of gunfire in the face. The rounds left floating star marks in my etheric shield, exploding nimbuses wreathing the hot metal. I ducked behind another pillar, spitting out dust and rock chips as more bullets chewed the column near my head. *In illo tempore.* I squeezed time for a brief instant, and the Chorus traced the trajectory of three bullets as they splintered through the stone. I retreated to the west wall as the Chorus scooped up the tumbling shells and brought them to my outstretched hand.

Hot and misshapen, they sizzled in my palm when I spit on them, and the Chorus outlined each bullet with violet light. Steam rose between my fingers as I squeezed them tight, marking them with saliva and flesh. *Videte nostros hostes,* I whispered to the Chorus, and noting the phantasmal positions of the souls in the room on my psychic overlay, I darted to my right.

René was closer than I expected him to be, and I didn't get my fist primed soon enough. He blocked the jab easily and countered, forcing me to react and step back. One of the bullets slipped from my fist, and without the proper motivation of my energized Will, it tumbled slowly through the air, turning end over end like a fat and lazy bumblebee. René ignored it, knocking aside my arm with a sweep of his own, before landing a solid blow against my stomach.

There was power in his fist, and I had to divert energy or he would have pulped my intestines. It was like getting kicked by a horse, and I was still recovering when Girard came at me from my left. Head down, arms wide. The Chorus folded over me, and I tucked my chin against my chest and tried to cover my head as Girard slammed into me. The Chorus groaned as the magus' Will slammed into me too, and I blinked…

…on the ground, Girard on top of me, his fists banging against my arm and shoulder. *Where had the last few seconds gone?* There was nothing there but a wall of white noise. Chorus noise. Girard was grinning, enjoying himself; René was not—why did I think he had been smiling?—I caught sight of him beyond Girard's wild face, trying to pull the Vaschax brother off me. Almost as if he knew what was going to happen in the next few seconds.

For a moment, the impact of Girard's hands vanished, and I felt nothing. Floating in a zone outside the flesh, outside time. I stared at René, and he stopped pulling at Girard. I couldn't see his eyes behind the glasses, but I knew he was staring at me.

He did know what I was about to do. Those damn sunglasses.

He let go of the other man as I spiked Girard with the Chorus. Right through the chest. All the blazing fury of his soul suddenly laid out before me. The Chorus slammed into his center, and he jerked back, as if I had suddenly become electrified. He wanted to hit me again, the fierce intent was still in his eyes, but his hand wouldn't move. He tried to open his mouth, but it wasn't his anymore. He had no control over his flesh, and as the Chorus lit up his spine to sever the connection between the soul and the flesh, the light in his eyes changed. He knew, too.

René reached across the nave with his Will and grabbed the wooden bench near the wall. He jerked it toward us with magick and the bench slammed into Girard, knocking him off me. The physical connection between us was broken, and the Chorus snapped hungrily at the tender core of Girard's soul, but they couldn't break it open. They had their hooks in him, but without physical contact, it was going to take them a moment to take him apart. A moment he was going to spend fighting back.

One of the pair with a gun came around the edge of a column, and René was already half-turned toward him when I rolled over, whipping my arm around. Even though I had lost track of time, I hadn't stopped protecting what lay in my hand, and as I moved, I transferred the energy in the two bullets. Potential becomes kinetic, and the bullets burned in my hand as I let them go.

Girard was on one knee, shaking and spitting as his soul found purchase in his flesh again. He was aware of what flew out of my hand, and he flinched. It was all he could do.

Not that it mattered. He wasn't the target.

The gunman gurgled—it was Jerome—and his head went back, a new hole opening in his neck. René caught the gun as it fell from his hand—having Seen that future—but he paused as something else clattered to the floor of the chapel. He stared at the black shape on the floor, the broken shard of an object that seemed out of place, and it took him too long to realize that it was a piece of his sunglasses.

Watch our enemies. The Chorus had been more accurate than I had anticipated.

René turned his head in my direction and his sunglasses, the right lens shattered and broken, hung crookedly on his face. "No," he whimpered. There was blood on his cheek from where the bullet had grazed him.

The Chorus blew through him as they dove for Jerome's soul, and he shuddered at their touch, knowing it was his turn next. They hit the coruscating column of light coming off the fallen gunman, and René shielded his naked eye from the sudden flare of psychic light as the Chorus devoured the rising soul. I felt it almost immediately, the cells of my body singing with all the energy coming back through the perpetual contact I had with the spirits.

Girard started shouting a spell, his mouth wide. I didn't even listen to his words. They didn't matter. He wasn't going to finish.

Fire nipped at my heels.

I vibrated with the energy of the three Watchers, and I was bright, a burning light. So enlightened, so engorged with the fresh influx of their souls, I could feel the approaching edge of the psychic storm with ease. The leys were filling in again, and the tsunami wave was coming fast. The stone of the mount was starting to howl with its eagerness to be made whole again. There was so little time left before the wave hit.

In the Chapelle Notre-Dame-sous-Terre, Marielle and Antoine had gotten out of the grotto, but had run afoul of Henri and Charles. As I strode into the room, my psychic senses fully extended, a blade of raw power spitting from my stiff fingers, the Chorus read the situation. Marielle was face-down, Charles kneeling on her back, his gun pressed against her head; Antoine and Henri wrestled for the Spear. It was still attached to Antoine's silver arm, but Henri was stripping the silver away, scattering sizzling globs of liquid metal across the floor. The wards of the hole were blindingly white; they, too, were reacting to the approaching thunderclap of energy.

Charles sensed me coming—I would have been surprised if he hadn't, I was so incredibly bright—and he looked over his shoulder. His grip on his weapon tightened, as if threatening to blow Marielle's head off would stop me, and she shifted beneath him. He glanced back at her, reestablishing his grip on her neck, and his gaze fell upon her face. She had turned her head enough that she could see his face. That he could see at least one of her eyes.

She hypnotized him, spearing him with the eyeball glamour like she had done to Jerome at the airport, and I kept my gaze locked on Charles' head. Veins stood out on his neck as he tried to break free of her suggestion to hold still, but he couldn't tear himself away.

As I came abreast of them, I ripped my hand forward. The blade of force projecting from my fingers sliced through the base of his skull, severing the top of his spinal column and sheering off the back side of his head. I didn't even slow down as he made a funny noise in the back of his throat and collapsed on Marielle.

Henri registered my approach, and he raised his right hand in a gesture of protection—three fingers up, thumb and pinkie touching. His intent was strong, but it wasn't focused. His attention was split between stopping me and reducing Antoine's arm into globs of hot metal. Antoine—ever quick to take advantage of an opponent's distraction—jerked his right arm back, and Henri found himself caught. Silver flowed over his left hand, coating his knuckles, binding him to Antoine.

I hit Henri's shield hard, pouring a great deal of the energy I had taken from his brother into my fist, and the Viator's knees buckled. Henri caught himself before he stepped off the edge of the pit, but barely. Antoine shifted his weight and brought his arm—and the mess of silver, Spear, and flesh—down. Sweeping around, he pulled Henri off-balance and the Viator's only option was to fall to his knees. Antoine kept pulling, crashing to the floor as well, and both men found themselves too close to the rim of the pit.

Antoine tried to pull Henri in with him; Henri struggled to

find some way to anchor himself, some way to get some leverage against Antoine.

"The key," Antoine Whispered, his voice ringing in my ears.

I was already on my way. I leaped over the struggling men, clearing the pit and landing next to the altar. On the floor, the mandala and starburst pattern of script glowed heavily in the thick air. At the center of the pattern was the twisted knob of the key, and I pulled at it, but nothing happened. The key was stuck; it wouldn't come out.

The air in the chapel gusted suddenly, a wave of pressure sweeping into the room. The stone wall behind the altar wept fat tears, beads of clear jelly that welled up from the cracks between the stones.

"You need the ring," Antoine Whispered. "The ring commands the key."

Henri snapped his head forward, smacking Antoine on the forehead. Antoine's focus wavered, and Henri pulled himself halfway free of the silver snare. The metal stretched between them, and I could see Henri's fingers straining for the shaft of the Spear. Antoine snarled and the strands of silver twisted into strands of barbed thorns, tearing at Henri's jacket and arm.

Behind them, the hall started to fill with a radiant glow as the walls reacted to the flood of energy coming back. Marielle was standing next to Charles' sprawled corpse, and she became outlined in light.

Steam rose off Henri's frame as he tried to find energy in the surrounding stone. Antoine held on, his left hand grasping for Henri's face. The light glittered off the band on his ring finger.

There wasn't any time. Not to separate them enough to get the ring from Antoine.

The Chorus filled my hand as I made a fist, and I slammed them against the stone floor. I couldn't get the key out, but maybe I didn't need to. Maybe I didn't need to worry about opening this hole ever again. If I could disrupt the magick of the key, then perhaps its purpose could be co-opted. If the key was acting as a shim that broke the integrity of the ward, then if I could shift it, the ward would seal again. I didn't need to command the key; I only needed to break it.

My knuckles shrieked as I played unstoppable force to the mandala's immovable object. My bones were the most fragile object in the collision and some of them shattered.

Antoine thrust his silver arm below the rim of the pit, hauling Henri closer to the edge. Henri slipped across the floor, and his shoulder and head passed the plane of the pit's opening.

The key broke too, and the ward snapped back. The last thing I saw was Antoine, caught in the stone floor, and Henri, his body twitching, with nothing left above his clavicle; then the storm reached ground zero and everything went white as the world imploded.

THE FOURTH WORK

"…down they fell,
Driven headlong from the pitch of Heaven, down
Into this deep, and in the general fall
I also; at which time this powerful key
Into my hand was given, with charge to keep
These gates forever shut, which none can pass
Without my opening."

— John Milton, *Paradise Lost*

XXIII

Once upon a time, in the Old Kingdom of Egypt, the sun god Ra was bitten by a serpent. Not the normal sort of serpent one finds in the garden, hidden among the trailing vines, but one with a malicious bite (a distant cousin to the sharp-toothed one who wound itself around the Tree in the Garden, in fact). When the serpent bites Ra, he is mystified as to why one of his creatures would wound him so. He kneels on the path and lifts up the tortured snake and asks, *Why do you inflict yourself upon me?*

The answer is, of course, an allegorical riddle: *Because it is my nature.* The snake knows no other way. It is narrow and perfect in its focus, and there are no diversions or branches on the path it knows. Ouroboros, the great Norse serpent, is the symbol for the re-occurring nature of the cosmological cycle, and he is drawn biting his own tail. Why? Because it is his nature, too.

Ra does not understand the snake's answer and so falls ill. Enter Isis, Osiris' wife, who—let's be honest—is the archetypal symbol for the Great Healer. She did, after all, piece together all the pieces of Osiris' body after his brother Set dismembered him and cast the pieces to every corner of the known world. Isis comes to Ra's bed where he lies stricken, and asks, *What ails you, my King?*

I have fallen ill, Ra says, *but I do not know the cause of my sickness.*

I can heal you, my Lord, but I ask a boon.

What is it that you wish? Ra replies.

I wish to know your secret name.

No man may know that secret, he says.

Isis opens the drapes of the tent in which Ra lies and shows him the darkness and sickness that has come over the land as the poison has come over him. The land, locked in the shadow of a perpetual solar eclipse.

The Land languishes, my Lord, and with it, your people, she says. *Do you not wish to save them?*

This poison will pass, Ra says, *I will be well again.*

As you wish, Isis demurs.

But he doesn't get better. The poison ruins his veins, causing him to weep internally, blood and pus flowing into his chest cavity. It ravages his lungs and he cannot breathe. It devours his stomach and he is assailed by an impossible hunger. It descends into his groin and he loses the power to create life.

Isis is summoned by her sister, Nuit, who is equally consumed with despair. *Heal him,* she begs Isis. *Bring him back.*

Isis bends over the ruins of the god, who does not recognize her as the poison has blocked the path light follows from the eyes to the brain, and whispers into his ear. *I only ask a small thing, my lord. Just one tiny word.*

Deep in his madness, some part of Ra hears her, and in the shrunken nut of all that remains of his glory, knows that, without Isis' aid, the light that is Ra will go out. He calls forth the only spark remaining in his heart and binds it to the last breath in his lungs. This chariot and cargo fly through the ravaged cavity of his chest, up through a hole in his throat and into his mouth. When it reaches his lips, the spark is transformed into a single word, and Isis, her ear next his lips, is the only one who hears it.

Empowered by the perfection of this word, made glorious by the presence of Ra's secret name, Isis opens her heart and releases her healing magic. Her love drives out the serpent's poison, and she builds him a new stomach, repositions his ribs, and even reaches down into his groin to warm the cold stone of his sex. She brings him back, and when he wakes, the sun is born again and the river flows once more. The Land continues on.

But she knows his secret name now. That can never be taken back.

As for who gave the serpent the secret of poison? Well, that detail may or may not be revealed by the storyteller. He may leave it up to the imagination of the audience, or he may dismiss all inquiries as to the identity of this miscreant. *It does not matter, he may say. The serpent is villain enough.* For many centuries, the initiates claimed it was Isis who gave the serpent its fangs.

I believe it was Ra himself.

When I opened my eyes, the light was all wrong, and I gradually realized it was soft and ambient and altogether normal. Daylight. I turned my head and discovered I was lying in bed. Next to Marielle.

I had been dreaming. A rocky spur, exposed by the wind from the vast sea of sand surrounding it, had wept water long enough for a verdant oasis to grow around this artesian upwelling. I had been sitting in the shade of palm trees, listening to Philippe tell stories. Cristobel and Lafoutain had been there too; all three were dressed in white—the reflective garb of desert nomads. Nearby, several camels had been contentedly chewing while Detective John Nicols—dressed in a similar fashion—fussed with the high saddles and bags.

I believe it was Ra...

Marielle stirred, and her leg moved against mine beneath the covers. A tiny smile creased her lips as she turned toward me. The comforter was bunched over her, and one of my feet stuck out on my side of the bed. The bed was like a European double, smaller than it should have been, and it was easy to spill over the edge. You also slept close. I moved my hand incrementally and my fingers brushed across her bare hip.

Close enough to touch.

She was as naked as I.

Orange and yellow was starting to bloom on the curtains, sunflowers of morning light. Dawn was less than an hour away; the light through the curtains over the French doors was no longer the monochromatic shadows of Nuit's palette. A long finger of darkness slowly retreated across the wall opposite the bed.

Marielle sighed, and her leg moved further across mine, rocking my hips toward her. My hand slid off her hip, my fingertips trailing across the slope of her stomach. Like running my hand across a warm stove, tingles of heat rose up to my knuckles, which didn't hurt.

Fumbling with the comforter, I extracted my right hand from the covers. My knuckles weren't bruised, and on my palm, there was a deep line that went all the way to the base of my thumb, a trinity of burn marks, and some striations that looked like the fading print of a typographer's stamp. *Half a word…* This was the room where Marielle and I had spent New Year's morning, but my hand bore incongruities, the marks of a different time. Last night—

No. *That* night. Not last night. The apartment in Montmartre had been five years ago. Last night I had been at the coast, in a stony chapel beneath Mont-Saint-Michel. Where I had killed men for their souls. Where the leys had come back in a tsunami-like rush of noise and energy.

Marielle's leg moved again, in a motion that wasn't unconscious. She was awake, watching me, rubbing the edge of her thigh against my leg. "Where are you?" she asked. Her voice had an oddly hollow ring, as if it was an echo.

"Right here," I said, closing my hand and sliding it back under the covers.

She flowed into my embrace, her mouth seeking mine. Breast

and belly and hip followed, and we floated away beneath a sea of white damask as the morning bloomed outside. In our room outside of time, we found each other again.

Is it real? I started to ask, but the words were lost in the sudden quickening of my pulse as her hand found my cock. She raised her head so I could kiss the hollow of her throat, so I could chase the line of her clavicle with my teeth. Her legs parted as she shifted her hips, my hand sliding under her. I pulled her closer, and she squeezed my shaft as I rubbed against the smoothness of her upper thigh.

Her arm around me, she held me close, astride the combination of her fist and my cock. My foot, caught in the sheet tucked around the base of the bed, thrashed and kicked free. Finding purchase on the edge of the bed, I pushed, extending my leg. She laughed as we burrowed further into the pillows.

I eased off, snatching her wrist and pulling her hand off me. Catching her arm between our bodies so she couldn't grab me again, I ground my hips against her, feeling her respond in kind. My cock slid between her legs, and she elevated her hips, inviting me to try again. I felt a tiny tremor run through her left leg as the joint at her hip popped, muscles both remembering and imagining another time and place. This time was easier, not so clandestine as the alcove on the boat, in not such an impromptu position. She rotated her pelvis, inviting me to find my way.

She bit my earlobe, exhaling heavily into my ear as I entered her. *Does it matter?* she moaned, fingers digging into my shoulders. What is real. What is not. It was like the childhood game of plucking petals off a flower. She loves me. She loves me not. She loves—riding a figure eight of motion, back and forth. From shadow to light and back again. From reality to unreality. From what could have been to what was. Back and forth, building speed. Building intensity with each shuddering passage through this central nexus of our cycle. She loves me; *is it real?* She loves me not; *this is how the world is made.*

Tell me, she whispered, and I can't answer for my mouth is pressed against her throat, bruising her with my teeth. Her legs wrapped around mine, holding me tight. *Tell me—*

A light exploded outside the room, the sun erupting into a super nova. Streaks flashed across the wall over the bed, and I reared up, throwing back the comforter. The curtain was flapping on its rod as the balcony door banged open. The sky was burning, a kaleidoscopic confusion of red and orange and black. A confusion of blood-tinged soap bubbles streamed into the room, obscuring the figure standing on the balcony. Outlined in fire.

Beneath me, Marielle shrieked, throwing her head back against the pillows. Her hands clawed at my chest, and her hips bucked savagely. A horrible void swam beneath her, and I was being bent at the middle, caught in the vortex. I tried to pull back, tried to stop from climaxing, but the greedy suction was too much. The pressure on my spine was too much.

For an instant, the room vanished, sucked into that void, and I hung over the Abyss, staring down at the lack of black fire where Choronzon dwelled. Hands held me back, even though my feet were slipping over the edge. Hands around my waist pulled at me, pulling me away from Choronzon's magnetic attraction. More hands followed as the slumbering Master of the Abyss started to wake. Someone grabbed my right hand, and their touch seared the three wounds on my palm. I pulled my gaze away from the fiery halo of the monster below and looked over my shoulder.

They were all there. Philippe, Cristobel, Lafoutain, and the rest. Pulling me back. John Nicols had my hand. *Not like this,* he said. His hand was burned black from where he had touched the theurgic mirror, black and so cold that his flesh burned against mine. I twisted around, grabbing his wrist with my other hand, and the Chorus cracked like a whip, pulling me free of the gravity well of the Abyss.

I fell off the bed, banging my shoulder hard against the wood floor. Sunlight danced on the polished wood, dazzling me. A line of bloody circles led back to the door, and as I managed to focus, more crimson bubbles floated down and popped. There were tarot cards scattered across the floor, spread out in a widening arc from me as if I had been holding them in my hands when I fell. I glanced down at my torso and found a number of them stuck to me like a half-hearted attempt at a loincloth.

On the bed, Marielle was still fucking me, though it was a younger man, an echo of a previous time. Laughing and shouting with delight, her legs wrapped around my waist, she was oblivious to the black shape riding my shoulders, its clawed feet digging into my back. It leered at her, panting with excitement, its one eye staring.

She doesn't see it. None of us could.

On the balcony, wearing a cloak of morning light, Antoine stood, watching. His silver hand was shaped like a bowl with a broken stem—a fragment of a cup—and he dipped a thin wand into the liquid it held. Missing a finger on his left hand, his motion was somewhat clumsy as he raised the wand to his lips and blew another stream of crimson bubbles. They floated into the room, and several popped against my chest, leaving red rings on the cards and my flesh.

"My *Qliphotic* shadow," I said as I walked out of the apartment, as I left sanctuary and stood, exposed, on the balcony with him. A distant noise, like the roaring, gnawing sound of a conflagration, vibrated through me, making my bones and teeth ache.

He nodded. *It was your wound that never healed. The pain which you refused to let go.*

"I know. I needed an anchor. I needed some way to understand."

Samael looked at me as if he could see me, his single eye squinting against the light; he knew we were talking about him. One of his long-fingered hands snaked under the chin of the man on the bed, squeezing his throat, and I swallowed heavily. I tried to remember that moment from five years ago; part of me wanted to think that was the way it had happened. As I had neared climax, I had started to choke, and because I hadn't been able to see him either—not then—my brain was already willing to believe it had been Marielle's hands on my throat. She had choked me as I came—

"No," I said, and Samael hissed as I moved his hand away. "That's not true."

In my revelation at the top of the tower in Portland, I had seen my initiation again, the night in the woods when I had first seen the Tree of the Sephiroth, when I had fallen through *Daäth* and into the nightside. But I had seen that lost child from a different angle, from an external viewpoint where it was obvious that the hand choking him had been his own. It had been my fear that had suffocated me, that had led me to invite the *Qliphoth* in.

That's what we're all afraid of, Antoine said. *We're all wondering what part of our experiences are real and what are nothing more than panic or dread.* He stared, unblinking, at the image of Marielle and me in bed. *Or lust. Or jealousy.*

I peeled a card off the left side of my chest and showed it to him. The Magician. Antoine smiled and copied the pose: left arm up, holding the soap bubble wand; right arm down, the bloody water in his silver bowl sloshing over the rim. *As above,* he said, *so be it below.*

On the hill behind him, the white shape of Sacré-Cœur flashed against the burning horizon. Black streaks, like the ashy remnants of burned clouds, smeared the sky. The crackling roar of the fire was louder now, as if it was chewing through timber and masonry a few blocks away.

"So what do we do?" I asked.

He shrugged. *The best we can, my friend.*

"And if that isn't enough?"

Don't fall into that trap, he said. He raised his wand and pointed it at the black shadow. *That's what he wants you to think. That's what he told me when I started to listen to him.*

With a bloody, ripping noise, Antoine vanished and it was Philippe standing beside me on the balcony. His cancer had advanced and it covered his left side entirely. His blackened hand had all of its fingers, and his signet ring glowed with white fire; the bubble wand was now a short stick with a long blade attached. The Ace of Cups was clutched in his right hand.

"I will not be your angel of vengeance," I told him.

It's too late, he said. *The final act is already in motion. What is done is done.*

"Why are you still here? Why are you and Cristobel and La foutain still in my head?"

It's isn't time for us to go. Not yet.

I looked back at my old self and Marielle—nearly invisible in the thick sea of the comforter—cuddling, their lust spent. The one-eyed shadow was gone. There was no longer anything for him to feed upon. "And when it is time," I asked, "then you'll go?"

Perhaps.

"Or I might be stuck with you for the rest of my life."

Would that be so bad? David and Hubert are good companions. They have served me well over the years.

"They knew they were going to die, didn't they? It takes an Architect to consecrate the Coronation, doesn't it? Either they take the Crown, or they recognize the one who does. That's why they're all being killed. So there's no competition."

There is always competition. That is the secret at the heart of Free Will. The Will to want something.

"If all the Architects are dead, then who gets the Crown?"

Whoever wants it the most.

"That's anarchy."

No, it is the old way. The first way. The oldest ritual. As old as our ability to dream and want. It almost exists outside our belief in it. We are simple animals; we cover the earth with our desire lines just as we invent stories to validate our mental and emotional needs. We make it all happen, and we take solace when the cycle starts over in the way we think it should.

"Fratricide."

No, that is the version written by the West. That is the way we invented because some thought it would be easier.

"Easier," I sighed. Brother against brother. Jealousy and rage allowed control of the flesh. That first sin, re-created time and time again through the ceremony of ritual combat. A justification codified by our elders as a rationale for our bloodthirsty instincts. As a shield for the lurking anarchy that lay deep in our hearts. "Is this what you meant when you told me to burn it all down? That I should come to Paris and bear witness to this annihilation of the rank."

No, I meant what I said, quite literally. He pushed the tip of the Spear through the Grail card, and red drops welled up from the wound.

"That's a metaphor," I pointed out.

What I say and what I mean are never the same, he laughed.

"I hate you, Old Man."

Et te amo, mi fili. He pressed the bloody card to my forehead where it stuck. *It is time to go back.*

The roaring sound of the world fire filled my ears and the blood running from the Grail obscured my vision. I reached for Philippe, but you can't grab a spirit. I reached for something, and as there was nothing there, I fell.

XXIV

"**B**ad dream?"

The stone floor was cold beneath me, and I sat up slowly, feeling like I had been beaten by a half-dozen men with sacks of rocks.

The chapel wasn't completely dark. The stones of the exposed wall behind me gave off a slight glow, vibrant with the returned ley energy. The room stank of blood and my pant legs were stiff with it. There were huddled shapes on the floor. In the gloom at the back of the nave, catching and reflecting what light there was, a pair of mirrored sunglasses, watching me.

I recognized his voice more than I knew his shape, and seeing that I was conscious, he came closer. Like Philippe, his bearing had that aristocratic aloofness that centuries of European breeding made instinctual, though the cut of his suit wasn't quite as traditional as the Hierarch's. He wore no tie, opting instead for a dark-colored shirt beneath the dark jacket. Disguising the male pattern baldness he had been suffering from for decades, his head was shaved, but the color of his pale eyebrows and the trimmed and oiled shape of his goatee gave away the fact that he was an older man. The rest of his face and neck were surprisingly smooth, but for a patch of blackness darker than the rest of the shadows in the chapel nestled at the base of his throat. He leaned on a metal-tipped walking stick.

"*Salve,* Architect Husserl," I said, naming him. *I know who you are. I know what you are.*

"*Salve, Adversari,*" he replied. *And I, say the same of you.* "Were you having a bad dream?"

The ward had closed, sealing the floor. I was sprawled beside the altar, my legs lying in the pool of blood from Henri's headless torso. My right hand hurt, and I could only move two fingers without a great deal of pain. Charles' body lay where it had fallen, also making quite a mess, and Antoine lay on his side, arm still caught in the floor. There was no sign of Marielle.

My forehead was wet too, and when I reached up to wipe away the blood, I found a tarot card stuck there.

"Yeah," I said. "I suppose I was."

Black marks wiggled around the Grail like the lines in comic books drawn to indicate motion. *Is it a bird? Is it a plane? It's the flying cup!* I wiped my fingers across the card, smearing blood with the ink, and the surface became a blur of motion. A riot of symbolic suggestions.

Reflections glittered off Husserl's glasses. "Ah, the Hierarch's cards. What do you see, blind little magus?" His voice still had that same mechanical precision, and I finally realized why. The thing on his throat was helping him speak. The trim throwback to the nineteenth-century fashion on his face was stuck there, like his eyebrows, with spirit gum. His skin was as smooth as a baby's because it was just as new.

Someone had hurt him recently.

"Blood and water," I said honestly.

"Yes, the Grail. I see it too."

I watched the motion on the card for a little while, and Husserl was patient. Why wouldn't he be? He knew the future.

"René didn't have much luck with the future," I said, remembering the earlier encounter before the storm hit and I had been swept into that inchoate conflagration. That tsunami of etheric energy that had hurled me into an out-of-body experience—a cosmological dream. "I don't think he saw me coming."

Husserl sighed. "No, he was too close. He was no longer in flux. He failed to look in the right direction."

"You didn't warn him?"

"It is difficult to change what you See. Dangerous, too, because one can become *tangled* in that Weave."

"Ah, yes, that whole seeing is creating thing." I glanced around again, and there was a glint of metal in the floor nearby, a shard buried in the center of a ragged circle that looked like an imprint of my fist. *The key—*

"You can't remove it," Husserl said.

"Remove what?"

"Even if you could," he said, "what would you do with it?"

"I hadn't had a chance to think it through that far."

"Trust me, then: it won't help you."

You need the ring.

I shrugged. "Okay, I suppose I can give you that one." I put the tarot card down, giving some thought to standing up. Not a lot. I examined Antoine, trying to find his left hand. In my dream, he had been missing his ring finger. He had taken the ring too, along with the key. *Did he still—*

"He doesn't have the ring," Husserl said. "Nor does it matter," he repeated, his voice hardening. "Even if you could retrieve it." The thought of trying to take it from the Architect had barely entered my head. "The lock is broken."

I relented, relaxing against the floor. "Okay, so no ring and no key. What are we doing here then?"

"That depends on you, M. Markham," Husserl said.

I spread my hands. "I suppose it does then, doesn't it?" The Chorus squeezed my neck, and I held them in check. As long as Husserl could play the Farseeing trick, he had the upper hand. I wasn't convinced that scrying would enable him to foresee every possibility—I had managed to trick René and the way I had touched Husserl's thread back at the Archives had seemed to surprise him—but he was anticipating everything readily enough at the moment that the best option might be to simply hear him out. The man had a propensity to talk. "What's on your mind?"

"The same thing as yours," he said.

I laughed. "I doubt that."

"Don't be so sure of yourself. I may not have the advantage of carrying spirits, but I have been privy to the Hierarch's plans for a long time. I knew every thread he was going to twist before he did."

"And you figured you'd let him do all the hard work, and then swoop in at the last minute."

He inclined his head slightly. "Perhaps."

"Don't you think Philippe might have anticipated that?" Husserl didn't seem inclined to answer that question, and a moment later, I found my own answer. The Chorus had uncovered a handful of memories and was feeding them to me. "Oh, wait, he did. At Château Neuf de Meudon."

He gripped the head of his cane. "Yes, M. Markham. The Hierarch and I had a discussion there—"

"A discussion?" I interrupted him with a snort of laughter. "That's not the way I remember it. Seems like someone got their face burned off." The memories weren't complete. They were stuttering loops like I was watching a short surrealist cut-up film. Fire, reflecting off the glass ceiling of the *Grande Cupole*. Husserl's cane with its knob of black glass. My hand on his throat, flames licking at the cuff of my shirt. His hair, burning.

Husserl took a step forward. "Is that all you remember? You are a very poor Witness, M. Markham."

There was more. Husserl had been smiling. Even as I crushed his throat and burned him, he had never stopped smiling at me.

"But shouldn't you be asking yourself why he didn't kill me?" Husserl asked. "If he knew what I planned, why did he stop with my face?"

Why hadn't I killed him?

Husserl cocked his head to one side, and the weak light reflected off his glasses. "You're not sure. I don't have to See to tell that you don't know the answer to that question. Your head is filled with spirits, but you still don't know anything useful. You don't know *why*."

If Philippe had known who the Opposition was, why hadn't he killed them? Why had he let them live?

A really troubling point intruded on my thoughts: What if everyone had been lying to me? What if there was no Opposition. Perhaps they were all scrambling in the vacuum to be the last one standing. *It is the first way.*

"Why don't you tell me?" I asked Husserl, shoving that possibility aside. That was too chaotic, too unstructured, and I couldn't believe that Philippe would have left so much to chance.

He laughed. "Why should I? Why don't you ask him? You're his master now, aren't you? Or are you just a simple tool?"

"You're trying to twist me," I said. "Just like he did. Everything you say is the same manipulative bullshit that Philippe used to pull on us. He read people very well, and he didn't have to know the future to know how they'd react in certain situations. You're doing the same thing."

"Of course I am," Husserl said. "We all do, M. Markham. It's a facet of being human: all that lying, cheating, and conniving. It's what makes our meat so sticky sweet to the pure light of our souls. All that corruption. All that filthy sin. What else would the Divine Spark soil itself in but that which is the very opposite of its purified innocence?"

"Don't make this metaphysical," I said, realizing that sentiment applied to my line of thinking as well. *Keep it concrete.* "I'm talking about the very specific mechanics of shaping events and people to your ends. You're just like Philippe: whispering what we want to hear; suggesting what we already know, but can't bring ourselves to want. The only difference between you two is that he was better at it than you. Even with your special glasses."

Husserl laughed. "Better than me? You think my actions are driven by jealousy, by some vague psychological need?"

"Are they?"

"Why do you think Philippe and I are at odds? How do you know this course of events isn't something that we planned together?"

"You—" And I stopped. Wouldn't that make sense? Wouldn't that explain why Philippe hadn't killed him. What about the others? Cristobel had accepted his sacrifice eagerly; and Antoine, burned by my actions in Ravensdale, had suffered that pain in order to receive his reward. Why couldn't Husserl's actions be considered in the same light? Who was to say that they weren't all so aware of the big picture that a sacrifice of the flesh was but a minor token if it moved the plan forward. Hadn't Husserl done exactly that when he had called me at the Archives, ostensibly from Tevvys' phone? He had claimed to have done so at my request, but I didn't know that Moreau had delivered that message any more than I knew how Husserl had gotten my phone number. What had that conversation accomplished? He had told me I was a singularity, a point beyond which no future was certain, and that realization had unlocked an awareness of the Hierarch's grand plan. He had moved Philippe's design forward in a manner that suggested he was aware of some of the details of that vision.

But this was the lie he wanted me to believe. A twist of logic that seemed so obvious and so natural, but when I looked at it more closely, it fell apart. So Husserl was privy to Philippe's plan, and Philippe knew that Husserl knew. But that didn't tell me who was ultimately playing whom. Husserl had as much opportunity—if not more—than any of the Architects. If he could read the future, then I would have been disappointed if he hadn't been able to anticipate what was coming. It would be easy to claim ownership of the plan now as I was the only one who could readily contradict him. Control didn't mean compliance or agreement. It simply meant knowledge.

Those who understand the big picture get to fine-tune the small details. One of the truisms of the Watchers. If you Know, you can act. If Husserl Knew, then why couldn't this all be an act? A misdirection for my benefit?

Which circled us back to the basic question: Why?

I put my hands flat against the floor, and the Chorus remarked on the rhythm of ley energy storming beneath me. Like the vibrations from the DJ's record, back at Batofar. A subsonic vibration, a confusion of echoes. In my own head, the same sort of mixture—too many histories, too many divergent desires. It became difficult to parse the *"why?"* out of the noise.

"Why did you call me when I was at the Archives?"

Stalling. Trying to think. Trying to put more of the pieces together.

"I've already told you."

"I don't believe it was just to tell me that I was the axis around which all of this turned. I would have figured that out eventually. You forced the issue, and you revealed yourself. I didn't know your involvement prior to that call. Why did you give away that advantage?"

"It confuses you, doesn't it? That we might not be enemies. That we might be working toward the same goal."

"What goal? Coronation?"

"It is the inevitable outcome of this course. A new Hierarch will be Crowned."

"And you think I should be showing more enthusiasm about giving you that opportunity."

"I know you will."

I shifted my weight forward and Husserl didn't seem bothered by the shift in my position. I considered the distance between us, and the obstacles: Antoine, Henri, the blood, Charles…

"Where's Marielle?" I realized.

He smiled, a motion made all the more sinister by the fact that no lines developed on his face. He really did have the skin of an infant. "That's a better question."

I repeated it.

Husserl inhaled deeply, like a hound scenting the approach of rain. "I won't try to convince you that she came willingly, because you won't believe me, so I will say that she is in my care, and will remain so until Coronation. At which time, I will put a knife into her chest and cut her heart out."

Her heart.

On the floor beside me, the tarot card twitched, the wet smear of ink and blood solidifying into a concrete picture. Hearing some echo in Husserl's words, I listened to the Chorus for a moment as I watched the picture on the card become clear. A woman holding up a cup, and rising out of the frame, only his crossed feet and the wide pole upon which he was crucified visible, was the Martyr. It was identical to the watercolor I had seen at the Chapel of Glass, though a close-up detail. The crucified man's flaming heart wasn't visible. But the cup was.

Philippe's spirit giving me a nudge, trying to bridge a gap and make a connection. *Drink from this vessel.* The Ace of Cups; I had drawn it on the chart of the Architects, an unconscious doodle while Vivienne had been mesmerizing me. Words and tongues; *tell me what ails you?* Earlier, at Batofar, I had sipped from a cup Marielle had given me containing a concoction that had driven out the poison in my system. But was that all it had done? Had it created some other connection?

Her hips moving, inviting me to try again. In the alcove on Batofar, the physical connection. I had been caught up in the moment, in the sensation of being alive and whole again, and I hadn't been paying close enough attention. Keys and locks. Opening doors and crossing thresholds; connections made across disparate spaces. Marielle hadn't been fucking me. She had been trying to extract something from me during the sex. She had tried to break open some mystery hidden within my heart. *What I say and what I mean are never the same.*

What had she tried to take?

"You won't harm her," I said.

His smile remained. "You are guessing, calling my bluff."

"No, I know you're lying."

"And how do you know that?"

"Because if you wanted to kill her, you'd have done so already."

He nodded. "Yes, in much the same way I would have cut your throat while you were busy dreaming that petty little dream of yours if that is what I had wanted."

"Yes."

"Very good. You are learning to think." He leaned on his cane, the light flashing on his glasses. "If I haven't killed you, then I must want something."

"I'm guessing you do. Why don't you tell me?"

"The Spear, M. Markham. It and the Holy Grail are required for the Coronation ceremony."

I glanced at the solid floor, and then at the circular indentation left by my fist. "Ah," I said, getting it. "And I suppose she is the carrot by which you will entice me to retrieve the Spear for you."

"Precisely. The sisters of the Archives will only release the Grail when the Spear has been retrieved."

The ground trembled. It felt almost like an aftershock of an earthquake, the faint vibration that seemed like nothing more than the sort of rumble caused by a heavy truck downshifting on the road outside, but as we were far from any major roadway, that was hardly the case. Something else had shifted.

"The Coronation was supposed to have taken place at dawn this morning," Husserl said, seemingly indifferent to the tremor.

"The first day of spring. But that was not to be, it would seem. The sun is already in the sky, and the Land is troubled by the lack of a Hierarch. We will have one more chance tomorrow to greet the sun."

The ground trembled again, more obviously this time, and I scrambled to my feet.

"What's going on?" I demanded.

"The Architect Spiertz." Husserl tapped his cane against the floor. "He, too, wants the Spear."

The Chorus tried to get a reading, but couldn't sense anything through the crawling web of etheric energy in the rock. "Where is he?" I asked, even though I had a bad feeling about the answer.

"Underground," Husserl said. "Though I believe he is trying to break out."

XXV

The next tremor was strong enough to make me stumble, and I lurched against the nearby wall for support. By the time I recovered, Husserl had retreated from the room. It was a good idea; Chapelle Notre-Dame-sous-Terre was directly under the nave of the main cathedral. There was a lot of masonry overhead that I wasn't too sure was built to withstand a major earthquake. It would pancake this chamber should it all come down. As I passed the mess of Henri's body, the Chorus registered a stuttering rhythm in Antoine's chest.

I considered not stopping for a second. Keep on going. Follow Husserl. Get the fuck out of this deathtrap before the ceiling comes down. Before *whatever* is down in the grotto gets out.

Antoine moaned as he rolled onto his back, ribbons of magick suddenly erupting out of his body and wrapping themselves around his severed arm. He gradually focused on his surroundings and moved further away from the sticky puddle around Henri's decapitated body. Chiding myself for the decision, I helped him across the floor until he could lean against the wall.

"Quite the mess," he whispered. His hair was stiff and a large bloodstain covered the right side of his head and neck.

"Effective, though," I said. "We won; they didn't."

He surveyed his arm, a rueful expression tightening his mouth.

"At what cost?" he muttered. The tightness held as his magick grew sharper and more focused, binding off his arm. When I had cut off his hand with the sword, I had only taken a little bit above the wrist, but now everything below his elbow was gone. Prior to the whiteout of the ley storm, he had managed to seal the wound with a blocking spell that had held during his unconsciousness, but now he was building a better solution. It was fascinating to watch him work as I had never been very good at healing magick. Chorus-sight revealed a profusion of etheric strands weaving about his stump. When I was flush with soul energy, I could undo massive trauma, but this fine detail work was the sort of skill I hadn't learned yet.

However, there were other pressing matters at hand. "We can't stay here," I said, tearing myself away from his work.

He grimaced as my words interrupted his concentration. A strand of magick whipped back like a wild tentacle and he neatly severed it near the central mass of squirming lines with a thought. It flew away, disintegrating into ambient dust.

"It's Spiertz," I said.

More strands broke free, and with a shudder, Antoine aborted his spell, holding all the strands in place. He squinted at me, licking his dry lips as he tried to focus on my words. "What?"

"Spiertz," I repeated. "He's still alive. Apparently."

Antoine stared at me dumbly. "That is not possible," he said slowly. "I killed him." He looked past me, turning his attention to the chapel. "Down in the grotto beneath the altar," he continued. "He attacked me as I was retrieving the Spear."

Down in the grotto.

"Where did you kill him?" I asked, wanting to be sure. Wanting to hear him say it again.

"Down there," Antoine said, his eyes darkening as he looked at me again. Wondering why I was so dense. Why I didn't know what he was talking about.

I spelled it out for him. "What happened to his body?" I

asked.

Pain crossed his face, and he put his left hand over the end of his stump. His magick wavered, and I noticed he wasn't wearing the signet ring.

"It exploded," he said. "When I stabbed him with the Spear. Some sort of…" He trailed off, lost in memory that seemed to be getting away from him.

A soul lock. "Yeah," I said. "I know what it was."

My body clenched, the Chorus reacting to a psychic detonation below us. The ground shook at nearly the same instant, and a shower of dust cascaded from the ceiling. Something fell over nearby with a loud crash. Antoine was on his feet instantly, an instinctive reaction kicking in and driving him upright. Wincing at the pain still rattling around my skull, I stood up too. Grabbing his good arm, I hauled him toward the door.

"You can tell me the story in a little while," I said. "But we can't stay underground."

Antoine's silver cap was still in the floor, the Chorus reminded me, as was the Spear. We would be leaving both behind.

Later, I thought. *We can't stay.*

The rock moaned beneath us as we fled from the chapel.

I got the story out of Antoine in fits and spurts, as if the telling of it revealed some secret shame he was loath to give life to by sharing. We hurried through the maze of vaults and hallways, working upward toward the top floor of the Merveille where the rectory and the cloister lay, where we'd be able to stand on the western porch of the church and have nothing over our heads.

He had been at Batofar, watching Marielle and me, and after she had given me the potion and we had lost ourselves on the dance floor, he had left. He knew of the relationship between the ring and the key and had driven out to Mont-Saint-Michel to retrieve the Spear. It had been simple enough to slip into the chapel undetected—and he had even set up a spell surrounding the Chapelle Notre-Dame-sous-Terre to keep any wondering priests at bay—and he had invoked the power of the key, unlocking the grotto. It had been filled with water—how full? I had interrupted to ask; a little more than half, he thought—and the Spear was imbedded in the chest of the statue. When he had pulled the Spear out, the water had started to drain.

When he made his way out of the hole, Spiertz had been waiting for him.

I didn't get the sense that Antoine had been surprised by the ambush; in fact, I suspect he knew the Architect was lying in wait for him. What Antoine didn't say, but which came across clearly enough in his tone, was how Spiertz had bested him magickally. Spiertz had dropped the hammer on Antoine fairly hard, and Antoine had been forced to retreat to the grotto. Spiertz had come after him, and tapping the energy in the surrounding rock more readily, Spiertz had been nearly impervious to any of Antoine's attacks.

Nearly.

One chink in the armor is all it ever takes. One missing link. One crack in an otherwise unblemished surface. Antoine had found that crack and had driven the Spear into it.

"He laughed," Antoine said, holding his stump and leaning against the wall of the last stairway. "He thanked me for setting him free, and then he exploded." He shook his head. "It was like the whole world was running away from me, my flesh included. Everything was blown back—quickly—and I barely managed to hang on to my sanity as his—what did you call it?—his soul lock detonated."

Spiertz was the one who had been bound to the strike team at the Chapel of Glass. It had been a geomantic spell after all. Sometimes the obvious choice is the right one. He had bound a lock to his soul too, though what he used as an energy source was unknown. The gunmen had been tied to him, and the fury of their detonation was linked to Spiertz's Will. What had he used to power his own soul lock?

And why had he thanked Antoine?

We staggered out into the open air. The sky was patchy with clouds, and the morning light colored them rose and gold. Any other morning, I would have stopped to admire the view to the west—the aquamarine and indigo texture of the ocean, the glittering play of sunlight along the curve of the waves as they approached the French coast—but this morning, there were other concerns.

The tremors were coming more quickly now, like rapidly approaching thunder, and each impact rattled the island. Distantly, we heard the sound of security alarms and the occasional scream. The thick silence that had cloaked the island had been shattered by the ley storm, and in the aftermath of the tsunami, the world was waking up again. Waking up into a geological nightmare.

Antoine squinted up at the spires of the cathedral. The gold angel of Michael atop the tallest spire appeared to be on fire, but it was only a trick of the light. "I killed his flesh," he said. "When I split his heart with the Spear, I only killed his flesh. His soul was still intact."

I nodded. "Accepting for a minute that Husserl isn't lying to me, that would seem to be the case," I said, recalling the crawling paranoia I had felt in the grotto. The sensation that someone had been there with us. Someone who I hadn't been able to perceive. But the Chorus should have been able to spot him. Bereft of body, his soul should have stood out—even against the furious static of the walls. So where had he been?

In the statue, Cristobel suggested. *He turned the grotto into a focus. The soul lock was a way to cause a radical influx of potential energy. He hid at the nexus of the power and waited for the wave to come back.*

It made sense. If we hadn't shown up, the grotto would have stayed open and the energy would have more readily flowed into the chamber below. Without Philippe's wards in place, the whole pit was nothing more than a reservoir waiting to be filled.

Spiertz had thanked Antoine, and I finally realized why. Physical death had enabled the Mason to become something else. Something not bound by the flesh. *Something...*

"...elemental," I whispered.

I became aware of a resonance that wasn't coming from the ground beneath us, but a vibration in the air around us. The storm had passed, but the atmospheric pressure remained.

"He's part of the Land now," I said. "Becoming one with Mont Tombe."

"Is that all?" Antoine asked, as if it was nothing more than a minor detail.

"So why does he need the Spear?"

Antoine sighed, and his shoulders hunched unconsciously, tightening in anticipation of an oncoming blow. I felt it too. "I guess we can ask him," he said.

The western façade of the church exploded.

XXVI

I got in front of Antoine, and the peacock shield of the Chorus flinched like a hundred eyes blinking in shock as masonry and granite hurled across the open expanse of the porch. The eruption was mainly directed upward, the result of a massive object throwing itself toward the sky, but there were still quite a few pieces that came straight at us. A cloud of grit billowed out from the broken church as one of the alcoves collapsed, and it was several long moments before we could see clearly.

A giant, walking through the wreckage of man's greatest architectural achievement—a cathedral built to inspire us to contemplate the majesty and enormity of Heaven's work—and here was a creature who could touch the ceiling of that vaulted space. With one of his hands. The statue from the grotto hadn't grown proportionally. The legs were as thick as some of the pillars in the various chapels, and the torso reminded me of some of the redwoods in Northern California. But one of the arms was long and thin, as if the mass ratio was correct but length was more important than girth, while the other was a stump, ending in something that vaguely looked like an open sore with a short nail protruding from it like an inflamed ingrown hair. The head was small too. The long braids coming off the back of its skull were long and very mobile—more like snakes all the time—but the rest of the skull seemed unfinished. A face had been roughed in, but with very little detail. As if it were ornamental, and not meant to be functional.

"Somehow," I offered, "I don't think it's going to be big on conversation."

The giant fought its way free of the walls of the church, knocking the last part of the west wall down, and I caught sight of its feet. It had two central legs that ended in flat columns, like the feet of an elephant, and sprouting from the upper part of its calves were a number of smaller supports that worked in the same way that the flying buttresses on the church behind it held up the central vault of the nave. These buttresses moved, accordion-style, in concert with each ponderous step.

Antoine and I remained still, hiding behind the staring eyes of the Chorus' peacock shield, as the giant turned its shadowy face toward the sun. The granite of the head flowed and rippled in the sunlight and the features became more prominent—a nose emerged, a slashing line opened into a mouth, and two sunken pits caught some of the sunlight and kept it. The jaw lengthened too, growing something that started as a beard and became more stalks like its hair.

"Spiertz," Antoine muttered behind me, recognizing the face even with its tentacled chin.

"So he's really in there." I couldn't help but be impressed. It was an incredible feat. Surviving without the flesh, Spiertz had bound his soul to the rock of the mount and forged it into a body. I wondered if the Chorus could even touch him. Could they even find him in the rock?

"How do you kill stone?" Antoine wondered.

"Wish I knew," I answered.

Spiertz swung his head in our direction. It was bigger now, more correctly proportioned with the rest of his body, and the face bore a frozen expression. Caught somewhere between amusement and horror, his open mouth gaped. The stone of his chest rippled like water and we heard a rattling sound like sand in a pipe a second before a stream of tiny rocks shot from the giant's mouth. The peacock eyes of the Chorus flashed crimson with the impact of a thousand stones, and I groaned as the Chorus squeezed my spine.

Behind me, Antoine whispered a string of words and the scattering spray of sand off my shield flashed white and fused into glass. He kept the spell active for a few seconds, letting the curve of glass build up as more sand scattered along the convex surface until we were almost enclosed in a protective bubble. He grabbed my arm and pulled me back, both of us ducking under the far edge of his barrier. A second later, the glass shattered as the giant brought a heavy foot down on the white dome.

Antoine raised his left hand and slashed it down, and a blot of blue lightning cut through the air between his fingers and the giant. One of the flying buttresses sheared off, sparks erupting from the cut, and the giant wobbled momentarily as the other supports slammed down, adapting to the new configuration.

I had a chance to get a better look at the stump, and I realized what was protruding from the center of the inflamed end. "The Spear," I Whispered to Antoine. "He's got the Spear already."

The giant swung its long arm at us, a wide sweep that would take our heads off if we remained standing upright. At first I thought I had miscalculated the length of its arm, but when the Chorus translated all the energy patterns into vectors of force, I realized the arm was growing longer as it moved. I sprawled on my ass and Antoine leaped forward, tucking his head and rolling clumsily. The arm whistled over my head, but caught Antoine's heel, knocking him to the side and spoiling his roll.

The giant tried to step on Antoine, and while it missed with its heavy leg, one of the buttresses hammered down on Antoine's leg. Lightning flashed again, and the buttress disintegrated into a spray of stone chips. The giant swept its arm down once more, striking the pavement of the terrace with a crack of thunder, and when it pulled the arm free, the long whip of stone was festooned with shards and splinters of concrete.

The Chorus attached themselves like a limpet mine to one of the remaining buttresses on the nearby leg, and with an acknowledgement from me, they detonated—an explosion of silver light that shattered the support. The giant whirled its spike-encrusted arm at me, and one of the ragged shards of concrete tore a hole out of the shoulder of my jacket. Got a little bit of me too.

Antoine blew off another leglet as the giant stepped away from us. That left four remaining on its left leg, and as it retreated, I thought for a second that we might actually bring it down before it managed to hit us with its spiked arm, and then I realized it wasn't making a defensive withdrawal so much as fleeing. It crashed into the building along the southern edge of the terrace, and its weight took it through the upper floor. It vanished into a cloud of debris, and we heard the crackling, shattering sound of falling rock as it tumbled down the side of the mount.

"Where the hell is it going?" I asked Antoine.

"Paris," he replied. He knocked some of the dust off his suit jacket, though it didn't much improve the condition of the garment. There were a number of tiny gashes on his face from rock chips. "You think he wants to be trapped in that body forever?"

I watched the cloud of dust that rose in the wake of the giant. "It seems like it is working pretty well for him so far."

Antoine limped toward the ruined edge of the terrace. His right pant leg was shiny with fresh blood. "The man is slipping away," he said. "Couldn't you feel it? Spiertz had moved his soul into the rock, but it's too foreign a substance. His soul can't be sustained; it is going to break up and become nothing more than an appetite."

I stood next to Antoine and looked down the hill. The giant was in the village below, thrashing its way through the buildings. Heading for the wall surrounding the base of the mount. Beyond that lay the shallow water of the bay, and then the mainland.

From there, straight toward the sun until it reached Paris.

I remembered a bit of trivia that Lafoutain had offered. "Les Michelettes." I pointed them out to Antoine.

"Medieval technology," he said. "It lasts forever, doesn't it?"

"Let's hope so."

Antoine did the heavy lifting while I prepped the projectile. A bombard was one of those medieval inventions that was simple in design, cumbersome in construction, and devastating in effect. The bombard was nothing more than a very heavy tube that, when filled with powder and a projectile, hurled a heavy object very far and very hard. They were very good at bringing walls down without the need of putting men within arrow range, and when engineers discovered that stone balls tended to shatter due to their velocity, they opted to make bigger guns. The supergun arms race went on—*bigger is better!*—until someone discovered how to mass produce iron balls, at which time the need for large-bore guns dropped.

The downside of a big gun was that it was heavy, and not so easily transported, as the English realized during the fifteenth century when they were getting the shit kicked out of them by a bunch of French knights. The two guns left behind were hauled back to the walls of Mont-Saint-Michel and mounted there, like trophies, so everyone would know the English had not only been beaten, but they had left their cool toys behind. At some point, an officious bureaucrat had ordered the cannons filled, but as they had opted to use fairly cheap cement, it didn't take us long to clean out one of the cannons.

Having positioned the re-bored cannon, Antoine sighted down the length of his good arm and took a distance reading on the retreating giant. It had started on the causeway, but by the time we reached the lower wall of the island, it had reached the first breach. The pavement had collapsed under its weight and it had fallen into the sea, where it had run afoul of an old law of alchemy: salt water and stone don't mix well. It had been slowed by the ocean's touch, and it had climbed back up to the road once more, but the next break had confounded it again, and the second time it had stayed in the water. Sluggish in the grip of the salty sea, it forged toward the shore, but it was moving slowly so there was little danger of it being out of range.

I packed the throat of one of the Michelettes with glass, sand, a car battery and gasoline, a bunch of scrap metal torn from the same car that I had taken the battery and gas from, and a ragged block of rusted iron I had scavenged from the ornamental gate. Submerged in several inches of blood-tinged gasoline, the armament was a solidifying mass of Chorus-tinged intent, waiting for the trigger of my Will.

"Make it count," Antoine said, squinting at the giant.

I bit my tongue, hard enough to taste blood, and nodded.

He closed his eyes, exhaled slowly, and raised his arm a few inches. His magick moved the cannon sympathetically, lifting the barrel off the shelf of the wall. Veins in his neck stood out as he held the cannon in place, and I gave him a few more seconds to dig his anchors in. Pointing the bombard in the right direction was only half the trick, the other half was making sure it stayed on target as the projectile fired. His forehead creased with exertion as his finger quivered for a second, and then he found his center. The jitter in his finger stopped and the skin of his forehead smoothed out.

"*Ignis,*" I whispered, and the cannon fired.

For the brief seconds of the projectile's flight, my perception was bound to it. The wind burned my hard skin, and I screamed as I tore through the morning air. I knew where I was going; I saw my target, and my focus never wavered. The shape of the giant grew quickly in my field of vision, too quickly, and then there was nothing but the shuddering blankness of impact. I gasped, hurled back into my own frame of reference, and the Chorus melted from my skin.

"You missed," Antoine pronounced. The cannon lay behind us, knocked askew by the force of the blast.

Shading my eyes, I stared out at the foundering giant. It couldn't get up, the sea's poisonous touch was too great on it now, and it thrashed about in the surf like it was caught in quicksand. "I guess that depends on what I had been aiming for," I said, glancing over at Antoine.

The giant's left shoulder and stump were gone, torn off by the impact of my improvised projectile. Somewhere near the water's edge was a piece of rock with the Spear imbedded in it.

"We have to destroy him," I reminded Antoine. "The tide'll go out enough for him to crawl to shore, and then he's going to repair that shoulder and start marching on Paris again."

Antoine nodded. "I suppose you have a plan?"

I did. While gathering materials for the cannon shot, I had realized something about stone. Mountains weren't permanent. They lasted thousands of millennia, but eventually, through erosion by wind and water, they could be reduced to a flat spot on the terrain. Given time and temperament, a mountain could be worn done, one grain of sand at a time. The trick was speeding that process up. Spiertz's soul was in the rock, diffused so widely that the Chorus couldn't find him, but what if the area and mass of rock were reduced to a smaller amount? If the statue was hacked up into pieces, could I find the piece that held Spiertz and break him?

"First," I said, "we're going to need the Spear. And then, well, you're going to have to trust me."

"Can you do it without the ominous theatrics?"

"I need a conduit."

Antoine grimaced, understanding the nature of my plan. "No. That's not going to work."

"You can ground yourself better than I can, and I know how to siphon energy from a living source. I'm going to need a lot of power, and your feeding it to me is the easiest way." I glanced at his shortened sleeve. "Besides, this plan requires two hands. You're missing one. It's like drawing the short straw."

XXVII

O ne of the skills taught young Watchers was how to channel energy. Building and executing a spell took a certain amount of concentration, as well as a source of ready fuel, and if the magus had to draw and convert power from the leys, then the effectiveness of his magick was diminished accordingly. Magi like Antoine strained that distinction with their ability to draw power almost effortlessly, but the rule still held: one part to feed, one to transform, and one to execute. The trinity of doing magick. Channeling meant you could offload two-thirds of the effort on to others, and depending on the number of conduits you could manage, it meant your available pool of energy could be much larger than you could draw on your own.

This is how armies are built. Singular in focus, endless in power. The sum of the group is greater than the individual.

We were two, and had to settle for a single stream. Antoine gathered the leys and bound their streams into a single point in his chest; I—very carefully—attached a Chorus leech, and opened the conduit between us. There was a little bleed, as much as Antoine kept himself hidden, the Chorus could still taste him in the flow.

The tide had gone out another foot by the time we reached the shore. Invigorated by the heady flow of energy from Antoine,

I swept through the mass of slippery rocks and wet sand along the water's edge with the Chorus. My senses were engorged with data: the hard light off the water, the laughing sound of the waves as they pulled at the giant, the smell of brine and decaying plant matter, the groaning thunder of stone under siege as Spiertz fought to overcome the cloying grip of the ocean, the stale scent of blood and sweat coming off Antoine and me. Somewhere in all that data was the cold hunger of the Spear.

It lent invincibility to those its wielder commanded, but there was a cost. Nothing was free in this Universe. It was a closed system, after all, and energy could neither be created nor destroyed. We existed in a constant state of transformation, and rewards were given in exchange for tribute. The pound of flesh is always paid. Wounds made by the Spear would never heal.

Unless they were healed by the Grail. This was the symbiotic relationship of the pair, and why they were required for the Coronation. One blooded the candidate, the other healed. Spiertz could be made human again if he could get to Paris.

In his elemental state, he was vulnerable to water. It was too fluid and the touch of it against the giant's stone skin was corrosive. The gaping wound where the giant's left shoulder had been was a mass of slag, now that it had been fighting the ocean. Many of the buttress legs were gone, melted away by the salt water, and the right arm had been compressed. Less surface area to be touched by the sea.

Near the edge of the sea, the water running up the beach and kissing the edge of my boots, I found the twisted remnants of the giant's stump. Sticking out of a mass of fused glass and steel was the sharp point of the Spear. The giant pounded the water, struggling to drag himself closer as I knelt beside the hunk of granite and iron and glass. The Chorus, fueled by the ready power streaming through my body via the conduit with Antoine, spat out of my clenched fist like an arc welder's hot torch, and the detritus around the Spear grew orange and red before it bubbled away. A cloud of white steam hissed around me as the liquefied materials hit the water.

The giant's arm rose out of the water like an octopus' tentacle, cracking as it grew longer, and it cast a shadow on the sand as it slammed down. I stepped aside, and its impact splashed hot water all over me; as it writhed in the shallow water, I let the Chorus guide my hand through the warm mist surrounding the melted rock.

The Spear fell into my hand naturally, and when the giant's hand whipped up again, I met its approach with the shining blade of the Spear. The Chorus covered the pitted and stained blade with a glaze of incandescence and the pair—Will and Spear—sliced through Spiertz's animated stone. The hand fell into the surf, and the giant made its first human-sounding noise.

The Chorus swirled around me, raising a storm of light, and I pointed the Spear at the giant, which had stopped fighting the surf. It was lying on its side, its head raised out of the water, and it stared at me. "That's right," I Whispered to the stone statue, on the off-chance that my magi-speak would get through to Spiertz. "You're going to have to get past me if you want a shot at the Crown."

The giant's expression darkened, its mouth widening to a ragged pit, and for a moment, I thought it was going to vomit sand at me again, but it jerked its head back and then forward again. The long strands of its hair snapped forward and two of them broke off. The Chorus tagged them immediately, reading their intent, and they deflected one. The other one came directly at me, and I moved the tip of the Spear to intercept it, and reached deep into the conduit. Power flowed through my arms and legs, bracing me, and the Spear vibrated with energy, singing a harmonic overtone that climbed in pitch as the missile struck. The stone exploded in a shower of gray dust, coating me with grit.

I flicked the Spear down, angled it flat, and then flicked it up, throwing a wave of energy in a wedge before me. The ocean receded, forced back by my command, and I strode out into the newly cleared beach. When the waves came back, I flicked them out again, and the giant recoiled from the edge of the psychic wedge I commanded. I sliced through two of the buttress legs, clearing my way to the central leg, and then I thrust the Spear deep into the stone.

Spiertz was in there; I could feel him now. He howled at me, a psychic charge I felt in my arm, and I responded, releasing the Chorus through the metal blade. They shrieked as they devoured the giant's leg, eagerly snapping at the wisps of Spiertz's soul they could find in the rock. The giant pulled its leg back, trying to get away from the Spear, and the stone crumbled. It turned white, like water leaching out of mud, and then crumbled into ash. A wave crested the giant's leg, washing over my hand, and the Spear came free of the stone as all the rock around the wound was swept away.

The giant tried to lash me a few more times with its strands of hair, but the Chorus, emboldened by the bits of Spiertz's soul they had devoured, caught each one of them and burned them into smoke. Spiertz couldn't grow another hand on the end of his arm, not past the cut made by the Spear, and so he grew a pair from his elbow; I cut them off too. I waded out further, and sank the Spear into the stone of his waist, and when the ocean claimed all the dead rock from that wound, Spiertz lost control of the lower part of the giant's body.

After an hour of hacking at his body, all that remained was the skull, and the features had been wiped off by the waves. I raised the heavy stone of the giant's skull out of the water—*reducam de maris*—and touched it with my free hand. Part of Spiertz swam in the cacophony of the Chorus, and because his personality and memory had been devoured piecemeal, most of it was incoherent noise in my head. What remained of Spiertz's personality was bound in the stone still, but there wasn't much left. A lot of the Mason was gone.

I drove the Spear into the center of the skull's smooth forehead, and the Chorus filled the stone vessel with their light. Steam rose from the skull, and Spiertz shrieked and thrashed within the prison of stone. He wasn't human enough to curse me, but I felt his rage. I squeezed the shaft of the Spear, flushing power down to the Chorus, and the rock exploded. What didn't vaporize in the blast was thrown into the water, and clustered around the burning tip of the Spear like glowing fireflies were the tiny remnants of Spiertz's soul, clutched in the thorny claws of the Chorus.

Antoine severed the conduit as I returned to the beach. *"Percutiam te et auferam caput tuum a te,"* he said, staring out at the gray stains in the water. The ocean washed the detritus of the giant away, the tide pulling the mud back out into the deeper water of the bay. *I will smite you and take your head from you.* David, telling Goliath how the giant Philistine was going to meet his end.

"Am I next?" Antoine asked.

I shivered. My skin was cold all of a sudden; the sunlight felt weak, as if the sun was looking elsewhere, and its heat was lost to us.

There's a memory I have of Portland, and I don't know if it was a dream or a vision, but it burns in my head. Antoine standing on the bank of the Willamette River, watching the water wash away the ash of Portland. "It is done," he says. The morning sun has burned away all the black, and none of the soul-dead have survived the dawn.

None but me.

"I am standing on the precipice of the Abyss," he says, "staring into the face of nothingness, and what do I see but the glitter of many lights. So many threads—undone, unbound, twisted free of the Weave." He turns his ruined face away from the ravaged cityscape and looks at the man standing next to him. "Where do they go?"

Philippe Emonet leans on his cane; his left leg, bent and twisted, pains him. His hair is in a disarray, and his face is slack and loose. He shrugs.

Antoine raises his silver hand and touches his face. The fingers come away wet, dappled with a pink smear of blood and water. "I am the Witness," he says. "I have Seen what has been done—what we have done—and I will carry this terrible knowledge with me for the rest of my days."

Philippe nods slowly.

"We're all responsible, aren't we?" Antoine says. He lowers his hand and the fingers dissolve back into the smooth shape of the silver cap. "But you are the lucky one, aren't you? You only have to carry this weight a little while longer."

Philippe's lips curl into something like a smile. *Long enough,* he says, his words clear to both Antoine and me, though his voice doesn't work. *There are others who will carry it longer than you and I.*

"Of course there are." A bark of laughter rips out of Antoine, a stab of noise that appears to be painful. "You still need me, don't you, Old Man? You've taken everything from me so that I am pure in my purpose, so that my desire is focused on one thing only. Markham may have been your salvation, but I am to be your vengeance. Is that it?"

In this dream, I am a ghost, a translucent vessel that is being filled with the morning light. A cup, not yet full of fire. I stand on the water of the Willamette River, and watch Antoine argue with his conscience.

"I will wait," Antoine says. "I will Watch. That is what I will do for you. I will be patient, until my turn comes."

As the light changes, as the vision becomes less like a dream and more like the morning after the death of Portland, I become more solid and the specter of the Hierarch vanishes. Antoine remains, standing on the edge, staring into the Abyss.

Am I next?

XXVIII

"Do you know the security code?" Antoine asked, leaning heavily against the back wall of the elevator in Tour Montparnasse. After leaving the beach, we had commandeered a car and driven back to Paris. Antoine had insisted on stopping at an open market outside of Caen where he had bought a bottle of expensive vodka. Something to dull the pain. I was still buzzing from the energy I had channeled and the sparks of Spiertz's soul; Antoine, on the other hand, was wiped out.

Or so he professed, and after drinking most of the fifth in less than two hours, it wasn't much of a white lie anymore.

"Yes," I lied. I hadn't seen the sequence that Marielle had entered, but it didn't matter. Every member of *La Société Lumineuse* had their own code—the heavy security lay on the hidden floor anyway—and, according to Lafoutain, all the code did was announce your presence. As I had the memories of more than three Architects in my head, I had a choice of codes to choose from.

I opted for Philippe's, and I was a little surprised when the code was accepted. I had half-thought they would have disabled his code already. With a tiny change in the air pressure inside the car, the elevator began to rise.

"Starts with a nine," I told Antoine. "You know, the number of Architects."

He looked at me, bleary-eyed, and pretended to not know

what I was talking about.

He wasn't as drunk as he seemed. I knew him now, better than he knew me. The conduit had been rather one-way in that regard.

The elevator opened on the empty foyer of the Archives. I walked up to the door and tapped on it lightly with the tip of the Spear. The noise was tiny in the empty space, like a marble falling down a drain, but the reaction was quite dramatic.

The walls went black and the lights went out. The only illumination was the yellow glow from the strip of lights along the base of the wall in the elevator carriage, and a violet pinprick like a distant star in the mantle of black space from each of the cameras set in the corners of the room. I held up the Spear, knowing it would register like a furious supernova on the magick-sensitive monitors.

There was a long pause, a moment where both Antoine and the Chorus became increasingly nervous, and then Vivienne's voice spoke in our heads.

"Why are you here?" she Whispered.

"I've come for the Grail," I replied out loud, not having the same visual luxury as she to pinpoint my response.

"A lot of men have sought the Grail," she Whispered. "A lot of them have stood where you stand and made the same demand. They all went away with nothing. You are no different than any of them."

Antoine had spent a good portion of the drive back, most of it after he had started drinking, trying to convince me that Husserl would have already retrieved the Grail from the Archives. He had the ring; why wouldn't he claim the Cup? I had argued that the daughters wouldn't have given it to him; I didn't have a solid rationale, just the intuition that Husserl's Vision of the future required him to maintain anonymity as long as possible. As long as he was only an observer, he couldn't be enticed to become part of what he Saw, thereby limiting his exposure to the chaotic possibilities.

I was starting to understand how scrying worked. Scryers remained in flux until they were forced to touch a thread. That was how they protected themselves from what they Saw. René had been too close to, too intimately involved in, the future he was Seeing, and as such, he hadn't been able to keep the bigger picture in mind, and had missed a critical detail that had cost him his life.

Husserl knew I needed the Grail too, and if I succeeded in retrieving the Spear—which he, apparently, had every faith that I would—then I would need to visit the Archives. Why bother getting it himself when I would bring it with me?

Though how I was going to get the Grail from the Archives was a bit hazy. Antoine wasn't too thrilled with my lack of a plan. Banging on the door and demanding it hadn't been his choice of methods, but as he hadn't offered anything better, it was the plan we had. He couldn't help but point out that the last time someone had tried to assault the Archives, they had brought an entire armored division with them. Hitler's occupation of Paris during World War II, Antoine had pointed out, had been an excuse to bring the heavy armor forward because the *Schwarze Sonne Gesellschaft* hadn't been able to crack the vaults.

Then I had pointed out that Hitler's copy of the Spear had been a fake. We were ahead of the game this time.

I tried to keep the conversation civil, though. No need to go ballistic. Not yet. "I have been designated as the Hierarch's representative," I replied.

"Designated by whom? I do not see any symbol of office on your hand." she asked. "The Hierarch is dead. The spring equinox has arrived, and there has been no Coronation ceremony. Whatever rights his name afforded you are no longer applicable."

I raised the Spear, and let the Chorus fill the blade. Not a fake. I was going to have better luck than Hitler's black magi. "Then I come under no banner but my own. I am *Adversarius,* and if you don't open the fucking door right now, I'm going to cut a hole in it with the Spear and come find the Grail *on my terms.*"

The dark got darker, as if ink had been splashed on the walls of the elevator and it slowly dripped over the emergency lights, dimming them by degrees. The Chorus flowed even thicker over my skin, giving me warmth as the temperature dropped, and Antoine bound a handful of leys to his Will.

"Very well," Vivienne Whispered to us finally. The darkness began to abate, a slow emergence of light that revealed the endless stacks of the Archives. "However, the Spear does not cross the threshold. You may enter, but that phallic symbol doesn't. Those are my terms, and they are nonnegotiable."

I made a show of hesitating for a minute, as if I were thinking it over. Much like she had with us. "Fine," I shrugged. I walked over to Antoine and held out the Spear.

"Nice plan," he muttered.

"Whatever works, you know?" I replied. "Could you sober up by the time I get back?" Keeping up appearances. Making him think I didn't know.

The Chorus felt him probe me, and they rebuffed his attempt. Let him wonder.

For a second, I froze, caught in a black panic that this was all a bad idea. A vision—seemingly prescient—that this would end disastrously. Then I realized it wasn't the Weave peeling apart and revealing the future, but just old memories caught in Philippe's past. When the Spear was brought out of hiding, blood followed. It was an old tradition, and I would have been more of a fool than I already was to think it wouldn't happen.

"Sure," he said, finally taking the Spear. An involuntary shudder ran through his hand, a twitch that scampered all the way up his arm and into his spine. The Spear was quiescent, but it was still an artifact of power and I certainly knew what he was thinking. I knew what he was remembering.

I'm sorry, Father.

Absolvo et amo te.

This would all be over soon. I met Antoine's gaze, and saw that he knew it too. One way or another, the end was coming.

Now that I had been invited, I stepped across the boundary and entered the Archives. The wall became solid behind me, cutting me off from Antoine and the Spear. The Chorus registered a complaint, a rippling unease that moved across the back of my legs. *Relax,* I told them, *this is all part of my cunning plan.*

They had grace enough not to laugh at me. Not this time.

It was like Antoine had said: even the Nazi occult troops hadn't gotten in. Like I could have actually bashed the door down. Marielle had said you needed to be invited in order to gain access, and if they actually did have the Grail on-site, I had a pretty good idea why the place was impregnable. And why being asked was the secret key to unlocking the front door.

Tell me what ails you.

Sometimes the answer is in plain sight. Right there in the old stories.

One of the other daughters was waiting for me, and without a word she led me through the stacks. The Chorus couldn't sync to the magnetic poles, and I knew she was taking more turns through the stacks than necessary, and somewhere along the way, I was pretty sure we had walked farther than the architectural plan of Tour Montparnasse allowed. The daughter, a muscular woman with long black hair who radiated a density of focus that informed the Chorus that she would—given the slightest provocation—be happy to break any bone in my body, led me to a free-standing room, a cube of stone that rested in the sea of stacks like a stone in the river.

There were cases along each of the cube's walls, and on one side, between two of the cases, there was an open space where an ornate and Romanesque mosaic of a portal had been laid. The tile work was detailed and precise, the sort of attentive workmanship that was only found in old Italian villages; the largest tile wasn't more than an inch or so across, and the whole mosaic measured at least six feet by eight feet. I marveled at both the detail and the rarity of such a large piece surviving so many centuries.

The outside edges of the mosaic were rendered as Ionic columns, pure white stone, and wrapped around each was a series of ribbons—red, yellow, and green. Hanging between the columns, suspended by iron hooks that, upon closer examination, were decidedly un-Romanesque clasps, was a tapestry. The Romans had always favored clean and simple lines, and the twisted knots of the clasps had a Celtic confusion to them. The tapestry depicted an idyllic scene, a Heavenly Garden, complete with a lush, viridian lawn, a grove of flowering fruit trees that were caught on the verge of exploding with color, and a sky, brilliantly clear.

My escort stood to one side of the mosaic and raised an eyebrow at me.

"What?" I asked.

"I cannot open the door for you," she said. Her accent was Turkish.

I glanced around, looking for Vivienne. Wondering if this was the punch line. I was invited into the Archives, but only so far. And she had already stripped the Spear from me, leaving me without that potent weapon.

"Mlle. Lafoutain will join you inside," my escort said. "But you must find your own path within. The door will only open for those who know its secret."

"You're serious," I said.

She smiled and nodded. Her hands hung loosely at her sides, but I wasn't fooled by their casual placement. I had been granted access to the castle of the Grail, but I still had to prove my worthiness of being in its presence. The woman standing next to me was a guardian of the Cup; if I failed to open the door, she was perfectly within her rights to throw me out of the Archives.

My guess is that she wouldn't mind doing so.

I looked at the tapestry again, and mentally snapped my fingers at the Chorus. *A head full of institutional knowledge, and no one wants to volunteer a helpful hint?* They twisted counter-clockwise, like springs unwinding, and remained silent. The Architects had too tight of a lock on the spirits wrapped around my soul. They weren't going to help.

The landscape looked familiar, but I had had the same impression after a few hours of crawling through the archives of the British Museum a few years ago. A complicated confusion of favors had gotten me into one of their archives, looking for a landscape by Alfred Sisley that had supposedly been lost since the First World War. Someone had approached my client—known to be an avid collector—with this landscape, and the provenance had been good, but something about the deal had seemed rotten, and my client had asked me to put to rest a rumor that had been haunting her for years. Either the British Museum had this landscape or they didn't, but they weren't telling; she wasn't about to pay $12M USD to find out.

I had spent hours looking at landscapes: works the museum hadn't catalogued because the provenance was suspect or entirely unknown; pieces so badly damaged they couldn't be restored, but which couldn't be destroyed either—curators collect and document, they aren't so keen on throwing things away; and, in a room deep within the byzantine subbasements of the museum, a collection of paintings the museum could never publicly admit they had.

I had found the landscape in question—a dreary picture of an empty lane; Sisley was big on the *en plein air* method of capturing the light, and his early works showed a lack of understanding that some periods of the day were better than others for creating an impression of nature—and saved my client a lot of money. I later learned she hadn't been the first to have been approached with this scheme. There was a scam going, involving forgeries of pieces buried deep in the gray area of museum acquisitions. My client had gone hunting, and last I heard, the underground market was still reeling.

A lot of art is a matter of learning by copying. Copies of other masterpieces, copies of the things the painter sees around him or her, copies of the piece they're working on in an effort to more fully articulate the idea caught in their head. Landscapes are easy: static, unchanging; you could come back over the course of a week, or a month, and the scene will be the same.

There was one eighteenth-century Impressionist who did more than a hundred versions of the same scene. Unlike Monet, who transcended the entire movement with the emotional verisimilitude of his watercolors, this painter's style was entirely unremarkable. My source at the British Museum had shrugged and said, "They're part of history; it's not our place to decide whether or not they're worth keeping."

The scene will be the same. Was this mosaic some view from Philippe's farmhouse? It had that nagging familiarity, as if it was the *other* scene: not the view out the front window, the one everyone remembered; but, rather, the view off the back porch. A vista seen but usually in context with something else. Something in the foreground that demanded your full attention.

A connection came together in my head. It was something I had seen, but not like this. Not so naked. Usually there was a stone in the foreground. A tomb marker. And other figures too. Shepherds, clustered around the stone, inspecting the inscription.

"*Et in Arcadia ego,*" I said. It was a painting by Poussin; the Louvre had it. Seventeenth-century pastoral piece, thought to be cryptically symbolic for a number of pseudo-historical conspiracies. This tapestry was the same view, minus the stone and the shepherds. The world, unmarked by man. Still pristine, still innocent.

My guide nodded, a glimmer of disappointment in her eyes, and stepped back from the mosaic. A breeze touched my cheek, a tiny caress of wind that wasn't the product of some HVAC system. A natural aroma of foliage and blooming flowers filled my nose and I turned toward its source. The tapestry fluttered, the wind coming from the other side, and the intoxicating scent of a pure land, untainted by exhaust or sewage, was a heady ambrosia. I realized the tapestry was nearly transparent. The landscape wasn't a picture detailed on the cloth hanging between the columns, but it was what lay beyond the curtain.

I stepped forward, and was about to touch the fabric when the Chorus sparked against my side, reminding me of the stone in my coat pocket. I stopped, and reached for the hot rock I had brought with me from the beach at Mont-Saint-Michel. "Here," I said, offering it to the daughter.

"What is it?" she asked, making no motion to take the stone.

"What's left of Jacob Spiertz," I said. "Lose it somewhere in here, will you? And never catalogue it."

When the Spear had shattered the skull, most of the pieces went into the water and most of Spiertz's soul had been harvested by the Chorus. But not all of it. A tiny nugget had remained, a twisted coal of an emotional resonance with the faintest hint of a malignant personality. It wasn't much; but it was the Architect. If there were other pieces, they would be devoured by the sea. This stone had fallen above the tide line, and I had picked it up. Just so it couldn't grow into something larger. Lost in the Archives, it would never have the chance to do so again.

A smile ghosted across her lips, and after she took the stone, she transferred it to her other hand so that she could hold out her right again. "Nuriye," she introduced herself when I realized what she was doing and took her hand.

"Michael," I replied.

"Vivienne warned me about you," she continued. "Said you

were the worst sort of bull."

I glanced around at the stacks. "This being her china shop, I suppose."

The ghost of a smile stayed on her lips as she raised an eyebrow, and that was as much confirmation as I was going to get.

"I'll try to be careful," I said.

"Please do." She hefted the stone. "This grants you some respect, but don't assume my vigilance is lessened in any way."

"Of course not."

Nuriye nodded toward the tapestry. "The way is open to you now. Go."

Dismissed and divested of my burden, I reached out to touch the fabric, expecting to feel the tapestry squirm in my hand, but all I encountered was marble tile. The picture still moved, but all I touched was polished stone. I had been fooled by an illusion. One that could even be nothing more than an image projected from behind me.

Turning to rebuke Nuriye about the bad joke, I realized I wasn't in the stacks anymore.

The world had moved, and only as I became aware of the shift, did it actualize and become solid. The stacks became walls, the tall ceiling lowered until it wasn't more than a few feet over my head, and the mosaic of the garden became a different picture.

Inside the cube, the Chorus hissed. They were riled up, unhappy about the sudden transition from one space to another, but my trio of wise men kept them calm. They had been here before. They were familiar with the way the inner sanctum admitted visitors.

The walls of the small room were made from large blocks of granite hewn from the earth with little grace. The stone was old enough that it no longer absorbed heat; it was just the cold and dead flesh of the Land.

Each of the four walls held only one picture, a large portrait centered so that the subject could look directly at the small sculpture in the middle of the room. The lower portion of the sculpture was about three feet high, round and vaguely Venus-shaped—like the archetypal figure found at Willendorf—though it was so old, any similarity may well have been a suggestion of the shadows on its mottled sides more than actual representation. The top was a basin, as if the supporting figure balanced a concave bowl on its head, and it was filled with water and light.

The eyes of the figures in the paintings reflected back the golden glow. I was alone, so I took a few minutes to examine the pictures. Three men, one woman: all done in medieval style. Earlier than Poussin's painting, but not so far back as to be the same era as the subjects therein. Later. Probably mid-thirteenth century or so.

The woman was clearly a nun of some kind, and she sat in a gold chair, surrounded by a host of fearful priests. The background of the painting was a series of concentric mandalas, done in oranges and yellows. Hildegard of Bingen, most likely, done in her style, as I didn't recall her working in this size.

The paintings on either side of her were priests, and the portraits, while sporting stylistic differences, were too similar to be accidental. Their poses were mirror opposites, right down to the curvature and spacing of their gestures. The one on the left hid his head under a miter and he stood before the ghostly outline of a church. At first, I thought it was because the painting was unfinished, and then I realized it was the church itself that wasn't done. The right-hand man stood in a library, and the distribution of color in the books behind him suggested the same outline as in the painting opposite, a ghostly presentation of the church.

The priest on the right was St. Bernard of Clairvaux, the man most directly responsible for the Templars. I didn't recognize the man on the left, though if I were to guess, he was an architect—a priest who showed his devotion by building temples. *Twelfth century.* I corrected my assessment. Bernard and Hildegard had both flourished in the twelfth century. Right at the beginning of the Gothic period. Lots of churches went up at that time.

Abbot Suger, Cristobel identified the other man, narrowing the field of candidates to one. *In front of the construction of Saint-Denis.*

As I walked over to the last painting, I glanced in the basin. It was empty but for the water, and the golden light came from the inner lining, a beaten layer of gold.

Hildegard, Bernard of Clairvaux, and Abbot Suger. I ran the names around in my head as I looked at the last painting. Contemporaries, so it would follow that the last one was as well, but I couldn't come up with a name. Nor did Cristobel or the rest of the Chorus provide one.

The pose was the stance of the Magician—one hand up toward Heaven, the other pointed at the ground—but I couldn't place his face. I stepped closer, peering at the object in his hand. It was smaller than a traditional wand. A writing implement of some kind. He sat in a plain chair, between two columns, and the landscape behind him was similar to Poussin's. Was it the same?

I didn't know, and I stared at his face for a long time, trying to divine his secrets. There was something about his eyes, about his sad, sardonic smile that hinted at a key. Hidden there on his tongue. Waiting to be discovered.

One of Houdini's great secrets was that his wife always carried the skeleton key that he would use to pick the locks. Just before he was thrown off a bridge, she would rush in and give him one last kiss. In that moment, their mouths locked together, she'd pass him the key.

I imagined Houdini's expression was much like the one in the painting as he allowed himself to be led to the edge and thrown into the river. Old lover, cold mother: hide me, and let me divest myself of my secrets. Let me be reborn from your darkness.

What sort of magician was he?

XXIX

"Have you identified them?" Vivienne asked.

She was standing beside the stone urn. The glow from the basin gave her skin a Mediterranean warmth, making her look more like a true sister to the daughter who had escorted me than a spiritual one.

"I have, I think."

"Do you know what connects them all?" she asked.

I glanced back over my shoulder at the mystery man one more time. "Not entirely. Hildegard, Bernard, and Suger were all contemporaries, but I'm not sure who he is. Some noble, perhaps. A patron? I don't know my twelfth-century nobility that well." An image drifted up from the deep well of the Chorus. An empty boat, its oars missing. A single pole resting across its bench. Something that could have been a spear shaft. Or a fishing pole. "The Fisher King?"

Vivienne inclined her head an inch or so. "Perhaps. The Hierarch was more invisible in those days. Not many knew who he was." She indicated the others. "These are the first Architects. The original trinity. The Visionary. The Scryer. The Mason." She pointed at each as she named them. Bernard. Hildegard. Suger.

The trinity. I let that sink in. Was it an accident that I had been directed to the Visionary when I had first arrived? That the Mason had been holding—though, in some ways, it could be argued that he had been, in fact, guarding—the Spear? That the one Architect still manipulating me was the Scryer?

Too many coincidences. This was the key to Philippe's master plan. Re-creating the cosmology. Recasting the original players. Which meant—

"You're part of the plan," I said.

Vivienne inclined her head. "We are all part of a 'plan,' Michael."

"No, I mean, *this one*. Philippe's succession. You knew what he was planning." The wheels turned in my head. "And so did Marielle."

Vivienne looked away, gazing into the golden water, and the light reflected from her eyes. "We are daughters," she said. "It is not our place to participate in the games of our fathers. In the games of *men*."

"Bullshit," I said, recalling something Lafoutain had tried to tell me before the poison had taken him. "You're just as capable as any of them."

A faint smile creased her lips. "That's very flattering of you to say so, but you are—if I may remind you—*Venefice*. Your vote of confidence carries little weight with your brothers."

I indicated the picture of Hildegard. "But she was one of the original Architects. Doesn't that count for something?"

"Not for a few hundred years, it hasn't."

"But aren't the Archives run by women? *Les Filles de Mnémosyne*. You said as much to me earlier. You are as close to pure knowledge as I will ever find. How is that not recognition of your roles within the organization?"

"We are nuns, Michael. Cloistered here, with all the other treasures. We can't leave."

An involuntary shiver raced up my back. To be trapped inside this building for the rest of my life. It wouldn't take long before the Archives—seemingly infinite—shrunk down to a room like this one. Ever-present walls and ceiling. No natural light. Not being able to feel the wind or the rain. I wasn't claustrophobic; rather, I was accustomed to having a sky overhead.

I had been raised on a farm in rural Idaho. We could see the Grand Tetons from the back porch of my grandfather's ranch. Every summer, I had slept outside, under the stars, more often than in my own bed. As soon as I had been strong enough to lift my own weight, I had started climbing. The apple trees in my grandmother's tiny orchard. The outbuildings of the ranch. The rocky bluff on the other side of the river; and later, when I was in high school, any cliff I could drive to, climb, and return from by nightfall. It was part of my upbringing, a facet of who I was that was so integral that I assumed everyone had the same access, had the same desire to explore and participate in the natural world.

After we had lost the farm and Dad had moved us to Seattle, I discovered otherwise, but I always felt sorry for those people who let themselves be trapped by the rigors of the city. They had chosen to be part of a system, a construct bent on self-perpetuation that spent more of its energy and fuel on keeping itself alive than on improving its world.

Maybe that had been part of my fascination with Katarina in the beginning. She was a city girl who wasn't afraid of the woods. We had met at REI, and even though she later confessed that her main interest in learning about rock climbing had been to meet me, she still went camping. We had even climbed the East Ridge of Buck Mountain together. She had looked up at the night sky and not been afraid; she had lain down beneath a talk oak and listened to it creak in the wind; she had seen dawn transform a black horizon into a field of fire and light.

But all of that was forbidden to Vivienne and the other daughters. It wasn't that they had no interest in the world untarnished by our hand; that world was a world they could never touch. Cloistered. Kept. Caged. Locked away. I thought of the sensations that had assailed me when the Chapel of Glass had been cut off from the leys, or the panic and fearful claustrophobia inflicted upon Spiertz in his oubliette in Notre-Dame-sous-Terre. Were these even in the same class as a lifetime of being kept inside a glass tower?

All the knowledge in the world and she wasn't free.

"I'm sorry." I didn't know what else to say.

She nodded absently. Her eyes were unfocused, staring into the water of the basin. "We have never needed for anything. My father, and the others assigned by him, are—were—kind jailers, but they were still allowed to come and go. No matter how much we bent our wills and our minds to the tasks given to us, we could never forget that tiny fact: when they were done, they could leave. We never could.

"It has been argued that the outside world offers nothing that we don't already have. That it is a pit of perversion, and all of its influences are foul. By keeping us here, our jailers are, actually, protecting us from the sin and degradation of human existence. By remaining true to our studies, we are closer to the divine. This life isn't a punishment, but rather a gift."

"But a gift you didn't ask for," I said.

"Exactly." Vivienne raised her head. "As I'm sure you noticed, the Archives are larger than the building they are housed in, but there are still boundaries. You recall that office we met in originally? It's part of the outer ring, a façade we maintain to look like any other multinational corporation housed in this building. Those offices are as close to the outside world as I am allowed, and even then, the wards are so strong that all I want to do is flee back to the inner sanctum of the Archives."

The shiver ran through my back again. No wonder she had been so emotionally tense in that room, especially when I mentioned her father. I wondered if I was wrong about the cemetery. Would she want him that close? So near and yet so inaccessible? Would it be worse to see the plot of land where he was buried, and yet never be able to visit it?

She looked at the picture of Hildegard. "She was cloistered too. Did you know that? She was supposed to spend her life in a tiny chamber not much bigger than this, contemplating God. Her parents offered her up to the Church, and I'm sure the idea was completely palatable in the twelfth century, but—" She took her hands off the edge of the basin and her tone hardened. "—it's hard to swallow such malfeasance now.

"Luckily, Hildegard turned out to be a gifted child. She had visions, and perhaps that is why her parents got rid of her. A daughter filled with the weirding light of Satan. Hildegard managed to rise above such abandonment. She recognized the power of her gift."

Vivienne took a piece of paper out of her pocket and offered it to me. I unfolded the page and looked at the color photocopy of a medieval drawing. A figure meant to represent God sat on the top of a tall mountain, and the mountain was filled with tiny windows from which people looked out at the sparks and rays of light emanating from His being. At the base of the mountain stood two figures, a child whose head had become a stream of light rising up to the foot of the angelic being at the peak. The other was a figure made entirely of eyes—

The Chorus flinched, and I crumpled the page.

Vivienne nodded. "I thought you might recognize it."

I shoved it back at her. When I inhaled to speak, I felt like I was breathing glass splinters. "What is that?" I gasped.

"Hildegard's first vision. She wrote about it in her book, *Scivias*. She recorded twenty-six visions, and wrote commentary on them all. Her record of this one mentions much of what you see here, and of the individual at the base, she writes: '...At the foot of the mountain, stood an image full of eyes on all sides, in which, because of the eyes, I could discern no human form.' Does this sound familiar to you?"

Portland. The tower with the bloody eye. The shining light of the theurgic mirror. The darkness that followed, sweeping across downtown. The wave of cold hunger, rushing down to the river, wiping out all the lights. The Chorus, shrieking and burning as they were torn from me. *An image full of eyes on all sides.* What was I but a confusion of identities, a proliferation of desires and needs held together by a singular foul purpose. What was I but a being with no shape of its own. Only a Will.

Does this sound familiar to you?

How could she know?

I cleared my throat. "It depends," I said, equivocating. "On how you interpret the image."

"Well, that's the question I'm asking, isn't it?"

She still hadn't taken the page from me and I let it fall to the floor.

"I'll take that as a 'yes,'" she said.

"That was over eight hundred years ago. I don't believe in prophecy. I've seen too many of them twisted to suit the needs of the oppressor."

"The Watchers have been waiting for more than eight hundred years. You can imagine how, after a few hundred years, they started to get a little frustrated. No one really enjoys being a footnote to history. No one wants to be one of the innumerable generations who—stoically, of course—kept the faith." She bent and picked up the page. "You don't have to believe in prophecy. For the record, neither do I. But you do recognize the importance of symbolism and ritual, don't you? You have to concede that power is nothing more than the energy of those who are realizing their desires. There is always strength in numbers. What does it matter if it happens to be a picture drawn last week or eight hundred years ago?"

Goosebumps ran along my arms. "Is this the justification for what happened? It was ordained more than eight hundred years ago. We aren't responsible. We're just carrying out our destiny. Is that it?"

Vivienne smoothed out the page on the edge of the basin and looked at the picture. "Perhaps. Would you want that to be true?"

"I'd like—" I stopped. She was right. It was all a matter of interpretation and of rewriting history. Did it matter why Bernard and the Hollow Men attacked Portland? Did it matter why the Watchers had allowed it to happen?

No. Yes. Neither. Both.

If Hildegard had Seen that event, if she had Scried that night in Portland, then she had brought it into being. According to Husserl's argument for the power inherent in scrying. See the future; make the future. The rest of us were only fulfilling the world already visualized. Thinking that I failed to stop Bernard or that I had somehow triggered a series of events leading to this fight for the Crown was to take on guilt that didn't exist. There was no fault to assign, no blame to carry, because there was no free will involved. I walked on a predestined track—we all did—and what I *thought* about my actions and my desires was a subjective hallucination. Every decision I came to as a result of reason and logic were pieces in a puzzle that was already cut. Every hard choice I made was no choice at all.

If I wanted to believe this line of thought, then there was no tragedy. No crime committed against humanity. It was all part of a predestined course of action. We were but tiny players in God's cosmic drama, one He had written at the dawn of existence and was now watching play out.

"I don't want it to be true," I finished.

She held up the picture so that I could see it once more and then dropped it in the basin. "So, don't believe it," she said.

The paper darkened immediately as the ink ran, the lines blurring and smearing. The image of the angel went first, and then the tower with all its windows. The child with the long neck became even more distorted as the page floated toward the bottom of the basin, finally losing all semblance of human shape.

Only the figure filled with eyes remained intact, and eventually it became invisible against the smear of ink. It looked, all too familiarly, like one of Philippe's tarot cards.

"Is it still there?" she asked, watching me.

I blinked and took a deep breath. *Was it?* I took a step closer to the basin and peered more closely at the page. The paper rested on the bottom, edges curling up along the slope of the bowl. The ink had run completely now, and some of it was bleeding off the page, tiny tendrils wisping into the water where they became bleached of their darkness. Fading strands of smoke that vanished as they became filled with light.

"No," I said. "There's nothing left."

"See? So easily dismissed. So easily turned into nothing more than a bad dream."

"You can't dismiss the vision as easily as that," I said. "You can't just throw it away and pretend it doesn't exist."

She leaned forward and looked at the nearly blank page. "I did, though. Besides, how do you know I was telling you the truth? Maybe that wasn't something Hildegard drew at all. Maybe it was something someone gave to me. 'Show this to him,' they said. 'See what he does.'" She shrugged. "Freaked you out, didn't it? How I got under your skin so quickly."

I took a step back from the basin. "No, now you're lying to me." The pictures on the walls seemed to flow, the faces changing into demonic visages wracked with laughter.

"Are you sure?" she asked. "Or is it more convenient for you to believe that I am?"

What do you Know, foolish magus? The faces all danced with mirth. *What do you Know?*

"I was there," I tried, my voice faint against the raucous laughter ringing in my head.

"Where?" Vivienne asked.

"Portland," I whimpered. "When Bernard activated the Key of Thoth and tried to talk to God."

"Were you?" she asked, pressing the point. Her words came hard and fast. "Not according to the Record you weren't. We had a Witness there. He didn't see you. Are you accusing a Watcher of falsifying a True Record?"

Antoine lied. He lied to protect himself and to elevate himself in the eyes of the Watchers. He hadn't done it to protect me; he had done it to take power for himself. His report gave him control of the situation. Whatever he claimed as the Record became permanent. I had been written out, like the shadow filled with eyes. Smeared into the background and then dissolved. *What's gone is gone.*

What was I doing now? Was I part of the cosmological rebirth that was coming? Was it my destiny to take up the Cup and drink from it at the Coronation ceremony? To be Crowned, thereby receiving the vision and wisdom of the Hierarch. Me—the untested, untrained, and uninformed magus—who had been given the keys of power by a madman. Or was that part of the lunacy of Husserl's interpretation: to twist me so much that I argued that I wasn't the Hierarch's tool, performed the tasks anyway, and when the end came, was pushed aside because, yes, I really wasn't his tool after all?

I didn't exist. I had died in the river, buried under all that water and flowing energy. There was no Record that I was still alive. Not if the Record was to be believed, and who was I to contradict the Record? To accuse a Protector-Witness of lying? I was a lonely voice in the wilderness, crying out to be heard, to be accepted, to be loved.

But why? Why did I want their affection? Their adulation? Hadn't I spent five years hiding from them, trying to get away from my past? Hadn't I tried so very hard to not be a Watcher? Yet, here I was: running errands for the Architects, killing the competition, and being twisted by the continued admonishment that I wasn't a real player, that I wasn't worthy of being initiated into the secret histories and occult mysteries of *La*

Société Lumineuse.

I took another step back and collided with the wall. My hand touched the painting and it felt warm and resilient, more like flesh than dried oil paint. A hand grabbed mine and I tried to pull free, the Chorus sparking down my arm and into my neck, but something sharp pierced the top of my skull and the lights went out.

XXX

A t first, I thought the lack of illumination had simply been a result of the bowl going dark, but when the light in the basin came back, I realized I was sitting down, back against the wall, with no recollection of how I got there. I reached up and touched the top of my head, expecting to find an entry wound, but there was nothing but a tender spot. Nothing was broken. The Chorus buzzed in my ears like angry bees, and my sense of balance was off by several degrees in the wrong direction.

Vivienne crouched next to me, and put her hand under my chin so as to lift my head. "Are you all right?" she asked.

"No," I admitted. "It's been a long day. Couple of days, actually." Now that I was sitting, I really didn't feel like getting up. The thought earned me another buzzing pass from the Chorus. Angry little bees.

"I'm sorry," she said. "I understand. I was a bit abrupt. I could have been a bit—"

"No, no. That's fine," I interrupted. "I… just… well, never mind. It's not important." I forced a smile onto my lips. "I get it, though. I'm not the white knight everyone expected."

She pursed her lips. "What makes you think we need one?"

I started to protest, and then wondered why I was bothering. "You know?" I said, "I don't really fucking care if you do."

My social filters were low, and I let the words out. I didn't care anymore. "I don't really care if Hildegard foresaw the Ascension Event in Portland. I don't care if it was *my destiny* to stop Bernard. All I know is that a lot of people died that night, and, really, there's no spin you can put on what happened that will alleviate the moral culpability of the Watchers. You were either Witnesses or participants, and both positions aren't acceptable to me. Both positions are reprehensible."

She looked at my face a moment longer, watching the movement of the Chorus in my eyes, and then she let go of my chin. "Very well." She sat back on her heels, and her hands fell into her lap where they unconsciously folded into a penitential prayer. "You came for the Grail."

I swallowed some of the bile backing up into my throat. "I did."

"You threatened to break into the Archives, to carve your way in with one of the old relics. Do you think you would have been successful?"

"No. I wanted to get your attention."

"Were you trying to impress me?"

A short laugh rattled in my throat. "No. I have a feeling you're far too cynical for me to woo you with a method as unsubtle as that." *The worst sort of bull.*

"Woo me?" Her hands unclasped and moved to her thighs. "Well, yes, 'wooing' me with the threat of violence is certainly the least effective way to grab my attention."

"Is that why you sicced Nuriye on me?"

She hesitated for a second. "There are two lines of thought suggested by your statement, M. Markham. Both of which are offensive to me and to Nuriye. Would you care to try again?"

I swallowed the rest of the rage, and took a deep breath. Her tone had gotten brittle, and it didn't take the Chorus to read an elevation in her stress level. She was right—it had been an indelicate question—but her protestation of affront was partially a cover. There was some validity to the question.

"Fine," I said, letting go of my indignation and moving on. We had gotten off-track once before, and I knew I could keep pressing her, but what would it gain me? Moral satisfaction? It would be satisfying, but it wasn't what I came for. I actually did need her help in this instance, and her permission.

"One must be invited into the sanctuary in order to approach the Grail," I said. "I know that. Just as I also know that I can't 'steal' the Grail; it has to be offered to me."

"And why would I offer it to you?"

"Because you're supposed to."

She stood and walked away; she walked back to the basin and looked down at the glowing light. "Is that right?" she said finally.

"All this bullshit about Hildegard and destinies aside—this endless argument of Free Will versus Determinism that is the topic on everyone's mind—we were talking about coincidences. You tried to distract me, but it's not coincidental that a Visionary died yesterday to put me on this path, that I had to take the Spear from a Mason, and that a Scryer asked me to bring the Grail to him. It's all part of Philippe's grand fucking plan to re-create the world: it's the cosmological re-creation of the original meeting between the twelfth-century trinity."

"You're reading too much into recent events," she said.

"That's a hollow sounding excuse," I continued. "Bernard du Guyon thought he was playing at God with his little soul harvester, but he's like a kid with his first magic trick compared to Philippe, isn't he?"

Vivienne shrugged. "I wouldn't know."

"Your father wasn't part of the plan, was he? He was a casualty in this war. He wasn't supposed to die." I paused for a second, making sure I had the right answer before I took the next step. Who thought he had Seen his victorious ascension into the role? Who wanted it the most? Who wanted to be Hierarch?

"What did he promise you?" I asked.

"Who?" Vivienne tried.

"Husserl."

"The Preceptor?" Vivienne shook her head. "Why would he promise me anything?" She wouldn't look at me. Her lie—*the Preceptor*—was so transparent that I wondered why she had bothered.

"Did he promise to free you?"

"No." I detected a note of sorrow in her voice. The expected outrage was there, as was defiance at being cast in the role of victim. But underneath all that, a hint of sadness. A resigned exhalation, an acceptance of some weight that she was to carry for the rest of her life.

"No, of course not." I said, as if I realized the error of my question. "Marielle was the one who dangled that carrot."

She tried to hide her reaction, but she knew I had already heard the sudden intake of breath. She knew I had seen her hands tighten on the rim of the basin. Vivienne laughed, a hollow sound devoid of any warmth or humor. "She has a great deal of faith in the blind devotion of her suitors. How many did she promise the Crown to?"

It was something Husserl had said at Notre-Dame-sous-Terre when I had asked him about Marielle. *I won't try to convince you that she came willingly, because you won't believe me.* I had been too distracted to listen closely to what he had been saying, but there had been time during the drive to reflect on everything. And the more I thought about the situation, the more it started to make sense.

Marielle had been frantic to get to Mont-Saint-Michel, not for Antoine's sake—though he was just as useful a tool as I—but to secure the Spear. When I had joined her in the grotto and the others had arrived, it had been my job to go fight them, and I had gone willingly. But, the more I replayed events in my head, the more I realized how eager we all were to fight for her. Even at the safe house where Lafoutain had died. Delacroix had practically thrown himself at her feet in an effort to please her.

The winner gets the prize. And they all knew it. She didn't care, or maybe she did—it was hard to tell anymore—and besides there was no end of suitable suitors. How many?

Me? Just one more in an endless line of suckers.

My bluster deflated, like a balloon with a sudden leak. The question of how many—how many others had been tasked before me?—revealed my indignation as the empty posturing that it was. Like the anonymous voices in the Chorus, I was just a face in the crowd. An able body who had been tasked with serving the whim of the Hierarch's Daughter.

Vivienne hadn't escaped Marielle's grasp either. The light from the basin only highlighted the bloodless resignation in Vivienne's face. We had all been used.

"Vivienne Lafoutain, Chief among the Archivists of the Secrets of *La Société Lumineuse,* I ask a boon of you. I ask that you give me leave to bear the Grail to the Coronation ceremony." I didn't bother trying to hide my bitterness. Just get it done. Just finish the task assigned you. Receive your pat on the head like a good soldier—*my ever dutiful wolf*—and go sit in the corner and wait to be called again.

Vivienne grimaced at my words, similar thoughts running through her head. "Landis Michael Markham, *solūte frater* and willing Quester for the office of Hierarch, I grant you leave to approach and take up the Grail." She stepped back from the basin, indicating it with a wave of her hand. "Should it find you worthy," she added, her words equally caustic.

I stood, and approached the basin. I looked in, but nothing had changed. There was nothing there but the gold lining. Nevertheless, I put my hand in the water.

The gold plating shivered, and at first I thought it was the water itself that was rippling and then I realized the motion was coming from the gold. It lifted free of the stone, crumpling and twisting into a smaller shape. I held my hand still, and the gold brushed across my fingers, wrapping and unwrapping itself across my flesh, and a tingling sensation like a mild electric current ran up my arm. I felt parts of my body twitch and itch. All the gashes and cuts and bruises sustained over the last few days were burning. As the gold Cup formed itself in the water of the basin, its touch healed me, including the cut in my arm from the Spear; the Grail healed all of my wounds, except for the one in my soul.

Nuriye was waiting for us as we stepped out of the tapestry, a long cloth of maroon and midnight in her hands. I wrapped the fabric around the Grail, and its light was strong enough that the gold threads in the fabric glowed, hidden veins of light. I carried it in the crook of my arm, almost as if I were cradling a child.

Nuriye fell in step with Vivienne, and they both fell back a few steps, herding me toward the foyer of the Archives. The route back was shorter; the Archives hadn't reconfigured themselves when we had been in the inner chapel, the daughters simply wanted me gone and guided me along the shortest route.

The script on the guardian wall glowed gold as we approached—not silver as it had the last time I had left the Archives—and the wall faded away when I raised the cloth-covered Grail.

The foyer was empty; there was no sign of Antoine.

"Where did he go?" I asked the women behind me.

Nuriye shrugged as she took two steps back. The shadow of a stack fell on her and her face became unreadable.

"He went back down to the car," Vivienne said. Her voice was flat, toneless, and the Chorus tightened in my gut. She had been withdrawn since the Grail had formed in my hand, and I didn't blame her. The only reason my heart was racing was because of the relic in my hand. She was lost in her own head, in her own guilt and remorse. The light had changed when I had lifted the Grail from the basin. It was still radiant, a glow that would transfix anyone who laid eyes upon the Cup, but it wasn't as bright. We felt the loss of light; we carried the memory of a brighter star, and everything seemed dimmer now. It was easy to let shadows prey on our minds.

I hesitated on the edge of the Archives. The floor beneath my feet was still polished wood. One step away from the cold marble of the lobby. The Grail hadn't crossed the threshold yet. I could give it back. I could put it down and walk away.

It is your fight, the Chorus whispered. *It is your right. Take it. Claim the Crown. She will give you her love. Above all others, she loves you the best.*

"What is it?" Vivienne asked.

"Why?" I asked. The Chorus hissed and attacked my doubt, silver snakes darting through the fog in my brain, slaying the rising phantoms of disbelief.

"That is a question without answer, M. Markham. That is an aimless question, one that has no purpose. Surely you are of a stronger *mind* than that?"

"Why me?" I clarified. If Marielle had so many suitors to pick from, why had she chosen me? Why had Husserl allowed me to be the one?

"Really, Monsieur. You expect me to know the answer to that question?"

I stepped away from the edge and returned to Vivienne. Close enough to examine her face. Searching for some clue, some idea as to where I had failed, because—the Chorus' elation at having the Grail in hand, notwithstanding—I had a nagging feeling that something was very wrong. The spirits in my head couldn't shake the sensation, much as they tried. In some ways, their eagerness to take the Grail across the threshold only increased my apprehension. Too many possibilities with thresholds. Too many chances for the world to change suddenly when you stepped across into another world.

"Goodbye, M. Markham," Vivienne said after tolerating my examination for a moment. "We have called the elevator for you. It is time for you to leave." Her face was a porcelain mask, smooth and without any lines or markings. There was nothing to read, nor did her eyes reveal any emotion. Just a blank wall.

"What have we lost?" I asked her, and her eyes went even colder. The light was hidden behind a thick veil.

"Please, Monsieur," Nuriye said from the shadows. "Respect our wishes. You have taken our light. Just go, and leave us in these shadows."

Vivienne remained frozen, though I could detect a tiny tremor at the corner of her mouth. A tiny quiver that, if I were to watch it long enough, might develop into a fracture. But I didn't stay; I let the Chorus pull me away, and I walked backward from the two daughters. Unwilling to turn my back on them. Not yet.

The Grail shivered in my arms as I crossed the threshold and the shining veins in the cloth went dark. The bundle in my arm was heavy, but it wasn't dead weight. There was still power in the Cup, but it was diminished even further now. It wouldn't show any radiance again until it was filled. Not until the morning light filled its golden bowl.

I waited for a second, but the walls didn't materialize. Vivienne and Nuriye remained still, watching me. Waiting for me to leave.

The Chorus swarmed and sparked, pulling me toward the elevator. Pulling me and the Grail. What was I waiting for? Nuriye was right. I had taken the light from the chapel. There was no reason to stay here, no reason to watch the shadows creep into the Archives. I had done enough.

The elevator, the Chorus reminded me as its bell rang. *It is time.*

I turned.

There was no elevator. The doors were open, but there was no car. Just an open shaft.

"It is time."

At the sound of the voice, an external echo to the internal vibration of the Chorus, I turned around. But something struck my lower back before I could reverse myself, before I could complete my turn. The Chorus, furiously tugging at me a second before, collapsed into a burning knot. Pinned, like an angry butterfly. The Grail, even though it was wrapped in the cloth, felt slippery against my arm, and when I looked down at the bundle in my arms, I was distracted by the bloody tip of the Spear protruding from my side.

My left side burned, and I couldn't even feel the Grail as it slipped away from me. Someone shoved me forward and I stumbled, tripping over my own feet that refused to respond to my mental commands. I was as clumsy as a bull in the ring, weakened by blood loss from the picador's lance.

The Spear was pulled out, a savage yank more traumatic than the initial thrust. My legs gave way, and I collapsed in a heap, banging my elbow and forehead on the floor. The Grail struck the marble and rang with a muffled note, almost a sob; or maybe the sound came from my throat. I wasn't sure.

The world was inverted. Gravity flowed in the wrong direction, and my ears were filled with a buzzing harmonic tone. In the distance, Vivienne stood upside down, clinging to the floor like a vampire bat. The Grail lay nearby, its cloth cover coming undone, like a partially unwrapped Christmas present.

It's not time, I thought. *Not yet.*

I reached for the trailing edge of the cloth, my fingers groping desperately for the fabric.

"No, my friend," Antoine said as he put his foot down on my arm. "Not this time."

With a smooth motion, he brought the Spear down and I thought I saw the sun break through the fog, but there was no fog, nor was there any sun. It was just the fiery touch of the Spear as it cut through the flesh and muscle and bone of my wrist.

Antoine, his body shivering and glittering with the fading magick of the spell which had hidden him from my sight, crouched so that he could look me in the eyes. "Endgame," he smiled—that old, feral grin of his. "Your part in this Weave is done. It is my turn now."

I tried to grab the Grail again, but my stump just shook and spat blood all over the cloth. I tried to find the Chorus—to make them heal me, to tell them to make the pain go away—but they were scattered in my head. Like single fireflies, strewn across an acre of open field. I couldn't catch them. I couldn't hold them. I couldn't hold anything. Long smears blurred across my field of vision.

Antoine put his foot against my side and shoved. As I slid across the floor, my head flopped around and I could see Vivienne, who hadn't moved. Who did nothing but watch as Antoine pushed me toward the open elevator shaft. I reached out to her, or maybe I just wanted her to see the stump of my arm.

My right leg went over the lip of the elevator, and my left feebly tried to find some purchase on the cold marble floor. My left hand scrabbled on the smooth floor, and when I couldn't grab something there, I tried for Antoine's leg as he shoved me one last time. I felt the fabric of his trousers slip through my fingers. Too much blood. Too slick.

Vivienne never looked away as Antoine shoved me into the elevator shaft. And what made me let go, what extinguished the fading hope in my chest, was her expression. She knew he had been waiting for me. She had known his plan. This was her revenge, allowing one suitor to murder another. Or perhaps it was deeper than that. Perhaps this was her message to Marielle. *You took my father; I will take your lover.*

But we both knew it was an empty message.

She had warned me, but I hadn't listened.

Goddess help you, Michael Markham, if you are that alone.

I was just the dumb courier. I was expendable. A piece to be used and then discarded.

Antoine had warned me too. *I will be patient.*

I hadn't listened.

THE FIFTH WORK

Felix Anima
> O libenter veniam ad vos ut prebeatis michi osculum cordis.

Virtutes
> Nos debemus militare tecum, o filia regis.

⊣ ⊣ ⊣

The happy SOUL
> Oh, let me come to you freely so that you may give unto me a kiss from your heart.

VIRTUES
> It is our duty to fight alongside you, o daughter of the king.

– Hildegard von Bingen, *Ordo Virtutum*

XXXI

In each corner of the room, squat stands with a dozen candles each provided illumination. Not enough to reach to the ceiling, not enough to reach to Heaven, but enough to light the lower realm. Opposite me, hidden by muslin screens, was a narrow bed, and shadows danced on the wall behind the bed, phantasmal figures partially visible over the top edge of the screens. Whoever lay in the bed was tied down. I could see enough through the gaps between the screens to discern that the figure wore a plain cotton habit, and judging by the shape of the bare foot I glimpsed, it was a woman.

Kneeling beside the bed—on the side where there were no screens—were three figures. Plain brown robes, belted with long strands of polished beads. Their hoods were up, hiding their faces. The one on the left was holding the long strand of his rosary, his fingers working the beads as he prayed. The one on the right had his hands clasped over his ample stomach, and from the angle of his hood, I wondered if he was praying or sleeping. The one in the middle leaned forward, his hands on the edge of the bed, listening intently to the sounds coming from the woman's mouth.

She was making guttural noises: not quite words, not quite moans of pain; growling as if there was something in her mouth, something obstructing her lips and teeth. Whatever she was saying was important enough that he listened, but not so important that he took the gag out. As if the sound of her voice was more important than the actual words she was trying to say.

What I say and what I mean are never the same.

Something cold touched my side, and startled by the invasiveness of the sensation, by the reminder of my own flesh, I tore my gaze away from the tableau of the madwoman and the priests attending her. There was a hole in my chest, one that wept blood, and for a moment, I couldn't remember how I had received such a wound.

I fell, John.

A fourth priest, kneeling beside the chair in which I was sprawled, was wiping the flow away with a blood-stained cloth. He held the rag over a narrow basin and wrung it out. Blood spattered on the dusty floor, leaving tiny blots of blackness.

My right arm ached; more blood-stained rags were wrapped around the truncated end, and around my forearm, a chain of glass beads—black as night—had been cinched tight. The rosary tourniquet. The silver medallion lay on the underside of my arm, pressed tight against my skin by the loops of the beads. The silver ball on the end of the chain—the sphere that hid the cross—hung from an inch of chain near my elbow. It knocked against the wooden frame of the chair as I shifted my dead weight.

The priest attending me pressed his cloth against my chest wound again and I recognized the blunt shape of his hands. I reached over and tugged back his hood. "Hello, John," I said. "Thank you for trying to save me."

Detective John Nicols nodded. "They say you can't feel anything, but I think they're wrong." As a spirit, he looked much more rested. More at peace with himself.

I looked away, directing my attention to the three wise men. "They've been pretty right so far."

"You're letting them be right," Nicols said. "You're believing what they tell you."

"Why shouldn't I?"

"Because they've also said everything they tell you is a lie."

Nothing is true; everything is possible. When Nicols and I had first met, I had thrown that old phrase at him. Mainly to rile him up, but there was some truth to its seeming contradiction. You could find some freedom in the chaos of that phrase. You could liberate yourself from the tyranny of those old manacles of William Blake's—those mind-forg'd ones—by adopting such an axiom as the foundation of your belief. Nothing is true, and so why believe in anything other than what you wish? Everything is possible, so why not dream of meeting God?

"Why are we here?" I asked.

"Because she Saw us," Nicols said.

"Who?" I looked at the woman on the bed. "Hildegard?"

"Yes," Nicols said. "She looked into the future and Saw us."

"You too?" I asked. "Eight hundred years of Western history preordained by this woman. I don't believe it. John. I can't."

"You can't dismiss it," he countered. "Remember the vision? The figure with all the eyes? The child who ascended into Heaven?"

"I can't trust anything Vivienne told me," I said bitterly. "Especially now."

"But you know, don't you? In your heart, you know she is right. You know who those two figures are."

"I'm sorry, John. I should have been stronger."

He pressed the cloth to my chest, and when he took it away again, there was less blood. "Strong enough," he said. "It's all right, Michael. I know it wasn't your fault."

"I can't subscribe to the belief that this all happened because it was supposed to. It makes it all so meaningless, and so many people died, John. There has to be some meaning to it. There has to be some hope that we could have made a difference." I closed my eyes as a wave of pain ran through me, a shuddering pulse that rippled from front to back. When it passed out of me, I choked and coughed, and there was blood in my mouth.

Nicols didn't say anything as he leaned forward and wiped my lips clean.

"She only had twenty-six visions," I continued when the shakes passed. "She saw key points at best. She couldn't have seen everything. Like Nostradamus. And look at his track record."

"True, but you're assuming you know everything he wrote. Maybe the material that was clearly the ravings of a madman are the only works that were made public. What of the rest?"

"Well, I guess I wouldn't know, would I?" I nodded at the three wise men clustered around the bed. "Not having all the answers like them." Now that I had acknowledged John's aid and that he and I were talking, I was stronger. More anchored in this dream. It was easier to breathe now, easier to speak.

"I'm willing to guess that the old batshit Frenchman didn't squirrel away a bunch of papers where he put things down in a much more lucid way. Even if Nostradamus had secret papers, deciphering them would still be a matter of interpretation, wouldn't it? Like the vision Vivienne showed me. It could mean anything. It doesn't have to be a representation of what happened in Portland."

Nicols smiled. "Of course, it doesn't. But that's the case with all of the secrets, isn't it?"

Through the gaps in the screen, I watched Hildegard suffer her ecstatic fervor. Was she Seeing the future? Like Husserl had said: scry reality and fix it in place by Witnessing it. Had her records been better than Nostradamus', or had they been the same sort of vague poetry that we associated with him: open to so many interpretations that it could fit whatever excuse you needed to justify your actions?

But the mission of the Watchers had always been to be True Witnesses, objective observers of history so that there was at least one record that was untainted by special agendas or personal biases. Or was that just the lie all of us eager neophytes wanted to believe?

How different was that from any history we learned?

I got lost in the woods, a scared little boy who was afraid of the dark and the monsters that might lurk within it, and so I invented a way to be strong. I invented a history for myself that would sustain me, that would allow me to understand this strange new world in which I had found myself. And what had that gained me? Wisdom? Understanding? Peace? Hardly. It had been a way to justify the pain.

Hildegard moaned and bucked on the bed, straining against her bonds. Her head moved on the bed, and there was a smear of blood on the mattress. Were her visions any different? What she saw, what she wrote down: Was it a record of the future, or a justification of her pain?

I looked down at my wound, now a pale hole in my chest. The bleeding had almost stopped, and the hole looked like a shadow on my skin. Nicols squeezed the rag over the nearly full basin, and pale blood spattered the surface of the pool. Like rain falling on the ocean. Why did we feel pain? Why had the Creator given us this failing? Why hadn't He made us stronger?

If you believed we were His eyes, distinct observers who could look upon His work and validate it by Witnessing it, then our purpose was to inhabit this world, to be part of its existence as a way of giving it all purpose. It is a grand extrapolation of the question about a tree falling in an empty forest: If no one is there to witness creation, has it really happened?

But was it more than that? Were we justification of His pain? Were our eyes, our minds, our hearts, our nervous systems, our souls a means by which the Creator expressed His own apprehension of being? Was our pain an infinitesimal part of His, split and shared across billions and billions of points of light?

"Of course, it is," Nicols said. He sat back on his heels. "All existence is suffering. Don't you remember the Eight-Fold Path?"

"Why are you here, John? And don't tell me that you're the guilty part of my conscience. I don't think I can take you parroting back to me everything I told you."

He smiled. "No, I'm a volunteer."

"Why?"

"To watch over you."

"What about them?"

"They're transient. They won't stay much longer."

I recalled Husserl's comment about the Architects. *They will leave you.*

"When?" I asked Nicols.

"Soon." He lifted his shoulders at my expression. "It's not my place to tell you." He looked at the three men and the possessed priestess. "You will know, I think. When it is time."

"But not yet."

"No." He shook his head.

I lifted my stump from the chair's armrest. The candlelight reflected from the silver medallion pressed into the pale flesh of my forearm. Cristobel's magick circle, meant to protect him from injury. What good had it done him when an entire building fell on him?

"I fell, John. Antoine threw me down an elevator shaft. I should be dead."

He took my shortened arm and turned it over so he could examine the medallion too. "You should be."

"But I'm not."

He smiled. "Not yet. Death isn't a part of this place. Neither is time. We are like that kitten. The one in the box."

"Schrödinger's."

"That's the one. Caught on the cusp. Neither one nor the other. Not until someone looks in the box and observes us."

"Who?"

"God, perhaps."

I shook my head. "I don't believe that. That would imply

that there is a place where I can go that He cannot. That would invalidate His existence. That would invalidate mine."

"Unless you were God."

"But I'm not."

"Are you sure?" he asked. "You thought you were once."

"That was different."

"How?"

"I was trying to rattle Bernard. I was trying to get him to doubt himself. To doubt that he was right. He was going to kill us all with his insane plan to harvest everyone's soul. I didn't have the power to stop him; I had to trick him. I had to plant a seed of doubt."

"It worked, didn't it?"

"Yes, but—"

"So why does it have to be a trick? Why couldn't it be the truth? One you were more ready to accept than him?"

"I'm—I'm not sure… What do I believe, John? What's the point of trying?"

Nicols laid the rag down on the floor and stood up. He offered me his hand, and waved his fingers when I looked at him dumbly. "Come with me," he said.

"I'm—" I indicated the hole and then, realizing I was pointing at it with the stump of my right hand, I waved that at him too.

"Those are the limits of your flesh," he said. "They don't matter here." He gestured again. "Come on, Michael. We need to wake her up or she'll never stop dreaming."

At first, I felt the pain of all my wounds, recent and historical: every bone ached, every joint complained; the old holes in my chest—imagined and real—burned like hot coals had been placed against my skin; the new hole, this one made by Antoine too, spewed a great rush of dark water—tears and blood; I lost sensation in my right arm again, a frost descending upon my nerve endings. The chair exerted a tremendous pull on me, like a mother's embrace. But I stood.

"There," Nicols said. "That wasn't so bad, was it?"

I looked back at the body sitting in the chair. "It looks pretty bad."

"Well, you were never easy on it. That's for sure. *Time heals; chicks dig scars.* That sort of bullshit."

"I had to be brave, John."

"I know, Michael. We all have to find our own way."

He led my spirit over to the bed, moving one of the screens aside, and as we stood at its foot, the bound woman visibly relaxed. There was blood on her face, in her hair, and on the mattress beneath her. There were old marks on her legs—this wasn't the first time she had been bound. A stick had been forced in her mouth, tied in place with strips of cloth around her head. Her hair, much longer than I had ever seen it, was in a wild disarray about her face.

It wasn't the woman from the painting. It wasn't Hildegard. It was Marielle.

The three priests looked up, their heads moving in such unison that it seemed like they were all working off the same marionette string. Cristobel. Philippe. Lafoutain. My three wise men. All looking very somber and stoic.

Their mouths were all stitched shut.

Nicols shrugged as I looked to him for an explanation. "You shouldn't listen to them. You know how they are. Schemers. The whole lot of them. I'll be glad when they're gone."

"Are they crowding you, John?" I found the idea funny, even in these circumstances.

"No," he said. "But you're still fragile. You still don't trust yourself. You'll listen to them because you think you need that reassurance."

"And I should listen to you instead?"

He waved a finger at me. "I hear sarcasm. That's good."

"Is this a pep talk, John?" I glanced around the tiny room. "Is all of this an elaborate excuse to cheer me up?"

He snorted. "You remember my last pep talk?"

I did. He had held a gun to his head and threatened to shoot himself if I hadn't shown him that I could care about someone other than myself. It hadn't been a hollow gesture. He would have done it. The fact that I was instrumental in driving him to the brink of suicide hadn't been lost on me, either.

"What am I supposed to do, John?" I sighed. "I couldn't stop Bernard. He wiped out more than fifty thousand souls. The Watchers let him. Even if Philippe hadn't known the others were plotting against him, he should have Seen Bernard's plan. How could he have been so aware of the little details but have missed the big picture?"

"He pushed you there, and because you were there, only fifty thousand died." He raised his shoulders and wouldn't meet my gaze. "It could have been worse."

"But that's no comfort," I said. "It's still too many."

"I know." His voice was almost a whisper.

Cristobel's glass eye was weeping, and Lafontain was looking down at his hands. Only Philippe was still looking at me. He didn't look away. *Burn it all down.*

I shook my head and when I looked away, my gaze fell on Marielle, tied to the bed. She was staring at me too, her expression filled with as much focused anger as her father's.

He was still there in my head, even though Nicols had gagged him. Part of him was still welded to my being. Part of me still knew why the Key of Thoth had been built. Why it had been activated. Because Philippe had failed. Because he had become too proud to accept that he was too old to lead them anymore. Too infirm. He had held on too long, and paid the price of that hubris.

"And what was I supposed to have done? Finish the job for you? Tear everything down because you failed. Was that it? I was supposed to wipe the slate clean? Kill all your friends because they betrayed you too. Was it all that petty?

"And you," I said to Marielle, my voice rising now. "What about your role? You used all of us. You preyed upon Antoine's jealousy. Upon Husserl's greed. Upon my naiveté. You used me, so that your fucking boyfriend could have it all. You threw me away."

I surged toward the bed as if I was going to throw myself on her, and Nicols forced himself between us. I raged against him for a minute, which was like throwing myself at a giant redwood, hoping to knock it down with the force of my frustration. When I ran out of steam, I realized there was another voice in the room, a whisper of sound that ran without pause, without breath.

Laughter.

I looked around for the source and realized the shadows on the wall weren't thrown there by the figures in the room.

"Samael," I hissed.

The black streams flowed together into a coherent shape, and the laughter from many throats became a single voice. "Still so bright, my pretty one. Still so eager to believe me. Are you ready for my help? Are you willing to accept my love?"

"Never," I said. "Never again."

He laughed once more, and more than anything else, I wanted to never hear that sound again.

"Don't listen to him," Nicols said. "That's all it takes. Just stop listening."

I pushed against Nicols slightly, more to make him give me some space than to try to shove past him. "Then who should I listen to, John?"

His eyes were bright, shining with a wet light that reminded me of the Grail. "I can't tell you, Michael."

"Because I'm not supposed to listen to you either, is that right?"

He nodded, and when I brushed against him again, he broke into smoke. Wisps of white light that streaked around me, that moved through me. He was both gone and everywhere. All at the same time.

On the wall, the shadow of Samael was frozen, a smear of black ink that begged for interpretation. A demonic Rorschach blot, waiting to be given shape and definition by an unknowing witness.

The woman on the bed wasn't Marielle any longer. She was younger, her face unblemished and unlined as if she had never felt any lasting pain. The wooden gag was gone from her mouth, and as she stared—unblinkingly—at me, her lips began to move. Her voice was so low and her words so quick, I couldn't follow what she was saying.

I wasn't sure I wanted to hear what she had to say anyway.

The three priests approached, and before I could pull away from them, they circled me. Cristobel took my shortened arm in his hands and pressed the rosary-wrapped stump against his lips. Philippe stood behind me, his hands resting on my shoulders so that his fingers touched in the hollow of my throat. Lafoutain took my other hand and placed it over his heart.

Listen, the Chorus said.

"No." I struggled in their grip. "I'm done listening. Not to you. Not to your proxies. I'm done. Let me go."

Be still, the Chorus echoed.

"*Tranquilla tuum animum,*" he said, and I looked over my shoulder at the chair in which I had been sitting. Just like the picture in the Grail chapel: one hand across his knee, palm open, fingers pointing at the ground; the other raised toward the dark ceiling, a tiny sliver of frozen light laid against his stiff fingers.

"*Omne imaginum meae cordis sunt.*"

Everything is an echo, the Chorus said, the whisper of their voices overlapping the magician's. But their voices trailed his by a split second. Echoing. *Everything is an echo of my heart.*

Philippe's hand tightened about my throat, directing my attention back to the bed. I let him guide me, and the flash of light from behind me wiped the black stain off the wall over the bed. The light went through me too, through the woman on the bed as well. Through all of us.

Phantoms. Every last one of us.

The light took my anger with it, and my pain and fear. All the shadows in my heart fled, and all that was left was the placid stillness of an untroubled pond.

Hildegard's lips moved again, and her words—in a language I didn't understand—fell upon me like a gentle rain falls upon water. Tiny drops that barely left any trace on the surface. They fell into the water, and vanished.

You can't see a raindrop as it falls, and you can't find it after it hits a pool of water. The only part of a raindrop's existence that you can participate in is the moment it hits the water. Even then you don't see it, you only see the reaction of the water to its impact. The raindrop, for all you know, may not have existed at all. But something went from above, down to below, and when it passed across the threshold between the two spaces, you were witness to its transformation.

It's a cycle. Water flows down to the sea, evaporates into the sky, becomes a rain shower, falls back to the ground, and runs down to the sea again. The only part of the cycle that we can perceive is the echo of its passage.

I fell, John. Antoine threw me down an elevator shaft.
I know, my son.
What is left? I've been betrayed by everyone I ever loved.
Not everyone. I have never forsaken you.

XXXII

I hurt all over, a persistent reminder from my abused flesh that I was still attached to it. Hermes Trismegistus, in his discussions with his son, liked to remind him of the nature and purpose of the flesh. The flesh is the anchor of the soul; it is the stone, water, earth, and fire that give the spirit shape. As long as you could feel something, you were still bound into this world.

The pain in my side. The wound from the Spear. It wasn't fatal. Not yet, at least, and the Chorus had—during my visionary blackout—staunched the flow of blood. This I could feel, and gradually, I remembered the way the world was.

On my back, resting at an angle on an uneven surface, I tried not to twitch as my spirit filled my flesh once more. The vision faded, falling away from me much like my spirit had risen free of the flesh at Nicols' suggestion. As above, so below: all things move in concert.

While my nerve endings all lined up to tell me how much pain I had recently suffered, I tried to recall the details of my fall, but after the first few seconds of despair and panic, there was nothing. Just the memory of waking up in a twelfth-century penitent's chamber with all my spirits.

The Chorus had carried me, obviously, while I had been off in Never Never Land, talking with John and witnessing the distorted history the ghosts wanted me to see. The world was filled with cycles, and the history of the Hierarch and the Watchers was no different. Too many iterations, too many loops: they all started to blur after a few generations. Minor differences cropped up, but the cosmological revolution always followed the same path. Like the leys—*what was it that Philippe had called them?*—the *desire lines* laid down by our persistent repetitions. Over and over again.

When my muscles seemed to be under my control again, I sat up slowly, and the change in position lessened some of the internal complaints, while giving voice to others. Tuning them out—the body was going to make that sort of noise for a while yet, I expected—I turned my attention outward, to the space around me.

Underground, the Chorus whispered as they slithered along the ground, tasting the soil. There was a ribbon of etheric force nearby and they tapped it, digging into the rich source of energy and information. North was just off my left shoulder, and I was near—I sniffed the air, recognizing that faint, but distinct, dry odor—an ossuary somewhere. One of the lost passages beneath Paris. With the cemetery close to Tour Montparnasse, I wasn't surprised there were tunnels similar to what led me from the Chapel of Glass to Père Lachaise

Invigorated by the trickle of energy from the ley, I summoned a spark and let it drift overhead. The room was roughly square, with niches in the wall that seemed too short for coffins, and the floor was a jumble of stone and timber. I was draped across one of the larger pieces. Laid out on a slab. The spark drifted higher, but the ceiling didn't materialize, and I was reminded of the ceiling in Hildegard's room. Was I still under Tour Montparnasse? Some subbasement of the elevator shaft? The walls looked too old, like hand tools had carved out this space, and none of the junk under me looked like it was a remnant from modern construction.

More importantly, I didn't see a door.

Of course not, Lafoutain noted. *No one has been down here for more than sixty years.*

"Lucky me," I muttered.

There is an access shaft, the spirit of the Scholar said. My tiny spark leaped upward, torn from my control, and it went so high that it seemed to vanish.

"That's a long way," I said.

It's not as far as it looks, especially for a climber like you.

I lifted my stump. "It's pretty hard to climb when you're missing one hand."

I guess you'd better get started then, shouldn't you?

"I'm really beginning to not like you guys."

His laughter echoed in my head until I started climbing. It gave me strength, as I think he knew that it would.

"Your turn," I told Lafoutain when I reached the access shaft. I rested on the edge of the hole, my legs dangling. My chest ached, and my stump had started to ooze blood from all the exertion. The Chorus had activated Cristobel's magick circle and used that energy to bind off most of the stump—the one thing that transferred from the vision to reality was the presence of the Visionary's rosary around my severed arm—but the seal was dependent upon my Will, and I was tired.

More tired than I had been in a long time.

My turn for what? the Scholar's spirit inquired.

Cristobel's argument was that I needed him so that I could understand the mystery of Philippe's plan, and as a spirit, he has managed to tease helpful hints here and there from the grip of the Old Man. Husserl probably should be in my head too, but he managed to dodge that trap. As had Spiertz, in his own way. I understood that part of Philippe's plan now. The Chorus, via the mechanism of the Lightbreaker, was to have swept clean the attitudes and personal histories of the Architects, leaving only their knowledge. The Hierarch wanted new leadership that wasn't tainted by all the petty bullshit and in-fighting that had gone on in the last decade.

The easiest way to accomplish this goal was to kill everyone, but that would mean that all the institutional knowledge they carried would be lost. That was where I came in. I wasn't his courier, or his candidate for succession. I wasn't even the spark that started the conflagration that was going to wipe it all away. I was just the guy who came through later and swept up the useful relics.

"Is that why you were selected to join the others?" I asked the Chorus. "You were his Scholar, Lafoutain. Is this your reward for a lifetime of service? To be turned into a schizophrenic figment of my psychosis?"

Lafoutain didn't answer, and the Chorus' only response was to vanish into the drain of my memory.

"I thought so," I said.

The whole situation was a mess. Everyone was trying to fuck everyone else. The Crown was the prize, and with it came the rest of the Watcher organization. And Marielle as well. That's all that mattered. Keep your eyes on the prize, and be the last man standing. As primal as it came. There is always competition, Philippe had told me in one of those lucid moments when he deigned to speak to me. The secret that lay in the heart of Free Will. The Will to desire. *Whoever wants it the most.*

Anarchy. Will untamed. Will unrestrained. The World as a billion points of light, all fighting to be the center of the universe.

Was this what he wanted? Was this how it was all supposed to end? In a chaotic squabble over the leftovers? After a lifetime of being a Witness, was that all he thought of us? Petty little animals, fighting over scraps.

One of the arguments Lt. Pender had articulated before Antoine had killed him had been that the souls of Portland had been better off as a combined unity focused on the realization of a single goal. It was a better use of their energy and their existence than they could have ever hoped to attain with their own small lives. Was such a unification not a better use of their lives?

I had disagreed with him—rather vehemently—based on the position that no one had asked them. Not that his argument was wrong, but that the methods were morally repugnant. And after I had killed Bernard and scattered all those souls to their final destinations, I had had a lot of time to think about that argument.

There is a place not far from the Portland Airport called the Grotto, one of the few active Franciscan monasteries in the United States. The main portion of the sanctuary sits on top of the bluff, looking north toward the river and the airport. You can't see downtown at all, the bluff hides most of the central core of the city from view, and when the wind blows east to west, the dry scent of the ruined city drifts out toward the coast. You could almost pretend the Ascension Event had never happened. The only indicator left is the psychic pain radiating through every ley line crossing the valley.

I had stayed at the Grotto for a few days, watching and reading the city as it tried to understand what had happened. Trying to understand what had happened to me between the first light of dawn and the moment Antoine had Seen me walking back across the water.

I had been given another chance. The black stain on my soul had been purged, and I had been given new guides. New angels to fill the hole in my chest. What was I supposed to do with this knowledge? With this experience?

More importantly, why had Philippe twisted the threads in a way that had forced me to be the one facing Bernard. What was I to have gained from that experience that would then be useful to him? Originally, I had thought he would have called upon me to serve him, and I had waited patiently for a sign that I was to come to his side. I had never anticipated that he'd come to me, especially to die.

Was that all I was supposed to be: his dumb pack animal? The transformation of the Chorus had afforded him a way to postpone Death. He had willingly become part of the voices in my head, and in doing so, had managed to retain his own identity. Was it a low-rent resurrection, a life beyond life? Or was it truly a means by which the knowledge of the Architects could be saved? If it was the latter, and I was inclined to think that was the case, then there had to be a way for me to transfer this knowledge. A way that wasn't the same as the manner in which I took souls.

A memory stirred. A fragment that unfolded into a blur of steel and shadow. Her hands on me. The cold kiss of the bulkhead against my skin. Her legs wrapped around me, pulling me close to her. So very close. Beneath all the pleasure of the flesh, that other sensation: that sucking, pulsating whirlpool. Trying to draw something out. Trying to take a part of me.

Marielle.

She knew. She knew they were in my head. She knew what they offered, what secrets they held. She had tried to draw them off while we had been at Batofar. In the hallway. That was what she had been trying to unlock.

She had tried, and failed.

After that, things had gotten out of our control, and there hadn't been another chance.

I leaned out of the shaft and looked up. *What time is it?* I asked the Chorus.

They touched the ley, synced to the geomagnetic pulse of the planet, and told me.

After nightfall. Not yet midnight.

Unprompted, they also reminded me of the date.

"Second day of spring," I murmured. The seeds, planted in winter, were starting to break ground today. The dead kings, buried in the cold ground, rising again. The world, broken and bleeding, made anew.

I laughed, and something broke free in my chest. I coughed, spat, and laughed again, my lungs clearer now. *You are a sentimental bastard, Old Man,* I thought.

He had waited until the last minute to come find me. So that everyone would be scrambling to find their new place in the organization. Within all that chaos, I would be able to move more readily, to be more able to accomplish the tasks laid out for me. But he could have initiated this plan weeks ago, in the cold death of winter, when everyone was hunkered down and waiting for spring to come. He could have surprised them all by starting early, but he hadn't. He had waited until the end of winter, until spring was imminent. For all of his education and enlightened thinking, he was still a vegetable god at heart. He was beholden to the cycle of the Land, and he wanted to be properly received into the bosom of that which waited for him.

In the old stories, the young lovers don't flinch when their goddesses tell them the price of being loved. They don't turn away when the ground opens up for them. They know, even before it is spelled out for them; they know what happens after that first kiss, and it never diminishes their love.

Leaning back into the shaft, I sent my tiny spirit light into the tunnel to see if there was any clue where it led. It went around a corner and bounced light back at me for a while. A route to follow at any rate; Lafoutain may have known where it went, but that knowledge was not forthcoming from the fog of the Chorus.

"What am I going to do with you three?" I wondered aloud. They were sulking, Lafoutain's suggestions about the way out notwithstanding, and the uneasy way the Chorus was boiling in my head said there was unrest in the rank. They were captive in my head, and it looked like I was going to miss the Coronation event; my presence wasn't required for it to proceed anyway. If I was supposed to give this knowledge over to the winner, then all I had to do was wait for someone to come looking for me.

Antoine would probably smack his forehead tomorrow and *suddenly* remember where he left me. Then it would just be a matter of cracking my head open and letting the spirits out.

Was this what Husserl meant when he said they would leave me?

I had a feeling I wasn't supposed to die in this hole. That would ruin everyone's plan. As much as I wanted to curl up and die, if I tried—if I leaned forward a little too far and slipped off this shelf—the Chorus would just save me again. I wasn't done carrying them yet, and until I delivered them, they'd keep me alive.

So much for Free Will, I thought, slumping against the wall of the access shaft. I could be pithed like a frog for all that my ego was needed. Just as long as basic motor functions stayed on. Just as long as the pilot light in my soul stayed lit.

Is that it? the spirit of Detective John Nicols asked.

"Pretty much," I whispered, fending off his insistent question. "I'm pretty sure I can see bottom from here. What else is there?"

What about the child in the woods? The one who was frightened of the dark and the unknown? How did he survive?

"Was that survival?" I asked. "Look where it has led me. All that darkness, and for what? To be a pawn in someone else's game."

We're all pawns, Michael. Another spirit intruded, another echo welling up.

"Fuck you, Old Man. You used all of us. Even your daughter. What kind of father does that?"

He didn't answer—probably thinking my question was rhetorical—and the Chorus stormed into a wall of white noise in my head. Nothing but noise.

What else was there?

There's a psychological oversimplification about men: they don't ask for directions. If you swallow that line, then there's a thousand more that follow, justifications and rationales for nearly every injustice or moment of human stupidity that can be read in our history. Men are too proud to ask for directions; their testosterone causes this hubris, this blindness to the world around them, and everyone else suffers for it. But if you look at our stories, the myths that have formed the basis of our society for generations, you find that part of the complex cycle of comprehending the Divine is getting lost.

If we knew where to go, then there would be no story, no crisis, no opportunity to transform our lives into something extraordinary. We would know all the secret portals to faerie, all the hidden paths through the black woods, all the secret signs that unlocked the sealed doors. Not knowing the path is an integral aspect of not knowing who we are, and being lost upon that path is critical to finding it, to finding ourselves.

It's not that men don't ask for directions; it's that most confuse the mundane journeys they take as being something extraordinary and special. Not every adventure from your front door to the supermarket or the deli or the shopping mall is symbolic of the great journey of self-discovery and initiation; some of these are errands. Some of them don't matter one fucking bit, and the sooner you get from point A to point B and back again, the sooner you can go about doing something that isn't a matter of fulfilling a baseline Maslowian need.

Neither is being lost an excuse for an existential meltdown. Sometimes being lost isn't anything more than not having the proper perspective on your situation, or not asking the right question about your current course and your heretofore destination. Being *lost* is a binary state, really, a frame of reference not much different from being *on track*. It's a matter of perspective. Flipping from being lost to being on track changes nothing about your physical state or your metaphysical location. You either know your orientation in space and time, or you don't. Light is either a wave or a particle. It all depends on the observer.

And his state of mind.

What else?

I still had the deck of tarot cards. The pocket they were in was somewhat inaccessible from my left hand (being on the same side), but eventually I managed to tug out the velvet bag. Everything else Philippe had given me was gone, but I still had the cards. I still had a way to *find* myself.

I tugged the bag open and spilled the cards into my lap. I didn't even bother trying to shuffle them; I moved them around for a moment, losing a couple to the long drop, and then picked five. I considered trying to get the rest back in the bag, and started shaping the pile into some semblance of the rectangular deck, but then a thought struck me.

Why?

Why was I bothering? They were Philippe's cards. What was the point of keeping them? John had called my attention to what I was doing in the beginning, but from his perspective, it hadn't made much sense. Keeping trophies. I was hanging on to the Architects. I was hanging on to the symbols of an office which was never going to be mine.

Why?

No more, I thought, and I pushed the cards off my lap and let them twist away in the darkness of the shaft.

I was going to do a five-card spread. Keeping it simple. One for me; two for influences, above and below; one for the past, and one more for the future. I arranged them on my lap, face-down, and then leaned my head back against the wall of the access tunnel for a minute. Reflecting on what I was about to do. *It all depends on the observer and his state of mind.*

Card reading wasn't the same as scrying, but it was close enough that I wanted to think twice before I committed to this course of action. Piotr would be the first one to point out that, invariably, the question asked wasn't the one answered by the cards. The reading always gave you a broader world-view than your tiny query encompassed; your subconscious' way of reminding you that your light was an infinitesimal dot in the vast sea of experience and being.

This is how it ends, I thought, and let my breath out slowly as I opened my eyes.

Valet of Cups. Reversed.

Hanged Man. Reversed.

Knight of Cups. Reversed.

Ten of Cups. Reversed.

The Emperor. Reversed.

"Not much Grail influence there," I muttered as I swept them up and put them in my pocket. Struggling to my feet, I crouched and duck-walked into the access shaft. I had some walking to do, and there was probably another climb in there somewhere. Time enough to think about what the cards revealed.

Time enough yet.

XXXIII

I was a child of the Crowley generation, those magi who came into an understanding of magick in the era following the Great Beast's death. In the era following the occult revival of the late 1960s and early 1970s, actually. We were symbolically aware, charged with an understanding that every culture had its own sigils, its own systems of magickal reckoning. Crowley appealed to us because of the illusion he provided of being a great synthesizer. He spent a great deal of his life trying to convince people of his identity, and in the end, he forgot even that.

Crowley's entire tarot deck was a living thing—highly stylized, overflowing with a profusion of symbols, always fluid—in contrast with the more traditional decks. Like the version of the Marseille deck that Philippe used. While occultists before Crowley like Etteilla and Waite opted for simple designs that plainly evoked meaning, Crowley layered his deck with excess baggage, hiding everything in plain sight so as to obfuscate the real meaning within a wash of noisy symbolism. His cards tended to explode any given query into a profusion of interpretations, but I liked having more than one choice. A selection made it easier for me to understand the true path I should take.

Philippe's deck, though, was one of the Tarot de Marseille designs, one of the oldest patterns still used. There were variations of the Marseille pattern—two primarily—and over the years, printing mistakes and bad color correction had turned those two variants into a dozen or so. In Philippe's deck, the Fool was missing the seat of his pants and the small feline prancing behind him looked like it was about to claw his scrotum and penis. There was only one deck that featured a Fool with a bare ass and dangling sex parts. The John Noblet deck.

There was only one specimen of the deck—in the Bibliothèque Nationale—and it was missing a few cards—half the Swords. Marielle and I had gone to see the deck once, and when I had pointed this out to her, she had said something enigmatic. Something that hinted she knew more than I. As that was a common occurrence in those days, I hadn't given it much thought.

She had been right, in this case. There were other copies. Philippe's deck was complete, and the cards had been made in the last twenty years. Like Piotr, Philippe had probably made his own deck, and the cards, while worn and creased and stained with ink, felt like modern cardstock.

The Noblet cards were simple, line drawings filled in with a few colors. None of the confusion and motion of Crowley's deck. And yet, even with these simple drawings, there were hidden meanings to uncover, hidden symbols that would influence the querent's mind. I hadn't touched the cards very much after I had chosen them; I didn't want Philippe's influence to start changing them. I wanted a pure reading. One without too much noise. A reading that would clarify my confusion, that would show me the one path through the chaos of Philippe's death. I didn't care who wanted the Crown more; I didn't care who was manipulating whom, or how deep the thread-winding went.

I wanted to know my own mind.

The cards were all reversed, and typically that could be read as an error by the fortune teller, an inversion of the deck that, by being endemic, indicated a full rotation. A full circle. But I wasn't inclined to use that excuse. Let them all be reversed. It had been that sort of week.

The Valet of Cups was an awakening. Crowley's card was feminine—the Princess of Cups—and she was the genesis of an Idea. The wellspring of the Imagination. She was—

Devorah.

In Nicols' last reading, the Princess of Cups had been a librarian figure. A woman who had given us guidance. The Chorus had tweaked her spirit, awakening the imagination in her, and she had become a rhapsodomancer—an interpreter of events filtered through a linguistic proxy. Devorah had found her voice in Milton's *Paradise Lost,* and she couldn't undo the damage I had done to her psyche.

What is done is done.

That was a debt I would have to pay someday, and the Valet of Cups was a reminder. Reversed, he was the closing of the springs. The shuttering of the mind. Water, buried beneath the earth, not yet allowed to bubble forth. Instead of being the awakening of the spirit to its higher calling, he was the loss of illumination. He was the soul, trapped in the flesh, bound to stay in this world a bit longer.

I had come back from the sky after all the souls had been freed in Portland. I had come back, because I hadn't earned the right to go on. Too much blood on my hands. Too much that I had to atone for.

But it hadn't been Death. Or the Tower. Or the Nine of Swords. It was the Valet of Cups. The postponed awakening. *Show me the way to the Crown.*

Les Filles de Mnémosyne. The daughters forever caged by the Watchers. If they were the wellsprings of the imagination—the Muses who gave us all our creative ideas—then what did it say about all of us that they were trapped in the Archives?

Show me the way…

Above the Valet was the Hanged Man, who, in being reversed, was the only figure that appeared to be standing right side up.

He was the Fisher King, and I had seen him in Nicols' reading too. He had been in the same place in the spread—the position over the card that represented the querent. He was the Heavenly influence, that which floated above. In being inverted, he was the antithesis of transformation. He was a magus caught by indecision—caught by too many choices, too many paths. Crushed by too much knowledge, he could not act. He was, indeed, trapped. His foot was caught in a loop of his own mental peregrinations, and he could not move. His hands were bound behind him, further symbolism of his failure to contain his wisdom (unlike the Magician card, a figure whose hands were free to indicate both Heaven and Earth). He hung over my head like the sword that hung over Damocles.

It had been hanging there a long time, hadn't it? Ever since the duel on the bridge. Antoine and I had fought over Marielle, and I had fled Paris, and the threat of discovery had been a persistent fear ever since. Stay hidden, and keep the deception alive. Don't let them find you; don't let them hunt you.

The Ten of Cups signified a fulfilled life, one filled with the contentment of family. In Crowley's deck, it was the Tree of the Sephiroth, the ten spheres of Life. Reversed, it was ten cups all spilling their wine. Noblet's wine was dark red, and it didn't take much to read the card as signifying the loss of life. All that blood, spilling out of all those chalices. Positioned behind the Valet, the Ten was all the history I had been fleeing. All that blood.

Below the Valet was the Knight of Cups, the physical manifestation of the mystical element arrayed above. In Crowley, he was an enigma. An individual who wore a mask and whose motives could never be ascertained. He was aloof, dangerous, and volatile. In another time, I would have liked to have drawn this card. He was the wolf, hidden among the sheep. The Noblet Knight carried the Grail and his expression was filled with sympathy and understanding. He was an insightful companion, an empathetic reader. One who intuitively understood the suffering of others.

Reversed, he was a buffoon. A man who was unaware that the contents of his cup were spilling out, splashing all over his clothes, his horse, and the ground. His expression became one of confusion, of chaotic frustration. The reversed Knight does not know why the ones he loves have hurt him so. He can't figure where all the blood is coming from. *What have I done wrong?* he asks, and no one will tell him.

The last card, in front of the Valet, was the Emperor. He stands outdoors, one leg crossed behind the other, leaning against a shield with an eagle symbol. He holds a scepter of office, topped with a globe and a cross. Though his beard is long and white, there is nothing about his countenance that suggests infirmity or dotage. He was the Hierarch, the leader of men and the keeper of knowledge. In Crowley, he sits on a throne, and his leg is crossed in the exact same triangular pose as the Hanged Man. They are not too different, these two men, though one is the king in power, and the other is the king in transition.

It happens every year. The old vegetable rituals. One king is buried, another is born. *The king is dead; long live the king.*

But my Emperor was reversed, because the office would never be mine.

By the time I discovered a locked door, I had the reading all figured out.

For the first time in a week—in a long time—I knew myself. I knew what my role was. I wasn't supposed to become the new Hierarch, nor was I just a tool. I was my own man. Neither angel nor agent. The reading showed me fear, the sort the fortune teller in Eliot's old poem held in a handful of dust.

Eliot cited Jessie Weston's book as an influence on *The Waste Land,* and her book, *From Ritual to Romance,* had offered an initiation into the Western mysteries via the Arthurian romances—the stories of Gawain, Lancelot, and Parzival. I saw the connections now; I understood the rituals Vivienne had enacted and which I had been completely oblivious to. No wonder she sacrificed me; I had let her down. I was not the knight she had expected.

There were too many reversals, though. Too many deviations, variations brought about by the flood of noise of our twenty-first-century lives. Too much chaos brought about by the passions of the body which we confused as being passions of the spirit. This was why Philippe used the old deck: it was pure.

I will show you fear in a handful of dust.

The dust comes upon us when there is no water, when we have lost ourselves in a desert of our own creation. Jesus wandered in the wilderness for forty days, according to the stories, where he was tempted by the Devil. All the temptations pursuant to the flesh. Not the Will. Not the spark. The Devil showed Jesus the desiccated flesh of the world, all the grains of sand running through his fingers, and said: This is all that you are, and all that you will be; why will you not take water from me and make clay from this dust?

I am not a Creator, Jesus said to the Devil. I am a Witness to creation.

The Chorus, emboldened by my focus, sparked through the lock of the door, and it swung open with a groan of ancient hinges. The spark of light fell into the room beyond, revealing the detritus of forgotten maintenance equipment.

A subbasement of Tour Montparnasse.

I gave the Chorus a new directive, and they flew out of my head, silver streamers penetrating the walls. *Find a working elevator.*

I needed to go back to the Archives.

I pushed the zero on the elevator keypad, and kept pushing it until the internal speaker in the car crackled to life.

"Why are you here?" Vivienne asked.

The same question again. The ritual started anew.

I held up the Hanged Man card so that the security camera could see it.

She didn't answer, but the light turned green on the keypad and the elevator started to ascend.

I reviewed the five cards as the elevator ascended, going over the interpretation one last time. Making sure I was ready to accept it. The Chorus started to boil in my head, the spirits of the Architects growing agitated as they became aware of my decision. I held them all down with a clamp of my Will. I had controlled worse in my head for a lot longer. They were smarter than me, assuredly, but I was their master now. They bound themselves to me with their choice, and now they would be bound by mine.

They had thought I would have been more malleable, more pliable, especially after losing the *Qliphotic* influence. I would have been bereft of purpose, of direction. I would have been eager to be given new orders. I should have been an easy tool to manipulate.

The elevator sang its arrival.

The wall of the Archives was translucent, shot through with silver threads, and beyond the barrier, Vivienne and Nuriye waited. Behind them, hidden in the shadows like the faded drawings on old temple walls, were other figures, the other archivists. The other daughters. My heart ran a little faster at the sight of them. They knew something was going to happen; they were hanging on the cusp of possibility. Like Crowley's Moon. That moment prior to transformation. All is possible; nothing is true. What comes next is not preordained, not scripted, not anticipated. What happens is the result of what is said and done in the next few moments.

You See it, Michael, it becomes so; that is the key to the ego of the Moon.

I approached the border between the external world and the *secretum sanctorum* of the Archives. I approached the thresh-

·old that separated the Grail Castle from the mundane world, that separated the daughters of Mnemosyne from the sons of Light.

"The Hanged Man," I said, showing them the card. "He's the Fisher King. The wounded magus who is the representative of the Land. Is that his role?"

After a moment of silence, Vivienne responded. "He is the spirit of the Land." Her voice carried the gravitas of ritual.

What happens next is all that mattered. What will be done will be done.

Juggling the cards, I showed her the Emperor. "And his role?"

"He is the guardian of the Land."

"They are the same, aren't they? Right now, it is the Hanged Man who is waiting to be recognized. He cannot become the Emperor until he is healed. That's what the Grail is for, isn't it? Every year, the Hierarch must renew his promise to the Land with the Grail. Every year, during the winter, he becomes the Hanged Man, and on the first day of spring, he is resurrected and reborn as the Emperor."

She nodded.

I dropped those cards, and held up the Knight of Cups. After a second, I reversed him. "You let me fall, because I didn't understand my role." When she didn't say anything, I shrugged. "It's all right. I get it. We're all trapped in our own cycles." Nuriye stirred at my words, glancing at Vivienne.

"Does she know?" I asked.

"Do I know what?" Nuriye inquired.

"The price exacted from your sister for your freedom." I paused. "Or is that a *promise* of freedom?" She didn't answer. "It hasn't happened yet, has it?" I asked. "You still need to be good in order to get your reward, don't you? Which one is it? Husserl or Antoine?"

Vivienne laughed. "You still don't understand, do you?"

I glanced at the Knight. "I guess I don't." I dropped him, and showed her the Ten of Cups. "Family," I said, and her face hardened.

Then again, maybe I do.

I dropped the Ten, and watched it flutter to the floor. I had one card left. One intuitive leap to make.

"I want to make a deal," I said.

"A deal?" Vivienne was incredulous. This wasn't part of the ritual. "What do you have to offer? It's over, M. Markham. The Crown has been given and received."

I glanced at the other women watching. "Has it?" I asked. The Chorus touched the ley and rebounded from the throbbing tension in the etheric channel. Blockage. The whole world outside was waiting, still caught on the cusp between night and day.

Antoine and I hadn't gotten the Spear until after dawn, and as a result, the Coronation hadn't happened. Nor had Antoine been able to accomplish it with the Grail after I had gotten it from Vivienne. We were all still waiting for the right time. The right moment.

"They're still waiting," I said. "Still waiting for dawn. That sounds to me like there is still time. Time enough to hear what I have to offer."

She scoffed. "You have nothing to offer. The outcome of the Coronation has already been Seen. What can you do to change that?"

"That's a very good question," I said. "I seem to remember you saying how you hated unanswerable questions. This time, though, I do know the answer to your question. In fact, let's not bother with that one, since I know the answer. Let's ask a different one instead." I nodded at the others. "Do you speak for all of them, when I ask you, Chief Librarian of the Imprisoned Sisters, would you rather wait until dawn to find out if the promises made to you are going to be kept, or would you rather make your own choice? Would you rather find your own path to freedom?"

Her mouth opened and closed several times before words came out. "You're a lunatic," she said. "Your mind has been shattered. You have lost too much blood, and don't have enough sense to die."

"Probably," I said as I held up the last card. "But I've got one card left."

"The Valet of Cups? What can that possibly signify?"

I spelled it out for her. "I have the spirit of the Hierarch in my head. A lot of his arcane knowledge, too. I was supposed to pass on what is in my head to whoever was Crowned. You can have all of it instead, in exchange for some assistance."

Vivienne was too stunned to say anything, and I heard a buzz of voices from the other sisters. Before Vivienne could tell them to be quiet, or even find her voice to admonish them, Nuriye spoke the all-important words. The ones that told me the answer to my question.

"What sort of assistance?"

"I need to crash the party. Before dawn."

"That answer is a non-answer. You must offer us some specifics if we are to properly judge the value of what you offer."

I went down the list. "I need a flight circle. From the roof of this building. Targeted to the roof wherever they are doing the ceremony." I laughed. "I only made Journeyman, remember. I don't even know where the ritual takes place."

"Sacré-Cœur," Nuriye said. "On the hill."

Of course. I should have known. It was in the background during my visitation to the apartment where Marielle and I had spent New Year's Day. The vision that was both memory and precognition, brought on by the etheric storm at Mont-Saint-Michel.

Vivienne whirled on the other woman, who stood her ground. "What?" she said with a shrug. "In the shape he is in? He wouldn't make it past the first rank. Telling him gives him nothing of value." Nuriye raised her eyebrow at me. "But the flight circle is a matter of conveyance, a way of easing your journey. Hardly a worthy trade for the Hierarch's knowledge."

"True," I admitted.

"If you only made Journeyman, I doubt you have the skill to inscribe one properly; plus, you need someone to anchor it for you, to keep the target aligned."

"Yes," I said, pretending that I knew the details of how the circle worked. It coincided with my plan anyway.

"But how do you suggest we help you with that? We cannot leave the Archives." Even as she asked the question, I could tell Nuriye got it. She knew what I was suggesting.

"I guess I'd have to give you the tools to let yourselves out, wouldn't I?"

Nuriye laughed as Vivienne's face grew dark with anger. "You go too far—" she started, but Nuriye cut her off with a stroke of her hand.

"I want to hear what he has to say, sister. He did not come back from the hole the Protector threw him into just to toy with us." She directed her attention at me. "But tread carefully, *solūte frater*. We are not caged animals. You cannot taunt us with impunity. Speak your offer plainly."

"I'll give you what I have in my head in exchange for whatever aid I need, and I acknowledge that part of that assistance will require you to be freed from your duties as keepers of the Archives."

"You can't release us," Vivienne ground out. "Only the Hierarch can do that. And until one is Crowned, there is no one who can release—"

"Not even your father?" I interrupted. The Hierarch may have been the one who could bring down the wards that kept them here, but I was willing to bet that Lafoutain—as Preceptor in charge of the Archives—knew as much as any man could about how the wards were maintained.

Her face went rigid, a mask of frozen emotion. I had just stabbed her, and she was trying to not show how deeply my jab had gone.

"I need to get to the Coronation," I said, listing the items on my fingers. "I need to get past the host of Watchers that are, obviously, standing guard to keep *soluti fratres* such as myself out."

"True," Nuriye acknowledged. "That's two." She noticed that I was holding the Valet of Cups with two fingers. With two raised, there was one left. "What's the last thing?"

"A pair of swords," I said.

"Swords?" she echoed.

I nodded. "All things must end the way they began. This started with a duel under the bridge five years ago. A duel over a woman. It's going to end the same way."

"A list of three," Nuriye said, with a curt nod. "In exchange for the knowledge of the Hierarch." She glanced at Vivienne and then at the other sisters. "We will have to consider your offer. It is a dangerous thing you ask of us, freedom or no." She returned her gaze to me. "I am not so stupid to think that the only thing you want is revenge against your rival. If we were to provide you access to the Coronation, we would be acting in opposition to the entire rank. We must consider whether the knowledge of one man is worth the wrath of all his brothers."

"I said that I would give you everything in my head," I said. "I've got more than one Architect up there. The Hierarch, the Visionary, and—" I looked at Vivienne. "—your father."

It was more than she deserved for what she had done to me, but I was past that now. My terms. Not hers. Not Philippe's. Not Marielle's. *This is what I offer you. This is how we embrace the future.*

"There is no need to consider this offer. I accept these terms, and the responsibility that comes with them," she said, and her voice broke.

The wall came down.

XXXIV

It turned out to be more than three things, in the end. Nuriye let it slide. The daughters of Mnemosyne were still getting a deal. In addition to the circle and the swords, I also asked for a corner in which to lie down for a few hours, some medical attention, and a new hand. Antoine was the better swordsman, and even though he was down a hand too, he had had five years to learn how to fight left-handed. If there was going to be a handicap, I wanted it to be in my favor.

I begged off on the transfer of the Architects for a few hours too, even though they were howling in my head. A slender daughter named Lusina brought me to one of the outer offices, and had me lie down on the leather couch in the room. With the lights off in the room, I concentrated on my breathing while she pushed and pulled ley energy through me, knitting bone and repairing flesh. She managed to apply a web of scabrous tissue to cover the wound made by the Spear, and although she couldn't do anything for my missing hand, she accelerated growth in the stump until it was a knot of scar tissue. Good enough.

Finally, she laid her hands on my forehead, quelling the restlessness in the Chorus, and for a little while, I slept.

When I woke, the sky was still dark, occluded with thick clouds. The Chorus, somewhat resigned to the fate in store for certain of their members, responded to my commands. They touched the ley, and felt the swollen frustration of the Akashic Weave. Dawn was only a few hours away, but you'd never know from the ambient light in the sky. The clouds were too thick, there was rain in the air, and the atmosphere around Paris was turgid with denial. The sun was going to break through the cloud cover when it rose, and if there wasn't a proper representative waiting to receive the blessing of the Land, the Weave was going to tear, and the grid was going to feel it. The psychic quake that had hit Mont-Saint-Michel was going to seem like hitting a bump in the road with your car in comparison.

The Watchers were going to be there. No question about that. Getting in on the party was going to be the best trick of my life.

The door to the room opened and Nuriye came in, carrying two wooden cases. She put one down on the floor beside the couch and set the other one on the seat next to me.

"Did you sleep?" she asked.

"Some," I replied. "Enough, I suppose."

A smile tugged at the corner of her mouth. "Never enough, is it?"

I shook my head.

"Vivienne is almost ready for you," she said. "But first, let us deal with your hand." She opened the latch on the case and lifted the lid.

The gauntlet lay in a velvet-lined casing. It was Renaissance-era, mid-sixteenth century, Italian by the looks of it. Two cuffs, six plates to the knuckle-plate, and the finger sleeves were solid pieces out to rounded caps. Silver and gold pieces, hand-etched with astrological symbols. The real surprise was the palm. Most gauntlets are metal overlays to leather gloves, attached via leather loops or ties to a pair of thin gloves. This pair had a hinged piece of silver that covered the palm as well, a piece that was covered with chiromantic markings.

"What is this?" I asked Nuriye. I caught sight of a tiny sigil in the bottom corner of the palm plate. It was the artisan mark of a well-known Italian armorer. "Caremolo Modrone?"

She nodded. "One of a kind. Built for a client who was fascinated by John ab Indagine's *Introductiones Apotelesmaticae*. The sixteenth-century bible on palm reading."

She picked up Cristobel's rosary from where Lusina had left it beside the couch as I had dropped off to sleep, and stroked the ball with two fingers while whispering to it. It quivered in her hand, but didn't trigger; she carefully fed it through the cuff of the gauntlet until it rested on the inside of the silver palm. She said one more word and the metal tines sprang out of the sphere, and with a metallic ring, the newly formed crucifix anchored itself inside the glove.

More words flowed from her lips and the Chorus tingled as they felt her magick. She stroked the beaded tail of the rosary, and violet light limned the black beads. When she wrapped the strand of beads around the cuff of the gauntlet, they stuck to the silver and gold plates. The whole hand started to shimmer with a violet light, and when she ran out of beads, she slipped the cuff over my newly healed stump. Wrapping her hands around both the cuff and my wrist, she squeezed, and the thousand pinpricks of her magick intensified for a moment and then vanished.

"Try it," she said as she removed her hands.

With some effort, I could make the hand open and close.

"You won't be doing needlepoint or brain surgery," she said. "But you can hold a sword." She smiled. "Or make a fist and hit someone."

"That'll do just fine."

"I thought it might." She patted the other case on the floor. "Speaking of swords…"

"Have I mentioned how much I'm enjoying working with you instead of against you?" I asked.

Nuriye cocked her head to the side as she turned the sword case around and flicked open the latches. "Don't get too comfortable," she warned.

Like the gauntlet, the swords lay on velvet-wrapped cushions. They were beautiful blades, and my heart leaped into my mouth at the sight of them.

I stammered something incoherent, possibly something about not being worthy of the blades, and Nuriye laughed. "You're not," she said, "Which is why I expect you to bring them back."

That made me blush, that vote of confidence. It was the nicest thing someone had said to me in some time. Funny how that sort of thing can spin your world so readily.

"Thanks," I said.

Nuriye nodded and shut the case. "Thank you, Lightbreaker. Your curse is about to become a gift to others. That may be the finest choice you ever make." She bowed her head, and the Chorus—for once—was completely silent.

The tiny room that had held the Grail seemed darker and smaller without the presence of the Cup, but there was a fine radiance gleaming from the portraits on the wall. Each of the figures was outlined in a luminescent halo, a dusty glow like the sort of iridescence found on fungal growths in deep caves.

Vivienne had changed into ceremonial robes, a simple frock of white and silver that left her arms bare. Her hair was down, cascading like a river of gold down her back, and on the inside of either arm were tattoos of stars. Constellations of her own invention, star charts for realms fixed in her imagination.

She stood next to the basin, and it was filled with something other than water now. Shiny, and less fluid than water, but not as stiff as Jell-O. *"Aqua vitae,"* she said as I peered at the surface of the liquid.

"Really?"

She favored me with the sort of smile a patient parent gives their underperforming child.

"Right," I said, straightening up. I rested my hands—both of them—on the rim of the basin. "Are you ready to do this?"

Her smile faltered slightly, and she swallowed. "Yes."

Vivienne was going to take all three spirits from me. There were a number of ways this exchange could go horribly wrong, not the least of which was me accidentally breaking her spirit. But Vivienne had argued if anyone was going to be put at risk, it was going to be her. And only her. She would take all three, and if she determined that she could pass them on to other daughters, she would consider it.

I hadn't mentioned that I doubted they would stay very long. I had a feeling the construction of the Chorus was what had enabled the Architects to stick around. Without that web, they would fade into the subconscious of whomever held them. Whether or not Vivienne kept what knowledge they still had was up to her. And them, I suppose.

I couldn't quite tell, but I had the feeling that Philippe wasn't as pissed about this as I had thought he would be. Lafoutain welcomed the transfer, and the impression I got from Cristobel was that the arrangement was more than satisfactory. Philippe was, I think, still reserving judgment. On both me and his fellow Architects.

Or not. For all I knew, we were still unwinding along the path he had laid out for us. I didn't know anymore, and I think—more than anything—that was all he had wanted from me. All his obfuscation had only been intended to keep me from doing what *I* thought he wanted me to do. *You will be your own agent; that is all you will ever be.*

Sometimes, what he said *is* what he meant. Which only makes everything he says that much more convoluted.

Vivienne put her hands on the edge of the basin as well, and stood there expectantly, waiting for something to happen. I took a few slow breaths—in through the nose, out through my mouth—until she caught the hint and started to mirror me. Once we synced up with the breathing, I began to slow them down, making each exhalation last a little longer; and with each inhalation, I took in a little more of the light in the room. Each time, a little more of her innocence died; each time, we got closer and closer to the ragged edge of the Abyss.

With each cycle, I broke a little more of her mental defenses down, and the change was so gradual, so incremental, that by the time she realized the Chorus was in her head—*what I know, I pass to you; what you know, passes to me; Father, daughter, Holy Spirit; let these secrets be revealed*—we were already done.

For a moment, I felt their reunion—father and daughter—and was filled with an overwhelming sensation that I had done the right thing.

Nurlye's hair stirred about her face. I had expected it to be windier at the top of the tower, but the atmospheric pressure was so heavy that nothing more than a thin breeze could survive. She faced east, looking toward the glowing white shape of Sacré-Cœur on Montmartre. Her cheeks were damp, and though there were goosebumps on her bare arms, she didn't seem cold. At her feet, in one of the clear spots on the roof, was a white circle, filled with squirming sigils.

"The light is coming," she said, nodding toward the faint line splitting the eastern horizon as Vivienne and I joined her. "It is nearly time."

"Right," I said, adjusting my grip on the case with the swords. "I guess I'd better get on with it then." I hesitated for a second as Vivienne touched my arm.

"Nothing has changed," she said, and I shivered at the echo in her voice. That echo of other egos, and I wondered again if that was how everyone heard my voice or if I was more sensitive to the sound. "The events that have led us to this place have not been undone. There is still culpability and responsibility for the choices that have been made. Innocents died because of the actions of those who were entrusted with the secrets."

"I know," I said. "We all still have a lot to answer for."

She looked at the gauntlet attached to my arm for a moment, and then her gaze moved up to my face. "Nevertheless," she said. "We may stand up in here in the open air because of your gift. Thank you."

I nodded. "You are welcome." I looked at Nuriye. "All of you."

Nuriye pointed toward the white shape of Sacré-Cœur. "The circle is calibrated to land you on the roof, near the statue of St. George and the dragon. There is an observation tower—a tourist lookout—nearby, with stairs that lead down to the side of the main chapel. You are still outside, but, at least, you are not at the bottom of the steps."

"Close enough," I said.

"I have called Viator Vraillet. Do you know him?" When I nodded, Nuriye continued. "He is friend of the family, and is willing to do us a favor in that memory."

"That is very kind of him."

"He won't kill any of his brothers. At least, no more than he has already. But he will aid you as best he can."

"Hopefully, it won't come to that."

"I hope so too," Nuriye said. She raised her face to the heavy clouds overhead, and the wind toyed with her hair again. Vivienne's long blonde hair danced around her shoulders, crackling with static electricity. "The wind is changing," Nuriye said.

The blackness of Heaven was fading, and the gray clouds that had besieged Paris for the last day were breaking up, fleeing the dawn. As if they knew what was going to happen in less than an hour. One way or another, the Land would make a choice.

It was too bad that I was probably going to miss the turning of the season.

Nuriye was thinking the same thing, but she kept the thought off her face—mostly—as she raised her fingers to her lips. She kissed them, and knelt to activate the circle. The white writing glowed bright, and the thrum of magick crystallized into the round sigil written onto the roof. The Chorus touched the conduit between the circle and its destination; they could sense the golden statue of the angel and the dragon on the roof of Sacré-Cœur.

"It is ready," Nuriye announced, as she stepped back from the flight circle. She kissed her fingers once more and touched them to the edge of my metal wrist, and the electric touch of her blessing lit the trailing edge of the Chorus. "Good luck," she said.

I smiled at her as I took a step forward and felt the tingle of the circle's magick take hold of my leg. I met Vivienne's gaze, and saw the glimmer of her Chorus watching me, and I nodded farewell to them. *Salve, patres. Nunc, meam viam indagabo.*

"*Salve, fili,*" she Whispered.

I focused my Will, and touched the storming mass of energy coiled beneath the circle. With a tiny exhalation, I said *yes* to the magick, and the rooftop of Tour Montparnasse fell away behind me.

The white basilica went from being a white dot on the horizon to a rounded dome that filled my vision. The green-colored sculpture of St. George and the dragon loomed, and for a second, I thought I was going to impale myself on the saint's upraised standard. The Chorus flowed into a swirling umbrella of energy beneath me, absorbing the shock of the landing, and I walked away from the jump as casually as if I had just stepped off an escalator.

Precision targeting: the joy of having a professional set the spell for you.

Vraillet, standing in the observation tower off to my left, whistled and waved to get my attention. I jogged over, noticing the heat radiating through the stones of the roof. The Chorus refused to fold back into my head; the heat made them agitated, even though there was no active threat.

In a little while, the sun would break the horizon and its light would hit this point, the highest point in Paris—Tour Montparnasse, notwithstanding. *Axis mundi,* I thought, trying not to dwell on the sensation that I had been in this situation before. Running in front of dawn, trying to stop those who waited for the light. *Over and over,* I thought, *until we got it right.*

I handed up the wooden box holding the swords and then grabbed the lip of the tower, hauling myself up and over the edge. Inside, the stone was black with age; it was like crawling into a tomb, and the Chorus collapsed into an even tighter array. The stairs were narrow and steep, and the ceiling was six inches too low, and I slipped more than once on the way down.

As Vivienne had warned me, the tower's egress was on the side of the church, and in order to reach the main chapel, I had to walk around the front of the church. The ground fell away quickly from Sacré-Cœur, and the view down the steps and out across Paris was phenomenal, all the more so with the radiant light from the souls of the Watchers who had gathered for the Coronation. Seeing the rippling wave of their lights as they zeroed in on me took my breath away, and for a moment, my courage wavered.

The Architects were gone, and I was on my own. Even though I had made this choice myself, even though I had come here of my own volition, the reality was a sudden shock. A moment of terror at the enormity of the task before me. Even more so than when I had climbed the tower in Portland to face Bernard. It had been different that night: I was the man for the job. I had been driven to that point for the very purpose of stopping the mad alchemist.

This was different. In a little while, the light of the dawn would inaugurate a new era of leadership of *La Société Lumineuse.* There were people inside Sacré-Cœur who were qualified for the role, who had fought hard to be there. What the hell was I going to do? I was one man, standing against the assembled rank. I had no allies, no support. I was all alone, and one man couldn't make much difference against a host of this size. Against all the forces arrayed against him.

One is a start, John Nicols reminded me. *Isn't this how you cross the Abyss? By being here—in the now—and anchoring yourself.* His presence was like a spike driven into the ground, and for a split second, the world revolved around this point beneath my feet. I could feel everything around me: the thick ocean of the Land banging against my spike into the Weave; the thousand points of light of all the other Watchers doing the same thing; the sun, behind me, creeping closer to the horizon as the planet spun on its axis. *Be true. Here. Now.*

The attention of the Watchers was now upon me. Witnesses, every one of them. Making True the Record. For a second, we stared at each other, marking this moment in time.

There were too many of them; fighting them wasn't the way. Just as pushing against the tide of energy flowing into the church behind me was equally as pointless. I could not stop the sun from rising. I could not stop the Coronation from happening.

Philippe's recommendation rose up in my mind, a burning coal of anger still resident in my head. *Burn it all down.* Floating above, buoyed aloft by the heat rising from this hot desire was John Nicols' demand from the woods outside Ravensdale. *Show me altruistic occultism.* Show me that one man can make a difference.

"*Salve, mi fratres,*" I said, breaking the silence, and offering them the traditional greeting. They were my brothers, after all. Against the vast etheric sea, they were as tenuous points as I, tiny outposts barely able to hold their ground against the battering waves of energy pummeling them. They were alone too, as frightened as I was as to what happened next. They were no closer or further away from understanding than I.

We were all Seekers.

"What is the meaning of this, Viator?" someone inquired

from the front rank.

Vraillet, still holding the box of swords, only shook his head. It wasn't his place to say.

But the question had been asked. The opportunity given. I would be allowed to answer.

"Five years ago—" I started, trying to reach as many of them as I could before someone decided to not wait and hear me out. Before they decided to incinerate the air in my lungs. The words were ready, almost as if I had been waiting a long time to make this speech.

Perhaps I had been. Perhaps this was what I had wanted to say to Antoine on the riverbank. Or to Philippe when he had come to die. Or perhaps it was what I had never managed to tell myself.

"Five years ago," I continued, "I was challenged to a duel by Antoine Briande. He was a Traveler at the time, and I was but a Journeyman brother. We fought, with swords, beneath the Pont Alexandre bridge. He claimed victory, and so was it inscribed upon the Record. Yet, I stand before you this morning. Am I ghost, or is the Record wrong?"

No one lit their spell. I continued before the moment broke.

"Two months ago, some of your brothers attempted to bring about the end of the world with a heinous device built from knowledge left behind by Hermes Trismegistus. Look around you, brothers; if you know nothing of this act, then consider the possibility that the man next to you did. That your brother condoned an experiment where thousands of innocent souls were harvested. That your brother cared so little for the lives of those he had sworn to protect from the mysteries that he allowed them to be torn from their flesh and transformed into energy meant to power the device.

"Antoine Briande, as a Protector-Witness of our fraternity, was there that night in Portland when the Key of Thoth was ignited. What did he claim when he returned as the Witness?

That he stopped the magi responsible from causing even more havoc than they had. Did he claim that the deaths sustained were a lesser of evils? It could have been much worse. Did he tell you that?"

The Chorus held its anchor against the chaotic churn of the Land. The waves beating against me were both thick and diffuse. There were too many magi present, all fighting to tap the currents without being burned by the profusion of power. Some were struggling to control their taps, more had given up and were listening.

"More than fifty thousand died that night. Have we become so inhuman that all we can say is that *it could have been worse?*" I shook my head. "But it got worse, didn't it? What happened after Protector Briande 'saved' us all? What came next?

"Your Hierarch, Philippe Emonet, was dying. That is what came next. Consider now, if you did not already know this, the cost borne by your liege for the death of a city. Ask the brother next to you what happens to the Hierarch when darkness devours the Land; ask your brother if he did not know how the death of those fifty thousand would poison the body and spirit of the Hierarch. And with the loss of his spirit, what followed?" I nodded. "Yes, we began to fight among ourselves."

Glossing over the fact that it had started several years prior, I think they knew what I meant. The Upheaval was a general shift in focus; the last few days had been war. The difference between Cristobel's long-range vision and Lafoutain's view from the rank.

"We have all lost friends recently, haven't we? Was it worth it? What have we gained from the death of our brothers? Have we gained knowledge? Does this blood on our hands bring us closer to the Divine? When the sun rises over the top of this dome behind me, will it bless you for all that you have done?

"There will be a new Hierarch soon, and whoever he may be, he will be the leader we deserve. I ask you now, *mi fratres,* do we deserve a man who has lied to us? Antoine Briande did not stand against Bernard du Guyon in the tower. He did not stop the harvest in Portland. Fifty thousand died because he stood by and did nothing. Yes, it could have been worse, but it did not have to happen at all. I was there, *mi fratres;* I went to the tower and confronted Bernard—not once, but twice, and that is more than your *Protector* did."

I turned toward Vraillet and opened the case. The gauntlet was clumsy, but I managed not to drop the sword as I picked it up. The fingers continued to tighten about the hilt as my Will meshed with the magick in Modrone's armor.

Turning back to the crowd of Watchers, I raised both swords.

"You could kill me now," I said with a laugh. "All of you. But, instead, I ask a boon. *Ritus concursus.* The Protector is a liar. He calls himself your Shepherd, but he cares not for the flock which he has been charged to protect. I challenge his right to participate in the Coronation. I challenge his right to claim the title of Architect and to approach the Land. Will you bear Witness to my challenge?"

Vraillet smiled, a wicked smile of satisfaction. "I will," he said, and his reply was picked up by others, spreading in a wave of sound down the hill. It wasn't unanimous, but the roar of approval was more than enough to consecrate my challenge.

"And I accept," came a voice in the silence that followed the shouts of the Watchers.

The tall door of the church was open and Antoine stood there, framed by the heat mirage blooming out of the church. "Ah, the rough beast has slouched his way here at last," he said. He beckoned with his left hand. "*Tempus fugit,* Michael. Bring your toys; I want to make you bleed a little before we end this once and for all."

He held the Spear in his right hand. *My* right hand. He had attached the whole thing to his arm, and much like Nuriye had magicked the gauntlet so I could operate it, Antoine had forced my dead flesh to respond to his Will.

So much for handicapping the fight to my advantage.

XXXV

"Kind of heavy on the rhetoric, weren't you?" Antoine noted as we walked up the central aisle of the church. My attention was drawn to the gigantic mosaic of Christ over the main sanctuary. I had forgotten how huge that piece was. Behind me, over my right shoulder, was the tiny rose window that held the sacred heart.

Sacré-Cœur. Built ostensibly to honor the dead of the French Revolution and, later, the dead of the Franco-Prussian War, the church was erected on the highest point in Paris, and was dedicated to the motif of the Sacred Heart of Jesus Christ. The symbolic representation of love for mankind by the Divine. Used by the Watchers as the center of their universe during the annual renewal of the Hierarch's promise to the Land. To Watch and to Wait.

"They deserve to know," I replied. "You lied to them."

Antoine was examining the sword I had given him. "There are worse sins, my friend. Besides—" He shrugged off the weight of my words. "It is your word against mine. When this is over, the matter will be settled." He glanced at me. "Once and for all."

"Once and for all," I echoed. "It'll be nice to be done with it, don't you think?"

Antoine didn't answer.

Inside the church, the presence of the Land was palpable. The leys came here, pouring all the world's energy to this nexus. Once a year. The abundance of energy beneath our feet was overwhelming; too much, in fact, for the ground to contain. It was almost like an inverse of the blank oubliette where there was no etheric energy to tap; here, there was such density of force that it was starting to collapse in on itself. Too much longer and who knows what would happen. A black hole of magickal force, perhaps. Or something worse. I didn't really want to find out. Nor did anyone else.

Tapping this energy would release an uncontrollable eruption of power. It would be like trying to stick a pin in an overinflated balloon and control the release of the air trapped inside. You can't control the release of all that pressure. It tears everything around the hole, and the entire balloon becomes a ragged scrap of cheap rubber.

That'd be my fate if I tried to tap the power. Turned inside out and spattered all over the church floor.

Antoine could tell what I was thinking. Sweat beaded across his forehead and on his upper lip. How long had he been standing in here, waiting for dawn? "It's too much, isn't it? Too much for anyone."

"And yet, here we are, fighting for it."

He raised an eyebrow. "Are we?"

I wondered if Antoine was strong enough. Was that one of the hallmarks of being granted the rank of Architect: being able to handle the touch of the Land? Was that why the room wasn't mobbed with all of the rank, fighting to be the one given the opportunity to take the Crown? Was Antoine's Will focused enough that he could control the etheric flow? Instead of a messy explosion of spirit and flesh, would he be able to control the flow in a tight beam through a pinhole of restraint?

"Maybe," I tried, seeing if he bit. Seeing how much he knew.

A smile tugged at Antoine's lips, as if he saw through my bluff. He fell back a step and swung the sword experimentally. The one he had taken was the more simple of the two: just a long blade, burnished steel, with a hilt wrapped in gold thread. Layers and layers of gold thread. In the pommel, a single, flawless diamond, about the size of a walnut.

"They're nice blades. Where did you find them?"

"The Archives."

Mine had a slight curve to it, an Arabian influence in its design, and the hilt was plain—black leather wraps worn with sweat and blood. The blade itself was mercurial, shifting in color as it cut the light in the chapel.

He pursed his lips. "A gift from the daughters?"

"Loan, more likely. They expect them back."

He caught me looking at his right hand. "The way I see it, you owed me at least one." He had cleaned up while I had been climbing out of the subbasement of Tour Montparnasse, and his suit was impeccable as ever. When he raised both hands and held them side by side, the difference between them was noticeable against the white cuffs of his shirt. "Though, it is a bit worn," he said. "But it won't matter later." He smiled. "When I am Crowned."

We were more than halfway to the front of the church now, and I let my gaze roam across the space beyond the low railing separating the nave from the sanctuary. The platform was low, only a few steps, and the altar was a simple marble block. Marielle and Husserl stood behind it, off to one side, watching us. The Grail sat on the altar in the middle, and it shimmered and wavered in the mirage-inducing heat. The gold chalice was bleeding energy off, acting as a release valve for the pressure building beneath the ground.

Antoine expected to be healed by the Grail.

When I received the Grail from the chapel in the Archives, I had been completely healed. Of course, since then I had been stabbed in the side and had my hand cut off by the Spear, but the wounds I had sustained earlier were gone. I suspected both of those wounds would be repaired by the magick of the Grail. I, too, had high expectations for the restorative power of the Cup.

"Yeah, about that," I said. "You realize Husserl is going to fuck you for it."

"Of course," Antoine said. "He will try. I'd be disappointed if he didn't. But I have the Spear, and once I am done with you, I will deal with him. He will wait until the very last moment to touch the Weave. That's how he brings about the future he has Seen. Besides, he thinks, given the choice between Marielle and the Crown, we won't sacrifice her."

"Really?"

He shook his head sadly. "She really wound your thread tight, didn't she?"

"No," I said, but it sounded false to my ears.

"She is her father's daughter, and I think he'd be proud at how she has manipulated all of us, but it only works—" He swung the sword back and forth a few times; the blade sang through the heavy air. "—if you let her in your heart." The sword fell back to rest against his shoulder. "I should thank you for that. Without you, I never would have realized how much I would have let her twist me."

"Well, I'm glad I didn't spend too much time feeling guilty about fucking her, then."

Antoine's first stroke would have split me from throat to stomach if I hadn't been ready for it. As it was, his blade skipped against mine with a clang of steel, and I felt the shock of his blow in my elbow. The fingers of the gauntlet tightened about the hilt of my sword, and I shoved his blade away.

"Never talk badly about a man's girl, even when he's protesting that he doesn't care about her anymore," I said as I stepped back to a more comfortable distance. I smiled at Antoine. "I learned that lesson the first time around."

He had thought I would have been lulled by the fact that he

was holding the sword in his left hand, but I knew, after all these years, it was now his dominant hand. The right held the Spear, and I had to watch out for that sharp point too, but the sword was going to be deadly in his left.

I was actually surprised he had waited as long as he had before taking a swing at me.

Antoine swung his blade—one-handed—in a butterfly pattern, clearing space more than trying to hit me, and we shuffled from side to side as we gauged the working space between the pews. Antoine had actually studied longsword techniques with a cousin a half-dozen steps removed who could trace his lineage back to fifteenth-century Doges. His cousin was a Fiore man, through and through, an old Renaissance throwback intent on bringing the old art of sword-fighting back into twenty-first-century vogue.

I learned my technique from too many black-and-white Hollywood films caught late at night at too many nondescript and insignificant hotels scattered around the globe. Basil Rathbone, Errol Flynn, Tyrone Power, and even the ubiquitous *Three Musketeers* film from the 1970s. No one was terribly surprised that I was a mongrel with the sword, a juggler with a sharp stick. I had hacked my way to a partial victory last time, and honestly, all I could hope for this go-round was to not get cut to pieces. At least not in the first few minutes.

Antoine waited for me, his sword moving back and forth. He knew I didn't have time to wait him out. He knew we were fighting the clock. I had to finish this duel quickly.

The air was thick and humid, hothouse-style moist, and already the light was changing in the church. The sun had crested the eastern horizon. It wouldn't take long before the light hit the high windows in the cupola and streamed down on the altar. On the Grail.

It was even harder for the Chorus to tap the ley now. It was like scrabbling against a flat slab of stone. There was nothing to grab. No seams. No ripples. Just a solid stream of force.

I turned and sprinted for the front of the church. Antoine shouted in surprise, and I knew he wasn't far behind me. I pivoted on my right foot, and turned into one of the last few rows of pews. Three steps down the aisle, next step on the seat of the bench, and then a long leap over the rows of pews. I felt his sword whip through the air behind me. Closer than I expected. I was dwelling too much on how close I had come to getting my ass sliced open and nearly blew the landing two rows up. I danced along the seat of the pews, and finally managed to face the other direction.

There was a little more space between us now.

"Where are you going, little lamb?" Antoine asked. He kept to the aisle, moving toward the altar. His Will was rampant, tightly focused about his frame, and there was no sense that he was drawing energy from the ley. He was still more adept than I, but at least he wasn't tapping the entirety of the grid.

Back when we had faced off in Béchenaux, he had used the grid to slide through space, moving more quickly than I could track him. He could probably still do the same here, but it would be a much tougher trick. One I would hopefully be able to see coming. Ripples in the etheric patterns. Disturbances in the grid.

He flickered, his body outlined in light as if someone had switched on a strobe behind him, and I dropped between pews, ducking below the height of the bench backs. Antoine re-appeared, not more than three feet from me, one row over, and his sword whistled through the space where I had been a moment before.

He was close enough to thrust with the Spear, and I turned its point aside with my blade as I skipped along the row. "I can see you coming," I panted. "You're leaving too much of a trail." He was forcing himself through the dense morass of energy, moving against the current, and a body moving in opposition to the vector of force tends to leave a wake.

Snarling, he whipped his sword around, underhand, and connected with the pew. The blade flashed as he cut through the wood, and splinters—arcing with blue lightning—flew at me. The Chorus absorbed them, its peacock shield rippling with meteoric death of the tiny missiles. The spent energy of his missiles slithered along my shield, collapsing into a storm of force. The Chorus kissed this knot and I threw it back at him. Antoine caught the ball of energy on his sword, splitting it, and the energy dissipated as water vapor, a tiny rain shower dashing across his chest and arms.

The Spear quivered in his right hand, its point seeking a target. It was active, a hungry blade seeking sustenance. Our magick was drawing its attention.

Antoine vanished, and the Chorus filled my eyes with their spectral overlay. I could see Antoine now, moving through the ether—a ghostly image impossible to stare at, but definitely visible in my peripheral vision. *In illo tempore*, I thought, and the Chorus responded, slowing everything down for a heartbeat. Within this bubble of slowed time, I moved forward, transferring my sword to my fleshy hand, and raising my gauntleted right.

Time snapped forward again, and Antoine appeared at my shoulder. My blade caught his on the cross-guard, stopping his strike before it even started, and I connected with a strong right hand to his face. His head snapped back, a cut opening over his left eye, and an involuntary grunt slipped from his lips.

He was preternaturally quick, slicing upward with the Spear. I twisted my fist over, and the point of the Spear skidded off the metal of the gauntlet, leaving a long gash in the cuff. The wound burned, ice on steel, and I snapped the hand around again, trying to connect once more, but one lucky shot was all I was going to get. He blocked my sloppy jab with a web of force swarming around the hilt of the Spear.

I backed off before he could press his attack. He let me go, and stood there, watching me like a tiger does a wounded canary. What was the point of distance really? With his ability to slip through space, distance was irrelevant.

"Seems familiar, doesn't it?" Antoine called.

"Like we never left," I offered as I put a hand on the back of a pew and vaulted over. One row closer. Only a handful remained. I risked a glance toward the sanctuary. Marielle and Husserl had shifted, drifting toward us, but they were still watching. Still waiting. Her expression was impossible to read at this distance, and I—

The Chorus shrieked, their colors darkening. Antoine—slipping into physical space again—on my left, and the Chorus caught the brunt of his sword strike, but they missed the Spear.

"Uh," was all I said.

I could see all the striations and tints in his irises, and there were dark rings under his eyes. So much strain. On both of us. *You will always be mirrors of one another.* We were both running on fumes. If I had been more prepared, if I had been better rested, this would have turned out differently.

As it was, I stood there, stupidly staring at the blade stuck in my gut. It seemed wrong, like it should have been coming from the other side, but this time I had seen him coming, and it hadn't made any difference.

A flicker of a smile crossed Antoine's face, and the muscles along his jaw tightened as he prepared to push the blade further in, but in the next second, we were both overwhelmed by a psychic wave of pressure. A scream that echoed throughout my head, scattering the Chorus, and making my teeth ache. Antoine staggered against me, and I sagged against the nearest pew, the wooden bench holding me up.

Distantly, I was aware of Marielle, Husserl reeling away as she shoved him back. She moved toward the railing of the sanctuary, the heavy weight of her magick rippling through the church. Light started to smear, and Antoine's form became a Technicolor blur.

I was still holding on to my sword, and when I raised it, Antoine knocked it from my metal hand with a sharp blow of his own blade. Blindly, I caught his wrist with my left hand, and we stood there, arms crossed, fighting over the remaining blade.

Dimly, I realized he was still holding on to the Spear, and I wondered why he hadn't let go. The Chorus, forcing their way through the haze of pain that overwhelmed my senses, forced me to focus on the sleeves of his suit coat. His arms were the same length, even though there was less of his right arm. *He took your hand at the wrist,* they shouted—a crackling, shrieking noise in my head. *At Mont-Saint-Michel, he lost most of the arm. How is he controlling the hand?*

My control of the metal hand wasn't very precise. I couldn't pick up pins, or pull the wings off flies. I could open and close the fingers. I could hold an object. I could crush an aluminum can. Or a sleeve filled with magick.

Antoine forced me back against the pew, pushing his blade closer to my face. His eyebrows pulled together as I closed my fingers about the right sleeve of his suit jacket, but he didn't realize what I was doing until I started to squeeze.

There was nothing in his sleeve but his realized Will, holding my severed hand in place. Much like the cuffs of the gauntlet around my shortened wrist, the fabric of his coat helped to anchor my hand. But because his arm ended just below the elbow, he had to re-create his missing forearm so as to anchor his new hand. The sleeve of his suit coat provided a framework through which he could bind his Will, and it worked well. To a point. Now I was putting pressure on it, pressure backed by the Chorus and my Will.

He struggled, trying to pull away from me, but I had his wrist still. And his coat. He tried to twist the Spear, and it moved slightly in my gut. Enough to send starbursts of pain into my intestines and stomach, but not enough to make me lose my focus. Not enough to make my grip slacken.

The fabric of his coat creased in my grip as he wrenched his left hand free. He brought his sword down in a heavy stroke, and I had no choice but to retreat. I couldn't block the blade, and I had no way to stop him. I squeezed with my right hand and stumbled back, twisting my upper torso to protect my head as best I could. The blade sliced across my shoulder, cutting deep into the deltoid. I took two more stumbling steps, bouncing off the pews and then tripped, banging my hip against a pew before collapsing in the central aisle.

"Stop!" Marielle was on this side of the railing now, running toward us. "Enough."

Antoine side-stepped through the ether into the space between Marielle and me, and forced her to stop with the point of his sword. "No," he said. "This is what he wanted." His right arm was crooked and bent, the forearm twisted. He still held on to the Spear, but his control of the arm below the elbow wasn't very good. As I struggled to get to my knees, he put his sword down and transferred the Spear to his left hand.

The floor was slippery with blood, and I fell again, pain shrieking in my back as I pulled my shoulders together. My vision was blurring again, and I focused on the blade resting on the bench two rows up. That was a goal I could still manage. *Adducite gladium mihi.* The Chorus slithered along the floor, ripples of magick nearly invisible against the heavy haze of etheric possibility.

There was a ringing in my ears, and at first, I thought it was an internal sound, but when Antoine and Marielle looked up, I realized they heard it too. The bells of Sacré-Cœur were ringing. It was dawn. Yellow light was shining through the square windows of the cupola, and a slow wave of gold was flowing down the western side of the dome.

I gathered myself together and got my feet under me. I was

a clumsy missile, but I was in motion. The Chorus wrapped around the hilt of Antoine's sword, making a connection between my Will and the steel. *Venite mihi.* The blade moved, and my metal fingers closed tight.

Antoine turned as I lumbered toward him, a gored bull making one last charge toward the victorious matador, and his Will compressed into a shimmering blue fire along the edge of the Spear. He realized his mistake at the last second; he realized I wasn't even going to try to stop his stroke.

The Spear slid between two ribs, missed my heart, and punctured a lung. The blade was a cold icicle in my chest, stealing my heat and light, and a sob escaped from my lips. There was no pain; there was just an emptiness that opened in my chest, a gaping void like one I had felt before. But whatever despair I had felt earlier at its earlier touch was nothing compared to the bleakness that washed over me now. This was the cold touch of betrayal, the final moment of your life when you realize there is nothing left. *Nihil est.* This was the black vacuum when hope has fled; this was the bleak nihilism of knowing how empty the Universe truly was.

Antoine flinched. He could read all of this in my eyes, and the desire for victory, which he had been so flush with a moment prior, fled, leaving him aware of what he had done. Aware of the price paid for his chance at Coronation.

I tried to smile. "You have no idea," I Whispered.

He realized what I was holding in my metal hand, and he tried to pull the Spear out, but it was stuck in my chest. Caught on a rib. He let go, raising his hand to deflect the sword, and my first blow opened his hand to the bone. I caught him on the cheek with the pommel, and he finally stepped back. Enough for me to get a decent swing. He twisted away and the blade took him in the side of the neck instead of the front. Blood spurted in an arc, and for a second, my vision went black.

What is done is done.

I staggered forward, bringing the blade back for one last swing, one last cut across his spine. To stop him from crawling away from me.

But Marielle was in the way.

Everything froze, and I blinked again, trying to figure out how I had lost track of a few seconds. She stared at me, unflinching, her arms lifted in a pose that seemed too familiar. I tried to let go of the sword, but my metal hand was slow to respond. The intent was already in the blade. My Will had already engaged. She didn't blink or flinch as the sword struck her; she only mouthed two words before she closed her eyes and crumpled around the blade.

I closed my eyes too.

And then the light of dawn hit the Grail and the world was lit with pain.

XXXVI

Someone slapped my face. "Wake up," Husserl said, hitting me once more. "This is not the time to get lost in a dream. There is no aid for you there. Not anymore. Your Architects have fled."

I groaned as the Chorus tried to silence the screaming sounds in my head—the echoes of the bells and the harmonic reverberations of my nerve endings. The room was too bright, filled with the radiant glow of sunlight. Husserl's glasses were like circles of fire on his face.

"I still need you to do something for me," the Scryer said, hauling me up to a sitting position. "I still need a Witness."

I tried to laugh, and found my mouth full of blood. I coughed, and it didn't seem to help. I couldn't feel anything but hot streaks on my cheeks from the tears; everything else was cold.

"Get one of them to do it," I Whispered, nodding toward the crumpled bodies of Antoine and Marielle.

He shook his head. "You are the one who Anoints me," he said. "I have Seen it."

"What if I refuse?" I asked.

"You don't," he said. "And we both know it."

I stared at his glasses, trying to see past the light caught in his lenses. He Knew the future. He Knew what was to come. Was all this blood and betrayal simply for his entertainment? Could he have made our paths easier by telling us what he Knew? Could he have spared us?

I had told the Watchers outside that I had come to fight Antoine for the right to be here, and that had been a large part of my intent. But there was still the unresolved matter with Husserl and my place in the bigger picture. I was supposed to have been the courier for the Architects, but they were gone. I had nothing to give the new Hierarch. I had already played that card. Husserl would get the organization, but a lot of its knowledge was hidden from him. The daughters—now free—would not be beholden to him. He would have to negotiate access to the Archives. He was going to get the Crown and become the new Hierarch, but what else?

The body has become diseased. It can no longer support life. It must be slain.

Are you happy, Old Man? Have I done enough for you?

He was gone, but I felt a tremor in the Chorus, a vestigial echo of his personality *No, they* whispered. *You were* not my angel of vengeance. You did it for yourself.

That is all you will ever be.

I nodded to Husserl. "I will be your Witness," I croaked, finding my voice.

"Good." He pulled me upright, and the pain of being moved brought me back. Standing was torture, and he pulled me roughly, not caring how each step wracked my spine and spirit. I only had to Witness; the state of the rest of my body was immaterial to him.

The atmosphere in the church was sweltering and turgid, the air filled with etheric force as the dawn boiled the ground, releasing the collected power of the Land. It was power without responsibility, force without direction, and it was going to smother us soon. All of us. Unless someone completed the Coronation ritual.

The Grail was too bright to look at directly, and my vision

bleached to pure emptiness as Husserl lifted it to my lips and gave me a tiny sip of the water held within. I gasped as the pain lessened, as my body found it had the strength to go on. The possibility of another sip from the Cup was promise enough. I took a deep breath and my left lung re-inflated; the Spear was forced out of my chest by the magick of the Grail and it clattered on the altar with a chime of despair. A few seconds later, I was strong enough to stand on my own, though I still leaned heavily against the altar.

My mouth watered as I focused on the gold light of the Grail.

Husserl ignored my fascination with the Cup and set it down. Picking up the Spear, he nicked his palm with the tip of the blade. It whined as it stroked his flesh, but his grip was strong and he only let it taste his blood. Returning it to the altar, he held his cut hand over the Grail. His blood sizzled and popped as it fell into the water of the Cup.

"By my blood and desire, I accept the Crown," he said. "By my Will and intent, I offer myself to the Land."

The waters foamed at his words, and the walls of the church groaned and trembled as the leys churned beneath us. The air grew thicker still, and it took nearly all my strength to draw that heavy air into my fragile lungs.

"There is but one Threshold," he said, "and there is but one Guardian Who Waits. There is but one Spirit, and there is but one Mind. I accept this purification by the water and the light. I accept this gift offered to me by the Land."

The waters subsided in the Cup, and the pressure of the Land around us lessened, as if we were in the calm eye of a hurricane. Husserl indicated that I should give him the Grail. His palm was red with blood, and a drop fell from his hand, spattering on the altar.

This was my role. I was to Witness his transformation. There was but one Guardian, but there was also one Watcher. God may have made the Universe, but it didn't exist until His Shadow observed it. All light is but a point in time and space until it has a direction, until it has a purpose. Nothing moves without a destination, and to have a destination, you must have a second point.

"Witness me," Husserl said. The fires of his glasses flickered and danced. "Attend to my Ascension."

He had Seen it, hadn't he? He had Seen this moment a long time ago, and everything had been a matter of waiting for it to arrive. The Silent Guardian Who Waits. He certainly qualified. He had been very patient. *You can't change what I've Seen.*

But he had been trying so very hard to convince me, hadn't he? When I had the Architects in my head, I had been a Singularity. A point past which he hadn't been able to See. Was that still the case? When I gave the Architects to Vivienne, had the future suddenly become clear to the Scryer? But that would imply that what he had Seen had been correct. I hadn't obscured him at all, in that case. I had simply caused him to be *uncertain,* but that hadn't changed the future.

And he had waited, patiently, on the edge of everything. Waiting until there was no way his touch could disturb what he had Seen.

"Give me the Cup," Husserl said, a note of tension creeping into his voice. He raised his blood-slicked hand, and his glasses shivered slightly as his palm entered his field of vision.

Why was he nervous? He Saw the future in his glasses. He already knew whether or not I gave him the Cup. He already Knew what was to happen. If I didn't give him the Cup, then why was he trying to hide that fact from me? The future was inviolate; once Seen, it happened.

Omne imaginum meae cordis sunt, the Chorus whispered. Everything is an echo.

It was all a matter of interpretation. Nicols had said as much. That was the case with all the secrets. What we Saw, what we

Knew, what we Believed was in our own heads.

We were observers of the world, tiny little lights who looked upon the mystery of creation and deciphered it as best we could. Wasn't this the whole course of human exploration and thought? Trying to figure out what it all meant? We didn't know, and we knew we didn't know, and that was why we kept trying. That was why we kept rising every day and looking toward the dawn. Would we see it differently today? Would we understand its secrets this morning?

Husserl was a Watcher. He was a manipulator of threads. Like Hildegard, he had visions, and that gave him an anchor to which he could bind threads. He could Make the future from what he Saw, but he had to create the connections. That is why we had been led to this point in time, to this place. So that his vision could be realized. So that his future could be created.

He had Seen me holding the cup. That was his vision. This was as far as it went. He and I, standing here. Me, with the cup; he, with the bloodied hand. This was the future, and all that remained was to interpret it.

I was to be his Witness. He was God, and I was to play the part of his Shadow, making real his world by agreeing to his interpretation.

I tilted the Cup and poured the water out.

"What are you doing?" Husserl demanded.

"It's not my future," I said.

"But it is," he said. "You can't change it."

"I can refuse to participate," I said.

He laughed. "What will that prove? That you want to be martyred?" He pointed at the Cup. "We're at the nexus of life, you idiot. You can't empty it."

He was right. The Cup was still full. I poured it out a second time and when I righted it, the chalice was still full.

"Give it to me," he said. "Witness me, and I will grant you whatever is in my power to do so. Defy me, and I will have any one of the men outside kill you and take your place." He smiled. "I am sure I can find a few volunteers."

He had a point there. I looked at the swirling waters of the Grail. What was my choice? Be party to his future, or be removed from it. Life, or death. What other terms are there ever with any choice, really?

Every moment, in every day, we make that choice, don't we? Do we continue to live, or do we give up? Do we take this next breath, look toward the next second of our lives, or do we shut our eyes and let it slip away? We no longer care to See; we don't want to Know; we are no longer willing to participate in this mystery. Our eyes will not record existence.

Hildegard's vision swam into my head—the one Vivienne had shown me, the one I had thrown into the Cup where it had dissolved. The angel atop the mountain of iron filled with windows and souls. The man who was nothing but eyes, staring in every direction, and the child who had been raised to Heaven where he was allowed to See of the Divine.

I had thought it represented the Ascension Event in Portland. I had thought I had been the man filled with eyes—the voices of the Chorus. But it was all a matter of interpretation, wasn't it? Why couldn't it be a vision of this moment? Why couldn't Husserl, with his scrying glasses, be the man filled with eyes. Why couldn't I be the one who had been raised up. The man who had been made into a child again.

Rede, mi fili.

Go back, my son.

I had been given another chance. I had to find my way home. I had to earn the right to be raised up again.

I was the child.

Husserl was the specter filled with eyes, looking in too many directions at once. Too many echoes. Too many reflections. Too many choices. *I am sure I can find a few volunteers.*

That was either an empty threat or he truly didn't need me. If so, then why bother with me at all?

Because it came down to a choice. To a matter of belief. Was the future his or mine? Or none of ours? Was it fixed because he had Seen it, or could there be an alternative? One based on a different *interpretation*.

He had Seen the future, but he needed me to believe in his vision of it. He needed me to accept it as the truth. Otherwise, it was just a dream, a mad vision born from his brain, a vision without anchor, without another soul to give it meaning. That was the crux of Hildegard's pain, wasn't it? She needed someone to acknowledge her visions, to hear her story, and to tell her that it could be true. Someone needed to believe.

I raised the Grail and flung the contents in Husserl's face. The fire in his glasses went out, snuffed out by sheets of falling rain, and his face went pale. "What are you—" he started, and then he shook his head. "No," he said. "No. No. No."

There was water on the inside of his glasses too. Water that disturbed his vision, that broke up the purity of his scrying mirror. He was seeing in too many directions now. Too many futures. Too many choices.

He ripped the glasses off his face. "No," he shouted. "I have Seen—"

I picked up the Spear and drove it into his throat, splitting his voice box. He gargled and squirmed around the point, his glasses falling from numb fingers. The light stayed fierce in his eyes for a moment, fighting to keep his vision alive. Until I leaned against the Spear and shoved it further in. Back, and up, into his brain.

The Land trembled as he collapsed, and the calm surrounding the altar vanished. The weight of the Crown—so very near his own head—came down on mine instead. Gasping at the immense weight, I let go of the Spear and reached for the Grail.

Marielle woke up first. Her eyelids fluttered a few times, and I watched as she came back to herself. Pain crossed her face, leaving lines in her forehead and at the corners of her eyes. I recalled staring at her face in bed that morning long ago when we had met at the dawn of the new aeon. I could have stared at it the whole day, and now, I felt time slow to a crawl as I watched her wake once again. She was a beautiful woman, and for a little while, I had been happy with her. For a little while, I had dreamed that I would be the one to stay with her.

Antoine groaned, and his hand feebly crawled toward his throat. The cut was there, but covered in a heavy scab that threatened to crack open again if he moved too much.

They were alive because I had wanted them to be, but they weren't healed. Not yet.

The Cup sat between my feet, and I waited for them to be aware of both me and the Grail, and the heavy weight of the Land, unrequited. The Coronation, unfinished.

"Now, the way I understand this ceremony is that someone needs to recognize the one who takes the oath. Is that right? Which means I only need one of you to be my Witness."

I watched their reactions: Marielle didn't look away; Antoine lowered his eyes.

"It may seem a bit brutal of me to heal you enough that you could attend to my choice, doesn't it? I mean, you were both busy dying here, and I could have just let one of you go, and skipped this drama. Right? That would have been kind of me." I leaned forward. "But, really? Do you think you deserve such kindness from me right now?"

"No." Antoine's voice was a gravely rasp.

"You really hate me, don't you?" I asked him.

His gaze flickered up toward me for an instant, and then slid away. "I'm not going to give you that satisfaction," he murmured. "Just end it, and be done."

"That would imply that what I want is to break your spirit and take away everything you ever wanted," I replied. "But, Antoine, *my friend,* I am not you. Even though we have been told—time and again—that we are the same." I heard Marielle's breath hiss in her throat.

"I know what you tried to do at Batofar," I said to her. "I know what you tried to take. And I know what you did to Vivienne. Here—*nunc*—I Know you, little sister."

I took a step back, taking a moment to let go of the steam building in my voice. "Frankly, I'm not all that happy with either of you being my Witness. I would have had Husserl do it, but he couldn't let go of his own vision. What about you two?" I watched them carefully as I crouched down and picked up the Grail. "Still scheming to take it from me?"

I had already drunk my fill and had my body restored, and they both watched—Antoine more greedily than Marielle—as I used my right hand to lift the Cup to my lips. The magick of the Land, flowing through the Grail, had made me almost whole again. I had been purified to be a ready vessel for the spirit of the Land. The Hierarch had to be whole. My right hand was still gone, but the gauntlet had become solidly fused to my wrist now. Once I took the oath, the Land would complete my transformation, filling the gauntlet with bone and flesh.

"Do you remember what you said to me when we were in Portland?" I asked Antoine as I set the Grail down. "We were standing beside the Willamette River, before I went back to face Bernard. You pointed out that I wasn't supposed to be there. I was—what did you say?" When he didn't leap to answer, I filled it in for him. "I was the 'dead man lost to us all.' Do you remember?"

His tongue wet his lips, and he nodded.

"It's true," I said. "And I should have listened to you then."

"Michael—" Marielle started, but I stopped her voice with a flick of the Chorus.

"There needs to be a Witness," I said. "And there is nothing you can say to me that can change my mind." I stood, and waved a hand toward the back of the church. "I could go out there and ask for a volunteer, but this choice, *my choice*—doesn't need to be that complicated."

I smiled at her. "It's pretty easy, actually. You two need to come to a consensus. One of you is going to be the Witness, and you have to decide who that person will be."

"Why?" Antoine found his voice. "Why should we choose which one of us dies?"

I shook my head. "I didn't say anything about killing one of you."

Uncertainty flickered across his face, and for a second, Antoine was naked before me, and I could see through his flesh. I looked on his soul, and there was no satisfaction in Knowing him because I realized, as I saw the light of his spirit, that he wasn't that much of a stranger in the end.

In the woods, lost, a small child, naked before the light and shadow, looking up. *Why?* had been his question too.

"My choice," I said with a little sadness, "is to reject both of you. I don't want the Crown. My choice is to be free of the responsibility of being a Watcher, and of being Watched. In a moment, you two will be all alone here, and then the only thread that you can twist will be the one next to you."

Marielle closed her eyes finally and lowered her head.

What is gone is gone.

EPILOGUE

The Chorus flew into the studio like an owl, darted around my head, and then left again, returning to their watch post on the roof of the barn. *Visitors.* A single car, coming slowly down the old road from the highway. Seeing the landscape around the farm through their psychic radar, I watched the sedan approach. Two souls: one in front, one in back; I recognized them both, though they had been changed by the coming of the spring.

I wandered over to the sink by the window to wash my brush, and looked out at the yard. The flowers were blooming in the old field; it was starting to look like I remembered it. Though there were no geese and no little girl to chase them.

The car rolled up to the main house, and Marielle got out of the back. Antoine stayed in the car. Driver's seat. The significance of their positions in the vehicle was not lost on me.

I had finished drying my hands by the time Marielle walked across the yard to the barn. It hadn't housed horses since she had gone off to school, and Philippe had turned it into a makeshift studio, complete with a small furnace for glass in one corner.

Someday I might try my hand at glass, to see how much of Cristobel I still had. Though judging by the way I was making a mess out of the watercolors, I was going to be a dismal glass blower. Probably just as well; the artist's life was a little too sedentary for me anyway.

When I had first arrived at the old farmhouse, I had spent a few days cleaning out the main house, getting it ready for habitation again. Philippe hadn't been here for a few years, and the whole place, while still sealed from the elements and curious locals with too much wine in their bloodstreams, had become filled with dead air and ghosts. It had needed a good cleansing.

I had then turned my attention to the barn and had discovered the canvases and the glass-blowing tools. A memory of Cristobel's initiation had given me an idea, and after a few days of poking through books in the extensive library, I had formulated a spell.

I hadn't taken the oath, in the end, and the Land had been generous enough to let me go with the healing magick of the Grail still upon me. My right hand was still gone, and the gauntlet was still attached to my wrist. I could have had Nuriye undo her magick and remove it, but I had wanted to get out of Paris. I had wanted to put all of my past behind me.

Besides, the daughters were undoubtedly busy. Vivienne had managed to breach the wards enough to allow access to the roof of Tour Montparnasse, but it was going to take a little longer, I suspected, to free them entirely from that building. They didn't need me underfoot.

The spell I had in mind required a lot of heat, and the glass-blowing furnace turned out to be perfectly suitable for my needs. After two nights of incantations and preparations, I had gone into Carcassone and stocked up on raw meat and fish. I was going to need a lot of protein afterward.

The glass-blowing furnace had come back to life with some reluctance, as if it was unwilling to serve a new master, but I stroked it in the right way and it slowly became a white-hot core. The Chorus had shielded my eyes and my flesh, and a heavy apron—inscribed with a number of seals and sigils—protected me from the brunt of the heat as the forge melted the gauntlet down. I shaped a new hand from the magick fire and bound it to the liquid smoke of Cristobel's rosary beads. I stole marrow and bone from my feet and made new fingers, I sloughed flesh off my thighs and ass to make new skin, and I kept John ab Indagine's chiromantic drawing as the foundation of my new palm.

The lifeline went all the way around the base of my palm, twice around my wrist, and ran up my forearm and bicep to my armpit. A tiny tattoo of black beads.

Afterward, for almost a week, all I had done was eat and sleep while the Chorus helped my body grow back the raw materials I had taken to make the hand. It was still a bit stiff, and the flesh was new and pink. There were no scars on the knuckles. I had wiped away my past.

Marielle knocked once before she entered the studio. She was wearing a green cashmere sweater and a pair of old jeans that were supple in their familiarity and comfort. She had dyed the color out of her hair; it was solid black again, as it had been when she was younger. Her father's signet ring glittered on her left thumb. It was clearly a man's ring, but she wore it well. It drew your attention, but not because it was an incongruity, but because it was an anchor. It grounded her, announcing how she was the rock upon which all the world turned.

"*Salve, mi soror,*" I said, tipping my head forward a touch. My sister.

"*Salve, mi frater,*" she replied. The slight of my honorific wasn't lost on her and her reply came somewhat awkwardly.

"I wondered when you might come," I said.

"We all needed some time to heal," she replied, wandering into the studio. She saw the canvas on the easel, and I wondered *what* she saw. I wanted to ask her; part of me still thrilled at the idea of hearing her interpretation, of being drawn in by her vision.

"It's going to take longer than a few weeks," I said, pushing that desire away.

Marielle nodded. "It's a new world, Michael. The old ways have been abandoned, but not forgotten. We needed a clean break, no matter how painful. We are not snakes; we don't slough off our old shells every year. It takes a little longer."

She caught a hint of the objection rising in my chest. "Regardless of how quickly our flesh regenerates. Broken hearts and spirits take a little longer." She shrugged. "But, children are resilient and eager to learn. They do heal, and they do learn to forgive."

"Is that what you're telling them? That they'll forgive you eventually?"

"Me?" Her eyebrows went up. "Why would they need to forgive me?"

"Did he ask you to kill him, or did you decide to do it on your own?"

Something that might have been a sneer started to move across her lips, but she hid it quickly, burying it beneath a sad smile. "A year ago, my father told me the Land had nearly rejected him at his last Renewal. He didn't think he would be strong enough to renew his oath this spring, and so he was forced to decide who would take the Crown after him, and how they would take it."

"Did he ask you to kill him?" I repeated.

"No child should ever have to bear the blood of their parents on their hands," was her response.

"That's not the way he remembers how the ritual goes."

"But he is gone, and there is no one to confirm what he thought, and so my way will be the way it is."

"Convenient."

"It is a better pattern, Michael, for all the threads. You See that."

I did. I had had some time to think about it since I had left her and Antoine in the church with the Grail. I had had time to figure out who was really playing whom. Whose vision w~ really the deepest.

Marielle came closer, studying my face. "In the end

are clean," she said, "and that is the way my reign shall be. That is the way they will know that I will always be smarter than them, that I will always See further and deeper than any of them. They may not like that a woman leads them, but they will not be able to dismiss the fact that I earned the right to do so. And from this point, we will work toward a future where they will understand. Where they will Know, and in Knowing, they will be strong."

"Why?" I asked. "Why the object lesson?"

She took up my new hand and raised it to her lips. They were warm and her kiss invigorated my new flesh. I wanted to pull away, but I was rooted to the spot, caught in the magnetic whirlpool of force she carried within her. That she had always carried in her. The Chorus flickered into the room, falling back into my skull, and the skin of my new hand began to tingle. The teeth marks on her right ring finger whitened, old memories coming to the surface. The opals in the signet ring on her left thumb glowed like the moon.

She looked at her hands, holding mine. "You and Antoine broke my heart a long time ago," she said, "and I made the mistake of going to my father and telling him of the pain. Do you know what he told me?"

I remembered the last conversation between Philippe and myself, burned into my brain from two perspectives. *Most die in darkness and in pain.* "I can imagine," I said.

"He told me I had made that choice. I was responsible for what happened between the two of you, and I needed to own that responsibility." She shook her head. "I knew he was manipulating me, that he was twisting my thread. He wanted me to be confused and angry. As if I could plant that guilt and water it with my tears. As if I could make it grow with all that misplaced frustration and hurt. He wanted me to hate both of you, because he knew—when it came time—that I would have to play you two against each other again."

She looked at my eyes, and I knew she saw the memory of

my own *Qliphotic* blackness there. "It is an easy choice, isn't it?" she whispered. "When you are bound in darkness. When you are frightened and willing to do anything to make the emptiness go away."

"It is," I said.

She leaned forward, hesitating for a moment, and when I didn't pull away, she brushed her lips against mine. All the air in my lungs vanished, drawn down into the whirlpool of her psychic beauty. "The sun has come back," she whispered, her lips still close to mine. Her face, so close to mine. "The world turned, and dawn brought light to our darkness. We can choose new paths now, can't we? We can put the past behind us and try again. Isn't that the opportunity given to us by the Land? We are the kings and queens of the world, Michael. We can choose any path we want. To walk into the light, or to stay in the dark." Her lips touched me again, flooding me with warmth. "Which path will you take?"

I pulled my hand out of hers and crushed her to me, kissing her fiercely. At some point, she broke away with a tiny noise, but it was a brief moment—an inhalation more than a reaction—and she then grabbed me again. I had already told her my choice, and I wasn't going to change my mind. No matter the allure of her words, or the touch of her flesh. No matter the path she offered.

Our lips parted eventually, but we remained close. Touching at chest, hip, and thigh. Hands lightly tracing each other. I wiped the moisture from her cheeks with my right hand and she tried to kiss my fingers once more. On her finger, the white ring of teeth marks. She would carry them forever, just as I carried Reija's hair about my throat.

We all carry our scars. Some of them are more welcome than others. Some of them don't remind us of pain, but of the things we once loved.

I thought of Lafoutain and Vivienne. *We can't control how*

other people love us, can we? Eventually we recognize that they do.

In his own way, Philippe had loved his daughter too. As best he could.

"Your father left me a memory of this place," I said. "You. When you were about eight. Chasing geese out in the field."

She nodded. "They came back every spring. As soon as the frost broke, I would leave my window cracked at night. So that when they came back, I would hear them. They always came at first light, chased by the dawn. I knew it was spring when I heard their voices again."

"Really? Your father was a very visual man. Most of his memories are like silent films. Little loops of imagery." The memory played again in my head. Little Marielle, laughing, chasing white shapes in the field of yellow flowers. This time there was sound, and I probably imagined it.

But maybe not.

"Thank you for telling me," I said.

Reluctantly, she let go and took a step back. A shy smile tugged at her lips. "I'm glad you know."

"Goodbye, Marielle."

"Goodbye, Michael."

After she left the studio, I didn't go to the window and watch her drive away with her Shepherd. What was done was done, and what was gone was gone.

Even though the equinox had passed, the sky was still empty of stars at night and the wind off the river was cold. When it got dark, I made a fire in the main house and read from a copy of Eschenbach's *Parzival* until I couldn't stay awake any longer.

The sun would wake me in the morning. The main sitting room looked toward the hills in the east. The dawn light would creep across the valley, stir up fog on the river, and steal through the large picture windows. It would wake me, and I would rise, free to make any choice I wanted.

Free to chose any path.

We all pass through Yesod.

I thought I might stay a few more days, though, in case the geese came back. Just to see them with my own eyes.

Acknowledgements

Emm, Ess, and Zee sustain me. As always.

My mother and father are thoroughly enjoying their retirement, and based on the pictures they keep sending along, I like to think of them as my location scouts. Even when they send pictures where they are going nose-to-beak with penguins. I know they mean well, and the angst such pictures generate gets redirected into the making of words, so it's all good in the end.

Jeremy Bornstein, Geoff Gibbs, Cooper Moo, and Jonathan Wood provided enthusiasm and asked pointed questions that I had to go figure out how to answer so as not to embarrass myself in this manuscript. Jeremy kept me honest with the Latin. Thank you, gentlemen.

Kristopher O'Higgins kept me on track when I caught the brain fever and wanted to wander, screaming, into the wilderness. Being an agent is, more often than not, like being the night intern at a mental hospital. Marty Halpern provided a stern editorial pencil, saving me from appearing like I can't hook two phrases together. I threw a lot of italics and outlandish phrases at him, and he took all of it in stride. The lads at Night Shade Books—Jason, Jeremy, and Ross—have given the Codex books a home, and I appreciate the continued opportunity to bring Markham's adventures to life. Jay Caselberg graciously went out into the streets of Paris and took pictures for me; I'm sure it was a real drag. Tom Dancs was, once again, an unsuspecting source of knowledge about jumping off of things. Thank you, all.

Barth Anderson, Darin Bradley, and John Klima provided moral support and were party to many a creative diversion. Somehow, even with them enabling me, the book managed to get done.

I listened to a lot of Fields of the Nephilim again (thank you, Carl), Die Warzau (thank you, Jim and Van), Laibach (thank you, brother citizens of NSK), Ulver (thank you, lads), and various incarnations of the Positronic Sound (Sister Machine Gun, Micronaut, and so on; thank you, Chris) while banging out the words. If the energy of the book is too manic, blame them.

As always, I have taken some liberties with various occult rituals and practices. For creative purposes, of course. You may blame me for oversights and errors. I do appreciate the interest and support from my readers, so thank you all as well.

Keep seeking, my brothers and sisters.

Salve.

Follow Markham as he continues to seek the light in *Angel Tongue: The Third Book of the Codex of Souls,* forthcoming in 2011.

ANGEL TONGUE
[An Excerpt]

I

"I have never seen a man eat a piece of pie as slowly as you." Serenity refilled my coffee cup without asking. She had a practiced pour, a tip of the wrist that released a full stream of hot coffee, and she snapped it off with equal precision. It didn't matter how empty the cup; she always knew how long to pour. Fresh pot, too. The aroma reminded me of the farms up in the Cordillera Occidental in Columbia.

The pie was cherry rhubarb—a local delicacy, Serenity assured me, though I wasn't quite sure what she meant by local. The truck stop was halfway between Wall and Kadoka, in the middle of the emptiest, and straightest, stretch of I-90 as it ran through South Dakota. Judging from the barren landscape along the highway, there wasn't a farm growing rhubarb—or cherries, for that matter—for a hundred miles.

Still, it was homemade, and fresh. "I'm savoring it," I assured her.

"Sure you are," she said with a wink. Incongruous as it seemed in this environment, "Serenity" could actually be her real name. She exuded a casual indifference to the fact that she worked in a Denny's knockoff inside a truck stop that took its name from the most remarkable local landmark: the Badlands National Park. As she wandered off to the next table, Serenity casually brushed her left hand across my shoulder.

The Chorus moved under my skin, tasting her. *You've been*

here too long, they whispered, *she's starting to get familiar.*

I glanced out the windows again, and very little had changed. The highway shimmered with heat mirages, the semis growled as they rolled across the dusty lot. The sun baked the paint on the cars parked in a haphazard row outside the restaurant. A pair of motorcycles, riders clinging like slick black beetles, glided around the gas pumps. Middle of nowhere; nothing ever happened here.

All in all, it was a good spot for a meeting, but only if both parties were on time. Whoever the three in the corner table were meeting was late, and they were starting to get nervous. This was the second roadside restaurant they had stopped at today; the first one had been about eighty miles back, and they dismissed it before I had even gotten out of the car. This one seemed to satisfy whatever criteria they had in mind. However, their contact hadn't arrived.

I had gone straight to the restaurant, taken a seat in one of the booths along the south-facing windows—where I had a good view of the parking lot, including their dust-covered Mercedes sedan—and did my best to be innocuous. The Chorus could have helped me, woven a glamour of redirection about my frame, but I was hesitant to run an active spell, not with the warding eyes that were starting to show up in public places. The truck stop was fairly remote, unlikely to be as closely monitored as the more heavily trafficked stretches between Seattle and Chicago, but it was better to rely on non-magickal methods of discretion.

They were sitting at a table near the eastern wall of the restaurant, back from the booths along the windows. The two men faced the rear of the restaurant, which opened into the rest of the truck stop, and the woman kept an eye on the parking lot, though she couldn't see as much of it as I could. I had caught her looking at me a few times, and I was starting to wonder if she had made me. I had been this close to them a few days ago, back in Illinois, but it had been a more crowded space and I hadn't been sitting in the same spot for an hour.

The Chorus tugged at the back of my tongue as she looked at me again. *No, it wasn't idle curiosity anymore. She knew something wasn't right.*

I carved off a big piece of pie and shoved it in my mouth. Time to start considering how and where to make contact. I couldn't keep shadowing them anonymously, not if they kept pulling these long drives. The woman was too alert behind the wheel, too aware of the other cars on the road. There wasn't enough traffic on the highway to escape notice if she was looking for a tail; and should she decide I wasn't friendly, I had a feeling she'd lose me within five minutes of hitting the first town with more than three cross streets.

Her name was Elizabeth Kimbrel. Tall and lanky, hair the color of sunburned wheat (usually pulled back in a single ponytail), narrow mouth that opened up her face when she smiled. Her hands were sure and capable, no rings, with a Rolex watch on a battered band that wasn't the original. Cosmograph Daytona. Black dials. She was the driver.

On the other side of the table, sitting on the outside edge, was Ted "Bear" Grumanski. Red beard, red tattoos of angel wings across the back of his shaved head, biceps like rocks shoved in the cheap sleeves of his shirt, knife clipped in the right-hand pocket of his cargo pants, old biker boots that were probably steel-tipped. He tried very hard to eat normally, but he couldn't quite shake the old habit of guarding his food. Bear had done time. He was the muscle.

The other guy was the thinker. Gray hair clipped short, cheeks pock-marked by old acne blemishes from a childhood marred with being labeled an outsider, an old scar at the base of his throat. He armored himself with a pair of Oakley wraparound sunglasses and a black leather jacket that was white with age along the seams. Judging by the way the jacket fit, he had either lost some weight recently or he was packing a gun; I was betting on the latter. Horatio Milestinger. His name had been familiar, and a Google search had reminded me of the late-night radio show I had picked up occasionally while out in the wilderness, on nights when the ionosphere was bouncing signals back. He hadn't been on the air for more than a decade.

I had been tracking the three of them for almost a week. I still didn't know what they were involved in, other than it didn't require hard merchandise. They revolved around Milestinger, though; the other two deferred to him, and aside from his fascination with the weather and radio signals, I hadn't been able to figure out what his obsession was. Or why they were all the way out here in South Dakota, waiting for a meet.

Information of some kind. That was the coin of the realm these days. Especially if it concerned rogue magi.

A black shape moved across the far side of the parking lot, and I squinted at it. One of the two motorcyclists, heading for the highway. Or a third one, just like the other two. The Chorus slithered through my jaw, and the mouthful of pie turned sour against my tongue. *Three is more than coincidence,* the spirit of Detective John Nicols whispered in the back of my head. *Three is too many.*

Moving the fork around the plate, I shoveled up the last piece of pie.

Kimbrel was openly looking in my direction, and something in her expression alerted the two men. Milestinger swiveled around in his seat to look, and was distracted by the sudden vibration of his cell phone, which had been silent for the last hour. He paused, half-turned in his seat, his thumb moving across the buttons of his phone. *Text message.*

The angry sound of a small engine caught my attention. One of the motorcycles came around the corner of the building, between the restaurant and the row of parked cars. The rider was the wrong shape—too many heads. No, it was a pair, and the second rider had a hand raised, holding a black—

I ducked as the windows started shattering from gunfire. Heat rolled into the restaurant, and the sound of the bike engine was suddenly loud. It revved higher, the bike picking up speed as it raced up the pavement. In the wake of its roar, there came pandemonium—screams and shouts from the people in the restaurant.

The Chorus, rampant and active, marked the gunman—the second rider on the bike—as he came through the window, his booted feet crunching through the broken glass on the table two booths down from me. He leaped to the floor and emptied the rest of his pistol's clip at the walls and ceiling of the restaurant, shooting more for the spectacle and shock than to actually hit anyone.

Though at least two people had been hit by the initial spray of bullets. The couple who had been sitting at the booth where the gunman entered were down. The woman was sprawled on the orange and tan carpet, her eyes open and fixed. Her soul was a rising plume of shimmering smoke.

I crouched by my booth and let the Chorus read the room.

The gunman was covered in black body armor that moved too easily to be leather, and his helmet was sealed tight and aerodynamic to a fault. When the Chorus reached out to touch him, there was resistance. *Quicksilver mesh*. Another of OPO's new toys. The fabric would harden and scatter magick in much the same way that Kevlar protected against bullets.

His gun empty, the biker ejected the clip and reached into a narrow slit at his waist for another one. His gloves were a bit bulky for the motion and he fumbled for a second with the second clip.

My trio were frozen in their seats, caught between surprise and despair, almost as if they knew who the biker was, or who he represented.

I was still holding my pie fork. The Chorus flooded down my

arm as I pushed off from the booth. They swarmed into my wrist, spectral electricity arcing along the metal in my fist.

The clip replaced, the biker indicated with his gun that he wanted the threesome to lie down on the floor. Muscles in Bear's jaw flexed as he slowly raised his bulk out of his chair. Kimbrel saw me coming, but she lowered her gaze immediately. It was Milestinger who kept staring.

The gunman saw something in the reflection off Milestinger's sunglasses and he started to turn as I bumped him, wrapping an arm around his body. His quicksilver armor solidified as I hugged him, reacting to the proximity of the Chorus. I found the front edge of his helmet, and jerked his head back. There was a narrow gap between the collar of the armor and the seal of his helmet, and I stabbed the fork into that space. Blood spurted over my hand, and through the connection between fork and flesh, the Chorus made their assault.

They roared into the gunman's body, swarming toward the coruscating cloud of his soul. They didn't even bother taking control of his central nervous system; they went straight for the hot, pulsating center of his Will. I hugged him tighter as his body went slack, following him down to the floor. The Chorus tore his soul apart, and an explosive rush of energy whiplashed through the metal connection of the fork, burning my palm. I ground my teeth as the flood of energy and memory poured into me.

I knew his name. I knew who he worked for. I knew why he was here. I knew what he was afraid of. I knew there was—

—a second target.

"Betelgeuse," I gasped, looking up at Milestinger. "He's here."

My words snapped them out of their frozen panic. Milestinger knocked his chair over in his haste. "Get the car," he shouted at the other two as he wove around me and the dead gunman. He jumped onto the seat of the booth, and with a hop onto the table, went out the broken window.

Bear and Kimbrel stared at me; there was something akin to respect in the tight line of Bear's mouth. I shoved the body aside. There was nothing left. Everything that had been Paul Adele, Agent-Investigator of the OPO, had been broken and transformed by the Chorus, the old soul-serpents bound to me. He was in my head now, a keening voice already fading into the general noise of the Chorus. The aspects of his identity that survived the transition would become part of their communal voice; everything else was raw power, my ready reservoir of magick energy.

I was the Lightbreaker, the master of the voices in my head; I had fought my demons and won.

"Who—" Kimbrel began.

"I'm your guardian angel," I said. I looked toward the parking lot. "You heard him. Get the car."

I followed Milestinger out the broken window.

DETECTIVE INSPECTOR CHEN IS BACK!

978-1-59780-123-2
Mass Market / $7.99

The Snake Agent returns in *The Shadow Pavilion*, the fourth Detective Inspector Chen novel from Liz Williams. When Chen's partner, the demon Seneschal Zhu Irzh, disappears, Chen must enlist all of his allies and assets in order to locate him.

Meanwhile, Zhu Irzh finds himself trapped in an unfamiliar jungle Hell, stalked by a rogue demon lord and his harem of tigress demons. An assassin from between worlds targets Mhara, the new Lord of Heaven. And a beautiful starlet holds a deadly secret...

From the strange streets of Singapore Three to the rough and tumble world of Bollywood, where money flows fast and emotions flare even faster; from the realm of the Celestials to the haunts of the Infernal and all the spaces in between, *The Shadow Pavilion* delivers the thrills, excitement, and near-future occult action fans have come to expect.

Find this book and many other great science fiction, fantasy, and horror titles published by Night Shade Books at your favorite bookstore or online at:
   www.nightshadebooks.com

WILLIAM HEANEY IS A MAN WELL ACQUAINTED WITH DEMONS.

How to Make Friends with Demons

Graham Joyce

"Anyone who isn't reading Graham Joyce is doing themselves a huge disservice. No matter what kind of story he takes on, his work immediately becomes the standard to which all others have to be compared. The only disappointment with a Joyce book is that, at some point, it has to end."
— Charles de Lint, World Fantasy Award–winning author of *The Mystery of Grace*

978-1-59780-163-8
Trade Paperback / $14.95

Find this book and many other great science fiction, fantasy, and horror titles published by Night Shade Books at your favorite bookstore or online at:
www.nightshadebooks.com

For demons are real, and William has identified one thousand five hundred and sixty-seven smoky figures dwelling on the shadowy fringes of human life, influencing our decisions with their sweet and poisoned voices.

After a series of seemingly unconnected personal encounters—a beautiful and captivating woman met in the company of an infuriating poet, a troubled and damaged veteran of Desert Storm with demons of his own, and an old school acquaintance with whom he shared a mystical occult ritual—William Heaney's life is thrown into a direction he does not fully comprehend. Past and present collide. Long-dormant choices and forgotten deceptions surface. Secrets threaten to become exposed. To weather the changes, William Heaney must learn one thing: how to make friends with demons.